THE BEST KIND OF
TROUBLE

LAUREN DANE

THE BEST KIND OF
TROUBLE

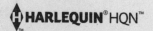

HARLEQUIN® HQN™

Recycling programs
for this product may
not exist in your area.

ISBN-13: 978-0-373-77934-5

THE BEST KIND OF TROUBLE

Copyright © 2014 by Lauren Dane

Printed in U.S.A.

Sometimes in your life you go through some rough spots, low points, places where you're not sure what to do or how to do it. This one goes out to every single one of you who have pushed me, supported me, placed wonderful opportunities in my path, who've checked in with a little bit of love, delivered a pep talk or a come to Jesus when I needed it. Thank you for reminding me in some way, big or small, just how blessed I am in my friends and family.

Tracklist for **The Best Kind of Trouble**

"Wanna Be Yours"—Arctic Monkeys
"Wait For Me"—Kings of Leon
"On the Chin"—Kings of Leon
"Lightness"—Death Cab For Cutie
"Arizona"—Kings of Leon
"Mouthwash"—Kate Nash
"These Days"—Foo Fighters
"Love Me Again"—John Newman
"Supersoaker"—Kings of Leon
"On Call"—Kings of Leon
"This is the Last Time"—The National
"I Want it All"—Arctic Monkeys
"A Lack of Color"—Death Cab for Cutie
"I'd Rather Go Blind"—Trixie Whitley
"She's Thunderstorms"—Arctic Monkeys
"Revelry"—Kings of Leon
"Undress Your Name"—Trixie Whitley
"Radioactive"—Kings of Leon
"Transatlanticism"—Death Cab for Cutie
"Titanium"—David Guetta feat. Sia

CHAPTER ONE

IT REALLY DIDN'T matter that the day was sure to be hot enough to melt asphalt; coffee was a necessity if she was expected to work all day at the library and not maim anyone.

Public safety was important, after all. That and her terrible addiction to things that were bad for her like caffeine and sugary baked goods.

Common Grounds was a daily stop on her way to work or other errands in town.

Bobbi was behind the counter, and when she caught sight of Natalie coming through the doors, she grinned. "Morning!" *So. Perky.*

Perky was not in Natalie's wheelhouse, so she aimed for amiable because Bobbi the barista was Natalie's pimp. "Morning. Hit me with something awesome."

Another luminous smile from Natalie's favorite barista as she got to work. "I have a new something to try. Are you game?"

"My vices are few, so I like to enjoy what I've got." She looked over the stuff in the case. There were no doughnuts, sadly, so a scone would have to do. "I'd like to enter into a relationship with that cinnamon scone there to go with my something new."

"It's early for you, isn't it? I thought the library didn't open until ten today?"

"It doesn't, but I'm doing story time for some pre-schoolers."

"Aw, that's nice of you."

Natalie had the financial ability to volunteer in her free time and a strong commitment to giving back, so reading to preschoolers once or twice a week was pretty fun as such things went.

Bobbi handed over the bag with the scone and her drink. "Latte with orange essence and a little shaved chocolate. Tell me what you think."

"Sounds fantastic." As for nice for reading books to kids? "It's a good thing when children like to read. Plus, they're adorable when they're three and four. They blurt out the best stuff. Usually shit about their parents. Last week, right as I finished up *Fancy Nancy,* one of them pipes up and says, 'my dad doesn't wear pants on weekends.' It was awesome."

Bobbi laughed. "My nephew's like that. My sister says she and her husband have to be careful about stuff they say now because he told his kindergarten class that he walked in on mom and dad *naked wrestling.*"

That made Natalie guffaw. "It's pretty hilarious when it's *other people's* kids ratting them out."

"Yeah. Our time will… Oh…*my.*" Bobbi's gaze seemed to blur as she gaped in the direction of the front door, and that was when Natalie heard *his* voice.

Not for the first time.

"Care to help out a man in dire need of some caffeine?"

She couldn't help it. Natalie turned to take in the ridiculous male glory that was Paddy Hurley. In jeans and a T-shirt, he still looked like a rock star. Though she'd seen him naked, and he looked like a rock star then, too.

His dark brown hair had lightened up, probably from being out in the sunshine. He'd put his sunglasses on top of his head, so those big hazel eyes fringed by gorgeous, thick sooty lashes had extra impact.

Impact that made Natalie's heart beat faster and her face warm as she remembered some of the things they'd done together. *To each other.* Dirty, filthy, naked things. Really good things the mere memory of had her libido sitting up and panting over.

Bobbi was entranced by him as she stood at the counter, blinking slowly, clearly caught up in her admiration. He kept smiling, as if he was totally used to that sort of attention. Of course he was.

"Can I get an iced coffee and a slice of that blueberry loaf for here?" He changed his tone a little from that flirty drawl to something more direct, and it seemed to do the trick.

Bobbi stood a little taller and cleared her throat. "Uh. Yeah. Sorry. Yes, of course."

"Thanks." He grinned, all white teeth and work-in-the-sun glow. *Good God,* he was beautiful.

"I'll bring it out when I'm done." Bobbi got to work but waggled her brows at Natalie, mouthing *holy shit, it's Paddy Hurley.*

Natalie tried to turn quickly and make an exit, but he'd caught the direction of Bobbi's look, and she saw the moment he recognized her, too.

"Hey, there. *Wow.*" He searched for her name, which was what allowed her to pull her mask on and pretend she had no idea who he was.

"Hello." She turned to Bobbi. "See you tomorrow!" Natalie put the lid back on her cup and gathered her things, but Paddy stepped closer.

"Natalie, right? You worked at that dive bar attached to the bowling alley near Portland."

A lifetime before.

"Sorry?" She cocked her head as if she had no idea he was talking about the two weeks they'd spent nailing each other as though sex was going to be outlawed any moment.

"It's Paddy Hurley. I'd know that mouth anywhere." He said it quietly. Enough that she appreciated his discretion.

That Natalie stayed in the dive bar. The Natalie she was now had risen from the ashes while she was in college, and she rarely looked back if she could help it. Paddy Hurley and those two weeks they'd shared were a great memory, especially the naked part. But she'd spent too many years and a whole lot of effort to be *more* and had no desire to go digging up that lifetime again.

"Nice to meet you, Paddy. I enjoy your music. I need to be on my way." She reached for the door, and he searched her features and shook his head as if he couldn't believe what was happening. Which was sort of charming, and she had to remind her hormones sternly to back off and let her brain do the work.

But he rallied. "I know it's you. Stay and have coffee with me so we can catch up."

"I have to get to work." She opened the door, nudging him out of the way a little as she did. The heat of the day greeted her, and she stepped out, covered her eyes with her shades and walked away.

The past was the past. She had a life now. One she'd spent a lot of time and energy building, and she needed to keep the door on who she'd once been firmly closed.

Even if it left a tasty bit like Paddy Hurley on the other side.

Paddy watched her retreat down the sidewalk, the hem of her skirt swishing back and forth, exposing the backs of her thighs. Thighs that had been wrapped around his hips more than once.

She had tattoos, matching ones, at the top of each thigh, right under each ass cheek. Pretty red bows like at the top of stockings. He smiled at that memory.

"Her name is Natalie, right?" he asked the barista when she brought him the coffee and pastry.

"Yeah. You know her?"

"She lives here in town?" He sipped his drink. He and his brothers had gone out for an early ride so he was hot and a little sleepy. The iced coffee helped with both.

"Sure. Works at the library. Comes in every morning before work to get coffee. Well, except Monday because the library is closed on Mondays. She's single. You know, if you were asking because you thought she was pretty."

He gave the barista a smile. He did indeed think Natalie was pretty. Her hair was short now where it had been long years before. He normally loved a woman with long hair, but on her that pixie thing worked. She had a great neck.

A great everything. She'd kept up with him on every level. They partied hard, fucked hard, worked hard. He and the band his brothers had formed, Sweet Hollow Ranch, had had a series of gigs at dives all over Portland and Southwest Washington. They'd managed to get two crappy hotel rooms included as part of their pay.

The motel had been right behind a bowling alley and the shithole of a bar attached to it. Natalie had been a waitress there, slinging drinks and dodging overeager hands when he'd met her.

It had been a matter of hours after meeting—the chemistry so instant and thick between them—until they'd stumbled into her studio apartment and into her bed.

She'd been underage, as had he, but they'd spent the next two weeks together around her shifts at the bar and his gigs.

And then he'd gone on the road, and she'd gone off to college. He'd thought of her over the years. One of their songs, "Dive Bar," had been about her and those two weeks.

Turns out she lived in the same town. Which meant it was fate. He continued to smile after he'd thanked the barista.

Why she'd pretended not to know him was the question. She had her reasons, and he aimed to know them, too. The woman behind the counter said Natalie was single, so it wasn't a boyfriend.

Paddy hadn't achieved the success he had because he gave up when things got hard.

He'd simply keep at it.

He leaned back in his chair and watched the street outside as he drank his coffee. A new challenge was always fun. Especially when it concerned a pretty blonde with long legs and a smile that invited a man to sin and not repent.

CHAPTER TWO

"YOU REMEMBER THAT shithole of a bar we hung out in just outside Portland?" Paddy handed a coil of rope to his oldest brother, Ezra.

"Dude, you've got to be more specific than that. There are dozens upon dozens of shithole bars I remember. More I don't." Ezra snorted as he hung the rope up on a hook just inside the stable door.

Paddy laughed. It had been fifteen years since they'd started out, and that particular shithole bar had been at least a dozen years before. "Back at the beginning. Right before we headed to L.A. and made the first record with the label. The bar was next to a bowling alley. We had two rooms in that rattrap of a motel that was behind it."

"Ah! Yes, I do remember that one. Damien got his ass jumped by those cowboys who heckled us and waited for him after the show."

"Then we all jumped in, and you got arrested."

"Wasn't the last time."

"And now you have pigs and dogs, and you only beat on your brothers."

"I'm too old to beat up anyone but you people. Plus, I have great hands. Why you taking me down memory lane?"

"There was a girl."

Ezra barked a laugh. "Yeah, well, you'll have to be more specific with that, too. Even more of them than shithole dive bars."

"Natalie. Long blond hair. Big blue eyes. Dimples. Juicy mouth. She worked in the bar. We had a thing. Hot, hard, fast, for two weeks before we left for L.A."

"Hmm, sounds familiar, but, Paddy, you have a thing for blondes. There are stories like that from coast to coast and across Europe. They all run together after a time."

"I do have a really fucking awesome life."

Ezra rolled his eyes. "Does this story have a point?"

"She's here. In town, I mean. This morning after our ride, I went down to get some coffee. She was there. At the counter. Hair is short now, but it exposes her neck."

Ezra hummed his approval as he put things away.

"She's a librarian."

Ezra's brows rose appreciatively. *"Well, now."*

"Right? But she pretended she didn't remember me."

Ezra turned and then laughed so hard he had to brace his hands on his knees. "Man, I wish I'd have seen your face when that happened," Ezra choked out in between fits of laughter. "I love how your ego paints it like she pretended not to know you instead of her just not remembering."

"Har har. She remembered me. There's no way she forgot it. It wasn't a night or two. It was two really intense weeks. Plus, asshole, I'm unforgettable. Anyway, she didn't deny knowing me. She just stepped around admitting knowing me. I know the difference."

Ezra stood up, wiping his eyes and settling down a little. "Thanks for that. Totally made my day."

"I'm asking you for advice. You give Damien advice all the time."

"He's an idiot. He needs it more than you do," Ezra said, referring to one of their brothers, the drummer of Sweet Hollow Ranch.

"Yeah, there is that."

"Okay, so hit me. What advice do you want? How to deal with the blow to your ego? Suck it up and move on. So what? There have to be dozens upon dozens of women who feel the same way about you, Paddy. You dumped her, and she does not have fond memories. You're lucky she didn't knee you in the gooch."

"I didn't dump her! It was fall, she was heading off to college and we were on the road. It was fine. No tears. No drama." He ran a hand through his hair. "I liked her. I liked her then, and I want to know if I'd like her now."

Ezra looked him over carefully as they left the stables. "So you want to what? Be this woman's friend? See if she wants another turn in the sheets with you? This is your hometown, Paddy. Don't shit where you sleep. If you charm her out of her panties and then it goes bad, then what? Do you really want some pissed-off ex-girlfriend who knows where you live?"

Paddy made a face. "It's not like that. I can't believe I haven't bumped into her before now. It's not like Hood River is a bustling metropolis."

"Yeah, well, you've been out on multiple tours in a row and traveling in between."

"True. Anyway, I don't just want to nail her, though she's gorgeous and all. Like I said, I want to see if we still click."

"Cut the shit. You're into it because it's a challenge."

Paddy sucked in a breath. "Okay, so maybe that's part of it. But not all of it."

"For whatever reason, you have an unhealthy level of self-confidence. You're okay-looking and all. Chicks dig you, and you hate to lose. So go for it, but don't be a dick."

Which, come to think of it, was pretty good advice.

NATALIE WALKED INTO Common Grounds with a spring in her step. She'd had a really great dinner with her housemate and best friend the night before. They'd watched a movie, and she'd gotten eight solid hours of really good sleep.

It was sunny, a breeze came in off the Columbia and she was well and truly prepared for an excellent Friday.

She waved a hello at Bobbi. "Good morning! I think I'd like an Americano today with lots of room. What sorts of delicious, calorie-packed goodness do you have left in the case?"

Bobbi looked over to her left. "See, like clockwork."

Natalie followed her gaze and nearly jumped when she saw Paddy Hurley sitting there with a grin on his face. The muted sunlight from the window he sat next to danced over his skin. Jesus H, he looked fantastic, his long legs stretched out, the denim straining at the thighs and over his crotch.

He packed quite a treat behind his zipper. Her belly and regions south tightened at that memory.

She snapped her gaze from his cock and tried not to blush.

"Have a seat." He pushed the chair across from him away from the table with one booted foot. Not cowboy boots, worn work boots she figured cost more than she made in a month.

She wanted to go over and sit. Wanted to flirt and chat and let it lead right back to her place. Something about the man had gotten under her skin right from go. He was dangerous. Wanting too much was dangerous.

"I have to go to work." With sheer force of will, Natalie turned her attention back to the bakery case.

Bobbi gave her a single raised brow but then got started on the Americano. The sounds and scent of the coffee-laden steam settled Natalie a little. "Ooh, I want one of those banana chocolate chip muffin things."

"Here's the thing, Natalie." Suddenly, Paddy was standing very close. How had he done that? *That* muffin is on hold. I'm a nice guy, though, so I'll happily let you have it if you'll sit and have coffee with me while we catch up."

In her head, her sigh was wistful, but on the outside, she added a little annoyance to keep him back. Natalie had a weak spot for charming men, and boy, did Paddy have that in spades.

She was careful not to turn to look at him. He was so close, she probably couldn't have kept her little resolution and stay on her Paddy Hurley–free diet. "I'll have the blueberry one instead, then."

Bobbi, clearly confused about the entire situation, shrugged and handed over the Americano and the muffin. Natalie thanked her and paid before heading toward the door.

Paddy caught up to her before she'd gotten more than a few steps. "Natalie? I was under the impression that when we parted ways before, things were okay between us. I guess I got it wrong. I'm sorry for whatever I did."

Natalie paused. She might know it was best to keep him at a distance, but she didn't want him feeling guilty or to come off looking disgruntled. "It was fine. There's no need to apologize."

His expression was smug for a moment, and then he caught himself with an easy smile. "So you *do* remember me."

There was no way she could stop her smile in response. "Yes. You're pretty memorable."

"So what's the deal?" He leaned a little closer. "You like being chased?"

With an annoyed hiss, Natalie stepped away. "*No.* I'm not interested in this…whatever it is. I don't want to play games. I'm not being coy. I have a nice, *quiet* life. I like it that way."

"There's no *whatever it is.* Not yet. We already had that. I just think we could get to know one another again. I promise not to trash your living room or put a guitar through your television or anything."

The charisma flowed off him in waves. It wasn't something he put on. It wasn't an affectation. It was impossible *not* to be attracted to him. They'd clicked all those years before, and it was still there, that chemical pull that made her a little sweaty and dizzy.

She stood a little straighter. "I have to go to work. I'm glad things are going well for you and your career. Have a good life, Paddy."

He grabbed her hand, twining his fingers with hers, and a shock of connection rang through her. She could *not* want this.

The heat of him sort of caressed her skin, and it wasn't even gross and sweaty because it was a thousand degrees outside. Was he some sort of sorcerer or something?

His attention shifted from where their hands were together to her face. "Wait. Let me walk you over. You're at the library, right?"

Using all her will, she slowly pulled her hand free, their fingers still connected until the very last.

"No. Really. I can't. I don't have room in my life for you and all that comes with you."

He flinched a little, but she had to give him credit for doggedness. "You don't even know me now. How can you know what comes with me?"

"I'm truly happy to see your success. You worked for it. But come on, I'm no dummy. I know what comes with a life like yours." She took a step away and then another until she was far enough to get a breath that wasn't laden with him. "Enjoy your Friday."

She left him there on the sidewalk as she kept going until finally, after she'd turned the corner, the squeezing pressure in her belly eased and she could breathe again.

She'd made the right choice.

She liked him. It wasn't like she could lie about that. But she'd spent years of struggle to make herself a life she wanted, too many to let her ladybits take over. Truth was, she let that fear remain. The fear that his wild life would be one cringeworthy experience after the next; the fear of all that chaos and insanity kept her steadfast.

The library beckoned, and she kept moving toward it. She had a direction, and it was forward, not back. There was room for pleasure; she certainly hadn't left sex behind, after all. But fleeting pleasure wasn't stable or strong. That's what he offered, and so she needed to pass on it.

But when she walked into the coffee shop on Tuesday, he was there. Natalie ignored him and once she got out to the street—and man, was she glad she'd driven that day so she could put a closed door and a bunch of steel between them—she saw he waited just on the other side of her car.

"*What?* God, I told you, I'm not interested."

His smile was slow, easy and effortlessly sexy. "You're not interested in Paddy the rock star."

Natalie frowned. "Is that so hard to believe? Not everyone wants to latch on to you for your fame, you know. I'm happy for you and your brothers. I like your music. But I don't party like that anymore." Hell, she didn't *live* like that anymore. "I'm not that girl."

He leaned against her car like a cat. "Darlin', none of us are those people anymore. If I drank like that now, I'd be seriously fucked up the next day. When I'm not on tour, I'm here in Hood River. Not exactly known as a place to do blow off a hooker's ass now, is it?"

She groaned. "I have no idea. It could be, and there could be a huge hooker-cocaine thing going on, and I wouldn't know it. This is my point. Why are you so set on me, anyway?"

"You're so suspicious. It's sort of sexy. I'm set on you because I like you. Let me take you to dinner. Somewhere low-key. Hell, I'll make you dinner at my house. No photographers. No keg stands. Just Paddy and Natalie."

"Patrick, just leave it be. There are a million women who would be happy to have dinner with you. I'm a librarian living in a small town. I don't have dinner with rock stars."

"I won't be a rock star at dinner. I'll be Paddy. Anyway, I love books. Come on. Give me a chance. While I'm impressed you'd think a million women would be interested in me, *I'm* only interested in one woman. You."

She got in and closed the door. After she'd started the car, she opened her passenger window a little. "Look, I'm flattered, I really am. But I'm not the woman for you."

She pulled away, and he gave her a cheeky wave.

In retrospect, it was right then that she knew she was in very big trouble when it came to Patrick Hurley.

CHAPTER THREE

"SO REALLY, HE'S JUST… It's like I keep telling myself I need to lose ten pounds before my high school reunion, but he's a dozen doughnuts. *Ooooh, Natalie, you know I'm delicious. Just one bite. I'm so good with coffee.*"

Tuesday, Natalie's housemate and best friend, broke out laughing. "I know how much you love doughnuts, too. So why not eat one? Or six? My point is, who freaking cares if you get a taste of Paddy Hurley? This isn't *Little House on the Prairie.* You're not going to get fired for premarital sex by the town elders."

"It's not that." She made no bones about liking sex. Natalie considered good sex as important to her life as doughnuts and coffee. Paddy came with too many complications and too much noise. He had *complicated* written all over him.

"Then what is it?"

That wasn't it, either.

"It's just…" Natalie licked her lips. "He's messy and complicated. He'd take so much time to handle, and I'm over handling other adults. I don't want to be a nursemaid, a psychologist, and I sure have no desire to parent him while I'm fucking him, too. Ugh. I spent years and years stepping over people passed out in my house. I had to call the paramedics more than once be- cause some random stranger, or my dad for that mat-

ter, had overdosed. I've had enough cleaning up puke
and pretending not to smell liquor on breath at nine in
the morning."

She'd lived a life utterly out of control until she'd
finally left home at seventeen, and even then it wasn't
until college that she finally got her shit together. *Control meant everything.* It meant you lived a life of your
own choosing and not at someone else's mercy, and
it meant not being responsible for keeping grown-ass
people from driving off a cliff.

It was the leaving that had been the key. The ultimate act of taking control of her life was walking away
from that house. That pretty, solidly upper-class shell
that was rotting inside. Just like her childhood had been.

"He comes with too much shit that pushes my buttons. Hot in bed or not, I just don't want to chance it."
Paddy was a walking-talking advertisement for out of
control.

Tuesday was careful to keep pity out of her eyes, but
she sighed heavily. "All I'm saying is that life is made
from chances you take. How do you know he won't be
worth it?"

Easy for Tuesday to say. Then again, her best friend
sat in the house making gorgeous jewelry or hiking
instead of going out on dates for her own messed-up
reasons. Still, being someone's friend meant knowing
when to call bullshit and when to leave it alone. Tuesday wasn't ready to confront those demons yet.

"I can't deny knowing he lived here. I found out
about six months after I bought the house here." The
fact that the dudes from Sweet Hollow Ranch lived in
town and were locals who continued to make the city
their home was a point of pride to Hood River. The

town tended to be protective of the entire Hurley family. People didn't call the paparazzi when one of them ate in their restaurants or shopped in their stores. There weren't pictures sold to the tabloids of them going about their daily business.

When she'd discovered it, she'd been mildly worried, but she'd already begun to put down roots. She had no plans to run off simply because some old lover was in the same area.

And then Tuesday happened upon a storefront on Oak that she'd decided to run a business from and share half of Natalie's house. Hood River had been a new start for both women.

"All this time I've lived here, and I never bumped into him or caught sight of him. I guess I had just hoped our paths wouldn't cross."

Tuesday made a dismissive sound. "Well, they have, and he's clearly looking for a taste. I'm gonna guess he'll eventually give up if you keep ignoring him. But what I'm saying is, why not see what he's got to offer?"

Natalie wasn't ready to admit out loud that maybe she was curious.

"Hand me the potatoes, and let's change the subject please."

Tuesday rolled her eyes but passed the bowl. "You did a pretty good job with these, by the way."

Natalie's cooking was an utter disaster, but over the years since she and Tuesday had roomed together in college, Natalie had developed a few not-awful dishes. Mainly easy stuff like sandwiches and soup, but she'd been working on mashed potatoes for a year or so, and she'd gotten to the point where nothing caught fire, and they actually tasted good.

"Now I can make canned soup, ham sandwiches and mashed potatoes. Maybe that's what Paddy is after. He's been waiting for a woman to make him mashed potatoes his whole life."

They both cracked up.

"At least between the two of you, you have enough money to get takeout every night. Or maybe he can cook. That would be a bonus to the good looks and success stuff."

"He's probably spoiled. He lives up there on the ranch with his family. Maybe his mother cooks for him or something."

"Maybe. But somehow I doubt it. But you won't know unless you let him in."

"I don't need to know to mock him, duh. Just let me have my fun imagining him eating overcooked Hot Pockets or clinging to his mom's apron strings."

"SO HERE'S THE THING," Paddy said as he sidled up to Natalie the next morning at the coffee shop. "I dig that you don't have to be at work until nine."

"Why?" She handed some money to Bobbi, who took in the daily Paddy show with apparent glee. "So you don't have to get up so early to come down here and pester me?"

He laughed at that. "I'll have you know I've been up since six-thirty when I helped my oldest brother deal with a fence problem. Have you ever dug a post hole? It totally sucks. Ezra is sort of insane because he seems to actually like it."

Natalie moved to grab some honey for her latte, but he kept talking. "It's good because I can get my work done and come down here in time for you to actually have breakfast with me sometime."

"See you tomorrow, Bobbi." Natalie waved and started for the door, which Paddy now held open for her.

"I don't like getting up early. Also, I don't eat breakfast very often."

He took up beside her, and she didn't stop him. "You have a muffin in that bag."

"That's not breakfast. Bacon and eggs with toast and maybe hash browns, that's breakfast."

"You're serious about breakfast."

"Not really. If I was, that's what I'd be eating. Mainly I have doughnuts or muffins or a toaster-pastry thing."

He wrinkled his nose. "Really? Those are like cardboard. Also, you don't look like you eat doughnuts all the time."

"I'm serious about doughnuts. But my favorite kind I have to go to Portland for. Which is why I don't eat them all the time. And my housemate is sporty. She drags me to hike and bike and windsurf. It's gross, but it enables me to keep my doughnut habit."

"You cut your hair. It was long before."

"You're good at the non sequiturs."

He snorted. "I'm not sure when you're going to run off, so I'm trying to get in as much chitchat as I can before that happens."

She stopped, turning toward him. "Why are you so persistent? I'm not even that nice to you!" It was hard for her not to be friendly to him. She liked him, for heaven's sake.

"You don't want me for my status."

She shook her head, trying to understand. "Status?"

"The celebrity thing."

She rolled her eyes. "You didn't *have* any status when I met you."

He grinned. "Nope. Just a shitty van that broke down a lot and some instruments my brothers and I played."

She paused for long moments and then started walking again. "I cut my hair years ago. Tuesday, that's my housemate, she went through a phase when she wanted to be a hairdresser. It lasted half a quarter. But she cut my hair, and I liked it short. Plus, I look great in hats, and short hair works that way."

"Did that hurt? You sharing that little fact with me?" He winked, and it was cute, and she ruthlessly tried not to show how amused she was but probably failed.

"So you two have been roommates since college?"

"No. We shared an apartment in college, and then she got married and I went to grad school. But three years ago, she came to visit and wanted to set up a business here, so I offered her a place to live for a while. She never moved out. Which is good because I can't cook, and she does and thinks it's fun."

"Like hiking?"

Natalie curled her lip. "Yes. Ugh."

"No husband?"

"I would not be allowing you to walk me to my job if I had a husband, Patrick Hurley."

Paddy's laugh made her tingle a little. It was a bawdy laugh. "You said that like you were going to paddle me or slap my hand with a ruler. You should know that'll only encourage me."

She pressed her lips together and then gave up, laughing.

He kept pace, but she noted his smile from the corner of her eye. "I meant your friend."

Duh. Of course he did. "She's a widow."

"Oh, damn. That sucks. I'm sorry."

"Yeah." They approached the library, and she handed him her coffee. "Hold that, please." She rustled through her bag until she found her keys. "Thanks." She took the coffee back and tucked the pastry bag into her purse.

PADDY REALLY DIDN'T want that moment between them to end, but he'd enjoyed a victory nonetheless, so he'd take that small step forward and get more next time. "Wow, I feel like we've turned a corner here, Natalie." He bowed. "Thank you for letting me walk you to work."

She appeared to be looking for something to say, and he didn't want her to say something about him not doing it again.

"Will you let me take you to dinner?"

She sighed, but it was a sigh of longing, so he pushed ahead.

"I mean, I was aiming for breakfast since it's the least datelike of the meals—unless you slept over, of course—and if that happens, I'll make you bacon, eggs, hash browns and toast. Maybe even biscuits. But since we're not at that stage yet, and you don't eat breakfast, dinner is a good alternative."

"Not lunch?"

Was she teasing him? That was a good sign. "I'll take what I can get. But usually during the days when I'm here in Hood River, I'm working. Either on music or on the ranch. Summer is a crazy busy time and my brother does so much when we're on tour, I like helping him out."

Natalie sighed long and then shook her head as she

looked him over. "Why you gotta be so human, Patrick Hurley?"

"Is that good or bad? I don't know with you."

She shrugged. "I don't know for sure yet, either. You can pick me up from here tomorrow night. I'm off at six."

With that, she unlocked the door and went inside. "Have a good day, Paddy." She waved one last time, locked the door once more and disappeared into the building, leaving him standing there with a dumb smile on his face.

CHAPTER FOUR

"I HAVE NO IDEA why I said yes. I should call him and cancel." Natalie paced in front of her closet, still only half-dressed.

Tuesday just rolled her eyes. "You don't even have his number."

"I have his mother's. She's got a library card. I looked her up in the system. I can call her, and I'm sure she can pass the message on."

"Sure, that's not creepy at all."

"Gah!"

Tuesday snorted. "Hush up. Wear that blue dress with the white piping at the neckline. You can wear it all day at work, and it'll still be nice when you're off. It says *I care enough to not look like I slept in a Dumpster, but I'm still casual enough to walk away from your ass if you start anything and look fabulous doing it.*"

Natalie halted and then laughed. "You should do red carpet shows on the entertainment networks. I like that better than 'I'm wearing blah from her spring collection because cerise is the it color' or whatever."

"It's why even after you marry Patrick Hurley and spit out his spawn, we'll always watch the awards show red carpet together."

"*Marriage?* No, thanks. I'm not even convinced I

should go to dinner with him. Anyway, he's not after marriage. He just wants to fuck me."

"Well, look at you!" Tuesday waved a hand in Natalie's direction. "You're all blonde and adorable, and you have great tits. Boys like those. Of course he wants to fuck you. Also, he *has*."

Natalie struggled sometimes with the balance between owning what she liked and feeling guilty about it, anyway. Breasts had a lot of power. She did have some nice ones, and Paddy seemed to be impressed. Knowing that filled her with a sort of taboo power. What that said other than she liked that he liked it, she wasn't sure.

She pulled the dress from her closet and looked at it.

"See what I mean?" Tuesday indicated the dress with a tip of her chin. "Listen and obey always. I know things. Now, I have to get ready to open the shop. Wear those flats, but take some heels in your bag. Don't argue with me about this. Heels are perfect with that dress and, like tits, everyone likes cute heels."

Tuesday kissed her cheek and left the room.

She did wear the blue dress, of course. With flats and the blue high-heeled sandals tucked in her bag to change into. On her way out the door, Tuesday tossed her a little drawstring bag. "I made those a few days ago. They'll be supercute with the outfit."

Her housemate, in addition to running a custom framing shop, made jewelry she sold in her store. The earrings Natalie spilled into her palm were dangly bits of blue. All together they made a dragonfly, one of Tuesday's favorite subjects.

Natalie took off the earrings she had on and replaced them with the dragonflies. "Thanks."

"Text me if you need me to save you. Otherwise, you

can debrief me tomorrow morning. If you sleep over at his place, text so I won't worry."

"I'm not sleeping over at his place." No matter how sexy he was. No matter how much knowledge she had about how good he was in bed. Sleeping with Paddy on the first date—despite their history—would be stupid.

"That's the saddest thing I've heard today, Nat."

"WHERE ARE YOU off to tonight?"

Paddy tossed the ball one last time, and Ezra's dumb but sweet-as-hell dog ran off after it, getting distracted by a butterfly.

He looked up at his mother, who stood on Ezra's porch with Damien's wife, Mary, and tried to pitch his voice low to avoid notice. "I've got a date."

"Is that a euphemism?" his mother called out. So much for trying to keep it quiet.

Mary laughed, and Paddy shook his head. "You're jaded, Mom."

"I raised you four! I'm an eternal optimist. You don't date, you go off and have your little flings and return home in a week or so."

"Well, I'll have you know I'm taking a librarian to dinner."

"Is *that* a euphemism?" Mary asked with a smirk.

"She works here in town, as it happens. I'm making her dinner on the boat."

"Do you need help?"

One of the best things about having Mary as a sister-in-law was that she was an amazing cook. The author of three cookbooks, she was their own personal tour chef, too.

"I'm grilling some salmon from the fishing trip I

took with Vaughan a few weeks back. I was going to have corn on the cob to go with."

Mary cocked her head. "You're going to serve your date corn on the cob? Is this a first date?"

By the scandalized look on his sister-in-law's face, he figured it was probably not a good thing to do.

"In a manner of speaking. I knew her before. Years ago. Before we hit it big."

His mother crossed her arms over her chest. "Oh, and she suddenly wants to go out with you?" Sharon Hurley was not one for any foolery that had to do with anyone taking advantage of her children.

He laughed. "Well, Ezra thinks this is pretty hilarious and all, but no. I ran into her in town last month, and she pretended not to remember me at first. I've been hounding her pretty much three or four days a week since then to get her to go out with me. She's utterly disinterested in me as a celebrity. In fact, it freaks her out, I think. That's why I'm doing dinner on the boat instead of taking her to a restaurant."

Mary perked up. "Oh, well, then. Wait. Natalie? Supercute little blonde? She's one of those who wears cigarette pants and flats and looks like an ad for a vintage clothing catalog?"

He kept looking back and forth between his mother and sister-in-law, confused by Mary's questions and hoping to get some sort of clue from the context.

His mother's brows rose, and then she nodded, patting Mary's arm.

That shared look could very well equal trouble for Paddy, so he wanted to nip it right in the bud before it could turn into a reality. "What is going on between you two? It looks like there's a caper brewing. *No ca-*

pers. For God's sake. It took me a *month* of following this woman around like a lost puppy just to get her to let me walk her to work. If you two rush in like Lucy and Ethel, you're going to ruin all my progress. Also, what are cigarette pants?"

Mary waved that away. "Never mind, it's her. There aren't any other blondes working at the library. Don't make her eat corn on the cob. Not on the first date. Even if you knew her from before." Mary came down the steps. "Come with me to the house. I'm sure I have some sides for you." She tucked her arm through his.

"Are you taking pity on me?" He liked to tease her. She'd come from an equally insane family and fit in theirs just fine. She was the sister he'd never had, and she kept his brother Damien in line and from burning things down. Plus, there was that really good cook thing, and she wasn't a chore to look at, either.

"That's what family does." She winked.

"Let's drive over. I want to get to the boat and get things set up. I'm picking her up at six."

He opened the door of his car for her, and she got in.

He wasn't stupid with his money, but he loved cars and had a special garage built at his place for his collection. He'd decided to take the Shelby fastback. He'd had it restored up in Seattle the year before, and he loved the summertime when he could drive it often.

It was a sexy car. And yes, he was showing off. A little.

Damien was out front when they arrived at his and Mary's house, just down the road from the main house their parents lived in. His brother's face lit when he caught sight of Mary. "Hey, there, Curly. Have you been keeping Paddy out of trouble?" Damien kissed his wife soundly.

"Impossible to keep the Hurley boys out of trouble. Only your mother has the fortitude for that. But he's got a date, and I've got stuff for him."

Damien slung an arm around his wife's shoulders as he took Paddy in. "Don't give him those potatoes. Well, you can't, anyway, because I ate them about ten minutes ago."

"Damien! Those were for dinner."

He laughed and Paddy rolled his eyes at his bottomless pit of a brother.

"I was hungry. How can I resist? They didn't even have a sticky note on them saying not to eat them like the other stuff does."

"You ignore those, too. I figured if I put the potatoes behind the beets you'd never see them." She looked back over her shoulder. "Come on in. Let's see what's left after Hurricane Damien has gone through my kitchen like a plague of locusts." Mary poked Damien's side. "Where do you even put it all? How fair is that, anyway?"

Paddy did what he was told, sitting at the bar while she put together a tote of food for him. Her colored-cotton totes were famous in his family. She had several, each with colored stripes indicating which of them got what bounty. His was blue, and she handed him three, one of which was insulated.

"Balsamic strawberries. They'll be awesome for dessert. Wild strawberries, even. There's a pint of vanilla ice cream in case she wants some to go with the strawberries. The balsamic is good on that, too."

He used to question her weird food combos. After

three years of her cooking, he no longer doubted that whatever she gave him would taste good.

She rattled off a bunch of directions for how to deal with this or that, and he just nodded and kissed her cheek when she finished up. "Thank you."

Damien finally roused. He'd been watching his wife through hooded eyes and Paddy tried not to think about whatever nasty stuff was going on in his brother's head. "Wait, date? Oh! This is the librarian?"

"You knew about this and didn't tell me?" Mary looked to her husband.

"Believe me, most of what I don't share you'd be scandalized by, anyway."

She rolled her eyes. "Come to breakfast tomorrow and tell us how it went. I may need to check some books out, anyway. I haven't been down there in some time."

"Don't meddle, Curly." Damien pulled on one of the long dark curls that were the source of her nickname.

"Pfft. It's not meddling when it's family."

Paddy grabbed the totes. "It *totally* is. She's skittish. If you poke around, just be discreet. I like this woman."

Mary smiled up at him, patting his arm. "I can handle it. Now go. Have a good time and use a condom!"

He found himself blushing and felt better when Damien cracked up.

NATALIE GAVE HERSELF one last look in the mirror in the staff bathroom. The earrings made her smile. Like a little bit of Tuesday was going on the date with her.

Date. With Paddy Hurley. She was so stupid.

And yet there she was, freshening her lipstick and finger-combing her hair. "Time to go," she told herself in the mirror before she waved goodbye to her coworkers and headed out to the sidewalk.

Where she heard the purr of an engine and knew it was him before the deep green classic car pulled into view.

He pulled up and shook his head so hard when she moved to open her door that she drew back as he got out.

"Wait!" He came around.

"Is it broken?"

Paddy snorted. "No. But my manners aren't, either. First things first." He took a long look up and down, and she was glad she'd worn the heels. "You look pretty. I want to say more, but I don't know if I should."

"Well, now you have me nervous."

He kissed her then. Nothing really untoward, a quick peck smack-dab on the lips. But those traitorous lips tingled and his scent was in her by that point. He wore cologne, which seemed odd, but it was nice. Sexy and masculine without being overwhelming.

He hadn't had a beard all those years before. She liked the slight scratch of it.

Paddy opened the door and indicated she get in. She managed to do so without showing her underpants or looking too ungraceful.

He got in just a second or two later and pulled away from the curb.

"You have great legs and cute toes."

He said this as his attention was on the road, so he didn't catch her blush.

"Um. Thanks." God, did he have a foot fetish or something weird? She thought back on their time and flushed, a sweat breaking out. Okay, so *that* was unwise because he was really supergood at sexy stuff. But he hadn't seemed unnaturally interested in her feet.

"Where are we headed?"

"My boat. I figured we could have dinner out on the deck. It's such a nice night and it'll be light until so late. I'll take us away from the marina. I know a nice little stretch just east of here. Deserted, so we'll be able to see the sunset and I'll have you all to myself. But not in an *it rubs the lotion on its skin or it gets the hose again* way."

She burst out laughing. "Did you just quote *Silence of the Lambs* at me? Serial killer dialogue meant to reassure me?"

He cursed under his breath, and she reached out to pat his arm to reassure him. "I know it was a joke. Really. I'm more concerned you have a foot fetish than with you being a serial killer."

"Foot fetish?"

"The toes comment? I mean, look, if it floats someone's boat, more power to them. But I can't even get a pedicure because people touching my feet weirds me out."

"Note to self, don't try to paint Nat's toenails." He turned with a grin on his face. "We're both being way more nervous than we need to be."

"Yeah. Probably."

"I like cute toes when they're painted and looking great in nice high heels. I don't want to lick them or anything. Yours would probably be worth it. But I can control my baser urges."

He parked at the marina, which was less than five minutes from the library, and walked her down the row, heading to a rather impressive boat.

"So, what's that? Fifty-footer? Nice."

"Someone knows her way around boats. I like to go fishing with my brothers and our friends. In the summer, if we're here and not out on tour, we can watch fireworks from the water. Have dinner out here. It's a good thing to have. You're okay with boats, right? No seasickness or anything?"

"I love being out on the water. My grandparents had a boat. Sometimes, as I was growing up, we'd go out on it. They lived on Lake Washington."

"Oh, Seattle locals?"

"Medina." Her grandparents had lived in a mansion with a sloping lawn to the lake where their yacht had been moored. Too bad they paid more attention to the lawn and their things than what their spoiled son got up to.

He held her forearm as she got on the boat.

"Oooh, swanky. What brought a rich girl from Medina to a shithole bar in Portland?"

"They're the rich ones." She blew it off, not wanting to get into it. She was rich, too, but it was their house and their lifestyle. The guilt would start if she thought about it too long. Guilt and anger and all the stuff she knew didn't belong to her, but she felt it, anyway.

He let her avoid the topic. "Come on, then. Let me get ready. Have a seat up there. Once we're away from the marina, I'll crack open some champagne."

She watched him, the sun behind his head highlighting him like a freaking angel. He was confident there at the wheel. Hands steady, sunglasses shielding his eyes and rendering him even more attractive.

THE TIME IT took to get away from the marina to the cove where they finally ended up had allowed her to get herself together and shove all that stuff about her family far away.

He handed her a glass. "Now, what should we toast to? New beginnings? Old times?"

"Dinner."

He smirked and clinked his glass to hers. "That's a good start. Come on over and sit while I work."

She managed to climb down and finally just bent to undo the shoes. Yes, they had been cute and sexy but walking barefoot was easier on a boat than in heels. "Hope you don't mind," she said when she caught him looking at her.

"I don't mind at all. They're sexy heels, I can't lie. But I like you making yourself comfortable on my boat even more. I'm hoping your skirt blows up enough for me to see if you've still got those bows on the backs of your thighs."

He'd licked her tattoos a time or three, if she remembered correctly. And she knew she did because it would be impossible to forget a man like Paddy Hurley licking the skin at the top of your thighs and then giving your ass cheeks a sharp nip. She shivered and was proud of the way her voice didn't betray how breathless he rendered her. "Those'd be some powerful gusts. The breeze isn't that strong and the dress is long enough to defeat what we've got now."

He looked back over his shoulder at her. "So, the bright red bows are still there?"

"I hear tattoo removal is pretty painful."

"Shame. Maybe I can see them later. Or next date you can wear a shorter skirt."

"Don't get your hopes up. I have to bend and kneel all

the time at work. Parents in Hood River tend to frown upon librarians flashing their panties at the library."

He groaned. "You're a wicked tease, Natalie."

He made her laugh. She hadn't expected to feel so relaxed with him. But she did. This was dangerous ground, but she couldn't help herself. Flirting with him was fun. And…it was easy because things just flowed between them.

He shook his head at her, still smiling. "Be right back. I need to put something in the oven and the microwave." He dashed down to the galley, and she contented herself looking out over the water. She loved being out on the water, but it had been years since she'd been on a boat. The last time had been when Tuesday had scattered Eric's ashes.

He popped back up a few minutes later. "Need a refill? I have juice and sparkling water, too, if you prefer."

Champagne was one of her favorite things, so on the rare occasions she did drink, she loved it. However, she needed to go easy because Paddy was like three glasses on an empty stomach just by existing.

"I'll have more when we eat."

He put a platter out on the low table in front of her. "Some snacky things. I considered taking credit. Once you taste them, you're going to love them and think I'm awesome. I'm all about that. However, it wouldn't be nice of me, and eventually you'd find out that my sister-in-law, Mary, is an amazing cook and gives us all food on a regular basis. She made all those little things and gave them to me. I was going to do cheese and crackers or chips. I particularly like those there. The ones that look like little sacks. They have cheese and spinach and other stuff in them." He pointed.

Natalie popped one of the phyllo bundles into her mouth. "Oh. Yeah, these are really good." She ate two more and then made herself try the other stuff. Dates stuffed with blue cheese, spiced nuts, cantaloupe wrapped in prosciutto.

After Paddy grabbed a few appetizers, he turned and got to work, oiling the grill as she settled on the rather comfortable couch on the deck to watch. He was at ease with himself, clearly at home in his skin.

"This should be done in like five minutes. You don't need to cook it very long."

"Want help? Not with cooking because I'd set something on fire. But I can lay out plates and that sort of thing."

"Nope. Table is set. If you want, you can take the pilaf out of the microwave. There's stuff in the cooler, but I'll bring it and the salmon in a minute."

She made her way down to the galley, guessing—correctly—at its whereabouts and grabbed the stuff he'd asked for and headed to the table on the main deck.

CHAPTER FIVE

PADDY BROUGHT THE salmon and the other things from the galley on a big tray but paused at the sight of her, the breeze playing with the hem of her dress and the hair at the nape of her neck. He wondered if she had any ink beneath the material of her dress.

Wanted pretty badly to see it as the sun rose, as she woke up in his bed.

"Hope you're hungry."

She turned, and it was a punch to his gut. The pleased smile, the ease on her face. She was so damned beautiful. Open in that moment, and he craved more with such longing, it alarmed him. There was something so alluring about her manner. Not when she was closed off, that sucked, and he hated it. Natalie was…elegant. Strong, sure, but she moved with a lithe grace.

Natalie padded over in her bare feet. And no, he wasn't a foot fetishist, but damn, she did have sexy feet, and he liked the way she looked. A little casual, rumpled by the wind. Distracting him with his nonstop imaginings of what was under her clothes. He had been with her before, sure. But that was over a dozen years past.

"I really am. I had a microwave burrito for lunch."

Snapping away from wondering what color her panties were, he pulled her chair out, and she sat. "I hope this is better than that."

She laughed, sipping her champagne. "The appetizers alone were better than that."

"Music. We need some music." He got up.

"I'll get started on dinner. You know, take one for the team and all."

Laughing, he found the remote for his dock and turned it on as he went back to join her.

"Wow, so you just go from zero to John Legend?"

"I'll take all the help I can get." He dished up some of the tomato salad.

Natalie had this way of pausing, he'd noticed. She considered her answers so carefully sometimes. Made him want to know more.

Finally, she finished her champagne and locked her gaze on his. "God save me, Patrick Hurley, but you don't need any help."

Oh, yes, that felt good. "Yeah?"

She sighed. "Yeah."

"Is that a good sigh? A bad sigh?"

She chewed her lip. "I don't know."

Then she shook her head and forked up some salmon. "I'm a liar. It's a good sigh. Also, the salmon is fantastic."

He preened a moment as he grinned before letting her off the hook. "So why are you eating microwave burritos for lunch, anyway? The library isn't that far from some pretty great little cafés."

"I'm a horrible cook. Sometimes I can't get away from work for an hour for this or that reason, and I need something quick. Plus, I eat out. A lot. It's better than a frozen diet meal, which tastes like tears and loneliness. I hate them. And yet, my freezer is full of them."

He wrinkled his nose and then gave her curves a

covetous look. "Why in God's name do you need diet meals?"

"I love doughnuts and I hate exercise."

"Sex is great exercise. I'm just saying."

"Hmm. I'm not sure it's a good selling point when you're trying to get one woman into bed to reference other women."

He cringed and then caught the twinkle in her eyes. "Oh, my God. You're teasing me."

She shrugged. "Some people think I'm funny. Even those of us who shush others for a living know how to laugh."

He snickered and then paused as he imagined her all stern in a pencil skirt and a button-down white shirt. Maybe with a ruler and some really high black pumps and stockings with the line down the back.

Leading up to those twin red bows.

Clearing his throat, he drained the rest of his champagne and poured them both some more.

"Why libraries?"

"I was in my third year as an undergrad and I went to a job fair. I wandered up and down the aisles, took brochures. Took notes. Asked questions dutifully. And I ended up at the MLIS people—master's in library and information science—spent forty-five minutes with them. I liked them. I liked what they did. Until that, I'd been considering getting a teaching degree. One of the folks I met that day urged me to apply to the graduate MLIS program, and I did."

They continued to eat as she spoke.

"So I looked around and kept at it, and he was so helpful and kind and open. I applied and got in." She paused. "Of course, by the time I was ready to graduate,

the economy had changed. With all the cuts to libraries, I wasn't sure what would happen. I'd been working
part-time in a library near campus, so I knew how tight
things were. I considered jobs outside public libraries—
law firms need librarians, for instance. Colleges, uni-
versities, that sort of thing. But…the public library is
important. I really wanted to pursue a position that way.
This job here in town opened up, and one of my friends
told me about it, and that's pretty much history."

"You probably could have made a lot more money
elsewhere."

Her eyes lost that teasing light and she got serious.
"Libraries are important, Paddy. Libraries are not just a
place to check out books. They're a haven, a safe place
for so many kids. You cannot undervalue that. Being
a place, a home for people who need to escape their
own unsafe places is something libraries provide. It's
a priceless thing. Some kids don't have any adults in
their lives who give a shit about them. They can go to
the children's librarian who does something as simple
as holding back a book she thinks that kid would like,
and it changes everything. I make enough to pay my
bills and fortunately, I have family money, too. That I
have the ability to be part of someone's safe place means
everything to me."

Right then, Paddy fell a little bit in love with Natalie Clayton with her ferocity about kids and libraries.

"Go down a layer or two and you're a fierce bitch
about kids. I like that a lot."

She shrugged.

"Family money?"

She looked away a moment and then nodded. "Yes.

I considered giving it all up, but in the end, I like using it to help other people."

"What does your family think?"

"Let's talk about you for a while. Why did you stay here in Hood River instead of heading to L.A. or Seattle or New York?"

"I like all those places. I actually do have a condo in Manhattan and a place in Santa Barbara, where I head when I need the ocean. But my family is here. We have enough land that I can be left alone when I need it, but my brothers and my parents are close enough that I can get on my bike or take a brisk walk and be on someone's doorstep in a few minutes. I help when I'm around. We built a studio in an old converted barn, and we do all our own production there. I know where everything is. No one bothers us in town, really. I guess at the end of it, this is my home. Everyone should have a home."

She smiled at him and it made him happy.

"I like Hood River a lot. Love it in the fall best. Love the colors of the leaves. So gorgeous."

"I thought you grew up in Medina?"

"No. My grandparents lived there. I grew up in Los Angeles, actually. I visited a few times every year, but I grew up in a world where the leaves never changed."

"Where at in L.A.?"

"Whittier. It's a suburb east of downtown. So you mentioned a sister-in-law? When did your brother get married?"

She was touchy about her family, obviously.

"Let's see, um, about a year ago. Yeah, they're coming up on their anniversary soon. Do you have siblings?"

"I grew up thinking no. But a few years ago, my

grandmother let it slip after five glasses of wine that a person I thought was my second cousin is actually my sister."

"Wow, that's some daytime-talk-show stuff right there. How did she react? Did she know?"

"She doesn't know and really, she's better off not knowing. Not like she's missing out on any sort of stellar parenting."

"You don't want to tell her? To have a relationship with her?" Paddy couldn't imagine not going to someone who was his brother or sister. He may fight like crazy with his brothers, but he couldn't imagine not having them all in his life.

A shadow of grief passed across Natalie's face for the briefest of breaths. "She grew up in a relatively normal household with both parents. She's married and has three kids of her own. She runs a stationery store with her husband in a small town in Nevada. Her life is good. Who am I to tell her that her mother had an affair and everything she's ever believed is a lie? What right do I have to do that?"

He sat back. He hadn't thought of it like that, but she was right. Took the weight of knowing, he'd figured, but she'd done it to protect her sister.

"I'm sorry. You didn't have such a great childhood, then?"

A shrug. "I have a good life now. That's what counts. So is it weird being a rock star?"

"Yes. Sometimes it's totally weird." Having a conversation with this woman was an intricate process. She'd revealed things, personal things, but there were other topics she wove around and avoided.

He wanted to know her. All her wounds and sore spots as well as things that made her smile.

"Like how?"

"Well, you know, I'm just Paddy. I've been me my whole life. So I'll be walking down the street in Manhattan and suddenly someone will gasp and call my name out and it's like…being recognized as Paddy Hurley from Sweet Hollow Ranch has its own unique tone. It's great. I mean, I'm happy people love our music and it pays my bills and enables me to do what I love and travel all over the world and stuff. But it's an odd thing to have someone shake and cry just because they've seen me on my way back from grabbing a coffee."

"Must make you feel responsible on some level, though."

He warmed, pleased she'd gotten that. "Yeah. I mean, normally, if you catch me before I've had coffee, I'm grumpy. I can tell my brothers to fuck off and leave me be, but that teenage girl? I have to dig deep sometimes because I don't want to be that guy. Even when I'm tired or hungry or pissed off."

"Must be exhausting to be on all the time."

"Another reason I live here and not L.A. or Manhattan. Anonymity is *not* overrated. I can go get groceries in a ratty pair of jeans and it won't show up ten minutes later online. I'm protected here. Once I'm out in the larger world, it's different. People you don't know just make shit up about you. I hate that. Two years ago we were on tour and I got food poisoning. Have you ever had it? It's the worst. I thought I was going to die. Anyway, so they had to take me to the emergency room because it was so bad, and so of course, it was reported that I'd overdosed. My mom flipped out." He stopped abruptly, and she reached out, touching his hand.

"I know. About Ezra, I mean. It's sort of impossible not to have seen all the reporting on it at the time."

Paddy swallowed. He was careful sharing things about Ezra, who was so powerfully private in the wake of his battle with addiction.

"Your mom nearly lost one son, so I'm sure it was very upsetting for her to read that about another one of her sons. You all do live pretty hard out there on the road."

"Did you look us up, then?" He wasn't sure if he was embarrassed or flattered or what.

She snorted. "Please. I live in the world. The modern world with television and media. You're supercute brothers in a rock band together. Of course it's common knowledge that you booze it up and carouse when you're on tour. I don't need to be Sherlock Holmes to know that."

"Oh. Yeah. Probably. It's not as wild as they make it out to be." Mostly. Since Mary, especially. She came with them on tour and there was no way she'd stand for any bullshit in her presence.

"Anyway, so yes, it's weird. But it gets me great tables at restaurants. I fly first-class. I don't have to worry about money because I have enough, and I have a great accountant who manages it for me and invests it for my future. I've met some amazing people, seen some amazing things. I do this thing I dreamed about, and we're lucky enough that we're successful at it."

They finished dinner and dessert.

"So, how'd I do?"

She looked back over her shoulder as she'd been standing, leaning to trail her fingers through the water.

"Dinner was great."

"Date-wise?"

"Not much to complain about. Gorgeous man. Really nice boat. Beautiful scenery. The weather is perfect."

He took her hand and took her down to the stern. "Gorgeous, huh?" He turned her to face him and got close, the rail at her back.

"Are we pretending you don't know how pretty you are?"

"Nah." She made him smile a lot. "Still, it's nice to hear from a beautiful woman I really hope to kiss a time or two tonight."

"I have such bad judgment." Natalie said it, but she had no plans to fight it.

"Really, now? That sounds like it'll be a win for me."

She laughed, placing her palm on his chest. "You're bad for me."

"I promise not to rot your teeth or give you diabetes. That means I'm way better for you than doughnuts."

She slid her hand up to his throat and around to the back of his neck. He stepped the last bit, bringing her to him, his arm around her waist.

He lowered his head, and she went to her tiptoes to meet him halfway for a kiss.

Ha, *kiss* was such a mild word for what it was.

She wove her fingers through his hair and tugged to keep him there. If she was going to make a really bad decision, she wasn't going to do it halfway.

Plus, he was really good at kissing.

He traced her bottom lip with the tip of his tongue and then nipped hard enough to make her gasp. That's when he barged right into her mouth and turned her knees to jelly.

And clearly, she needed to work as hard as he was working, so she hummed and sucked his tongue. He arched into her body, holding her tighter. She lost herself in him, in the way his hands felt on her body. In his taste as it filled her up and rendered her useless to think about anything else but his mouth on hers.

Out there, it was just the two of them. The stars overhead, the sound of the water, the breeze, Paddy and Natalie, and it was perfect, so she didn't fight it.

That kiss slid into another and another until her head spun, and she clung to him, taking it in, savoring every moment until he finally broke away, though his arms remained around her.

"Yeah. So that was fucking awesome."

She laughed as she tried to catch her breath.

"Do you want to go for a swim?"

"I didn't bring a bathing suit." Also, she sure as heck wasn't going to wear some cast-off suit from another chick he brought out there.

"There's no one around. You don't need a suit."

The sexual invitation in his voice wrapped around her, caressing, teasing.

"It's been a really hot day. I've got fluffy towels and a shower here to rinse the river off if you want."

He pulled his shirt off like a challenge.

"Live a little dangerously."

He unbuttoned and unzipped his jeans, easing them down, and she wasn't surprised in the least that he didn't have any underwear on. Or that he was *really* interested in that swim.

He followed her gaze to his cock and looked back

with a grin. "Yeah, well. You're sort of irresistible. But I promise it's just an invitation to swim. Not that I really don't want to fuck you, because I do. But we'll take it at your pace."

He popped a cushion from a nearby couch free, revealing a stack of neatly folded towels. He pulled two out. "What do you say?"

She needed to say no. Needed to say she had work in the morning and should really go home.

But she found herself saying, "You go in first."

With a grin, he jumped from the deck into the water with a splash. "I'll even keep my back turned until you get in."

She unbuttoned her dress, slid from it, her bra and panties, folded them and put them out of splash range and took a running jump from the boat into the river.

CHAPTER SIX

"So, IT WENT GOOD, huh?" Tuesday paused to examine a pair of hand-beaded slippers. They'd headed to a craft fair in Portland and had sucked down coffee and sang along to the radio on the way.

"It was… Yeah, it was good. He made me dinner and wooed me a little."

It had been a few days since the date, but she and Tuesday had barely connected between work and other stuff, so this was the first time they'd been able to talk about it all.

Tuesday put the slippers down, and they moved on, this time it was Natalie who paused to look at a framed photograph that had been hand-tinted. "Wow, this is fantastic." She turned to Tuesday. "This would look perfect in the front hallway, don't you think?"

Tuesday nodded, and Natalie bought it, tucking it carefully into the rolling cart she brought to fairs, green markets and swap meets.

"Did you sleep with him?"

Natalie snorted. "You're so shy."

"Whatever. Did you?"

Natalie shook her head. "Nope. We did get naked, but it was to swim. And it was dark so I saw some—well, okay a lot—when he just stripped off and jumped in." A smile came unbidden, and because it was Tuesday, Natalie gave in. "Everything is how I left it last. We kissed a lot. He felt me up. But we got out, and I dried off and got dressed and so did he, and he brought me home."

"Ugh. Lame. You said his cock was still nice and sturdy, so what's the story?"

Natalie laughed. "Sturdy?"

"Like a farm work truck, I'd imagine."

This made Natalie laugh so hard they had to stop so she could get her breath. "You're so broken and wrong, Tuesday. Thank goodness for you. We didn't because I wasn't ready."

"*Ready?* You've already fucked him. What's the holdup? It's not like you're a virgin."

"You should get laid yourself, since you're so invested in what I'm doing. Jeez."

"Mine are better," Tuesday said in an undertone as they left the jewelry stall they'd stopped at.

"Duh." This particular craft market had a wait list, and Tuesday was on it. Hopefully soon she'd be able to get a stall at some point.

Tuesday waved a hand. "Anyway, you like sex. He's gorgeous. Why aren't you ready?"

"I needed a little time and he gave it to me. That said a lot. We talked. We flirted. We kissed. It's all good. The pace works. If he was only after me to fuck me, he won't come around again." Just as he had been concerned about people after him for his celebrity, she needed him to want more than sex from her.

"Ah. I get it. I guess that's fair. If he passes your test and calls to ask you out again, will you go?"

Natalie couldn't afford to lie to herself, and Tuesday would know it, anyway, and call her out. So she went with blunt. "Yeah, definitely. I like him. He's funny and obviously talented. Plus he cooks."

"Always a plus."

"He's nosy, though. I ended up telling him more than I had intended to. Back in the day, we just had a lot of sex and drank. This talking thing is new."

They laughed at that.

"So you're… This is you dating him. For real?"

"Yeah. Maybe. I don't know. So far it's one date. But I just needed to do it like a real person. I wouldn't have banged some random dude on the first date, either. That doesn't erase all the other things I pause over. He's still…" Natalie whipped her hands all over the place. "A tornado? A storm? He's messy, and he comes with a lot of stuff I don't want or need."

"Whether you need it or not is a whole different conversation, Nats. Anyway, he didn't ask you to marry him or go out on the road with him. Right now he's farmer Paddy, and you're the librarian. Come to think of it, that sounds like a really hot book I'd totally read. So live a little. It's not that serious."

Natalie blew out a breath. She wanted him, at least for the next little while, so it was really in her best interest to let Tuesday talk her into it. Tuesday rarely steered her wrong.

Tuesday linked her arm with Natalie's. "We've spent enough money, and now I'm starving. I need a lot of pancakes and pork products."

"Yes, please. Let's go put this in the car, and we'll get brunch."

PADDY WAS UP EARLY, needing the physical activity to ease the burn. Even masturbating in the shower hadn't made it better, so he'd been out with Ezra in the orchards since the sun had risen.

The work, being outside and the cool morning air that would be gone in just a few hours, all combined to make a far more relaxed Paddy, along with Ezra, making their way up the front steps of their parents' place for breakfast.

The sound hit him immediately. A smile broke over his face as he remembered his nieces were with Vaughan that week.

Kensey and Maddie looked up from where they poured pancakes with their grandmother and squealed at the sight of two of their uncles coming in.

"That's how I wish I was greeted every time I came into a room." Paddy knelt and held his arms open to get kisses and hugs from the girls. "You guys are getting way too big. Stop that now."

Vaughan grinned at his daughters. "Second and third grade already."

It was a little bittersweet because they didn't live there with their dad. Instead, their mother had primary custody and lived in nearby Gresham. But Paddy had to hand it to Kelly. She'd had more than one opportunity to leave the area for school and her job, but she'd turned it all down so their daughters could see their dad on a regular basis.

They'd married too young and divorced too quickly. Vaughan and Kelly's marriage had been a casualty of their lifestyle as well as their age and inexperience at being in a relationship.

Paddy looked over at his brother. Vaughan had never truly let go of Kelly. There'd been plenty of women so it wasn't as though it hindered him in the sex department. But there'd been no one he'd been interested in for longer than a week or two, and he only rarely went out.

Kelly and Vaughan had gotten together for the same reason they split; they had an intense connection and chemistry. But at twenty-three and twenty-five, neither Kelly nor Vaughan had known how to manage it, and it had exploded.

Paddy stepped to the side as the girls moved to Ezra, grilling him about the animals he kept. "Yes, of course we'll go horseback riding after breakfast. You can come over and see the goats, too. Violet herds them."

The girls thought that was hilarious. A pig herding goats? And yet, that's exactly what Ezra's crazy, bossy pig, who thought she was a dog, did.

"Coffee just finished." His mother motioned to the coffeemaker with a spatula. "Mary and Damien are on the way up, too, so you boys need to put the extra leaf in the table."

They all moved to obey their mother, and ten minutes later the dining room was filled with the happy noise of a family eating a big breakfast.

"How'd your date go?" His mother never forgot anything, which made her awesome and frightening at the same time.

"Good. Mary's food went over well and only made my salmon look better. We drank champagne, went swimming." He attempted what he hoped was a nonchalant shoulder thing. It *had* been a pretty nice date. And he rarely had nights like it. Just regular, fun get-to-know-you dates.

"You gonna ask her out again?" Ezra asked, dropping pancakes on Kensey's plate.

"Yes." He hadn't even needed to pause to think it

over. He'd sent her wildflowers the next day. She'd called him to thank him but got his voice mail. He'd returned the call and got hers.

He would totally ask her out again and hopefully this time, he'd end the date the next morning. The kisses they'd shared had been a taste of heat. Their chemistry was still there in a big way. But they were both different.

Natalie especially. The carefree girl he'd dallied with for those two weeks had never shared anything personal, and he had to admit, he'd never asked. She'd said a lot but not much had been intimate.

"The way she talks about her job? So much passion. It's more than a place she goes to pay her bills. This is her calling. It was awesome."

"Is this your girlfriend, Uncle Paddy?" Maddie asked.

"I'd like her to be. She's a librarian here in town."

Kensey's eyes widened. "For real? Can we go check books out from her, then? I love the libary."

"Library, darlin'." Vaughan kissed her head. "And sure, I think checking books out is a great idea."

His mother went back for another pass at information-gathering. "So how does she talk about her work, then?"

"She talked about the library like it was a haven. How she wanted to be part of a safe place for kids and others in the community. Said the library was more than just checking out books."

His mother smiled and Paddy knew it spelled trouble.

"I like that. Girl's got a good heart. So you knew her when you two were young and silly, and now you've grown."

"Yes." The good thing was that because the girls were there, his mother wouldn't bring up safe sex or anything else embarrassing and cringeworthy. But that didn't mean she wouldn't find him later to do it.

"Is she pretty?" Maddie snuck a piece of bacon off her dad's plate, and he pretended to be scandalized.

"She's really pretty."

"She likes books, and she's pretty, too. Is she smart?"

He nodded. "She has a master's degree. You know what that is?"

Maddie shook her head.

"You go to grade school and then high school. She went to college after that. That's four years. And then she went to school for more years after that to get a special degree in being a librarian."

"That's lots of school! Smart and pretty. My momma says pretty fades but smarts last forever."

"That's what she says when Maddie doesn't want to finish her homework," Kensey added.

"Well, your mom is right." Vaughan laughed, winking at his brother.

WHEN SHE WALKED into Common Grounds Monday morning, he sat there at his regular table.

"There you are. Morning, Natalie. I took the liberty of ordering for you." He pointed at a very large mug and a plate with two spice doughnuts.

"You're the devil."

He laughed. "How so?"

She sat and looked at the pretty design Bobbi had made on the top of her cappuccino and then back to the masculine glory of his face. "Doughnuts? Two of them, even."

"It's Monday. If an extra doughnut is what it takes to

get through unscathed and without violence to another human, I say eat two."

Because he had what was probably 2 or 3 percent body fat, it was clearly easy to say. Which did not stop her from eating that first doughnut in what felt like three bites. Maybe it was four.

She hoped so.

He just grinned at her.

"What?"

"I like watching you. Did you have a good weekend?"

"Went to a craft fair with Tuesday. Bought stuff for my house. Ate too much. We planted stuff in our front yard, and yesterday she made me go on a hike. I just pray for winter when I don't have to hike up hills for a few months."

"Aw, come on now. You wouldn't do it if you really didn't like it."

She nearly choked on the second doughnut. "I hate to break it to you, but I do it because my best friend likes it. I don't like being really sweaty." She sipped her cappuccino. "Well, outside of a few examples. Some kinds of sweat are worth the exertion."

He leaned closer. "Please tell me you're talking about sex."

She blinked, keeping her expression serious. "No, I'm talking about raking leaves. Of course I'm talking about sex."

He wiped his brow theatrically. "I'm going to change the subject, or I'll be useless for hours. Bobbi says you never drink iced stuff. Now that September is here, that's one thing, but in full summer, too?"

"Are you a coffee spy, Paddy?" She raised a brow.

"If I am, can I capture you and do whatever I have to to get you to cooperate?"

The words fell over her, heated, dirty innuendo. "Maybe." They watched each other as they sipped their coffee.

"Tuesday says my dislike of iced coffee means I'm broken and tragically weird. I'll eat coffee ice cream, because I'm not *that* tragic. But I'll happily guzzle hot coffee all year around. I'm a traditionalist that way."

"Did you know you have a dimple?" He reached out to brush a fingertip over the space to the right of her mouth. Of course she wasn't smiling then; she was probably looking like a deer caught in the headlights because he set her aflame.

She ducked her head. "Did you have a good weekend?"

"My nieces were visiting, so we rode horses and went on picnics, and I endured three DVDs worth of animation. So yes, I had a good weekend. You should go out with me again."

Her head spun at that quick change of topic. "I should?"

"Oh, yeah. Do you like movies?"

"Yes, again, not *that* tragic."

"Our manager is dating a producer so we just got a bunch of stuff that's just released. I have a home theater. Why don't you come to my house? We'll have dinner and watch movies."

"I can't tonight. Monday night is my book club."

"Book club? What are you reading?"

"We have themes. This month is graphic novels, so we've been doing all the *Walking Dead* issues."

"Really? Amazing. Is this open to new members?"

She laughed. Nearly choking on her drink. "We'd never get anything done if you joined my book club."

"What? Why do you say that? I like to read!"

Natalie waved a hand at him. "You're far too charming, flirty and sexy. I'm the most steadfast member of the group, and *I* can't even concentrate around you. The rest of them would dissolve into goo. No book club for you, Patrick."

He laughed. "I'd say you were mean, but you did compliment me and say I messed with your concentration, so I'll let it pass. How about Wednesday?"

"Okay." She looked at her watch. "I need to get moving."

He stood with her. "I'll walk you."

She could have refused but she didn't want to.

"All right."

He walked on the outside, her barrier from the street. His gentlemanly ways surprised her at times.

"I admit it's way nicer now that you don't reject me over and over. Would I be pushing my luck if I tried to hold your hand right now?"

"Yes. I'm on my way to work. I like to keep my work and my private life separate."

"Hmm. We're going to need to talk about all this."

"Hmm." She mimicked him. "It's going to have to wait until Wednesday."

"Fine." He chitchatted about silly stuff until they got to the library.

"I take it a kiss would not be okay according to your rules?"

"You're learning. Oh, I need directions to your house for Wednesday night."

He took her phone and put the information in. "I'll

see you Wednesday, then. I can't be at the café tomor-row morning. We're doing an interview, so I'll be busy doing that for a while."

She didn't want to be disappointed, but there it was, anyway. So reckless of her to go getting attached to him like that, but her brain didn't seem to care. The other parts of her had lost that battle weeks before. "Okay. I'll see you Wednesday, then. Have a good interview."

She turned with a wave and headed into work.

CHAPTER SEVEN

HE SPENT MOST of Wednesday preparing for his date. He went in and got a haircut and a beard trim. He picked up snacks and supplies for dinner. He also picked up extra condoms. It was like a talisman. For luck.

They'd end up in bed. He hoped it'd be that night, but even if it wasn't for another month, it would happen. They had so much sexual energy between them, it sizzled.

He cleaned the house, changed his sheets and bedding. Aired everything out and moved furniture three times.

He was officially ridiculous, and he didn't stop even after he'd realized that.

There were three movies. Horror, a thriller and some comedy bro-flick. He'd let her choose.

In the shower he considered jerking off so he'd be more relaxed. Thinking about her had him tense and agitated, but in a way he sort of dug. He hadn't had to work this hard for a woman, well, ever, actually. He'd had her before, which only spiced things up. He knew what it was like to be inside her. Knew what her lips felt like wrapped around his cock. Knew what she tasted like.

He'd thought he'd remembered her body. He'd seen it naked an awful lot. But in the brief glimpses of her he caught out at the river, he'd noted curves. More than she'd had then. He had tended toward tall women with big tits and a lean look. But Natalie was voluptuous. He hadn't realized he had a thing for all that swoop and dip, but he was utterly converted. Nicely though, the big boobs part was there, too. He'd been so focused on the curves, he'd only barely noticed the ink and hoped for a far closer inspection very soon.

So yeah, he soaped a hand up and wrapped it around his cock as he imagined her naked. Wet, but not from swimming. Flushed from orgasm. On her back in his bed. Her lips swollen from his kisses and from sucking his cock. Her eyes half-lidded and dreamy.

"Open those thighs."

She complied with that smile of hers. Unashamed of what she wanted, of what he did to her. She was slick, dark with desire and when he fed her his cock, pressing in slow and steady, she made a sound that wrapped around his balls and tightened.

She wound her legs around his waist, grabbing two handfuls of his ass and pulling him closer, urging him on. She loved fucking as much as he did. That wouldn't have changed. Tight and hot, her inner muscles would flutter around him as she got closer. As he got closer. Her nails dug into his skin as she arched, her neck bared to his lips as he licked and nibbled.

Climax shot through him, yanking him from that fantasy as his dream Natalie dissolved, leaving him alone and still half hard as the water rushed over his skin.

SHE'D GONE WITH casual that night. Her favorite super-soft T-shirt with the V-neck and some jeans. No heels this time. He lived on a farm so if he wanted her to walk or do something outdoorsy, she'd be better off in the sneakers she'd chosen instead of sandals.

Of course, as she followed the road, drove through a gate that he'd given her the code to and continued on, she realized the word *farm* probably wasn't adequate for the land, the orchards and fields in the distance. She saw lights from a few houses and passed two until she saw the turnoff for his.

Off the main road, she could see the river in the distance as she parked in his driveway. All glass and gorgeous, warm wood, his house was Northwestern modern. The opposite of her Victorian, but it fit him.

She didn't get the chance to knock; he opened up with a smile before she'd even been able to raise her hand.

"Hey, you found me."

"Yes. Your instructions were perfect, thanks."

He opened the door wider and motioned her inside.

"Are you a shoes-off house?"

He snorted. "No. If you want to, go on ahead. I'm not wearing shoes because I don't want to. But it's your choice." He paused and bent to kiss her quickly. "Sorry to burst your foot-fetish suspicions."

She laughed and put her bag down in the entry.

He took her hand. "Want a tour?"

"Yes, please."

It was a great house. Clean. Very modern but warm at the same time. His living space was great with big couches and chairs.

"Is yours the house everyone hangs out at?"

"We split it up pretty evenly. My house is the middle point between Ezra, who is closest to the big house where my parents are, and Damien, who lives the farthest from it. We spend more time at Damien's these days because Mary is such a great cook." He paused. "Want to see the upstairs?"

Natalie nodded, and he took her up the stairs fronted by a wall of glass. "This view is insane."

"We all worked with the same architect who took the land and views into account as she worked. All our houses are unique and fit our individual tastes, but they're on the same continuum so you can see the thread. It's a light touch. Each room has something about it that I love. My work space has excellent afternoon light. My bedroom gets the sunset. Kitchen gets morning light. All that jazz."

He opened the door to a huge room with several guitars on stands, a large desk with two monitors, big chairs and a wet-bar-sized sink and fridge. "This is my work space."

She went in, impressed. "Wow."

He blushed, brushing his fingertips over the neck of a guitar. "I spend more time in here than any other place but my bedroom. I can run tracks in here. We're all hooked into a network with the board in the barn, that's our studio here. I write here. Ezra sleeps on that big couch a lot." He snorted a laugh.

"You and he do the writing?"

"About eighty percent of it is me and Ezra. Ezra does the bulk of production. Damien and Vaughan write a song or two each album."

"So you're closest to Ezra, then?"

He laughed. "Ezra and I collaborate really well, but we're too much alike in some ways, so we fight a lot. In the old days, it was nose-breaking sort of fighting, but now it's more pissy bickering. Though we do occasionally get physical. He knows how to push my buttons. He and Damien are closer. Vaughan and I tend to pal around more, but he's been away a lot over the last month. His girls just went back to school, so he's been spending time with them. But, and don't tell Ez this, Ezra is the person whose advice I seek out when I need an honest take. He's pretty wise for a dick."

She shook her head, imagining what it was like for their mother to have four really handsome sons who got into all the trouble they did.

He opened another door.

"My bedroom."

She walked into the room, spinning slowly. Stunned.

"What? Why do you have that look on your face?"

"I never expected this." Where the rest of his house was modern though comfortable, his bedroom was homey. His huge bed dominated one wall and was dressed with fluffy bedding. Heavy drapes were pulled back to expose sheers and windows looking out to the fields beyond, and if she was right, Mt. Hood on clear days.

Floor-to-ceiling bookshelves lined two walls. She traced her fingertips over the spines. This was the bedroom of a hedonist. Of the kind of person who spent the entire day in bed reading and watching movies.

Fucking.

"Never expected what?"

She turned to him. "This warm, inviting, comfortable space. It's womblike. I want to take a nap in your bed right this instant."

The worry on his features wisped away with a pleased grin. "Well, go on ahead. But only if I can nap with you. I love a good nap."

"I can tell." Napping was one of her biggest vices.

There was a big chair near the fireplace with an otto-man and a blanket on the back. She pointed. "Where'd you get that chair? I want one like it in my bedroom so I can read and nap on rainy days."

"If I told you, I'd be discouraging you from com-ing here on rainy days to read and nap, instead. That's self-defeating, Nat."

"You travel a lot. How can I leave my napping needs up to chance? You're quite heartless to make me, Pat-rick."

"Your sense of humor turns me on." He stepped closer. "You've been in my house for about twenty min-utes now, and I haven't really gotten a good kiss yet. Have a heart."

"You're the one who won't even tell me where to buy that chair. Mean."

"You're all breathless." Paddy cupped the back of her neck and slowly walked her into his chest. And she let him.

"I have asthma and you made me walk up stairs."

He laughed. "I swam with you a few days ago. You're in excellent shape. But goddamn, I love your body."

She gulped. "Oh."

"You need to be quiet so I can kiss you now."

She nodded.

He started at the corner of her mouth. Just a brush of his lips. When she smiled, he licked at the spot, making her draw a breath. That's when he used her distraction to sneak his very talented tongue right into her mouth.

Just a quick flick, and then he was gone again. He nipped her bottom lip, tugging until she moaned softly, digging her nails into his biceps where she'd been grasping him to stay standing because her knees had gone to jelly.

"You taste like cinnamon."

He backed off, and she was sure she should have been glad, but she really liked his mouth on hers.

"Gum. The cinnamon, I mean. And maybe two boxes of Hot Tamales." Perhaps three, but that wasn't something she could confirm as she tended to lose count.

He grinned. "Come downstairs. Ezra went into town, and he's picking Thai food up for us. He should be here shortly."

She followed him from the room and down the stairs. He had a great back. And a great butt, too.

"I should have asked if you liked Thai food. If you don't, I can make something. I went to the grocery store, but then I realized I'd rather order in and have more time with you."

"Thai is good. I order it all the time, but I haven't had it in a few weeks. Tuesday got a slow cooker and she's been making all sorts of great stuff in it. It's pretty awesome that one of us can cook."

"How come you can't?"

She started to answer, but there was a knock on the door.

"Hold that thought. Ezra's here."

Paddy bellowed out a *come in* as he jogged toward the front entry. When Ezra came around the corner into the room, she totally recognized him from before. Where Paddy was gorgeous, Ezra was ruggedly handsome. Big and brawny, he looked every inch the rancher he was. She bet he looked really good doing sweaty things like baling hay or riding a horse.

He flashed her a smile. "Hey! I remember you."

It was impossible not to smile back. He thrust the bags at Paddy and headed to her, taking her hands in his. "It's good to see you after all these years."

"You, as well. Paddy's been telling me about the job you do here on the ranch and also the collaborative way you put out Sweet Hollow Ranch's music. I'm totally impressed."

Paddy made a sound, and they looked up at him. He had puppy-dog face, and it was very cute.

"You can tell he was the spoiled one. He can't deal if everyone isn't fawning over him all the time."

"Shut it, buttface."

"Notice he didn't dispute my statement."

"She's my date. Go away."

"Thank you for bringing us dinner, Ezra." Natalie patted his arm.

He sent Paddy a face, and she burst out laughing.

"I'd love to have dinner with you guys, thanks for asking." Ezra turned to her and led her into the kitchen. "Gives me a chance to catch up with Natalie. I don't suppose you have that Mustang anymore?"

"Oh, my God, you remember that? I kept it for years, wanting to get it restored, but I never had the time or inclination and I ended up selling it."

Paddy turned and pulled her into a hug. "I forgot about that sexy fastback you used to have."

"So you both love cars, clearly. Given the one you drove the other day, I should have guessed."

"Paddy's past love and working his way into obsession. But, as far as obsessions go, classic cars isn't a bad one." Ezra pulled out a chair at the table. "Sit."

She did, trying not to laugh more as Paddy frowned at his big brother.

"Hey, we understand that you need to *go home*. Thanks for understanding I'm on a date and all."

"I headed Mom off so I think the phrase you're looking for is, *thanks, Ezra, for saving me from an evening of baby pictures and stories about the time I yarked on that Santa at the Bon Marche.*"

"I don't know which is worse," Paddy muttered.

"Please. Don't lie. Sharon Hurley nosy about her baby's date is way worse than me eating all your crab rangoon and leaving after I know I've given you an eye tic for a few hours."

Paddy thrust plates into his brother's arms. "At least set the table." Paddy turned to Natalie with a far friendlier look than he gave his brother. "What can I get you to drink? I've got waters, juices, orange soda, beer, wine. I can do mixed drinks, too. I have champagne for later, but not until Ezra leaves."

"I'd love some orange soda." The two men moved around the kitchen—and each other—with ease, saying far more about their bond to each other than their bickering had. It was clear the two spent a lot of time like this, just hanging out.

"So—" Ezra grinned her way for a moment and continued eating "—you're a librarian. Why Hood River?"

"Well, there were a few places that had openings. I visited several cities in a few states. I visited here in May, so it was so pretty and warm and everyone was friendly. I liked the library here. Liked the programs. But to be totally honest with you? I was driving around, you know, just checking the area out, and I drove past a big blue Victorian with a for-sale sign out front."

She'd slowed, looking up at it and had wanted it with a greed she rarely allowed herself to feel. The curves of all the bay windows, the lattice work; the house was like a childhood dream come true.

"It was the house that sold me on Hood River. Don't tell my boss that, though."

Ezra laughed, but it was Paddy who spoke next. "So? The house?"

"I went back to my hotel and contacted the listing agent. I made an offer the next day after I did a walk-through. Moved in sixty days later. It's a really big house, though, so I lived in half while I did a lot of re-modeling on the rest. And then my best friend came to visit, and she fell in love with it, too, and she now lives in the other half."

She wanted to ask him why he'd chosen to run the ranch, but she didn't know him well enough, and she didn't want to push any buttons about his past addiction. Addiction talk often made her antsy, anyway.

"I think I know the house you mean. It's not blue anymore, though. It's green and white. That's the one. Overlooking the river, right?"

She nodded. "Yep. It was that color originally, and when I saw the swatches, I knew I wanted it that way again."

Ezra stayed long enough for her to know he wanted to check her out and be sure she was okay. It spoke volumes about the closeness of this family. But it sure was nice when he finally sent a grin to Paddy as he stood, patting his belly.

"That was awesome, kids. I'm off home."

She rose, and he kissed her cheek before they followed him down the hall to the door.

"Make good choices." Ezra winked, and Paddy rolled his eyes, opening the front door.

"Yeah, yeah. Thanks for bringing the food. See you later."

CHAPTER EIGHT

"I THOUGHT HE'D never leave." Paddy leaned back against the door, flipping the lock. "I'm sorry about that."

"It was totally fine. I like Ezra and so do you. He checked me out because he wanted to be sure I wasn't going to hurt you or your family in some way."

He paused before he grabbed her hand and began to pull her down the hall. For all the smooth, supercontrolled way she acted, there were times she was utterly unvarnished. It kept him on his toes. "Nah. He knows you're fine."

"I was some chick you fucked for a few weeks years ago who suddenly resurfaced in your life. For all he knew, I was a stalker out to try to con you."

She was pretty perceptive. He hadn't even realized that until she'd said it. Of course Ezra, being the oldest and yes, being the guy who caused no small amount of drama and harm to their family, would take it on as his responsibility to protect them all.

"Does that offend you or bother you?"

She tossed herself onto the big couch in the center of the media room. "What? That your big brother did what big brothers are supposed to do? I'm guessing I must have done okay, or he'd still be here."

"If your family did that, I don't know that I'd be that easygoing about it."

"Well, that's not going to be a worry for you, so you can put that out of your head. But let's face it, you have a lot to lose. More than the average random woman who shows up in one of your lives. Not all of us are going to have big fat bank accounts and trust funds."

"You're going to tell me that story." He moved to the projector.

"Maybe. Maybe not. But right now, I'm here for the movies and popcorn."

"Is making out on the menu?"

"If you're nice to me, and you've included some peanut M&M's in the offerings, I might let you get to second base."

He was very glad he'd grabbed snacks of all types when he'd gone grocery shopping earlier.

"As a matter of fact, I did. So sit back and let me get everything set up."

She raised one brow and then shrugged, settling in and getting comfortable.

They chose a movie— the thriller—and he popped some corn and tossed her a bag of M&M's before finally joining her on the couch.

She put her head on his shoulder as they watched, and once they'd finished the popcorn, he pulled her close, and she fit just right against his side.

The credits finally started to roll, and she shifted to her knees, getting in his lap astride his body.

"Well, now."

She slid her hands through his hair and pulled him close, dropping her lips to his, claiming a kiss. He hummed, his hands sliding up her thighs to her hips, where he held on as she kissed the hell out of him.

Her skin where her shirt met her pants was warm

and soft, and he didn't stop himself from touching, caressing up her spine as she arched into him.

Higher and higher until he popped the catch on her bra, pausing for a moment to be sure she was on board.

She broke the kiss, leaned her upper body back, pulled her shirt up and off and tossed her bra aside, leaving him totally speechless and *very* pleased.

"Damn."

He grabbed her back, pulling her close, her breasts brushing against him, making him hiss as his hands roved all over her bare skin.

She arched into him like a cat before nipping his earlobe. "You take your shirt off, too."

"I want to spend some time on you first."

She made a sound and, grabbing his shirt at the hem, pulled it up and off.

"Man, oh, man." She flicked the bar through his right nipple with her thumbnail.

It was his turn to arch just then. "What brought this on?" He moaned as she kissed across his cheeks to his ear.

"I wanted you, and here you were."

"Well, that's very true."

"I like sex. I know already that I like sex with *you*. As long as things are private, I'm totally on board with this thing going wherever and for however long."

He wanted to frown, even though her words were good ones. As far as he could tell, there were no good reasons not to do more than just fuck. He opened his mouth to press her, but she made a sound that tore at him.

With a groan, he skimmed his hands up her belly

to cup her breasts and drew his thumbs back and forth across her nipples.

"Yes," she breathed into his ear before she licked the outer shell and gave him the edge of her teeth against that very sensitive skin.

She was lush there in his lap. The weight of her perfect against his cock. The heat of her pussy teasing him.

"You have new tattoos."

"You have nipple rings and more ink."

"I want to see you."

"Earn it."

She pulled away enough to look into his face, a smile of challenge on her lips. He snatched a kiss, accepting her challenge. Eagerly.

He shimmied to the edge of the couch and stood, setting her down on her feet. "Now, stand there while I look at you awhile. Whet my appetite because I'm starving for you."

"Mmm, that's a good one."

There was some of the woman he'd been with before in that moment. He liked it. Her ink was perfectly placed so no one would have been able to see it while she was clothed.

Starting at her right hip there was a spill of pink climbing roses. Unfurled as they flowed up her side and up her back. He circled her, taking it in. "This is gorgeous."

"Thank you. I get a little more once a year."

"You'd never know these were here when you're dressed." He pressed a kiss at the highest knot of blooms at her midback.

"That's the point."

He kissed his way across her shoulder until he'd come to face her again. "Is it?"

"The ink is for me. No one needs to know about it unless I want them to. I don't need everyone to see it or know about it to enjoy it."

He unmoored the top button of her jeans and slid the zipper down. Panties the same color pink as the roses on her body.

"I wanted to look at you the other night on my boat when we skinny-dipped, but I didn't want to scare you away."

He shoved her jeans down, and she stepped from them. Then she turned slowly, her ass tipped slightly toward him. She slid her fingertips over the red bows that were inked at the tops of her thighs. "I believe you were asking about these." It wasn't until she looked at him back over her shoulder that his control slipped. He dropped to his knees to get a better look.

He caressed up her legs to that spot where each bow lived. Gooseflesh rose, beading her skin as he breathed over it, and she squeaked prettily when he licked each one.

"You taste good."

She moaned, fisting her hands at her sides.

He hooked his fingers at the sides of her underpants and pulled them down, spinning her once she'd stepped free to face him, gloriously naked.

"I'm naked, and you have your pants on still." Her voice was breathy again, and it made him smile.

"I know. How fucking lucky am I?" He lifted enough to lick over the ink at her hip, his body warming when she held his head to her, her fingers cradling his skull.

"You could be even luckier if your pants were off."

"That'll come soon enough." He licked her belly, circling her belly button. "First you need to come and then we'll move to step two." He stood and walked her back to the couch, a push to get her seated again. He put a pillow on the floor and knelt on it. "Don't worry, the pillow can stay for when it's your turn to be on your knees."

Dear God, he was going to melt her. Her bones and muscles and skin were just going to drip into a puddle of wordless, turned-on goo at his feet.

He kissed the inside of each knee and then up her thighs, pushing them wide. She didn't have time to worry or be embarrassed or hesitant. He moved quickly, licking through her until her breath came out as a stutter.

"You like that?" He spoke, his lips against her labia. Enough that she felt his smile, and it sent a shiver through her.

"What's not to like?" she managed to say but felt like her tongue was three sizes too big for her mouth.

Maybe one of the reasons he was a lead singer was that he was really good with his mouth. Like stellar fantastic. He'd been good before, but clearly, he'd been practicing on a few women in the interim.

He teased her until her thigh muscles trembled. There was something so delicious about the way he held her thighs wide, the strength in his forearms as he held her open and down at the same time, the slight callus to his fingers—forbidden and dark and oh, so good.

He changed his pace. Slow, with licks with the flat of his tongue, fast, hard flicks with the tip of his tongue against her clit. He drove her to the edge, and then he pulled back over and over until she was a trembly, sweaty mess.

"If you don't let me come, I'm going to take over and do it myself!"

He pulled back, nipping the inside of her thigh. "I'd love to see that. But right now, your orgasm is in my hands, and you'll get it when I want you to have it."

She opened and closed her mouth a few times, trying to muster up outrage, but it never came.

He waited, brow raised. "Nothing to say? Good."

He bent and got back to work. But this time he didn't tease her. He kept a relentless rhythm that sent her spiraling into climax so hard, she saw stars.

When she managed to open her eyes, she found him resting his chin on her thigh, smiling.

"Someone learned more than a few new chords out on the road."

He burst out laughing.

"Just when I think I've got you figured out."

He got to his knees, and his hands went to his top button on his jeans. She sighed happily. "Finally."

"I'm sensing a theme here. You're impatient when there's something you want in view."

"Have you looked in the mirror?"

He stood, slowly dragging the zipper down, each click of the teeth nearly a drumbeat in her head.

"I have to laugh at that comment when you're spread out on my couch like the most luscious piece of cake a man ever saw."

He was a ruthless flatterer.

"Doughnut may be more apt."

He laughed again as he pushed his jeans down his legs, along with shorts.

"I see you wore underwear today."

"I do from time to time. How did you know I didn't?"

His cock tapped his belly, it was so hard. The belly was hard, too. She sighed her pleasure at the sight of him. "You and I went naked swimming just a few days ago. A gal notices things like that."

He was tall. Hale and hearty. She cocked her head, taking him in. Flat, hard muscle covered his body. It was a testament to living on a ranch she supposed, but damn, he looked good. Both of his nipples were pierced; silver bars running through each. He had a number of tattoos, far more than he'd had before.

"Wait." She got to her feet, wildly flattered by the way he looked at her.

"I'd rather leap on you." He leaned in and took a deep breath at her neck, kissing her there.

"You looked at my ink, I want to look at yours. Then you can leap. Though I'd really like to get this—" she grabbed his cock, squeezing it "—in my mouth first."

He groaned. "Hurry up, then."

She looked at the owl, wings stretched across his back and the muscles of his shoulders. There were subtle shadings of red and green here and there on its feathers. Masculine and yet, still focused on the inherent beauty of flight and the feathers. "This is fantastic work."

"Thanks. It's relatively new. A friend of my sister-in-law runs a tattoo shop in Seattle. He's a freaking genius."

On his right biceps, he had a tattoo of a wing; there was another on the left. "What bird is this?"

"Peregrine falcon."

"Birds, huh?"

On his hips he had musical notes. "First gold record, *Try Me*. On the left is first double platinum, *Ride*."

"I love that one."

"You listen to our music?"

"Hard not to. You're sort of a big deal. And you're good."

He had a labyrinth on his right thigh.

"It's one I walked at a really hard time in my life. Whenever things get bad or overwhelming, I just look down."

He got to her and she was past freaking out over it. His charisma scared her without a doubt. But she was charmed, and she wanted more.

She kissed his shoulder, and he slid an arm around her waist and pulled her close.

"I have condoms right there in that little table. I think you should grab one and then ride me. Right here. Right now."

She raised a brow as she looked at the table he indicated.

"I just put them there earlier today because I live in hope. It's not my fuck-company table or anything."

It was exactly the right thing to say. She pushed him back to sit on the couch before grabbing a condom. But she didn't use it right then.

"First things first." She put the pillow between his feet and he grinned.

"Oh, that. Well, I'm not going to argue with a really good idea."

She got to her knees, and he had to count to fifty to keep from blowing just from the sight of it. She licked up his thigh, her gaze locked on his, and he gulped at the carnality in it. She knew exactly what she was doing, which made it even hotter.

This was a woman who owned what she wanted.

This was the woman he'd been with years before.

Then she licked up the line of his cock, and he huffed out a breath, giving in to his desire to get his hands in her hair. He loved the cool softness of it against his skin. That her mouth was currently on his cock certainly didn't make it worse.

She teased him, taking her time. He'd been so eager to get inside her, he'd been in a blind rush. But this… this allowed him to wallow in the pleasure of the entire experience. She was doing to him what he'd done to her.

Her taste had been so freaking good; the sounds she made had been so hot, he hadn't wanted it to end. But it was the way her pupils had swallowed the color in her eyes when he'd told her he was in charge that had nearly killed him. She was so controlled, so in charge, he hadn't been sure how she'd react to his tease.

Her mouth was so hot and wet as she swirled her tongue around the head and took him so deep he grunted, his fingers tightening in her hair.

She moaned around his cock, and it vibrated to his brain.

He was torn. This was good. Like really, really good. She was a goddess here, her curves on display for him, those pretty blond curls bent over his lap, mouth on him. But he had been dreaming of being in her since he'd bumped into her at the café over a month before.

Once she scored her nails over his balls, he made a choice. He urged her back with his hands on her shoulders. "Wait. Stop. I want in you."

She pulled off with a slight pop of sound and licked her lips. "You were in me."

He swallowed hard as he grabbed the condom, ripped it open with his teeth and rolled it on quickly. "Now I can be in your pussy. Come on and ride."

She scrambled, straddling his lap. One-handed, she reached back to hold him where she wanted, and then he nearly blacked out when she slowly lowered herself on him.

"Jesus." Orgasm clawed at his guts, and he pushed it back because there was no way he'd finally gotten here, inside this woman, to come in a minute like he was sixteen.

She rocked back and forth, and he dug his fingertips into the muscles at her hips. Her bottom lip caught between her teeth as she moved.

"Mmm, yes. More."

A demand.

He held her down at her hips as he began to thrust up into her body, slow and steady. Staying deep.

The light was on in the hallway behind her so it glowed around her body as she moved. So beautiful, this woman.

He let go of her hip with one hand to cup one of her breasts, taking the weight in his palm before pinching and tugging her nipple until her head tipped back, her mouth, still swollen from his kisses and his cock, opened on a sigh laced with desire.

Her inner muscles gripped him and fluttered, and he nearly lost his mind. He held on, not wanting the moment to end. The scent of her skin, of her sex and desire rose and grasped nearly as tightly as her body did.

He slid the hand at her hip between them, finding her clit swollen and ready. She hissed. "I can't."

"Yes, you can. Come on, let me make you come again."

"I just did." But her voice had gone deeper as he

began to lightly slide the pad of his finger back and forth over her clit.

"I really need to come, Nat. But I won't until you do. Do it for me." He grinned, and she groaned, moving to lean her head on his shoulder.

"Is that your version of do it for America? Or just the tip?"

Startled, he snorted a laugh until her body tightened around his, and she bit his shoulder hard as she came. He snarled, pulling her down on him, holding her in place as he pushed deep, as hard and deep as he could and followed her.

He kept his arms around her until he had to get up. He carefully settled her back on the couch. "I'll be right back."

She pulled a throw over herself, snuggling against the pillows.

In front of the mirror in the adjacent bathroom, he stared at himself as he washed his hands. He wore a flush on his skin. Not the first time. Not even the first time with her.

But things were different somehow because he wasn't thinking about how he'd get her out the door. He couldn't get the sight of her all naked and curled up on his couch out of his head.

He wanted more of that. More of sleepy, relaxed Natalie Clayton in his house and in his life.

He didn't want to splash water on his face to snap out of his little fantasy. Because he didn't want her off his skin.

He forced himself to do it. He didn't know why he was acting like a fuck-drunk dumbass but he needed to snap out of it.

"Hey." She smiled up at him when he came back into the room.

"Hey, yourself. You should sleep over." He wanted to punch himself for blurting that out.

"I can't. I have to work tomorrow."

Oh. Well. He should be glad. Women stole covers, and if you let them sleep over they assumed stuff. She was doing him a favor.

But he found himself saying, "I have an alarm clock. Believe me, things get started early on a ranch. I'll make you breakfast even."

She stood, the blanket she'd been using fell away, and he had to step closer to touch all that pretty, naked skin. She leaned into his touch briefly, tiptoeing up to kiss him.

"Offers of breakfast are always appreciated. But I really do need to go home."

"Fine, fine. Deprive me of sleepy, warm woman for morning sex."

She snorted a laugh and then moved away, getting dressed.

"You're going home now?"

"Well, I got what I wanted. I'm going home to notch my bedpost. Where I record all my wild sexual encounters with celebrities and stuff. See you around."

He blew a raspberry. "Be sure to mark two notches."

She grinned. "I'll do that. Should I bring you a gold star the next time I see you?"

He hugged her again because he could, and because he would see her again. And because she made him smile so much.

"As long as it's not an edible one."

She snorted and swatted his butt.

After she'd gone, he'd gone to his bed to read awhile before going to sleep. Her scent rose from his skin, and when he woke up the next day, the faint stamp of her presence was still on his hands.

CHAPTER NINE

NATALIE WALKED OUT of work at the end of her day, and he was waiting, leaning against his car, legs stretched out. It had been a week since she'd had dinner at his place and the sight of him, long legs encased in denim, was just what her day had needed.

"Hey, you. I was thinking we could go and get some dinner. What do you say?"

"I have laundry to do."

He started, clearly confused by her refusal.

"Did you just turn down a date for washing clothes?"

She patted his arm. "No. You showed up unannounced and asked me to dinner. I already had plans to wash my clothes."

He frowned. "How about if we have dinner at your house so you can do your laundry? Work with me here. I have doughnuts."

She was going to gain ten pounds if he kept doing that. But, hello, doughnuts.

"Follow me to my house. We have a funky driveway so pull in behind me so Tuesday can get in when she gets home."

She ducked his kiss and headed to her car with a wave. Once she'd gotten her belt done, and she was on the way home, she allowed herself a smile at how handsome he'd been and how flattered she was.

He made her belly flutter. Belly fluttering was vastly underrated.

Tuesday wasn't home when they arrived. She'd left a note for Natalie on the fridge that she'd headed up to Olympia to see her family and would be back Sunday night.

Natalie hung her stuff up. "Tuesday won't be here. She left a note saying she'd be away for the weekend. She'll be sorry she missed meeting you."

While he wanted to meet this Tuesday she talked about so much, Paddy wasn't going to complain at having her all to himself.

"Bummer. Well, next time."

"Come on through, then."

Paddy walked through her kitchen, the floorboards creaking in a way he'd always thought of as welcoming. "Wow. This is beautiful."

She smiled at him, and he was instantly glad he'd said it. Truly, the place couldn't have been more opposite of his home. It was old-fashioned and fancy in places he'd deliberately chosen to be clean and simple in.

But someone had clearly put in the time to restore it to its Victorian glory, but it was also inherently comfortable and homey, too.

"It looks a little bit like layer cake outside, but in here, it's more casual. Lived in." The kitchen windows let in a lot of light and gave a view of a backyard with a pretty garden and seating area.

"Thank you."

He stepped closer and slid his arms around her. She melted against him, snuggling against his body. He kissed the top of her head, and she tipped back so he could get to that mouth.

It had been a week since he'd seen her last. It was…odd; he had to admit to himself that she seemed just fine with her life and with his intermittent place in it.

He kissed her long and slow, enjoying her taste.

"Give me a tour?"

"Sure. I don't have a home theater, though. We only have two televisions, one in my room and one in Tuesday's."

"Are you trying to get me in your bedroom?"

She laughed. "I have to do laundry. I wasn't lying. But there's time after I get the first load started."

He swept her into another hug. "You know, you could just have more clothes, or do laundry more often. Are you a procrastinator?" He might have pegged the Natalie he knew before as a woman who waited until the last minute to do laundry, but this one? Not so much.

"I have a presentation tomorrow afternoon that I just learned about today. I need to wash clothes for that. I have clean stuff, but this is important, so I need to look professional, and I have exactly one professional outfit for that sort of thing."

"Okay, so let's get that in the wash. I was going to take you to Nora's for dinner. How about I call in an order to go? I'll go pick it up and maybe a bottle of wine, too?"

"All right."

He followed her through the house and up a set of stairs. "This is my side of the upstairs. Tuesday has the other side. Her stairs are back in the kitchen, but there's also a landing that connects both sides where we have a little reading loft."

The walls going up the stairs were full of photographs. He pointed. "This is Tuesday?"

Natalie smiled. "Yes." She paused with a smile. "This was us back in the day. She was the first person I met when I started school. Other than staff and stuff, I mean. I went to my dorm room and she was there already. I knew within an hour that she would always be important in my life. Funny how that works."

He understood it, though.

"This is our group." She indicated a series of photographs. "Delia, Zoe, Eric, Rosie, Jenny, me and Tuesday. We're 1022 because that was our room number. We had a five-room suite thing. One shared main room and a bunch of bedrooms. Eric was honorary because he lived next door. He and Tuesday married a year after graduation."

"He's the one who died?"

"Yeah. He was all sporty, like Tuesday. They did all this crazy stuff, like every year they did a bicycle trip from Seattle to Portland. They kayaked and canoed. It started when he was tired a lot. But he was a busy dude, so for a while they just attributed it to his job. And then he got bruises that didn't go away."

She swallowed hard, the emotion clear in her voice. He brushed his knuckles down her back, wanting it to be better.

"Typical dude, he didn't want to go to the doctor, but finally he was really bad off, so he went after Tuesday pestered him relentlessly about it. They learned a week later that he had cancer. He died three months after that.

He was a great guy. He and Tuesday were right. You know what I mean? Anyway, that was four years ago."

"I'm sorry. I can't imagine."

"It sucked. But we all go to the doctor now if we're sick for longer than seems normal." She moved again, and he followed.

"The rest of your group, 1022 I mean, do they all live local?"

"Delia is a documentary filmmaker. She lives in Portland. Zoe and Jenny are in Seattle. Zoe is a biologist. She's a freak about cetaceans. Orcas mainly. Jenny's a schoolteacher. Third grade. Rosie lives in Brooklyn. She finds locations for commercials and advertising shoots."

"Wow, you guys are all so interesting."

"We went to a liberal arts college with no letter grades in the middle of the forest. It's our kooky wheelhouse." She pushed open a set of doors leading to a rather large bedroom with a sitting room attached. "This is my room."

Not surprisingly, the entire room was neat and orderly. The only thing that showed any messiness at all was her bed.

"I'd have pinned you for a make-your-bed girl."

"Why? I'm just going to get back into it, anyway." She disappeared into a closet and came back out holding a bundle of clothes.

"Can I look in your closet?"

She took him in warily. "Why?"

"I want to see if my suspicions are correct."

"I'm going to put my stuff in the wash. You have at it." She waved in the direction of the closet and then left.

He poked a head in and smiled. Ruthlessly organized, just as he'd figured. Her shoes were in neat boxes, her things hung according to type and color. He opened a drawer and hummed.

"Someone likes sexy underwear." He didn't touch the rainbow of silky panties, which would have been sort of creepy. He'd need to propose removing them from her body with his teeth, instead.

"So, are you stealing my shoes or my socks like a foot fetishist does?" She poked her head into the closet, and he jumped. "Wow, guilty people jump like that. Should I be scared? I have mace."

He snorted a laugh and then indicated the drawers set into the walls of the closet. "I'm far more interested in your panty collection."

"Lipstick, a pretty bra, some nice underwear, little things that can totally make a crappy day better." She shrugged. "Just started the laundry. We could stay in instead of eating out. We could just order pizza. There's soup, which I can do relatively well. And stuff for sandwiches. I'd say we had junk food but other than doughnuts, I'd be lying because Tuesday thinks apples are living wild. But I do have a stash of Hot Tamales in my dresser."

"I have plenty of junk food in my pantry. And a washer and dryer, too. I'm just saying."

"The clothes are already in the washer. Plus, in about five minutes, I'm going to be in yoga pants and a T-shirt."

He tossed himself on her bed after he toed out of his shoes. The scent of her skin rose from her sheets, and he didn't stop himself from burying his face in her pillow to breathe her in.

"I'll supervise. You don't need a bra for just being around the house. I'm not really company, after all."

"You're so thoughtful." And with that, she unzipped her skirt and stepped from it, folding it over her arm.

His mouth dried up. "Are those…are you wearing… stockings?"

She looked down at herself and then back at him with a smirk. "I do believe so, yes. Can I tell you a secret, Patrick?"

He gulped and nodded. She laid the skirt on a chair and pulled her blouse off, leaving her in nothing more than a pretty bra, barely there underpants and stockings.

She moved to him, climbing on her bed, hands and knees to him. She straddled his lap, and he leaned forward, burying his face in her cleavage until everything was perfect.

"Tell me your secret, then, Natalie."

"I like wearing stockings. I like it when the breeze blows up my skirt and I can feel the difference between where my legs are covered and where they aren't. It's like a dirty secret right there under the fabric."

"Christ."

Her mouth canted up at the right corner, and he licked over the dimple. "You're so dirty. You wouldn't know it from first glance. But holy shit, you make me hard as hell."

She reached back and undid her bra, letting it fall down her arms. "No one else has to know about a secret, Paddy. That's the point. I can be dirty here with you. Like this. No one at my job needs to know I'm wet for you. No one at the grocery store needs to know I chose my showerhead not only for the way it massages my *back*."

He might have whimpered, but it was hard to hear over the roaring white noise in his head as he imagined her in the shower, one foot up on the side of the tub as she pointed the showerhead at her pussy.

"What I am here—" she took his hands and placed them on her breasts "—belongs to me and to you. It's not for anyone else."

He licked over one nipple and then the other. "I love to live my life at a hundred miles an hour. I love the wild freedom of it. But I can most certainly appreciate this perspective, too."

She paused, clearly wrestling with whatever she wanted to say next. He reached up to brush the pad of his thumb over the dent in her chin. "You can say anything to me, you know."

"I don't actually, but that's not the problem."

"What do you mean you don't? Know that you can trust me to be honest?" He wrestled between a little bit of hurt that she would feel that way and pleasure that she'd share her feelings at all. "I'm feeling my way around here. I don't know how to do this very well. Mainly because I haven't done it before."

"Done what?" She rolled her hips, grinding the heat of herself against his cock. "This? Because oh, yes, you have. I've been there more than once when you have."

"Stop that. It makes it hard to think when you do that. I mean a relationship. I haven't done it. I date around, and I have great sex, and I move on. This is different."

One of her brows rose, and he smoothed it with his fingertips.

"*Relationship* seems like it might be rushing things."

He snorted. "I've been on your trail since July. It's mid-September now. I haven't gone out with anyone else. Haven't even thought about it. You're what I think about. All the time. I'm not saying we're engaged or anything, but this is a relationship, Natalie." He kissed her because she was delicious, and he needed that after his declaration. His anxiety softened when she kissed him back, her fingers sifting through his hair.

He nipped her bottom lip. "You can trust me to be honest. How can we do this right if we don't talk stuff through?" He sounded so emotionally mature, he wanted to call his mom and tell her about it. Ugh, maybe not thinking about his mother when he was in Natalie's bed would be wise.

"Part of me loves that you're wild because it's who you are. But I have… I just don't have the best feelings about that sort of life. I don't mind wild, I just like it in private."

She had said this all to his ear, and he gently touched her chin to get her gaze. "Thank you for saying that. What happened to you? Something in college? You seemed nearly as wild as me back in the day."

She sighed. "In a manner of speaking. But it was more that I figured my shit out in college. Not having choices or options is to lack control. Lacking control makes me feel helpless. It leaves a person vulnerable."

"So you put yourself in a place where you could give yourself control and you make your own choices."

"This is a weird conversation to be having right now."

"We've already established that you're weird and tragically broken, Nats. Keep up. So. Control?"

"I spent a lot of time responsible for other people. From a very early age until I got the hell out of there at seventeen. That was a step, a huge step in yes, taking back control and owning my life and my future. And then later, I also found a measure of safety and a huge helping of control when I chose to make firm boundaries in my life. My private stuff is for me. That's how I want it. That's how I need it."

"Okay. Well, tell me about your childhood."

She grabbed his shirt and pulled it off. "I'd rather fuck."

"Come on, talk to me."

"I've talked all I want to right now. I'm nearly naked. We're in my bed. Alone in my house. Show me how wild you are, Paddy."

He wanted more from her, but he could see she was past her comfort zone. Desire drove him hard. So hard, he should have feared it. So hard, he let her change the subject.

He shifted enough to land her on her back, and he loomed over her, quickly getting out of his jeans and shorts. He kissed up her ribs and across her belly, up the valley between her breasts, pausing to lick the curves there. He drew his tongue up her neck, closing his eyes at the hum of pleasure she gave him in response.

He took her lips, and she wrapped herself around him, her thighs around his waist, nipples against his chest, arms around his shoulders so her nails scored into his back.

He hissed and she arched, brushing the heated silk of her panties against his naked cock.

He took her bottom lip between his teeth and pulled. The rush of heat at his cock made him even harder. "Someone likes it a little rough."

His lips found the place where her pulse thundered, the sweet spot just below her ear. He swirled his tongue there and gave her the edge of his teeth before he moved down to her nipples.

He pushed her breasts together so he could easily travel back and forth between both nipples. The sounds she made tore at him, tore at his self-control.

"Please fuck me!"

"I was going to make you come first." He worried her nipple between his teeth.

"Yes," she muttered, holding his head in place. "Coming is mandatory, obviously. But you can do it while you're in me."

"You're bossy."

She squirmed, getting a hand between them and grasped his cock, fisting it a few times. Reason and patience scattered like birds.

She reached out, one-handed, and rustled through a drawer in her bedside table. Finally, she cheered and held a foil packet aloft. "Victory!"

He laughed, taking it from her and using it quickly. Then he didn't bother stripping her panties off; instead, he shoved them to the side and thrust into her body in one stroke.

She sucked in a breath, nearly choking at how good it felt. At the dark thrill of being handled like that. He was rough. Not to harm, but like he couldn't stop himself because he wanted her so much.

This was wild. And she was a grown woman who liked what she liked. He made it easier to do that. When she was in a relationship, she had a high libido and most definitely Paddy matched her in that department What they had when they were like this was wicked-hot chemistry. It made her feel so alive.

He put most of his weight on his forearms, resting his forehead against hers for long moments. He looked right through her. She wanted to close her eyes against it, but it was too real; she was so connected right then, it would have been a lie.

"You said you were going to take care of it yourself. The last time we were together, I mean. You should do that now."

Maybe she should have blushed or been embarrassed. But that didn't happen. The burst of heat wasn't from embarrassment, but desire.

He pushed himself to his knees, holding her calves around his butt. She was totally open to him. Above her, he was like an inked, pierced sex god. She was honest-to-goodness having superhot sex with a rock star, and it was everything others had it cracked up to be.

A lock of his hair fell forward over his forehead as his gaze seemed to burn her skin. She slid a hand down her belly as he leaned in enough to roll and tug one of her nipples.

Her hand went under the material of her underpants, and she gasped when her fingertips made contact with her clit.

"Jesus. I've never seen anything hotter than this right here. Your hand moving as you touch yourself. Your skin flushed. Nipples hard and dark. Your body keeps gripping my cock so hard, I see stars."

She wasn't usually one for dirty talk. It often made her cringe, in fact. Maybe it was that it never rang true, or the men she'd been with who tried it sounded like bad porn dialogue.

Whatever the case, his words wrenched something loose inside her. Sent sensation hurtling through her even though she'd barely touched herself. She said something incoherent and he snarled, fucking into her body in hard, sharp digs, his gaze flitting between where her hand was in her panties and his fingers on her nipple because her boobs bounced merrily with each thrust.

It seemed to stretch—climax and this moment between them where she was laid bare to this man, where he was open to her because he allowed her to see inside him. Whatever it was, she'd never experienced it before, and it left her raw. In the best kind of way.

He groaned, pushing so deep, the muscles in her thighs burned a little as he held them wide with his hips. Her name was a snarl on his lips as he came, and she liked it that way. Liked knowing she filled him with the same sort of savage need he did her.

As he pulled out, he took her hand, the one she'd been using on herself, and he licked her fingers. She stared, transfixed, her skin heating all over again. With a wicked grin, he kissed her fingertips.

"Be right back."

CHAPTER TEN

"WHAT ARE YOUR plans today?"

"Good morning, Paddy," she mumbled, pushing the hair from her face.

He kissed her. "I mean, I know you have your presentation, but what about after?"

She groaned, throwing her arm over her eyes. "Are you perky in the morning? Because if you are, we might have to break up."

"What's not to be happy about? I'm here in your bed. You're warm, and you smell good, and there's a good chance of morning sex."

"You have to make me breakfast for that." A smile hinted at the corners of her mouth.

"It's really a good thing I can cook."

"It goes well with the big package and the ability to make my knees turn to jelly with it."

He laughed and snuggled closer. "So? This afternoon?"

"Why?"

"I forgot to tell you Mary invited us to dinner. It'll be all my brothers. My parents may stop in, but they've been away this week."

"You forgot? Really?"

"I came into this room, and you took your clothes off. I forgot everything after that."

She moved her arm away and gave him the eye. They both knew he hadn't forgotten.

"Mary is a really, really good cook. I'm not kidding. Her food will change your life. And it would make me happy for them to meet you."

She rolled her eyes, but kept smiling. "All right. I'll come up there tonight. Just tell me when."

He made them both breakfast and after a rousing bout of morning sex, she shooed him out, saying she had to prepare for her presentation.

He paused at the door. "Stay with me tonight. You're off tomorrow. We can sleep in and go do something fun afterward. We can go out on the boat or ride horses. Whatever. Things are about to get busy on the ranch. It's nearly time to harvest the pears, so I want to get as much time with you as I can. Let me be selfish."

"You have to make me breakfast again."

He laughed, pulling her back into his arms to kiss her soundly. "I will happily make you breakfast. And lunch, too. What do you say?"

"Okay. Now go. I need to go over all this PowerPoint junk. I'll see you tonight."

It wasn't until he got back to his car that he saw the doughnuts on his front seat. He'd give them to her later. After dinner. When he could lick off any of the cinnamon sugar that got on her.

This was stupid.

She looked at herself in the mirror, yet again. "I don't know. Maybe I should just call and say I don't feel well," she said over the phone to Tuesday.

"Really, Natalie? Really? Come on. You're a grown-ass woman. Why is this man making you act like you're in tenth grade? Jeez. Has he been saying mean things to undermine you?"

"What? No! My God. He's not a jerk. He's actually a nice guy. It's just…dinner with his family? Are we even at that point?"

"Now that we've established the rock star is a nice guy who isn't being mean to you, we can move on to the next issue. I should charge you for this therapy."

"Eat it, Eastwood."

"Ha! You wish. Anyway. So obviously you *are* at that point since it's happening. It's not like you just met him today. It's not like you just met him a week ago. You knew him years ago, and you've been circling each other for the last few months. You like him and not just because you want to make it okay to do naked things with him. You guys are dating. And people who date meet one another's families and friends. Just don't have sex on our kitchen table because I eat on that table."

"Uh, okay. Sure." Natalie rolled her eyes. "I gotta go. I'm supposed to be up there in fifteen minutes. Thanks for the pep talk, coach."

"I'll see you tomorrow night. Have fun and make good choices."

"Love you."

Tuesday laughed. "Yeah, I love you, too, woman. Let yourself have fun tonight, or I'm gonna be so mad at you."

"Fine. Fine."

Natalie hung up and looked at herself one more time. She'd gone with an outfit that was right on the line between casual and dressy. White pants and a red blouse. She had on a necklace Tuesday had made for her. She'd done her hair to slick it back a little from her face in waves.

With a sigh, she brushed the front of her clothes and applied lipstick. She hoped it was the right tone. She should have asked. She looked toward the phone. Maybe she could call.

No.

If this was any other guy, she'd just trust her sense of style and go for it and that's what she'd do, damn it.

She grabbed her bag, the flowers she'd picked up on the way home and headed for the door. She could do this like a grown-up.

SHE KNOCKED ON his door, and he opened up with a smile. "Damn, Nat, you sure look pretty tonight." He kissed her cheek so as not to smear her lipstick. "And you smell really good, too."

He had on jeans but a button-down shirt. Nothing overly dressy by any means, but he'd rolled up the sleeves to expose his forearms. And they were really hot forearms.

"Can I get your bag from the car? We'll walk over to their house if you don't mind. It's a nice night, and it means we can have a few and not worry about driving."

"I can be a designated driver if that's what you're worried about. I don't drink much. I have an occasional glass of champagne because it's the best thing ever, but I don't plan to drink tonight."

He looked her over carefully but said nothing else for a moment.

"My bag is in the trunk, and I have flowers for Mary."

He grinned as she popped the trunk open. "It's a nice

night so I vote we walk, anyway. You stay right here and I'll get your stuff." He dashed to her car and grabbed everything before returning. "I'm going to run this up to my room." He held up the bag and handed her the flowers. "These are pretty. She'll like them."

She waited in his entry while he took her things up.

"So are you okay if I drink? I mean…are you in recovery or something? It shouldn't be crazy or anything. Ezra will be there, and he doesn't drink. He doesn't care if other people do, but if you do, that's okay."

"Am I making you nervous?"

He kissed the tip of her nose. He played off being silly but she saw a glimpse of vulnerability in his eyes, and she reminded herself to be careful with him.

"I just want you to be comfortable. I want to make you happy."

She shrugged. "I don't know what to say to that. It's very sweet, but an awfully big job really only I can do. Thank you. I'm okay. I just don't get to *oh, no, can't drive* point. It's not what I do. You can drink. Other people can drink. I drink sometimes. I'm not in recovery, and now I'm ready to walk over to dinner."

He put an arm around her and shut his front door. "Let's go, then, gorgeous."

TURNED OUT DAMIEN only lived about a three-minute walk from Paddy's house. His was more Northwest-styled than the modern elegance of Paddy's place. Music filtered from the house as did lights. She heard laughter as Paddy opened up and hollered that they were there.

A beautiful woman with pretty, dark curly hair came around a corner holding a bowl, which she shoved at the hottie who was obviously her husband. Natalie remembered Damien. With a face like that, it would have been impossible to have forgotten him.

The woman came forward with a smile, and Natalie could have sworn she'd seen her before. "Welcome. I'm Mary, Paddy's sister-in-law. I've seen you around the library, but we've not met formally."

Natalie handed the flowers over. "That's why I recognize you! Thank you so much for inviting me. I'm Natalie. It's nice to meet you."

"Oh, these are so pretty! Thank you." Mary linked her arm with Natalie's and drew her through the house.

"The farmer's market was closing up when I finished with work. I grabbed these and some lemon curd while I was on my way home."

"I was just there earlier today! Wanted some cider and some honeycomb." As they entered a large, open kitchen/living area, the people there turned to see who'd come in.

"Everyone, this is Natalie, though I suppose you all might remember her from before." Mary looked to Natalie. "Paddy told us all you two knew each other from before they went to Los Angeles to make that first label album. Were they totally adorable then?"

"God, yes, totally adorable in that way they have. They were always getting in fights. With each other and with the patrons of the bar. The girls loved them, though."

One of them laughed; she couldn't remember but she thought it was Vaughan, the youngest. "You cut your hair. I like it. Vaughan, the most handsome and talented of the brothers. It's nice to see you again." He waved from his place at the table. "Can I get you something to drink?"

"Sure, what do you have?"

PADDY BREATHED EASIER when she simply tossed herself into the mix. Vaughan flirted with her, and she batted him away. Paddy kissed Mary's cheek as she put the flowers in a vase and headed to where Vaughan was pouring a soda for Natalie.

"Back off. This one's taken."

"If you change your mind, I'm younger as well as more handsome and talented." Vaughan winked.

She sipped her soda as Ezra said hello and Damien reintroduced himself. His brothers were being goof-balls to make her feel comfortable, and she got it. And he loved that she got it.

There was a lot of food and a lot of trash talk, too, over dinner at Damien and Mary's big huge dining room table.

"When I first moved in here, he had this dinky little table. Imagine a family this size, and he has a dinette set that seated maybe four people," Mary said.

"I was only waiting for you, Curly." Damien winked at his wife.

"So anyway, you're a librarian. I was just in last week, but you weren't there. Yes, I was going to get a look at you and figure out a way to introduce myself, I admit it."

Paddy groaned, but Natalie squeezed his hand where he'd been holding hers.

"What day?"

"Wednesday afternoon? They said you were at the elementary school doing something."

"I go to talk about kid lit. All the books we've got-ten in recently that they might like. It gets me out of the building and third graders are adorable. They get so excited about stuff. The first graders are great, and they spill their parents' secrets like crazy. Mom drinks beer, and she and daddy take naps with the door locked. That type of thing."

"I have a second and third grader. I can attest to that." Vaughan grinned.

She drew Vaughan out, chatting with him about his girls, and there couldn't have been anything better to have done to make Vaughan like her. He showed her pictures, and she asked all the right questions.

Ezra gave Paddy an approving look as she and Mary disappeared into the kitchen.

"Thumbs-up. I have no idea how you landed a woman like her, but good job, and don't fuck it up."

"Um. Thanks, asshole." Paddy punched Ezra's arm. Mainly he thought it was funny teasing. The same type they did to one another daily. It was how they communicated most of the time. But in a corner of his heart maybe it sort of sucked that they seemed so amazed he was capable of being with a woman like Natalie. "Some people happen to think I'm a catch."

"Ha! Yeah, but you run from them usually, so don't get pissy with us. She's done some mellowing. I mean from before," Damien said.

"She was nineteen years old. I hope to hell I've done some mellowing since then, too. Anyway, I thought you didn't remember her."

"Dude, we *all* remember her now. It was two weeks, she was with you pretty much daily. She took pity on us and rustled free drinks. She was as wild as we all were. Plus, it's difficult to forget a face that pretty."

"All *were*."

Damien put his hands up. "I'm not attacking. I have zero double standards when it comes to wild youth."

"I like that you're defensive on her behalf, though."
Ezra raised a brow.

"I just—" He lowered his voice. "She's sensitive
about her private life. She's not that girl anymore. I
don't want her upset."

"Fair enough." Damien nodded. "Ten bucks says
Mom and Dad arrive within the next five minutes."

A flurry of bets were placed as he looked toward
the kitchen.

"YOU HAVE A really gorgeous home here. I don't even
cook, and I have to say how much I love this kitchen."
Natalie loved the warm tiles, the pots hanging from
the ceiling, all the gadgets and things. It was lived-in
and beautiful and clearly someplace this couple spent
a lot of time.

"I can't take credit for the basic bones. Damien had
it built before I met him. Between us? This room was
a huge factor in why I said yes when he asked me to
marry him." Mary winked, putting Natalie at ease. "I
spend more time in this room than any other except our
bedroom probably. You're holding up well, by the way.
My first time meeting all the brothers was when I was
surrounded by my friends. Took the edge off. I mean, I
suppose you knew them all before, but this is different."

Natalie laughed. It *was* different. "They're all nice,
and they clearly care about one another. I guess I was a
little worried they'd expect me to be the same as I was
back then. But none of them really are, either. I worried for nothing, and my friend Tuesday will poke me
and say I told you so."

"As best friends do. What were they like then?"

"Like Dalmatian puppies. Long and tall and in trouble at all times. They didn't just come into a room, they sort of spilled into it, all legs and hair and elbows. They had it then, too, that whatever it takes to make someone into a star. Charisma."

Mary nodded with a grin. "They all have this intense personal gravity that pulls you in. Okay, just tell me if I'm being nosy, but I hear you don't cook?"

"I'm awful at it. It's not that I don't want to. It's certainly not that I hate food." She waved a hand at her body. But she never had a mom around, or even a dad who did any time in a kitchen longer than it took to get more beer. She had to make due growing up, and maybe sometimes that was more than she wanted to dwell on so she avoided the kitchen. Maybe. Or it was something her therapist said and was probably right.

She took a mental-bracing breath. This woman was just trying to be nice. And normal.

"I'm, like, cosmically bad at it. All the jokes about burning water? That's me. Luckily, Tuesday can cook, so I do more cleaning to even things out."

"I'm dying here. I want to offer to give you lessons, but it seems sort of rude. Is it rude? Because I love to cook and I feel like an evangelist right now and also? I like you. I don't know a lot of people in Hood River, even though I've lived here for about a year and a half now. I tend to get caught up in stuff, and I don't leave the ranch and even when I do it's there, this big neon sign over my head that says, *Damien Hurley's wife,* and it's odd. I'd love to hang out. Is that weird?"

It would be weird, too, if Natalie burst out with *thank God you're weird, too!* So she waved a hand. "It's totally not weird. Tuesday has tried over the years to teach me how to cook. I've managed to master mashed potatoes, but it took her a year of patience to get me that far. To be honest? It stresses me out. I am so bad at it and I fail at it over and over, and every time I pass by my kitchen when I'm trying to learn something, I feel dread and guilt." And like she couldn't even be good at that one basic thing. "I think I might just be cursed. Or doomed. Or something equally dire."

Mary paused and nodded. "That's fair. I hate it that you'd feel bad about not being able to get it right. Cooking should be fun. I won't pester you, but if you ever change your mind, let me know."

"Thanks. But a definite yes on the hanging-out thing. I have a book club here in town. There are about eight of us. We read across a lot of genres and have themes. We potluck at each other's houses. Of course, I always bring chips and dip. Yes, I'm that person. But they're a fun, smart group of women. I think you'd fit in well."

"Oh, I'd like that, thank you."

She helped clear stuff as Mary put together the dessert.

"I can actually do coffee well. Want me to make some?" Natalie pointed to the coffeemaker.

"Good idea. There's decaf in that orange container."

Natalie got that started and moved to join everyone in the dining room. She paused at the doorway, just looking at them all. Paddy and Vaughan sat next to one another, hatching trouble; that much was clear.

"My in-laws are sure to arrive anytime," Mary said as she came in from the kitchen. "Michael will have kept Sharon away long enough for us to have gotten comfortable."

"She'll be nosy, but don't take it personally." Damien grinned at his wife.

"Sharon asked me how I'd feel about signing a prenup in the first ten minutes I knew her."

Paddy got up and moved to her, putting his arms
around Natalie's waist. "She did it to see what Mary's
reaction would be. Stop scaring Natalie." He looked
back at his brothers.

Natalie tried not to panic. She knew it would be a
possibility that she'd meet Paddy's parents, after all. She
just had very little experience with mothers. Tuesday's
family had sort of taken her under their wing over the
years, but there'd been no mother in her life growing
up, and her grandmother was certainly not much of an
example. She found mothers mystifying in most cases.

And that's when the front door opened and a boom-
ing voice announced new arrivals.

"Buck up. I promise they're nice people." Paddy
kissed her forehead, and she managed a smile.

Natalie recognized Paddy's mom immediately, and
some of her nervousness eased.

"Sharon, I had no idea you were Paddy's mom!" She
moved to Sharon Hurley and accepted the hug. She
looked over her shoulder to Paddy. "Your mom is one
of the community volunteers in one of the elementary
schools I visit regularly."

Sharon shook her head with a grin that looked an
awful lot like her son's. "Natalie. I can't believe I didn't
put two and two together. This is my husband, Michael. Michael, this is Natalie but I don't know your
last name."

"It's Clayton. Natalie Clayton. Nice to meet you."
She held her hand out to Michael Hurley, who, Mary
had not lied, stood at least six and a half feet tall. His
hair was dark like his sons', but his was salted liber-

ally with gray. He was a big man, broad-shouldered. The kind of hale that men who worked the land tended to be. He took her hand, enveloping it in both of his.

"Pleased to meet you, darlin'."

"There's pie." Mary kissed her mother-in-law's cheek and then accepted a hug from her father-in-law.

"See? I told you if we waited a bit we'd arrive in time for dessert." Michael pulled out his wife's chair and waited for Natalie to sit before he did, as well. Damien got up to help Mary in the kitchen.

Paddy put his arm along the back of her chair and Natalie appreciated the support.

Vaughan snorted. "I was looking forward to Mom making Natalie nervous." He looked to Natalie, who was trying to figure out if she should be offended or not. "No offense." His grin was pretty much a carbon copy of his brothers'. "She's just so devious, it's fun to watch her in action."

"Don't mind him. He was dropped on his head a lot as a baby." Paddy thumped Vaughan. "So you know my mom?"

It was Sharon who answered instead of Natalie. "I do some mentoring for fourth and fifth graders. We see each other from time to time at the school." Sharon then smiled at Natalie. "I figured you were a community volunteer, too. I can't believe I missed that connection." Sharon looked up at Damien, who brought in a tray of coffee poured into mugs. "Look at your manners. Nicely done, Mary."

Damien rolled his eyes.

"I did the same thing. I go to a few schools. Sometimes for the library, sometimes on my own. I know everyone by their first name but rarely by their last. Anyway, yes, I know your mom."

"So she's been prescreened?" Vaughan teased.

"Vaughan, watch your manners, boy. Your brother is going to punch you in the nose." Michael forked up some pie and watched his family with an easy smile.

"Wouldn't be the first time," Paddy added cheerfully.

"You're not even going to ask if she'd sign a prenup?" Mary asked, repressing a smile.

"She's got a trust fund that's worth more than I am." Paddy waved a hand. "I'm probably the one who should sign one."

Anger and worry warred inside her. That was something she should have shared, or not. Money made people feel differently about you. She wanted them to know her before they found out about the trust fund. It was hard to fight preconceived notions, and it just added to the weight of establishing a relationship with other people.

PADDY FELT THE muscles in her back tighten, and she moved away from him slightly. Shit. He'd done something wrong. Was it the teasing? Maybe he should have punched Vaughan. His brother was only playing, but he didn't want Natalie to feel bad.

The prenup talk?

She'd gone a little more formal in her manner, and his mother shot him a look.

Ezra started talking about his goats, which shifted the conversation, and she relaxed a little but never completely moved back against him like she was before.

They stayed another hour. When his parents got up to leave, he and Natalie walked out with them. She was warm to his mother and father, but once they'd gone around the corner, he stopped her before she could go back into the house.

"What's wrong? You're upset about something. Is it the teasing? Vaughan didn't mean anything by it. He's a shit stirrer. He wouldn't have teased you if he didn't like you."

"I'm really uncomfortable with you telling everyone I have a trust fund. What your brothers know of me is pretty limited to who I am now, and your parents don't know me at all. You just told them something deeply personal that could change the way they see me."

Oh. Well, that wasn't what he'd expected at all.

"I wanted her to know you had no financial interest in me. Not that way. She's very protective of us. Worried people are trying to take advantage. I figured once she knew you had plenty of money, that wouldn't be an issue."

"She could have figured that out on her own. After all, she knows I volunteer and have a job here in town. She figured it out with Mary, who doesn't have a trust fund obviously."

"Why are you ashamed of it? Who cares? They don't. I don't."

She poked her chest. "I do! It's my business, Patrick. I want to decide if and when that information gets shared. Money is tricky. People hear you have a trust fund, and they assume you're lazy. I like for people to know me for me. Knowing my net worth complicates things. I have to work against it."

He took a deep breath, surprised by her vehemence. "None of us cares. Don't you see?"

"You're the one who isn't seeing. I need to make my

own choices. I told you this before. If and when I talk about money to someone, I'll make that decision. This isn't about how you feel, Paddy. It's about how I feel. It's an intimate fact, and it's *mine*."

He chewed his bottom lip and thought for a bit. He wasn't sure how to make it better or all right, but she'd just given him some major insight, and he needed to really hear it. "Okay. I'm sorry."

She crossed her arms over her chest. "Is this a real apology or are you just saying you're sorry to get past this argument?"

"What difference does it make? You're unhappy. I made you that way whether I meant to or not. I'm sorry you're unhappy."

Her brows flew up. "I'm sorry for how you feel is not a real apology. You can't own my feelings. If you're sorry, be sorry for what you did, not how I feel about it."

"You're being impossible."

She shook her head and sighed. "Maybe I am." She licked her lips as she paused and then spoke again. "I have a button, I admit it. I can't deal with fauxpologies. You know the *I'm sorry you feel that way* statement which isn't *I'm sorry for what I did*. I just… I guess I have a lot of buttons and issues."

After being quiet awhile, she exhaled long and slow. "I think I'm going to head home. I'm going to say my goodbyes. I know how to get back to my car."

He took her arm. "We were just making some headway and you're leaving? Do you always run out on fights?"

Incredulous, she blinked back at him. "Do you think fighting is normal?"

She didn't? "Yes, I do! It's normal and healthy.

Jesus." He let go of her and shoved both hands through his hair. "I grew up in a house where my parents argued. Not every day. But they're both strong people and they share a life, so sometimes they'd butt heads and they'd work it through. And they made it through. That's normal and healthy. Should we just eat how we feel? Or do you believe people in relationships never fight about anything?"

THE PROBLEM WAS that Natalie didn't know what normal was. Discomfort weighed her down. Off-kilter. Absolutely *not* under her control. Yet his question was valid and asked openly. She owed him an answer.

"To be totally honest with you? I have no idea. I can't tell you what's normal. I don't know what I'm doing. You pissed me off, Paddy."

"Okay, that's fair. We're going to fight sometimes, Nat. I'm a pain in the ass, so yeah, I pissed you off. Everyone has hot buttons. I can't know yours unless you tell me or until we go through something like this, and I learn that way. I don't judge you for your trust fund. I know you work hard. I know you volunteer in your community and so does my mother. That's what counts in my world. I'm sorry my actions made you feel bad. I didn't intend that at all. It was meant to say to my parents that they had nothing to worry about. But it is your personal business, and I did share it without asking, and for that I am sorry."

She sighed, chewing her bottom lip. It was a really good apology. Earnest. "I don't know how to do this. I don't know how to be with someone."

He laughed, stepping closer and hesitating before he closed the distance entirely, hugging her. "Me, either.

The only way out is through, right? Isn't that the saying? We'll have to learn as we go. No way around it because we're both total noobs in the relationship department."

"You're being very reasonable. You make this seem so easy. It's really not."

"I'm faking it. I like you. I think you're worth the work, and I hope I am, too." He gave her a quick grin. "You wanna tell me about the trust fund? Why you're so uncomfortable with it? Is it from something horrible? Blood diamonds or apartheid or something?"

"The money isn't any more horrible than other old money tends to be. My great-grandfather and his brother invented several different medical and scientific devices when they were young men. Then my grandfather invested smart when he was very young and got a huge return on it."

He stepped back, sliding an arm around her shoulders. "Okay, then. You're staying the night, right?"

She had a choice. To step forward and be in this relationship with him. Just dating, yes, but it was a conscious choice, and she couldn't do it if she didn't intend to try her best. She could walk away and say it wasn't worth the trouble. It was trouble. Paddy Hurley had trouble written all over him. His loud, nosy family, too.

But.

She liked him. A lot. And his nosy, loud family, too.

"Yeah. I'm sorry I started to run off."

He kissed the top of her head. "We both have learning to do. Luckily, sex helps."

CHAPTER ELEVEN

"SO WHEN'S HOTTIE MCROCKSTAR showing up to shower you with attention?" Tuesday grabbed a windbreaker from the closet and tossed Natalie's in her direction. The day was warm enough, even for the end of October, but things got cold out of the direct sun.

They hadn't been out on a hike in a few months because of how busy they'd been, but Tuesday had used her amazing gift for guilt and ambushed Natalie that morning at breakfast with a promise of girl time and the beauty of fall in the Columbia Gorge.

Frankly, she'd have been just as happy looking at it from the car or in some pictures, but Sporty Spice wouldn't have allowed such a thing.

"He'd love that you called him that." Natalie tied her shoes. "Don't say that stuff in front of him. He's bad enough as it is. The man has no shortage of self-esteem." He'd been…courting her she supposed, over the past months. Since their dinner on his boat, he'd just inserted himself in her life.

Which was why she and Tuesday hadn't been able to spend as much time together. He knew her days off and often showed up to sweep her off somewhere.

"I think he's off doing something band-related today. They're writing material right now, so he and Ezra are hanging out. Probably punching one another in between lyrics."

"I'm really going to have to meet this brother of his." Tuesday snorted.

"He's gorgeous like they all are. My God. Big and brawny. He loves animals, too. But he's got a darkness to him. Anyway, I'm sorry I've been caught up in him."

They walked out to the car and headed out to one of Tuesday's favorite trails to the east of town.

"You really haven't, you know."

"Haven't what?"

"Been caught up in him. He wants more, and you're pretending not to notice."

"Am not! Yeah. Maybe. I don't know. He's... complicated. He's a man, yes, but he's also an artist, and so sometimes he's all refreshingly honest and up front and other times he's broody and emo, and then I get a little panicky."

"Panicky that he'll turn into Bob and make you clean up his messes?"

"I never claimed to be well-adjusted."

"Who the hell is well-adjusted, Natalie? God, cut yourself a damned break sometimes. *Everyone* is shaped by how they grew up and who was influential during those years. What you dealt with made you into who you are today. It created your triggers and buttons. It makes you resentful over certain things and hesitant to confront others. And it's made you strong. You are a fierce woman. Seems to me any relationship is going to be about two people, each with a bunch of shit they don't know how to deal with appropriately but whose tolerance of that works to keep things together and on track."

It was difficult sometimes to be known so well.

"Are you honest with him?"

They drove out of town. "I'm working on it. I mean, yes, I'm honest but it's taking time to feel okay revealing things to him. We're both learning, I think. He's better at this stuff than I am most of the time, though sometimes he messes up."

"You mean the trust-fund thing?"

"No, not really. That was three weeks ago at this point, and we're past it. I talked a little about why I need to be the one who makes the choice to reveal that sort of thing. He's trying. So I'm trying. He just sort of throws himself at life."

"And that makes you nervous."

"Yes. It makes me nervous that he's just rushing headlong through his life and since we're dating, I'm along for that ride sometimes. I like his brothers. They're all funny and welcoming and stuff. But when they're together, it's sort of overwhelming. It's loud and slightly out of control, and it pushes my buttons."

"So tell him."

"No way. They're not doing anything wrong, Tuesday. They're *my* buttons, and they're there because *I'm* messed up. I can't make him responsible for that. I just have to find a way to be used to it."

"I think you can tell him without it making him responsible for your issues," Tuesday, ever reasonable, suggested. "Eric and I had our share of stuff we had to get past. I had to tell him about the racist shit his brother would say when he wasn't around. You're the one who told me to."

"Well, you were worried he wouldn't believe you! Eric loved you like crazy. He knew you wouldn't have made up something about his family like that. And he believed you and supported you."

Tuesday nodded emphatically. "Yes. That's my point. If you just said, *hey, you know my childhood was sort of insane, and when you're like this with your brothers, it sometimes reminds me of that.* You're not telling him not to be that with his family, you're letting him know why you might react a certain way. He digs you. He wants to do the right thing."

"I can't make him responsible for my bullshit. I *won't* make him responsible for it. It's my stuff, not his. Maybe it'll, you know, normal me up, just being around it and getting used to it."

Tuesday heaved a put-upon sigh. "Here's the place in our program where I underline how it's not your fault that you were raised the way you were. The adults in your life fucked you over. It's not your stuff, either. It's theirs. He could help you with that."

"Ugh. Can we talk about something else?"

"No. Come on, Natalie. You had a chaotic life, but you overcame that and made yourself into something better. Why be ashamed of that?"

"I'm not ashamed of that. I'm proud of what I've made out of my life. But I don't want him to feel bad for the way he is. It's normal to roll around and punch your brothers and all that stuff. If I told him, he'd want to stop to make me feel better. That's not fair to him. Eventually, he'd come to resent me for it. His family would. I don't want to get between him and his obviously healthy and close relationship with his family because of my unhealthy relationship with mine. Anyway, why are you on this topic so hard?"

Again the sigh. "Bob called this morning while you were in the shower."

"He what?" Her stomach revolted. "Why didn't you tell me?"

"I'm telling you now."

Bob was Robert Clayton the third. Her father.

"What did he want? Or do I really even need to ask?"

Tuesday shrugged. "The usual. He swears he's been clean for ninety days. Wants to talk with you."

She'd done the making-amends step with him many times now. Sometimes he was genuine. He *meant* to keep himself clean. Sometimes he meant it when he said he was sorry. But eventually he'd end up a mess, and she'd be sucked back into his life, cleaning up after him.

The past two times she'd refused to hear it. Building walls around herself where her father was concerned was a self-defense, and one she didn't feel bad about anymore.

"Damn it. My grandmother must have given him the number." Natalie had changed it because she didn't want him having it. And she'd told her grandmother she didn't want him to know it.

"You know how she is."

"Yes, well, that's why *he's* the way he is."

"You'll call Monday and change it. I told him not to call again."

"You shouldn't have to deal with a changing phone number every year or so because of this."

"Whatever. You're not him. Thank God. If you want, we'll change the phone number and you can decide to tell your grandmother or not. She's going to give it to him regardless. She can't say no. So if you give her the number again, she'll do the same to Bob. You know how it works. I don't care either way. I just want you to keep your guard up."

Damn it.

PADDY WAS WAITING on her doorstep when they got back from the hike.

"I bring Fran's Chocolates." He thrust a box her way, and she took it with a quick kiss.

She wasn't always super affectionate in public so when she was, it made him extra happy.

He waved at Tuesday. "How was the hike?"

"It was good. The leaves are starting to change."

They went inside, and she popped the lid off the box and they gorged on chocolates.

He leaned back in his chair and watched Nat and Tuesday enjoy his gift. Paddy liked Tuesday a great deal. She protected Natalie fiercely but also seemed to push her when she needed pushing.

"You two want to come up and watch movies at my place? We just got a bunch of new DVDs. There's that sci-fi one you were talking about last week." He'd called in some favors for it, but the way her eyes lit, he was glad he had.

"Really? Awesome. Tuesday and I were going to hang out, though. We haven't had much girl time. Maybe tomorrow?"

Tuesday scoffed. "We can have girl time watching movies in your boyfriend's giant swanky screening room. He has a movie-popcorn-popper thingy. Way better than microwave popcorn."

Natalie smirked in Tuesday's direction but then let her off the hook. "Okay, then. I need a shower. I'm sweaty and gross. We'll be up in a bit. Should we bring anything?" She tiptoed up to kiss him again.

"Bring an overnight bag. You, too, Tuesday. The guest room is ready for you. No need to bring anything else. Mary's doing some sort of menu thing. She's been working on her new cookbook, so this is part of it. I don't know all the details, but I do know I'll happily eat the results of whatever it is she's doing."

"Oh, good, you can finally meet." Natalie spoke to Tuesday. "You're going to like her."

"Cool." Tuesday grabbed another chocolate and headed out. "Meet you down here in a few minutes."

"You could shower at my place." He nuzzled Natalie's neck once Tuesday had left.

"I'd just get dirtier." Natalie stepped back. "Go on now. I'll see you in about half an hour."

He kissed her again because he could and headed out.

WHEN SHE AND Tuesday arrived an hour later, Vaughan answered the door, greeting Natalie with a hug. "Hey, there. Paddy will be right back. He had to run up to my parents' to drop something off. Ezra won't be here tonight. He's off in Portland for a few days. Which is good because he always hogs the big chair in the screening room."

She introduced Tuesday to Vaughan and then to Damien, who was in the kitchen.

"We'll be right back."

Natalie took Tuesday upstairs and pushed open a door to the guest room where Paddy had kindly put a basket of fruit and crackers on the dresser and a pretty carafe for water on the bedside table.

"He's got good manners." Tuesday put her overnight

bag down. "You sure you're cool with me staying over-night? I can go back home when we're done with mov-ies."

"Totally sure. I want to hang out with you and I want you to get to know his family, too. And you've seen his kitchen, right? He makes the best breakfasts."

"Okay. I just didn't want to horn in on your time with your dude."

She dropped her things off in Paddy's room, and Tuesday whistled. "Wow. So this is some room. It's a wonder he can even leave the house. I wouldn't if this was my bedroom."

"I tease him about that all the time. His bed is the best. He doesn't skimp on good linens, either."

They headed down where Mary was preparing root beer floats in Paddy's kitchen. Natalie introduced Tues-day to Mary, who held up her ice cream scoop. "I'm trying these out with this artisan root beer Damien and Ezra brought home after a fishing trip to Alaska. Also, I need your input on those tacos."

"I knew it was a good idea to accept when Paddy invited me along tonight," Tuesday said as she picked up one of the tacos and took a bite. "Holy cow. What is this?"

Mary beamed. "A new recipe. Carnitas."

"I approve. Natalie tells me you write cookbooks?"

"I do. This is for a new one I'm working on now. Party food."

"Tell them about the web-show thing." Paddy came in. "Hey." He kissed Natalie and waved at Tuesday. "Sorry, I had to run some mail up to my parents. It ended up with my stuff by mistake."

"We had tacos to keep us company. And root beer floats. You can't compete, Paddy." Vaughan shrugged.

"So tell us. Web show?" Natalie asked Mary.

"Oh, it's in the idea stage right now, but my agent and I had this long talk about doing a web series. I could do one from the road, which would be cooking for a crowd or cooking on the go. I have an appointment to go to several wineries next weekend to see if one or two of them would be a good venue to host a winery cooking episode. I don't know if it's even feasible, but it's a new thing, and I'm excited by it."

"That sounds awesome. I'm excited for you. You're so photogenic, and you're good with people. I bet you're a natural on camera, too."

They all stuffed their faces with tacos and root beer floats before heading in to watch the movie and stuff their faces more with some popcorn thing Mary created that sort of tasted like a caramel apple.

After everyone had left and Tuesday had gone to bed, Natalie stood on the deck outside Paddy's bedroom, Paddy at her back, his arm around her waist as his chin rested on her shoulder.

"This was a good day. Thank you for inviting us over. I like your family a lot."

"They like you, too. And Tuesday. I didn't say it in front of everyone, but I know Mary would love it if you came out and did the winery tour with us next weekend. For the moral support. She's got us obviously, but having a friend there would mean a lot."

That touched her deeply. That he'd ask and that it would mean something to her. She was finding her place there with them, and that meant most of all.

"I'll be there."

CHAPTER TWELVE

THE FOLLOWING WEEKEND, Natalie had been rushing to get out the door on time when she realized it just wasn't going to happen. She called Paddy's cell.

"Hey, I'm sorry but I just got a call about a grant we're trying to land. I need to add some more documentation and it's going to take me another hour or two. You guys go without me."

It was the winery-tour thing. Natalie wanted to support Mary and be there, but their funding was greatly supported by grants, and this one was a really good opportunity.

And of course, Paddy understood that. "Well, I know how important this grant is. I'll send them all ahead. Just come to my house when you finish."

"No, no. You go. Be there to cheer Mary on. Tell you what, I'll drive out when I finish. Okay? I'll get there as soon as I can. I'll text you when I get close and you can let me know which winery you're at."

"Yeah, that'd be cool. Mary will feel better that way, too. Thanks, gorgeous."

"Mmm-hmm. Now go on. I'll see you as soon as I can."

They'd been going out for three months. She saw him several times a week, slept at his place or he slept at hers. It got rocky sometimes as they both tried to work through their stuff. They were both off balance, and sometimes they had to carefully find their way back on track. But it was unexpectedly good. Because they put in the work. No one had done that for her before the way he did.

She pulled together all her stuff, finished all the supporting paperwork with one of the other librarians, and they got it all together to be sent to the grant people. An hour and some change later, she headed out, looking forward to the rest of her day with Paddy.

Only to have it all come crashing down at the sight of her father standing at the front doors of the library.

She *hated* that he still had the power over her to make her feel this way. Hated that every time he came into her life, it was to create chaos and destroy her carefully built life.

Being around him meant having to play games. Meant having to pretend away what was real and true. The weight of those secrets had torn her up as she got older. She was too tired to play make-believe.

For a long long time, she'd hoped it would work. Each try. Each failure cost more, and she didn't want to pay the tab anymore.

"Why are you here?" She kept walking toward her car and thank goodness, he followed. This was her job. If anyone came out, he'd play proud daddy happy to meet her coworkers.

No one could play pretend normal like a junkie.

"I tried calling, but you won't take my calls. I emailed, too."

"My work email isn't for personal use. I've told Grandmother to let you know that." Not that it made a difference. He wanted what he wanted, and so the needs of anyone else meant little.

"I'm trying to make things right." He stepped in front of her car door.

She hardened her heart and kept that wall between them as thick as she could. "Too late. I have to go. I'm expected somewhere." She'd been very careful not to tell her grandmother anything about Paddy or her dating life so at least there was that.

"My sponsor says I can't be held accountable for your hate of me. I did the best I could, Natty. My addiction made those mistakes. I accepted that, and you need to, as well."

She didn't rise to the bait. He played the *oh, you hate me* card all the time. It never worked for her to respond to it. It was a dead end. "Don't call me that. I don't want you in my life. Why don't you tell your sponsor that? I'm not responsible for you or your recovery. I wish you well. I truly do. But you need to respect my boundaries." She reached around and pulled her door open, moving him in the process.

"It's not fair of you to hold grudges. I'm trying to do the right thing."

She closed the door, locking it. She rolled her window down a crack. Enough for him to hear her. "I'm not holding a grudge. I'm protecting myself. You need to stay away from my home and my workplace. Don't make me get a no-contact order. I hope you can stay clean. I truly do. But I don't want your amends. I don't want you at all. Please respect that."

HER HANDS SHOOK for a time, but when she pulled over to text Paddy, she was more solid.

She hadn't seen her father in three years. He'd made his amends to her more times than she could count, and it had been a really long time since she'd believed his apologies. Or hell, a long time since he'd made any genuine amends at all. Mainly it was more of the same.

Bob Clayton was raised to think no matter what he did, it wasn't his fault. He could have gotten past that as an adult, but he never had. So when he got to the amends part, everyone got the faux apology. The *I'm sorry you felt that way.* Or the *I'm sorry my addictions made your life hard.* Which was why she hated the fake apology so much.

Gah, another stupid button living with her father had left her with.

It had been enough at one time. Back when she had room to believe he'd get himself clean and they could move forward with a mainly decent relationship. But that point passed years ago. He wasn't capable of the change she needed, and so to protect herself and her life, she kept him out of it.

And if people thought she was heartless for it, they could have a relationship with him and commiserate about how mean she was. But she'd be protected from being disappointed by him yet again.

Paddy replied to her text to say where they were, and a quick look at her GPS told her it was just two miles from where she was. Smiling, she headed his way.

It was getting colder, but the day was clear and sunny, so she turned her collar up and put on a hat and headed toward the main building. Being with Paddy and his brothers would be good. She could wash away this melancholy with something happy.

"Blondie!"

She turned in the direction of the shout when she got inside to see Vaughan spill out of a side room, all smiles.

Paddy followed him. "Hey, there you are."

Her stomach fell at the sight when he stumbled, nearly losing his balance. He grabbed his brother, and they both laughed.

She stood, rooted to the spot.

Paddy made his way over, talking overloud. Clearly drunk. Messy drunk.

"You're here."

And she wished she wasn't. All the powerlessness she'd been dealing with at the reappearance of her father came roaring forward. It didn't matter that Paddy wasn't Bob. It made her nervous all the same. Made her feel out of control and cast adrift.

This wasn't normal, she knew. Understood, even as the rest of her didn't care. So she tried to hold it together.

"Yes." She needed to control the panic and get over it. As she'd told Tuesday that day on their hike, she just needed to get over her own shit.

He grinned, and she was nearly charmed, he looked so sweet. "Want a glass of wine? They just moved to the reds. I'm sorry to say Vaughan and I have been drinking your share in your absence."

"I can tell. Where's Mary?" Natalie knew she was locking up, but it was the only way she knew of to get through it.

He took her arm, moving in closer, and the stench of him hit her hard enough to make her shrink away. Bile rose, and she gagged. Her control fraying, she tried to pull free but he cocked his head.

"Nat? What's wrong?" He'd gotten close, holding her tighter.

Everything suddenly felt as though it were happening outside her body, as if she watched herself on a screen. Clearly, she wasn't fit to be out of her house, and she needed to go.

"Let. Go."

She tried to pull her arm free. Now that she'd accepted leaving, the need to do it *right then* banked in her belly.

"What's going on?" Damien came strolling over, looking between them. He'd been drinking, too, but not nearly as much as Paddy and Vaughan had.

Her teeth clenched, she managed to speak. "Paddy needs to let go of me right now."

Damien's posture changed as he seemed to catch the edge of panic in Natalie's tone.

He put an arm around Paddy. "Dude, you're going to wrinkle her clothes. Let go."

Paddy let go, and her heart slowed a little.

Then he slung an arm around her shoulders, hugging her to his body.

That was it. It was officially too much, and she ducked, pulling away. She turned to Damien. "Please tell Mary I was here to support her. I need to go."

Paddy grabbed her again, taking her wrists. "Hey, wait. What? Are you okay?" He'd sobered a little as he realized there was a real problem.

Natalie knew she was being unreasonable, but she panicked and the words spilled from her lips. "This is over. Don't call me or come to my house." She simply wasn't ready or able or whatever to be with someone like him. Maybe she wasn't ready to be with anyone at all.

She tried to extricate herself, but he held on. Not

to harm or coerce, she knew that on one level. He was confused and trying to figure it out. But he couldn't because he was drunk and not in full control, and it felt way too familiar.

So familiar it made her skin clammy and her head hurt.

"Let go of me." She made every effort to keep her voice down and calm.

"Paddy, let go. Go back inside. I'm going to walk Natalie to her car." Damien put himself between them but Paddy was...well, Paddy.

"Why are you leaving? Are you breaking up with me? What did I do?"

Mary came out, hurrying over.

They were a minute, maybe three, away from a full-on scene, and that was more than she could take.

"Please let me leave before this turns into a scene." She turned on her heel and left, shoving her way out the door as Paddy bellowed after her.

Mary caught up with her at her car.

"Natalie! What happened?"

"I can't. Not like this. I don't want this in my life. I wish nothing but the best for you, and I hope we can still be friends, but I can't do this. I can't."

"Can't what? What happened?" Mary started to reach for her but must have sensed her body language screaming not to, so she let her hands fall by her sides. "You're freaking me out."

Paddy came out, calling her name, and she got in her car. "I have to go."

She drove away, not stopping until she got home.

"WHAT THE FUCK is going on?" Tuesday demanded as she burst into Natalie's bedroom an hour later. "Paddy has called like fourteen times. There are notes on the door." She tossed them on the bed. "Do I need to help you kill someone and hide the body?"

Natalie sat up with a sigh. Thank goodness for her friend.

She told Tuesday everything, and Tuesday hugged her tight at the end of it all.

"Wow."

"Yeah. You told me to tell him, and I said I was the one who needed to get over it, instead."

"I love you so much, I won't even say I told you so. But now that this has happened, what are you going to do?"

"I did it. I can't be with him, Tuesday. I can't. The way I felt today? I haven't felt like that for years. Years. I never want that in my life again. I worked my ass off to get my shit together so I never had to live that way, and in one afternoon, it all came back."

Tuesday nodded. "But he made a mistake. He didn't know. About Bob, I mean. And to be totally fair, it was Bob who set you off, not Paddy. I just think you're being stupid. And scared."

"I can't have this shit in my life. He's stumbling and fucked up and I'm remembering all the times I led a stumbling Bob or one of his *guests* somewhere. I just...I don't want to live worried if that'll happen again. And it will. Dude, his life is full of that stuff. If that means I'm broken and fucked up, so be it. I am scared, Tuesday."

Her friend blew out a breath. "I get that. So much I get it. But—and you knew that was coming—you're in love with him. You like him and his family, and you're good when you're with him. Tell him you're scared.

Help him understand. Don't let Bob ruin your happiness. Not like this."

Natalie pinched her bottom lip as she thought about it.

"All I'm saying is, what you have with him is good. It's hard and rife with bumps here and there. Neither of you knows how to be with someone else. It's going to be work, but all the best stuff is worth the effort."

Could she do it? "I need to think about it."

"You're off tomorrow. Pack a bag. Let's go to Portland. We'll have a fancy dinner somewhere. See if Delia can join us. Maybe see a show. You can enjoy yourself while you think, and deal with him on Monday."

CHAPTER THIRTEEN

IT HAD BEEN two days and dozens of calls, and he still didn't know what the fuck happened between him and Natalie at the winery.

He'd gone out early with his dad to look at some new equipment, and they'd ended up at a diner for an early lunch afterward.

"So, you want to talk about it?"

He should have known news about the breakup would have reached his parents by that point.

"Everything was fine. I'd spoken to her a few hours earlier. She got caught late at work for a grant thing. I was going to cancel and meet her at my house, but she said to go on and she'd meet me there when she finished. She wasn't mad when we had that call."

He sipped his iced tea and winked at the server who'd been flirting up a storm with him.

"Did you do that in front of her?" His dad indicated the server as she swayed away.

"All I did was wink at her. And no, I'm not rude. I never even notice other women when she's around. Anyway, there weren't any other women around then."

"Damien says you and Vaughan were drunker than skunks."

"It was a winery tour. We'd been to two other wineries before that one. I didn't throw up on her or any-thing." Also Damien was a dick for tattling.

"But you were drunk."

"Yes. I didn't drive! Mary drove, and she wasn't drinking at all. I was going to drive home with Nat because she wouldn't have had much if any to drink."

"Do you know why that is?"

"I asked her once, you know, if she was in recovery or something. She said no. She's..." *Got a thing about control.* She'd told him, and he'd listened, but it hadn't really occurred to him until that moment that being around him when he was like that would have pushed her buttons. She'd told him she had them.

Question was, could he deal with that? Did he want to push to make things right or let it go and be glad he got out before things truly went bad?

"Just figured something out?"

He groaned at his father. "Did you know already?"

"Nope. I'm a mere male mortal, too, you know. Your mother can get in a right-old snit from time to time, and I have no idea what I did. Usually because I needed to think about it some, and I figure it out a while later. Sometimes because she's weird and she just gets pissed off about stuff for no apparent reason, but if you ever say that, I'll deny it. The thing is, women are compli-cated creatures. But really, if you pay attention, you can figure them out. Mostly. And when you can't, throw-ing yourself on their mercy and presents usually help."

"She could have at least told me what was wrong."

His father thanked the server when she dropped off their burgers and fries before turning back to their con-versation.

"You can pout about it if you think that'll do the

trick. Or you can give it another try and open with, *I'm sorry I was out of control the other day, can we please talk about it?*"

"How was it between you and Mom? At the beginning, I mean." He knew the basic story, that his parents, both from small towns in Tennessee, had met and married within six months and then ended up loading up two of their kids in a truck filled with their belongings and moved west to Hood River.

"I love women. And before I met your mom, I loved a lot of them." He grinned. "I was *not* interested in settling down. Not a single bit. Oh, sure, lots of women tried. I think I was a project. But I liked being free. I liked my wild life working the land, bedding whoever I liked whenever I liked, and I had no plans to change. And then one day, I was in town at the record store. Back when they had such things." His dad snorted. "And she came in. She was laughing with someone. Your aunt Cathy. Anyway, she was just beautiful. And so I sidled on over and introduced myself because I wanted some of that in the worst way. She said no when I asked her out. I was twenty-four years old and I'd never been turned down before. Never."

They continued to eat as the world outside passed by. "Anyway, so of course, I wanted her even more. It wasn't in my hometown but one a few over. Small enough, and I knew several folks so it wasn't long until I found out who she was and that she worked at the JCPenney, and I showed up there until she finally agreed to let me buy her lunch. I tell you, once I kissed her, in the alley behind the JCPenney, not very romantic, I know. I knew she was different from that first time

I saw her, but once I kissed her, I knew she was it for me. We got married five months after that."

"You said you married six months after you met. It took you a month to kiss her?"

"Yes. But between you and me, she was pregnant with Ezra when we got married." His dad laughed at that. "We didn't know for another few weeks, but I'd have married her a week after that kiss if she'd have let me. I never expected her, but I knew once I had her that she was it. Your brother was the same way with Mary. Hurley men know what they want and we rarely fail at getting it. Seems to me, Paddy, if you fail with Natalie, it's because you didn't try hard enough. Don't give up on her if you want her."

So HE FOUND himself waiting outside the library at her quitting time the next day, holding two dozen roses of all different colors and a bag of takeout.

His phone buzzed in his pocket and he pulled it out, glancing at the screen. *Natalie.*

He answered. "Hey."

"So I've been thinking."

"Me, too. I'm sorry about that scene at the winery. Will you talk to me?"

"I'm calling you, aren't I? I was calling to see if you wanted to talk to me, too."

She came out, and he knew he'd done the right thing because seeing her made him so damned happy, it wasn't even funny.

She headed down the steps and was halfway to him before she noticed him standing there and froze.

She put her phone in her bag.

He peeked around the roses. "I told you we had the

same idea. I have milk shakes. And Thai food. I went to Voodoo, too, so I've got doughnuts in the car."

"I can see you mean business. Follow me to my place. We can eat and talk."

He handed her the flowers before he went back to his car and followed her to her house.

When they went inside, Tuesday looked up from where she sat at the kitchen table, and her brows rose. "It's about time. I'm going to a movie. I'll see you later."

She kissed Natalie's cheek, grabbed her coat and purse and headed out.

"Wait. You don't have to leave. We can go upstairs to talk."

She rolled her eyes at Natalie. "Hush. I'll be back later."

Natalie watched Tuesday go and turned back around with a sigh. "I'm going to put these in some water." She hung up her coat in the closet and then put her bag down near the bench at the back door. She grabbed the flowers, and he followed her.

"I'll get plates out."

They walked around each other, sort of tiptoeing around the subject for several minutes.

"You have a thing about control. I mean, you told me about it, but I didn't really hear it or get how it connected with the winery, but I see it now."

She started, going very still, and he waited. He could do most of the work, but she had to give him something.

"And you saw me when I was not in full control and it pushed your buttons."

"Yes." She blew out a breath. "Look, I'm sorry I left without explaining myself."

"Will you tell me? I know I upset you, but we can't do this unless you share with me."

She swallowed hard and took a deep breath. "I grew up in a house that was chaos all the time. My dad was, is, was—who knows— The entire time I was growing up, he was an addict. For long years it was alcohol and then it was cocaine and then he was an IV drug user. He loved speedballs. My house was not a safe place. My house was not filled with adults who were good examples. My dad was fucked up all the time. We got our furniture stolen on a regular basis. I had a padlock on my door to keep my stuff safe, and my door was broken down on more than one occasion. We lived in a nice house in a nice neighborhood so I had that, which is more than a lot of other people did, I understand that.

"I've seen enough out-of-control people on the nod with their rig still in their arm, enough overdoses and random assholes lying in pools of vomit in my living room to last several lifetimes. I see that sort of thing, and it brings my past back to me and I drown in it. If someone else is out of control, that means they're not taking care of their business. It means someone else is cleaning up after them. Not just bottles and needles and puke, making sure the bills got paid, dealing with the school so child protective services never got suspicious. I'm just…done taking care of other people. I don't want to look back, Paddy. That scene triggered some stuff that had already been partially reawakened that day." She put her fork down.

He didn't speak as he tried to process. As he fought rage at the way she'd had to grow up, there was still no denying her opening up to trust him with part of her past warmed him. And then he got freaked out that he'd mishandle the next step. And then, maybe part of him was hurt she hadn't just come to him before.

"I'm far from perfect." She cut her gaze to his. "I know in here—" Natalie pressed the heel of her hand over her heart "—that what you were at the winery was not even in the same universe as what I grew up with. But here—" she rubbed her stomach "—keeps tripping me up. I saw you that way, and it all came back to me. The powerlessness of it. You didn't do it on purpose, and I understand that. I don't know if it's going to happen again and your life…well, your life is wild."

He took her hand, tangling his fingers with hers, and that connection simply clicked back into place. He knew she felt it, too, because her eyes widened slightly.

"I'm sorry. I was sloppy drunk, and I didn't get all the cues I would have if I hadn't been. Damien says you were really upset, and I saw it but that I kept making it worse." He licked his lips. "Look, I have a brother I watched descend into the worst kind of addiction. I watched him change into another person. Someone I hated. But I had him my whole life up to that point. I knew it wasn't him. And then he got his shit together and cleaned up, and he was more like the Ezra who was my brother. But he's changed forever because of what he did. And we all are, too. If you want, I can just not drink around you."

"It's not that. I have a glass of wine here and there. You know I like champagne. I'm not opposed to people drinking. Not at all. I just… It triggers me and all that helplessness when I see people who are sloppy and out of control. I guess I didn't realize how bad it was until I saw you. I just don't always know what's going to make me upset. I'm finding out myself as I go. It's not fair to you to try to deal with that."

He snorted. "I'll let you know if I think you're a burden or not. You're entitled to your feelings on this. Perfectly valid feelings, I might add.

"I want this to work. I don't think you'd have let me in the door if you didn't want that, too. So what I'm saying is, why not try? I like you. You like me. We're adults, and at least there's one of us with some measure of emotional maturity."

She rolled her eyes, and he felt so much better for it.

"I meant you, if that wasn't clear. I think you should give us a chance."

She squeezed his hand. "I'm sorry."

"For what?"

"For my reaction. I know you didn't mean to upset me. I'm sorry I can't guarantee something else random won't freak me out."

Tenderness chased away his amusement. He hated that she had all this baggage, hated more that she seemed to blame herself for it. "Beautiful, I was a dumbass. A drunken dumbass, and I manhandled you on top of that. You don't have anything to apologize for. But I do appreciate the explanation. I can be better at this if I know more about you."

"You weren't trying to hurt or control me. I knew that on one level. I just don't know, Paddy. I don't know if I can do this and not make mistakes."

"That makes two of us. In fact, I'm sure I'll make mistakes. I don't know what this relationship gig entails." That was something he'd had to work so hard to accept. He didn't know how to put someone else first. Not other than his family. "I'm feeling my way through. I want you to trust me. Even though I'm not perfect, either."

"On one condition."

"Name it."

"I'm going to need that spring roll."

He laughed, handing it over and then turning the bag over on her plate. "Have 'em all."

She hadn't realized how much she'd missed him until she'd walked out of the library and seen him standing there. A phone call meant she'd have some distance from him. But Paddy Hurley in the flesh? That smile?

As they cleaned the kitchen up, she was glad, so glad, she'd brought him home. Glad she shared with him. Glad he was there with her. Tuesday probably would say *I told you so* for that.

"So. I have a proposal."

She looked back over her shoulder as she tucked the hand towel on the ring. "That so? What is this proposal, then?"

"I have doughnuts. I think we should go to your room and eat them naked in your bed."

She paused. "As proposals go, that's a pretty good one."

She walked past him, swatting his behind on the way. "Let's be sure that sex is on that menu, too."

"That goes without saying when you're alone with me and there's naked involved."

She left Tuesday a note saying things were okay between her and Paddy, and that they were busy for a bit. She figured Tuesday would know when she got home if Natalie wasn't around and her door was closed, but it never hurt to be extra sure. The last thing she wanted was Tuesday barging in and catching her and Paddy in bed.

Awkward.

Paddy kicked her door closed and backed her to the bed. "Maybe you can eat that doughnut while I eat you. It's been like a week since I've tasted you."

She swallowed hard. "I might choke. Maybe we can eat them afterward."

"Damn, you're putting doughnuts aside for me? You really are trying."

She laughed as she pulled his sweater off, tossing it in a nearby chair. He undid her blouse and slid it from her arms, kissing her shoulder and across her collarbone. He paused at the hollow of her throat and breathed in deep. "I've missed you like crazy."

It had only been a few days rather than his exaggerated week, but she'd missed him, too. Missed the way he'd been part of her life.

"I missed you, too." She petted his beard.

She realized she'd started doing that recently. Petting it and soothing herself. It made her laugh and he paused.

"Um. Should I be concerned you're laughing?"

"I just realized your beard is my comfort object. I pet it like a blankie, and it soothes me."

He kissed her fingertips. "Whatever gets you hot. Feel free to pet me wherever and whenever you please."

They ended up in a tumble on her bed as they stopped pawing at each other long enough to struggle out of their clothes and return.

He felt so good. Warm. Solid. Hard against her. He tasted her, his lips teasing her mouth, her jawline, her ears. Her heart sped at his attentions.

She moved to reach between them, and he grasped

her wrists and pulled her arms above her head, pinning them there while he rolled atop her, kissing her until she was dizzy.

"I think—" he paused to kiss her again "—you need to give up control. Not all the time. Not in your day-to-day life. But here. Just between us. Give it to me."

She tested his hold, a thrill rushing through her. This wasn't anything she'd ever really considered before.

He watched her and she knew he'd let go if she asked. Her head spun with it.

"Please."

He paused before kissing her again. "Please stop or please don't stop?"

"Please don't stop."

He tightened his hold at her wrists and she arched, brushing her body against his like a cat.

"Mmm, you feel so good." He sucked her bottom lip. "Taste good, too. But there are other parts of you I need to taste because I've been denied you for so long."

"So long? Three days. Jeez."

He laughed. "Technically, it's five days because we were nookie-less for a few days before the wincry. Five days is close enough to a week. So hush and lemme lick you."

She closed her mouth because she had no real argument with that plan.

He slid his hands from her wrists, pressing her forearms into the mattress. The breath left her lungs in a shaky exhale.

"Yeah, I like that, too." He leaned some of his weight against her, enough to hold her down, not nearly enough to hurt her.

She struggled, but not really, and they both smiled at one another when he realized what she was doing.

He moved her arms to her sides, still holding them against the mattress as he licked down her chest, over her nipples.

She gave over to him, falling into the way his mouth felt on her belly, over her hip bone, at the way his tongue felt sliding through her. And when she came, she opened her eyes to find him looking down at her.

"You're beautiful when you come."

He made her feel beautiful. Powerful, even as he held her arms down.

"You should let me taste you."

"Nope. Maybe later. Right now, even as alluring as that mouth of yours is, I have other plans for my dick."

He let go long enough to get a condom on and returned to her. "Roll over. Put that pretty ass up in the air and keep your head down. Arms above your head."

Oh.

My.

She obeyed, and he caressed his hands all over her back. "This work is so beautiful."

She made an inarticulate sound because she didn't know how to speak with his hands on her like that. He reached around and slid his fingers through her.

"Trust me. Remember? Just want to make sure you're ready."

As if he hadn't just made her come less than a minute before.

She pushed back against his fingers, and he stretched her a little before he pulled them out and replaced them with the blunt head of his cock. He left it there for long moments and then pressed in slowly.

Oh. So. Slowly. She had to force herself to be patient, digging her nails into the sheets. Wanting more and making herself wait, trusting him to give it to her. She wasn't used to that. She took what she needed because who else would make sure she got it otherwise?

And he did in one glorious thrust, finally entering her fully.

Then he pulled nearly all the way out only to press back in again. Over and over. So slow and deep she thought she might die from how good it was.

He gripped her hips and fucked into her body exactly how he wanted, and she loved every second of it.

He thrust into her over and over, drawing closer. Even through the latex of the condom, she felt him harden, knew he was nearing climax. The fingers of his left hand dug into her flesh as he reached around.

She briefly thought about protesting, but she knew he wanted another climax from her, and she tightened up her muscles, reaching for it with her whole body. And it broke over her, sucking her under as he sped with a mumbled exhalation of her name. She came and he came, hard, and it went on for so long she started to lose feeling in her knees.

He groaned and pulled out slowly. One-handed, he helped her settle in the blankets, quickly going to the bathroom to get rid of the condom and return, snuggling into her back, holding her against his body.

"I missed you. That wasn't just something I said to fill the silence." He kissed her shoulder.

"You sound sort of unsure of that. A little angry."

"Sometimes." He sucked in a breath. "If I want you to be open with me, I should be, too. So yeah, at first I was angry. I've… This is not what I'm used to."

"Angry at me?"

"Angry at everything. It made me vulnerable. Missing you made me realize this wasn't just me dating a woman I enjoyed. Your absence made me confront how much you mean to me. How much space you take up in my life. I wanted it not to matter but it did. And then my anger shifted."

"Yeah?"

"Some things just are. You're in my life and I like that. I hated that I'd done something to upset you. More than I was mad you didn't just tell me what it was."

She sighed, closing her eyes as she thought about all he'd said. "You scare me, Paddy."

"I do?"

"Not physically. But…anyway, you matter to me and only people who matter to you can really hurt you."

"I'll try not to. But I will, anyway. I'm an amateur at this stuff. But I want you to tell when I do. Even if you think I'm the biggest asshole ever. I can't fix it if I don't know, and if I don't know and you're hurting, it's not fair to me. Or to you."

She blew out a breath, snagging his hand, kissing his knuckles. "I'll do my best."

"You hold your control like a shield. And I get why. But you can let me in sometimes, you know. I *want* you to trust me enough to do that. To let *me* be your shield. Isn't it heavy? Exhausting?"

She nodded, her forearm over her eyes.

"So what I'm suggesting is that between us, when it's quiet and intimate, you give me some of that control. Let me manage things, and just relax."

Eyes still closed, she nodded. And jumped. "Yes."

CHAPTER FOURTEEN

"I LOVE HORSEBACK RIDING. Thank you so much for having us out today." Tuesday turned her face up to the mid-November sleet as if it were awesome.

But since her best friend really was in heaven over all the outdoorsy stuff the Hurleys seemed to eat, sleep and breathe, Natalie pulled her hat down a little more and thanked the heavens she'd worn her gloves.

Vaughan and Paddy kept racing with Damien as Mary hung back with them. "God, they're like kittens."

Natalie laughed. "If he's all tired out, he'll sleep better and stop being so cranky."

Mary snorted. "This is the second time I've been through an album production with them. It's just getting started. It'll get worse before it gets better, I'm sorry to say. They're in each other's faces so much, judging, creating, leaving themselves so emotionally open to one another, it makes them all tense."

Natalie nodded. "I hadn't thought of it like that, but it makes sense. I'd be cranky, too, I guess. It's just... weird to have Paddy be the cranky one. I'm usually the cranky one in our relationship."

The sex, though, it had been...endlessly inventive, yes, but far more intense. She supposed he was burning off all the stuff from his brothers that way.

Tuesday chortled. "Yeah."

Natalie took off her hat long enough to swat Tuesday with it. "Hush, you."

"Whatever he's doing has calmed you down. I say it like I don't hear it on the other side of the house. It's better to pretend."

Blushing madly, Natalie shook her head. "Stop that! There's no way you can hear from your side of the house." Or she hoped so.

"I know. It's just fun to make you turn red."

"I'm glad we have our own house with no one close enough. I can't imagine what goes on at Vaughan's place. Ezra, well, he keeps his business away from the ranch, and I know what Paddy is getting up to." Mary winked at Natalie, who groaned.

"One of these days, I'm actually going to meet the mysterious Ezra face-to-face."

"It's pretty impressive. I mean, Damien is hard enough to manage, Ezra and all that darkness he carries around would be a full-time job. But he's no chore to look at and his voice is pretty fantastic."

Natalie nodded at Mary's reference to Ezra. "Nice and gravelly. And he loves animals. That's so sweet."

"He's the driving force behind Sweet Hollow Ranch. Even though he doesn't go out on the road. He's their big brother and they depend on him."

Natalie thought there were more layers to Ezra than anyone would ever truly see. "Paddy said he and Ezra do most of the writing?"

"Yes. But things are evolving. Ezra and Paddy are used to doing most of the writing themselves, but this time Damien and Vaughan are doing more." Mary shook her head as she watched the brothers cavorting all around.

LAUREN DANE   157

"So far there've only been two fistfights. I'm told this is a record. Of course, Damien is the most laid-back. Paddy and Vaughan, my God. I had to use the hose on them day before yesterday."

Natalie gasped and then choked, laughing. "Really? You have to tell us all about that."

Mary snickered. "It's a time-honored way of ending disputes in my family, you understand. I have two brothers, and when they got into fights, my mom would turn the hose on them. Anyway, Paddy and Ezra work together well. Mostly. Paddy's a perfectionist. He makes them do things over and over and over again until he's satisfied. When they're in the studio, Ezra is the leader of the group. Paddy is usually okay with that, but sometimes, you know, he's fussy. So he and Ezra were pissy with each other, and Vaughan took Ezra's side, and Damien threw up his hands and walked out, and Vaughan and Paddy started all that pushing and trash talk, and it spilled out of the barn to where I'd just come out. Vaughan tripped on the bottom step, and he took Paddy down with him.

"Then it just got stupid, and it upset my pig, damn it."

Mary seemed to share custody of a pig named Violet with Ezra. The damned animal grunted in this happy, singsong way anytime she caught sight of Mary.

"So the dog is barking, and the pig is squealing, and Ezra is yelling at them to stop it, and Damien is off to the side laughing and throwing dirt clods at them, making it worse, so I went over, turned on the water and started squirting them. It's pretty cold so I imagine that water was freezing. It broke up pretty fast after that."

Natalie laughed so hard, she cried. She'd slowly gotten used to the raucous noise the four Hurley boys made

whenever they were together. At heart, it was affectionate and protective. She could deal with that. Plus, they
were all sort of hot grunting and rolling around.

The three of them laughed and laughed until the
brothers noticed and turned, riding back to where the
women were.

"What are you guys up to?"

Mary waved a hand. "Never you mind about that.
How about we go home? I have stew making."

"Seconded." Natalie held up a hand.

Paddy pulled even with her. "I think given the shade
of red Nat's cheeks are, that a roaring fire and some hot
stew is in order."

"Fine. Joy killers." Tuesday winked at her, and
they headed back to the stables before walking over to
Damien and Mary's.

MARY SENT THEM to the store with a list and strict orders, but Paddy was pleased, anyway, to get her alone.

"How's the album coming along? I heard about the
fight between you and Vaughan."

He laughed. "Which one?"

"The one Mary had to break up with the hose."

"That little fucker tripped and took me down with
him. After messing up his freaking bass line four times
in a row."

"You're a harsh taskmaster."

"Hmph. Live is one thing. You know everyone puts
their all into a show, and it can be uneven, but it's okay
because that's the beauty of watching live music. But
an album is different. If he wants to write this time out,
he needs to bring it and to work his ass off."

"Makes sense."

"Really? I figured you'd say I was being mean."

"I think you're one of the most relaxed, laid-back people I've ever met. So if you're intense about this thing that matters to you so much, this thing you do and put all your life blood into? What's wrong with that? I figure your brothers will punch you in the face if you go too far."

"I didn't expect you to react that way."

"How did you expect me to react? Shock? Because I don't do something really creative, you think I can't understand it?"

She was so provocative sometimes. There were times he knew she did it on purpose. It used to offend him, but really he'd begun to realize she didn't do it with most people, only with people she liked and trusted. She wanted more from him in her own way and her raw, honest questions were about that.

"My music is this intensely personal thing. It's hard to put it into words. I guess I just expect people to judge me when they hear I'm precise."

"Well, if they know you and your brothers, they know you guys are intense with each other all the time. I imagine it's hard to expose yourselves to each other over and over. I imagine Vaughan wants to impress you, and I imagine you want the best from him and you wouldn't be giving him this chance if you didn't think he could do it. He's your baby brother. He wants you to respect him and believe in him. And when you get too harsh, he punches you in the face. And Damien throws dirt clods and laughs, and Ezra yells at you both to stop because he's the big brother, and that's what he does."

He laughed.

"But he should punch something else because I like your face."

"I'll be sure to tell him that. Maybe it'll save my face from being punched in the future."

"I doubt that. It seems to be a popular mode of communication between you Hurleys."

"You and Tuesday wouldn't punch each other in the face if you disagreed."

"No." She shrugged. "We have a rhythm. We always have. But we get into fights sometimes. Mainly we use humor to poke at one another. We push each other when we don't want to confront ugly truths. She was the one who pushed me to go out with you back in the summer. She said I should give you a chance."

"I knew I liked her for a reason."

"Anyway, I think the people you love most and are closest to you have an immense power to really hurt you because you let them in. Strangers can say something to me that won't hurt, but if Tuesday said them, or you, for that matter, they could slay me. I'm not going to second-guess how you make records. You've been doing this with your brothers for years and years. Given your success, you're all good at it."

"We're having some growing pains." *There, he said it.*

"How so?"

"Until the last album, Ezra and I did the lion's share of the writing. We come up with the raw material and then we meet as a band and work through the songs. We always have more songs than we have room for, and usually we do those songs as bonus singles for our fan club around the holidays. Anyway, we bring the lyrics and usually a basic track to the group, and we all work on it. Everyone is good at something different. Damien lays a beat, Vaughan funks it up, I create the texture and Ez, he puts it all together into something coherent.

"Last CD, Damien was falling in love. His life had gone a revolution. He had two of his songs on the album, including the title song. This time, though, he and Vaughan both came to the meetings with material of their own. Some of it was good. We've been able to take it and in one case, we melded a few ideas together into one. One will most likely make it onto the CD. Vaughan's is too rough, and he's super touchy about criticism."

Paddy found a parking space near the front doors of the grocery store.

"Well, if he wants to do what you guys do, he has to be open to the criticism you all get from each other."

He got out, walking around to her side where she waited for him to open her door. He knew she did it for him. She was perfectly capable of opening her own door and that sort of thing. But he liked to do it for her, and she made room for it. It never ceased to make him smile.

"See, you're right. And we try to tell him that. But he takes it the wrong way and punches me in the face."

"Perhaps Damien can tell him that? I mean, you and Vaughan are close. And you're a lot alike in temperament, so maybe a different voice saying it means he can hear it better."

"It seems underhanded to go behind Vaughan's back like that. He's a big boy."

She grabbed a cart. "Or, you can realize this is a business as well as a creative endeavor in your family, and that sometimes we hear things better when they're delivered by a person who comes at us in a way we don't react to negatively. Humans are crazy that way, Patrick. Sometimes their emotions get in front of their logic."

He bumped her with his hip.

"While we're being honest, can I tell you how much I hate it that we can't go anywhere without women eye fucking you?" She said this casually as she put cartons of milk into the basket.

"You've never expressed a single bit of jealousy before. I like it."

She frowned. "I don't. It sucks. I like to think I'm above that stuff, and I am so not. I mean, I'm guessing you'd be getting female attention even if you weren't who you are. You're pretty nice to look at, and you're flirty and sassy."

He didn't stop himself from kissing her temple. "You know it's just how I am, right? I mean, I might smile and nod but you have absolutely nothing to fear. I'd never do that to you, nor do I even want to. You're all the woman I can handle."

"Yeah, yeah. I imagine you guys would freak out if your women got the same level of attention you do. I mean, look at Mary, she's absolutely gorgeous. Full-stop beautiful. I bet if men touched her the way women touch Damien, he'd flip his lid."

"Well, of course!"

She gave him a raised brow. "On the way from the front of the store to here, a woman walked close enough to you to brush her entire body against yours. There was plenty of room in the aisle for her to pass without touching you. And you're here with me. Jeez."

"I'm sorry." He was sorry she was bothered, but he

couldn't help but want to preen that she'd expressed some level of possessiveness over him. It felt like a victory to him.

"Meh. It's okay. I get it. Maybe if I was another person, I'd rub all over you, too. You're pretty rubbable."

He leaned in, his lips against her ear. "You just rubbed against me a few hours ago."

She blushed hard. "Quit it. Rogue."

"That's me, baby. Rogue. Rebel." He hooked his thumbs in his belt loops exaggeratedly.

"Come on, then, Pirate Paddy, we need to get all this back to Mary. I'm starving."

They headed to the checkout lanes. This time he pushed the cart so that he'd be out of prime random-women-rubbing-against-him space.

Once they got to his car, and he unloaded the bags into the trunk, he heard someone call her name.

She cursed but didn't turn. "Let's go.

"Someone is calling you."

"I'm aware. Just ignore him and unlock the door."

"Are you afraid? Has that dude hurt you in some way?"

The guy reached them. He was in his fifties, though the lines on his face indicated he'd lived hard. His hair was thinning but he had it in a ponytail in the back like a lot of guys his age who tried to hold on to how old they were a decade or two before. He had a soul patch and wore tinted glasses and a diamond stud in his ear.

"Natty, I've been looking for you. I was just stopping here to get some lunch."

"I told you to stop calling me that. Paddy, the door, please."

HE HEARD THE tension in her tone and unlocked the door, opening it for her. "You need to tell me if I have to introduce this douchebag to my fist or not."

She shook her head. "No. I have it handled." She looked around him to the guy. "Go. Away. I've been totally clear with you on this point."

He turned his attention from Natalie to Paddy. "Who are you, young man?"

"I could ask you the same."

"I'm her father."

Natalie got between them, and Paddy didn't like that at all.

"Jesus. Shut up, Bob. Paddy, let's go."

"How can you be so cold? I raised you, and this is the thanks I get? Your mother ran off, maybe you're like her."

Paddy spun at the calculation in the man's voice and the intake of her breath in response. His hands were already in fists as he stepped around her and toward the asshole.

She touched his arm. "No. Patrick, I'm not kidding. Get in the car. Don't engage with him. That's what he wants. Please. For me."

It was the way she called him by his full name and the pain in her plea that finally enabled him to unlock his muscles and get in the car. She hit the locks.

"Drive before he can get in his car and follow."

He blew out a breath but obeyed. They were both silent on the way back to the ranch. Paddy made sure no one was behind him when he took the main road up the hill and then the main drive to the house. At the main gates, he used the code and then made sure the security was set. He'd need to tell his parents so they didn't go setting it off when they came and went.

"Even if he found us, he can't get in," he reassured her.

She nodded, looking out the window.

He drove to his place. "It's cold enough. The stuff will keep while you tell me what the hell just happened. Do we need to call the cops?"

"So that's my biological father, which you probably guessed. Every three years or so, he gets clean for a while. And then he goes NA and AA and he gets to the make-your-amends point. For many people in recovery, this is the point where they have to own their shit and work on rebuilding relationships they've destroyed while they were using. It's hard, I get that and so the first time—God, that was when I was fifteen or so—I wanted him to be different. I wanted him to be healthy. So it wasn't a perfect apology, but I just wanted him to get himself straight. Five months later, he and one of his girlfriends overdosed in the living room. That's when he added oxycodone to the mix of his addiction."

Paddy took her hand, squeezing it.

"It got really bad. So bad I moved out when I was seventeen. I entertained trying to find my mom, but he didn't lie about that. She did run off. Occasionally, a card would arrive from her with no return address. Mailed from all over the southwestern U.S. So I worked a bunch of shitty jobs around my school schedule and getting high. He was an excellent example so when I needed to be up to work and go to school, too, I used speed to get through.

"He got clean again. About six months before I moved to Portland and managed to get into college.

That time lasted about four months. Pretty much it was the same pattern. I wanted to believe him, I let him back into my life and he wasn't there when he'd asked me to come up to my grandparents' at Thanksgiving."

"Christ."

"So I had contact with my grandparents and he found where I was going to school through them. He showed up when I was in my third year. I'd gotten my life together. I had a job, and I had friends, and I was doing really well in school. By that point, I was healthy enough that I could see and hear all the cracks in his facade. I wanted him to do well, but I had to keep him back. Letting him get close hurt too much. I kept communication with him, but eventually, after all the calls at two in the morning when he was high and needed me to talk him through stuff the same as I had over and over, I just changed my number and told him to leave me alone."

"So he just turned up again?"

"He showed up the day we got into the fight at the winery."

"What? Damn it, why didn't you tell me? Why don't you trust me more?"

"Because you were stumbling drunk, and it pushed all my growing-up-with-a-stumbling-drunk-asshole-as-a-parent buttons."

She clapped a hand over her mouth, shocked she'd actually yelled it. "I'm sorry. That was totally out of line. I didn't tell you because, as I've learned after some therapy, I'm ashamed of it."

He sighed. "Just when I work up hurt feelings that you don't trust me enough to be a man you can rely on, you reveal something else that breaks my heart and fucks with my perceptions."

Paddy took her hand between his to stop it from shaking. "I was indeed a stumbling drunk. I'm sorry I asked that like an accusation. You don't need to apologize for having feelings. I can't tell you not to be ashamed, though I don't think you should be. We all went through some counseling while Ezra was getting clean."

She snorted. "Ezra isn't like Bob. Not at all. It took me a while you know, before I could see the differences. I tended to think all recovering folks were selfish jerks. But really, *Bob* is a selfish jerk. He's not evil. That's too simple. He just doesn't have the ability to understand anyone else's feelings. Or even that he should. Even when he's clean, he's going to be an asshole. I don't hate him. I don't wish bad things for him. I just want to be free of him. I want a life without him in it."

"Do you think you could ever have a relationship with him? I mean, does he get credit at all for coming to see you?"

"This isn't a loan. I'm not interested in credit. That's not how it works. There comes a time when you have to own your shit. Truly. Can I own what I did in a house like mine? When I was twelve and fending off druggies who wanted to fuck me? I won't own that. I own my rejection of him now. If that makes me heartless, so be it."

His mouth flattened into an angry line. "I hate that you lived that way."

She shrugged. "It's over and done."

"The library was *your* haven, wasn't it?"

She sucked in a breath. "I can't do this anymore. Not right now. I'm scraped raw and embarrassed, and we're going to be caught up in hurricane Hurley in a few minutes. Tuesday will be protective if she sees I'm upset, and I want her to have a good day."

"I want to make everything better for you."

She put her face in her hands as tears threatened.

"Now I'm making it worse, and I don't know why or how. Jesus, I'm fucking up."

She sniffed, willing the threatened tears far away, straightening to look at him. "No, you aren't. You're doing just fine." There were things she wanted to say to him but was so freaked out by the fear. What if he thought she was stupid? What if she cared about him more than he cared about her?

"Remember? Trust."

"No one has ever wanted to make everything better for me." She rushed the words from her lips before she could take them back.

He pulled her over the console and into his lap. Her ass hit the horn, and he opened the door to swing his legs out, holding her close. "You wreck me. No one has ever wrecked me. You don't mean to. It's not calculated. You just do it because you're brave and honest and Christ, I'm falling in love with you. And I do want to make it better because you're so much to me. You ask me questions, and you care about my life, and you have this heart that fells me." He spoke as he spilled kisses across her face. Over her eyelids and cheeks. She held on because he filled her up and made her light all at the same time.

"I want to take you in my house, strip you naked and show you how much you mean to me. With my lips and my tongue and other parts."

"I'd love that, too, but you know people are waiting for us."

Paddy sighed, standing and putting her down so carefully, the tears she'd managed to put away threatened again. "Sometimes they're a pain in my butt."

"But you love them."

"Mostly. But not when they're cockblocking me."

She grabbed her bag. "Do you want to drive over there or walk with the bags?"

"Get in. We'll drive over since there are so many bags."

HE WATCHED HER for hours. Seeing her in a new light made her even more beautiful to him. But he couldn't get the look on her face as she'd nearly lost it out of his head. Or the way she'd yelled and then apologized for it.

She was so afraid to fight with him, and he didn't know what to do about that. Because he wanted her to feel safe yelling if she had to sometimes. Wanted her to realize he wasn't going anywhere if she lost her temper from time to time. He'd been sort of a butthead, anyway, even though he was just expressing worry.

At the same time she'd unburdened herself to him. She'd opened up and trusted him with a piece of her story that had exposed her hurts and fears. In that act she gave up control in a different way. He *could* hurt her with what she revealed, but she did it, anyway. Letting go.

The longer they were together, the more he understood what a huge gift that was. Her confession that no one had ever wanted to make things better had nearly brought him to his knees.

She was made to be cherished. So that was what he tried to do, and he bungled it up sometimes. But they got past it when it came to that. And it was a victory every time they disagreed, and she didn't run off or close up.

That trust she showed was as intimate as the clasp of her body around his when they made love.

But it was the issue of her father that had him the most perplexed. She didn't want the man in her life, and that was all Paddy needed to know. From what he'd witnessed that afternoon, she was truly better off without a man so petty and vindictive.

Paddy wanted to know about the mother, too, but Natalie was fragile just then. He could see it in her features. So he waited. He'd be what she needed.

They'd started eating when Ezra showed up. He'd gone to Portland for the day and was more relaxed than he had been when they'd worked that morning before they'd gone on their ride.

Paddy didn't know exactly what Ezra did when he left for hours. He knew his older brother wasn't using again. But he got something there that he needed because he came back calmer than when he'd gone.

Ezra clicked with Natalie. He and Mary were close, but there was a certain synchronicity between his big brother and Nat. The addiction thing tied them together in complicated ways. Ezra reminded Nat that recovery could be good and lasting and true. But he reminded her that her father hadn't done that. And Paddy was pretty sure Ezra saw in Natalie the sum of all the shit he'd done to his family and friends when he was an addict, as well as someone who understood his struggle in a unique way. Maybe through her, Ezra could see himself as a better person than he gave himself credit for.

Natalie smiled as Ezra came into the house. She watched as each brother adjusted himself in their little family ecosystem. It was adorable and also a little awe-inspiring that they had such rhythm.

Ezra gave Mary a kiss on the cheek and grinned at Natalie. "Hey, you."

"Hey, yourself. You're finally here when Tuesday is around." And even better, he looked ridiculously hot in a black turtleneck and worn jeans with well-worn cowboy boots.

Tuesday came in from the front room where she'd been watching something with Vaughan, and she and Ezra seemed to freeze up a moment when they caught sight of each other. Natalie's brow went up for a brief moment, but she held back a smile.

"Tuesday Eastwood, this is Ezra Hurley. Tuesday is one of my oldest and dearest friends, and I swear she was beginning to think we made you up because every time she came up here you were off doing something or other."

Ezra shook Tuesday's hand, and the stack of silver bracelets she wore jingled.

"Nice to meet you. Natalie talks about you all the time. You have great hair."

Everyone stared because Ezra was normally gruff, sometimes smooth, but never blurty.

Tuesday's smile, though, well, she was clearly pleased. It was the throaty purr of a woman who'd been flattered by a man she was interested in. "Thank you."

They dropped their hands, but it took several more seconds before everyone started talking again. Damien called Ezra from the other room, and he seemed to have to tear himself away, saying he'd be back shortly.

Natalie followed Tuesday into the kitchen. "Dude."

Tuesday just smiled. "What?"

"You have great hair?"

Tuesday touched her hair. She'd forgone the braids she'd had for the past few years and let it grow out into her natural curls. Her hair was fantastic. Big and bold and fucking gorgeous.

"Clearly the man recognizes great hair when he sees it. Now, until you got all titillated by Sir Hotness and his clearly wonderful taste, you were upset about something. What's up?"

Natalie sighed. "Bob was at the grocery store."

"What? Are you kidding me? What happened?"

Natalie told her quickly, and her friend just shook her head. "That is some kind of fuckery. But I'm glad you told Paddy more about the situation. He's good for you."

"Yeah. He is."

She walked Tuesday out and told her she'd see her at home in a few minutes.

"I NEED TO get working." Paddy brushed a fingertip over her chin.

"I know. Go on. I'll see you later. Thanks for today." She paused. "And thank you. For defending me. And for listening."

Tuesday had gone home already, so Natalie had a few stolen alone moments with Paddy.

"Oh, wait, you left your coat."

She'd put it in his front closet earlier.

He walked her in but kicked the door closed and gave her *the look*.

"Patrick, you're giving me the look."

"Am I?"

He backed her against the closet door, hands at her

hips. "I guess I am. I'm afraid that doesn't bode well for you."

"Or maybe it bodes *really* well."

He leaned down to kiss her and she gave over to it. He had to go and they both knew it, but he made no move to break away.

"Can you be very quiet? And quick? Hmm?" He spun her and her palms slapped the door, the sound so loud in the quiet of the entry. "You never know who might come to the door looking for me."

She should not be turned on by any of this.

But holy cow, she totally was.

He licked up the back of her neck, leaving her skin extrasensitive as gooseflesh broke out. His hands skimmed around her belly, unbuttoning and unzipping her jeans. The cool air made her shiver, but not as much as the moment did. He shoved her pants and panties down, pressing her body against the wood.

The edge of his teeth grazed her ear as his fingers teased her clit, readying her body. She tried to be quiet, but he was driving her crazy, and when she heard the jingle of his belt and his zipper going down, she may have whimpered. She *knew* she did when the crinkle and tear of a condom wrapper sounded.

He pulled back a moment, her body cool suddenly where the heat of him had been scorching.

Her ankles hobbled by her pants, she couldn't do much more than rise to her tiptoes, thrusting her ass out when the tip of his cock brushed her butt cheeks.

"Yes," she moaned.

"Shh."

His hand clamped over her mouth right as he positioned himself and thrust into her body.

She was so wet, it went easy, even as the friction was delicious because her thighs were together.

Something about it was so taboo it sent a dark, delicious thrill through her as she groaned.

In and out, he thrust hard and fast as her fingers scrabbled against the wood. Looking for purchase and finding none.

"You're going to need to come. It's been a hard day. I want you to come all over my cock."

She cursed against his fingers, and he laughed softly, knowing exactly what he was doing to her.

With his free hand, he danced his fingertips around her nipple, through her shirt and bra. But it was enough. Enough to send waves of pleasure through her body, centering between her legs.

She whimpered when he moved his hand away, but he walked his fingers down her belly to her clit.

Three brushes of his middle finger and she was coming with so much sudden intensity, she had to close her eyes against it. He bit her neck where it met her shoulder as he joined her in climax.

Moments later, he pulled out and ducked into the powder room across from the closet, and when he returned, she'd managed to get her muscles working enough to pull her underpants and jeans back into place.

He looked carefully at her. So sweetly clear, he wanted to be sure she was all right with what had happened.

If it had been another man, she wasn't sure it would have been. But it wasn't any other man, it was Paddy. And what it was, was hot. Dirty and filthy and really delicious.

"You should go make music. Try not to punch anyone." She tiptoed up and kissed him. "I feel much more relaxed now."

He slid his arms around her waist. "Yeah? Everything okay?"

"Yes. Perfect. Now go on. I have to get home. I'll talk to you later."

He walked her to her car and watched her drive away.

CHAPTER FIFTEEN

"I VOTE WE walk right over there. I could use some soup and a cup of coffee." Sharon Hurley had shown up at the library the week following dinner at Damien and Mary's to invite Natalie to lunch.

"Sounds good." The little café was a place she ate lunch at all the time, so she knew the food was excellent.

"You look pretty. You're not afraid to wear color. I like that."

Natalie blushed. Sharon always said the nicest things. Oh, sure, she could be sort of scary sometimes, but usually to other people, which was always fun to watch.

They grabbed a table and settled in and once they'd ordered, Sharon leaned closer. "So I work with this group that does drives for different shelters and low-income programs for kids. Sometimes it's through the schools, too. I'd really like to get the community as a whole more involved, and I thought maybe you could help me with it."

"Really? Me? I'd love to help, but what makes you think I'd be so good at it?"

"I look at you when you're with kids, and I see someone who wants them to have a relationship with reading. I sense—and please don't take this the wrong way—but I sense that maybe you didn't have the greatest home life growing up."

Natalie swallowed, hard. *Trust.*

"No, I didn't. Reading was a way for me to travel. To be in places where people wanted to hear what you thought, wanted to know how you felt. Reading took me away from my reality, which wasn't safe, wasn't warm, wasn't filled with people who wanted to protect me."

Sharon took her hand. "I think you can relate to these kids, and they can relate to you. That's why I think you'd be good at it and I think they'd be good for you, too."

Natalie ducked her head.

"I'm a mother. I can't imagine not doing right by my kids. It makes me so angry to imagine that your parents didn't."

"My mother left when I was three. I sometimes got a birthday card from her. But I haven't seen her since she left. I don't even know what she looks like. My father is a weak person in every way. But I didn't grow up in a shelter. I had things those kids don't. I had money and opportunity. I'll gladly help you. I'm really excited to be involved."

"You have a trust fund, but that's not a substitute for love of family."

"I do. So I always had something to fall back on. Because, no it's not a substitute, but it's what I have. Which means I can help financially, too."

Sharon laughed and waved it away. "Oh, no, honey. Here's the funniest thing. I grew up on a farm. We didn't have much, and now I have sons—and let me tell you, I wasn't always sure they'd ever graduate from high school—who are millionaires. I make them all support my various projects and they do without complaint. I was just being nosy. I do that. I remembered Paddy mentioning it awhile back when we first met you. I'm sure my boys have told you scary tales about me."

"Your sons adore you. They're a little afraid of you, but they all adore you."

Sharon snorted. "They better adore me. They nearly killed me when they were growing up. I wore out the road between the ranch and the schools. Everyone knew me by sight. I started off pretty much every single conversation with a school employee with *I'm so sorry.*"

Natalie had to stop eating because she was laughing so hard.

"And they're still wild. Jeez-a-lou. Fighting and causing a ruckus. We used to have the window and glass place here in town on speed dial because they broke so many windows. Then Michael started making them do it themselves. But those scamps, they loved cutting and fitting the glass. That one sort of backfired, but having giant sheets of glass to use to replace broken panes did save us a passel of money. Then we got vinyl windows for better insulation and they're harder to break.

"Thank heavens for Mary because at least she keeps Damien from doing too much damage. Paddy, well, he's always gone his own way. You were quite a surprise. But a good one. I wondered about him. You've settled him. You know, it's hard when they're as pretty as Paddy. They're all smart and clever and too charming for their own good. Girls came as easily to him as playing the guitar. But you? Oh, he has to work for you. He was pissy about that at first." Sharon thought that was hilarious.

"But the thing about Hurley men? They're floozies, and I'm sure you're not unaware that those boys sure do love the ladies. In any case, they flit around and flit around but once they find the one, that's it. Over and done. They will dig in like a tick and stick with you forever and ever."

"Forever might be jumping to conclusions. I mean, we've only been going out since August."

"His father met me once and never saw another girl. We were married six months later. It's been thirty-seven years now. His parents were pretty much the same. He's got three brothers. They're all the same. It's written into their genetics, the rogues they all are." Sharon took a few bites of her sandwich before speaking again.

"Between you and Paddy? I know you two knew each other from before, so it's not like he just met you in August. Anyway, it's nearly December. He says things like, *I'll see you later on. Make sure you save a piece of that pie for Nat.* If my son saves you pie, he's in it forever. Trust me on that."

Point made, Sharon changed the subject back to the project. She was sneaky, and Natalie liked that about her. She cared about her family and her community, and she was a strong woman. There wasn't much not to like about that.

On the way out, Sharon paused. "Since Paddy might have forgotten, we'll sit down to eat at one or so. But in the way of things, we'll start eating at ten or so while the games start, so don't bother with breakfast. We'll be at my house this year."

Confused, Natalie racked her memory and finally just admitted it. "I'm sorry?"

"Thanksgiving dinner. Paddy *did* remember to invite you, didn't he? He and I just talked about it two weeks ago."

"Oh! Yes. Yes, he did. Thank you for having me. I'd

offer to bring something, but we'll all be better off if that doesn't happen. How about I bring some flowers and stuff to drink?"

"That'd be perfect. I'll be seeing you soon enough. On Thursday, if not before." Sharon kissed her cheek and headed one way while Natalie headed back to work.

"PATRICK, THERE YOU ARE. Come over here and help me unload all this stuff." His mother waved to him from where she stood at the back of their truck.

He jogged over, shooing her from the way. "I'll get it all. You just point where you want it."

"In the mudroom, please. It's donations for the family shelter. I have a few more things to pick up, and then I'll meet someone who'll take it to them."

He stacked boxes. "I can do that for you."

"I think you can come with me, just to lug things. Natalie is helping with a collection center at the library, too, so she'll most likely need you to help her get what she collects to me."

He gave his mother a look. "What have you been up to, Sharon Hurley?"

"I've been doing my civic duty, Paddy. And you?" She planned to dodge his real question until she was good and ready to answer it.

He sighed. "I've been out looking at trees and checking for fungus after a morning spent working with your sons, who are all pains in the butt."

She laughed. "Come on in and have some tea with me. I know Natalie isn't done with work for another hour, so that means you're not off to see her just yet."

"Not off to see her for a few hours more, if at all. We're still working on trying to finish a song, but we needed a break before we got into a fight. But I always have time for tea."

"Is that because I have pecan sandies?"

He grinned and walked her into the kitchen, his arm around her shoulder. "You wound me. So maybe to make it up to me, a cookie or three might help."

"Lordy, you're full of it. You get that from your father, by the way." She pointed at the cookie jar and he headed over, jamming two in his mouth before putting a few more on a plate.

"I had lunch with Natalie today."

There it was. Fear made his skin clammy. "Oh, God."

"Why you looking nervous, boy?"

"You almost got into a brawl with Mary's mom. I just worry about you sometimes." The time Mary broke things off with Damien, and their mother went with him to Mary's house and got into a confrontation with Mary's mother was sort of legendary in his family. Mary's mother was a hell of a lot like Sharon, so they were great friends now, but back then, well, Paddy was sorry he'd missed seeing that in person.

"That was a misunderstanding. She was protecting her child, and I was defending mine. However, I doubt I would be so close with Natalie's parents. Sounds to me like they both need to be driven over with my truck a few times."

"She told you?" That surprised him, though his mother could have worked for the military the way she could get secrets out of people.

The anger on his mom's face softened. "A little bit. She's so strong, but she's hurt inside. She needs some mothering."

He went to his mother and hugged her, bending to put

his head on her shoulder. She rubbed circles on his back just like she'd done when he was a kid, and it worked just fine when he was an adult, too.

"Thank you."

She kissed his cheek before he straightened and resumed being half a foot taller than she was.

"She's a good girl. And she has a big heart. I was worried you'd end up with a moron with big boobs and a tiny brain."

He winced. "Why? Why not big boobs and a big brain? I'm an overachiever."

She used the hand towel to whack his behind. "You. Anyway, she's going to help me on this project of mine. She has some excellent ideas. I invited her to Thanksgiving. She said you already had, so that's good."

"I just assumed she'd know she was invited. When I started talking about it like it was a done deal, she was all shocked. Tuesday is heading to San Diego. That's where her sister lives with her family. Natalie usually spends the various holidays in Portland or Seattle with her group of friends from college, I guess. I claimed her this year, told her she'd be expected here at Christmas, too." Though he did want to meet the rest of her 1022 group at some point since they were all so important to her.

SHE PICKED THE phone up, smiling at the tone. "Hey, Zo, what's up? You callin' from the road or are you back home?"

Zoe Marsden was one of Natalie's favorite people, a close friend of many years. She and her partner, Jenny, another member of their 1022 group, lived in a great old house in West Seattle where Jenny taught school.

Zoe's job sometimes took her all over the world to study whales. She'd recently been in Norway.

"I'm home at last. I've missed you guys like crazy. You're coming up for Thanksgiving? Jenny will make something vegetarian, but I'll have turkey, I promise."

Once back in college, Jenny made them all tofurky for Thanksgiving dinner. Natalie actually liked tofu, but she was of the opinion that it didn't need to be shaped like pretend meat, especially when it didn't actually taste good. Over the years, though, Jenny had remained a vegetarian and her cooking skills had improved, so turkey day with them usually meant something awesome not pressed into a loaf.

"I'm actually not this year. I'm…I'm going to my boyfriend's house. Well, to his family's house."

"Boyfriend? Wow. When did this occur?"

Zoe made sure Jenny got on the other line to listen in as Natalie filled them in.

"So bring him on Friday. We're having leftovers and watching movies as we always do. We want to meet him," Jenny said.

That might actually be good. Natalie's friends were people whose opinions she trusted. Paddy would no doubt charm them all, but she'd be able to see how he related with people outside his circle who weren't fans or whatever.

"All right. I'll ask him. They're working on a new album right now, so I don't know what his schedule is."

"Even if he can't, you can," Zoe reminded her. "It's been since the Fourth of July when we had my farewell dinner before I left on my trip."

"Yes. I'll definitely be there. I've missed you guys."

"Yay! You have to look at lots of pictures and pretend to be fascinated with dorsal shape and marking."

"Always."

They talked awhile longer before hanging up. The house was quiet. Tuesday had already left for her sister's in San Diego, so Natalie was alone. She headed downstairs to make some tea. It was cold, and she wasn't sure if Paddy was coming over or not, so she may as well tuck in and get warmer.

She put the kettle on the stove—after all, it was something she could do without damaging the stove or the teakettle—and put a bag in a mug. She considered digging out the bag of cookies hidden in the pantry but decided against it.

The phone rang again, and she picked it up expecting it to be Jenny or Zoe calling back.

"Natalie, it's your grandmother."

She held back a heavy sigh. She'd known this call was coming after all this stuff with her father. He'd have run up to Bellevue to whine to his mother, who had neglected him as much as he'd neglected Natalie. Now her grandmother would try to manipulate her.

Thing was, she'd reached a stage in her life where she was pretty over being manipulated by people.

She took a deep breath and searched for her manners, though. "Hello, Grandma. How are you?"

"I'm calling to invite you to Thanksgiving. Your father is in town, so it'll be the three of us."

"Thank you but I have plans." And she sure as hell didn't plan to spend an entire day watching her grandmother drink herself into oblivion while she fretted about Bob and what a waste of Natalie's life it was to work for such little pay at a library.

"With *family?* This is a family holiday, Natalie. Not a day to wear sweatpants and lay around with your roommates."

Natalie gritted her teeth for a moment. To be lectured by a person who knew what her life was like and never worked to get her out of it was unbearable.

"Yes, actually. With family."

"How can that be? I'm your family. Your father is your family, and we are both here inviting you, and you're rejecting us. I don't think you were raised to be so ungrateful." Her grandmother piled on the haughty, and it only strengthened Natalie's resolve not to give in.

"It can be because family is more about what you do than who you are." Natalie knew her tone had gone frosty, but it was better than saying something she couldn't take back.

"What does that mean?"

"It means I'm spending the day with people who are there for me when it counts. Someone isn't your family simply because they contributed to your DNA. Family is how you act. These people *are* my family and it would be terribly rude of me to cancel at the last minute."

"That sounds like something you read in one of those self-help books. But *we're* your family. Surely these friends can understand that. Why would you hurt my feelings to protect someone else's?"

Ah, there it was. And suddenly, it was just too much to bite her tongue yet again, even if she was an elderly woman and Natalie's grandmother. Because she'd spent a lifetime the victim of people who never acted to put anyone's feelings first.

"Understand what, exactly? I don't want to hurt your

feelings, but it's time we were honest with each other, don't you think?"

"I think it's time you got over your silly, infantile anger at your father. He loves you. He's trying to do right and your refusal to let him do that is hindering his recovery."

It was just…enough. Years and years of just letting it pass. Of taking it to keep the peace and suddenly, she had nothing left to do it anymore.

"Well, here's what I think. I'm not responsible for his recovery. He is. *I think* it's time you realize that he spent my entire childhood in a drugged-out, drunken stupor. *I think* it's time you realize that those times when I begged you to let me live with you and you sent me back to *keep an eye* on my father and keep him safe, you turned your back on me and made me raise him when that was your job to start with. *I think* it's time you re-alize that I had to step over used needles and pools of vomit strangers left in my living room. *I think* it's time you realize that he's done his *I'm clean now* routine seven times now. I'm done. I'm done with all of it. I'm not coming to your house on Thanksgiving to listen to how nothing is his fault. Jesus! He's not the only per-son on earth who has gotten clean. He's got money in the bank and more chances than most addicts ever will. *They* can do it. They do it every damned day because they work on it. I think he's not interested in working because that means he'd have to, for once in his life, stand up and accept what he has done and really want to change it."

There was a knock at her door, and she was so mad she just let Paddy in, not caring that he might hear this silly bullshit.

He leaned to kiss her forehead and rustled through cabinets to get tea ready, getting the hot water poured in her mug and one for himself, too.

He smelled good. Like late fall. Crisp air, wood fires, the cold. He was real, and he was good.

"I had no idea you had so much anger in you. Robert told me about it, of course, but you've never said." Her grandmother was a top-notch guilt artist, right down to the wobble in her voice.

"I think it would be more appropriate to say you've never listened to me when I attempted to talk to you about it."

"I can see this boy your father says you were with has had some negative influence on you. You have responsibilities to your family. No one is perfect, Natalie. Your own mother certainly wasn't."

She slammed her hand down on her counter, and Paddy stilled, his eyes going wide and then narrowing.

"I'm done paying for everyone else's transgressions! She left. Why, I don't know. But I do know I sure as heck wanted to leave plenty of times. Maybe he drove her away. She's selfish and a terrible mother regardless, but she's not me. I'm me, and I'm done with this conversation. I hope he is truly clean once and for all, but I want no part of any of this. I am not his rock bottom, I am not his keeper. I am not his rock or his reason to be clean. He has to make his own damned life choices. Good night, Grandmother, and have a good Thanksgiving."

"You want that money."

It shouldn't have hurt, her grandmother had done much the same to her father. But it did. It also took that flame of anger and simmered it, allowing her to withdraw from the conversation without any more damage.

"It came to me, legally, on my twenty-first birthday. If you didn't want me to have it, you should have challenged it instead of pushing me to take it. I won't let you manipulate me like this. I need to go. I do love you, and I hope you and Bob have a nice Thanksgiving."

She hung up and turned the ringer off.

PADDY LOOKED AT HER. "I don't know whether to give you a hug or a high five. I take it that was your grandmother?"

"Yes. Inviting me for Thanksgiving. I'm sort of embarrassed you heard that. I'm not usually like that with her."

"Sounds to me like she said a lot of stuff to provoke a response like that."

"She does it on purpose to poke at me and back me into a corner. I'm stupid to have let her do it."

He stepped close and pulled her into a hug. "You're lots of things, but you're not stupid. And I don't even know your family, but holy shit, I don't like them one bit. No one gets to upset you like this."

She smiled, snuggling into him. "I think I shocked her. I've never actually told her off like that. Jeez, all she did was call to ask me to Thanksgiving dinner. I'm going to hell."

He leaned her back so he could look her in the face. "Baby, hush. I heard part of that. I know you. It is not a child's fault that a parent leaves, and your dad and your grandmother both seem to use that to hurt you. That's not right. And you're not going anywhere near Thanksgiving dinner with them. Unless you really really want to, in which case I'll be coming along."

"Wow, you must really like me to volunteer for what would most assuredly be a pretty nightmarish day for you. But I said no and it wasn't hard. I don't go there for holiday dinners and I haven't in some time. I do see my grandmother a few times a year, usually at really stilted lunches where she drinks too much and tells me things I'm not supposed to know. But I don't need her to be my family. The fact is, when I needed her to be, she wasn't. I can forgive that, like I can forgive my father. But I can't forget, and I won't let them ever get close enough to hurt me like that again."

"I want to punch someone on your behalf."

"To be fair, you've been with your brothers all day, so you'd want to punch someone, anyway."

"Ezra made me and Vaughan sit on opposite sides of the studio today."

"You're really cute when you pout about not being able to fight with your brother."

"I tried to remember what you said about how he wanted me to respect him and be proud of him. You're probably right. Even if he is a lazy fuck."

She rolled her eyes.

"I'm hungry. I have Mary leftovers in my fridge, so I think you should pack a bag and come to my place. Spend the next few days with me."

"I have to work tomorrow for half the day."

"So? I'll drive you in. After I make you breakfast, even. Then I'll pick you up, and we can spend the night together. I'm going to have to make you come a lot so you're plenty relaxed for turkey day with the Hurleys."

"You'd really just use anything you could to have more sex, wouldn't you?"

He grinned. "Take a look in a mirror, gorgeous, and you tell me how anyone can resist all those curves."

"Oh, wait, what are you doing Friday?"

"I didn't have anything planned. Please don't tell me you want to get up at four and wait in some long-ass line to get socks on sale."

She cringed. "It's like you don't know me at all."

He laughed. "Hey, I should get credit for even entertaining the thought of doing such a thing for you."

"You were going to try to get me to do it with your mom or Mary or something, anyway."

He ducked his chin, blushing. "Okay, so I know it's not that. What are we doing on Friday, then?"

"1022 has a day after Thanksgiving day. We eat leftovers and lay around and have a movie marathon of some sort. I don't know what it is this year, but it should be fun. I told Zoe and Jenny about you tonight, and they wanted me to come and bring you, too, so they can meet you. I know Delia will be there. I forgot to ask about Rosie."

"Yeah, I'd love that. I've been wanting to meet your friends for a while. And relaxing all day watching movies sounds like the perfect activity."

"And you'll be surrounded by women."

"Clearly, I've been a good boy this year, and Santa is hooking me up. Lucky for me, I'll have the prettiest one in my bed already."

"Nicely done."

CHAPTER SIXTEEN

AFTER A THANKSGIVING day full of food, an announce-
ment of a brand-new generation of Hurleys on the way
from Mary and Damien and much more thankfulness
and food, Paddy closed and locked his front door, setting the alarm. He had kooky fans but mainly, he had
a need to protect Natalie that seemed to grow daily.

Her father had been lurking around town, and Paddy
didn't like that he'd gone to Natalie's grandmother to
manipulate and hurt her that way. He didn't put it past
the man to track her down up on the ranch if he decided
it was his right to.

Then again, the man would be lucky to be caught
by the alarm before one of the Hurleys got hold of him.
He hadn't shared with anyone else, but Sharon knew,
and once his mother knew something, his father did,
and while Michael Hurley was utterly laid-back in most
things, the man would kill to protect what he felt was
his.

And because Natalie was Paddy's, she was Michael's,
too.

"Big day, huh?" He followed her upstairs where she
headed straight to the master bathroom.

"It was a good day. I like your family, Paddy."

She got undressed while the water for her shower
got hot.

"They like you, too." He tipped his chin toward the shower enclosure. "Want company?"

She gave him a look over her shoulder that got his attention nearly as well as all that pretty naked skin did.

She got in and he followed, sliding his skin against hers until he felt better. Taking the shampoo—her shampoo she now kept here at his place—he took over, lathering it into her hair as she tipped back into him.

This moment was everything. Everything he'd needed and never knew it until she came into his life.

Her eyes closed, she leaned on him, let him take care of her. This woman who did everything on her own— born from necessity at a really early age—letting him take care of her.

And it didn't feel predatory. It didn't feel calculated. It didn't feel overwhelming or clingy at all. Putting her first, wanting her to be happy and taken care of had a sort of comfort to it.

He rinsed the shampoo away, and she stood under the spray for long moments, her eyes closed, one hand touching his hip as he stood under the opposite showerhead.

When she finally opened her eyes, that shock of connection roared through him as her gaze locked with his.

Two steps was all it took for him to touch, to pull her close and drop his mouth to hers. She met him halfway, tiptoeing up. Instead of wrapping her arms around him, she slid soapy palms all over his torso and back before finding his cock.

"Yes." He thrust into her hold even as he kept kissing her lips, her cheeks, her chin.

She added her other hand, cupping his sac. He leaned back against the tile, watching her, his gaze moving from the look of concentration she wore to the way she handled him.

She loved touching him this way. He arched into her like a cat, taking what she offered without any shame. In this, between the two of them, they worked perfectly. Their bodies saying words she wasn't sure either of them was brave enough to speak yet.

He'd get impatient soon enough, but until then, she'd tease him, drive him upward toward his peak. He liked being in her when he came. This flattered her for reasons she wasn't sure of, but it didn't matter. It worked. Made her feel sexy, and that was good, too.

She added a twist each time she reached the head and he groaned, taking her upper arms and spinning them so it was her back against the tile.

"Don't move."

He got out and returned quickly, wearing a condom. "Probably need to leave these in more places since you're here more often."

He drizzled her liquid soap all over her breasts, following with his hands, his fingers pulling and rolling her nipples on each pass.

Her eyes drifted closed as she allowed herself to fall into his touch. It was beautiful and reverent and yet, he didn't wrap her up like she'd break, either. It was the perfect line he walked.

He kissed her as one of those slippery hands found her center, fingers teasing her clit, her hips jutting forward to get more.

Again, he turned her. "Hands against the tile," he whispered in her ear. He nibbled the back of her neck, his fingers still busy on her nipple and at her clit until she could barely stand.

It was too much and not quite enough until he nudged her feet apart and the head of his cock pushed against her, entering her in one slow but insistent thrust.

The joy of it filled her, arced up her spine, swelled her heart. He held her, bringing her pleasure as he made love to her. And as dirty and hard as it was, it was making love. Even when it was fucking, it was that. She wasn't a faceless, nameless groupie; she wasn't meaningless or a person he was with to pass the time. She was someone with him.

Someone *to* him.

Orgasm seized her muscles and then let go as it flowed through her, taking her under as she rested her head against his shoulder.

His body curled around hers, his hands, less busy now, splayed over her skin. Holding her up. Keeping her where he wanted, how he wanted.

"I love it when you come when I'm in you. The way your body clutches around my cock. So good. Nearly too good."

He took his time until the water began to cool.

He shifted, his hands leaving her body, joining hers on the tile as he picked up the pace. Harder. Faster. She writhed against him until little aftershock orgasms rolled through her. He snarled her name and pushed in one last time, as deep as he could, and came.

But he wasn't done. Because they rinsed off and he got out first, bringing her a towel that was nice and warm. He wrapped her in it, rubbing her gently until she was dry and warm. She watched him, a smile on her face as he got dried off and then, surprising her totally, he bent, picked her up and took her into his bedroom.

She managed to get her underpants and some pajamas on as he took care of the fire.

"I have champagne if you want. Or we can have tea or hot chocolate."

"You don't have to be so careful about offering me alcohol. I told you, I don't have a problem with drinking in and of itself. Champagne would be lovely, I think. It's been a day full of stuff to celebrate."

He poured them each a glass, turned on some music—The National—and came to join her. Of course he wasn't wearing pajamas, which she had no complaints about.

He clinked his glass to hers. "Thank you."

She cocked her head. "For what?"

He snorted. "For putting up with my family. For caring about people. For being what you are to me."

"Oh." She blushed. "Well, thank you for letting me be part of your crazy family and for being a person I can care about."

He kissed her and settled back against the pillows. They watched the stars through the skylight and just lay with one another. It had been a really good day.

HE'D NEVER IN his life been nervous to meet people before. Not even label people when they were first trying to get signed. Well, he did get a little bit of butterflies when he met Neil Young, but Neil Young was the closest thing to a deity on earth Paddy could imagine, so that was different.

Natalie had met his family and had found her way to fit into their world, and this was her family. He already knew and liked Tuesday, but this was the rest.

She took his hand as he juggled a bag full of gifts she'd brought for them all.

The house was a typical 1950s Seattle split-level. Steep stairs from the sidewalk out front wound through a pretty garden to a front door that burst open with a squeal of Natalie's name.

Bright red hair streaked toward her. Nat's face brightened and she opened her arms. "Dee!" They hugged, laughing and talking in that way women did. At hyperspeed, interspersed with shorthand and a bunch of stuff Paddy knew nothing of.

And another layer of this woman unfurled. Like a flower. Like art. She was fucking beautiful.

He smiled because he rarely saw her like this. Open and full of joy.

She turned to him, her arm around her friend. "Delia, this is Paddy. Paddy, this is Delia."

Delia gave him a long look and side-eyed Natalie. "Nicely done." She held her hand out to Paddy. "Nice to meet you. Come on in. Everyone wants to meet you, but they're all pretending they're too cool to peek out the windows."

Paddy grinned, taking her hand and shaking before they all headed in.

A chorus of Nat's name went up, and she was engulfed in hugs for a few minutes before she managed to get free and send him an apologetic smile.

"Okay, everyone, this is Patrick Hurley. Better known as Paddy. Paddy—" she pointed to the redhead "—you know Delia. She lives in Portland and makes documentaries. Standing next to her is Rosie Morgan. She lives in Brooklyn."

"The one who scouts locations, right?"

Natalie nodded and looked back to the tall brunette. "We don't get to see her as often as we'd like. But we take what we can get."

Two women, clearly a couple, stood forward. One of them with a no-nonsense ponytail and gorgeous blue eyes behind cat-eye glasses grinned at Natalie and then over to him. "I'm Zoe. I'm glad to meet you. If you're not nice to our Natalie, we're going to hunt you down and maim you."

Natalie rolled her eyes. "Never mind her. She spends too much time in the sun without a hat. And last but never ever least is Jenny Dan. Schoolteacher and all around awesome woman. This is Jenny and Zoe's house."

He loved being around them all. They had that sort of shorthand born of many years of a relationship. They finished each other's sentences. They knew who liked what on their sandwiches and popcorn.

They didn't fawn over him, but they sincerely wanted to know about him.

"So you knew Natalie from back in the day?" Jenny's brow rose. "My first day at Evergreen, my parents dropped me off at housing. When I got up to our apartment, Nats was already there. She had this long blond hair and this body. Wow. I was like, hubba hubba, I hope she's gay because I want some of that."

Natalie laughed, blushing. "Then Zoe came in, and suddenly, Jenny realized blonde wasn't her type, after all."

Jenny looked to Zoe, and he saw that depth of connection they shared.

"Sweet Nat and Delia were wild back then. They'd party all the time and yet kick ass in school, too."

Delia grinned. "That first year we all grew up. Which is lucky, because I really need those brain cells."

"Most of us ended up staying in Oly that summer. We got a house on the west side of Olympia, right off the bus route. We lived in that house until after graduation."

"Oh, I thought you guys stayed in 1022?"

Natalie stole one of his chips. "It might have been on the 10th floor and had multiple bedrooms, but it had a shared kitchen with the other rooms on ten. And it was loud. Tuesday's parents live in Olympia, and her dad knew someone who was looking to rent a house. They did not really jump for joy when they saw five women wanted to rent it. But the Eastwoods vouched for us, and we paid a huge security deposit and promised to never have animals. Sometimes when we go to visit Tuesday's parents, we drive by it and get all nostalgic. Over the years it's been the home of other Evergreen students. It sort of passes from one group to the next."

"So she was wild?" He waggled his brows and everyone laughed.

Delia snorted. "We were nineteen years old. Hell, Tuesday was eighteen, as was Jenny. We were all wild in one way or another. By the time we graduated, we'd all grown up."

He'd known her then, in that wild time before she'd gone off to college. She'd been a flame, burning fast and bright. He'd responded to that. To all that silky blond hair and her big blue eyes. She'd been game for everything he'd wanted and had had plenty of her own ideas.

But this Natalie? Behind closed doors, she was still game for everything he wanted and had plenty of her own ideas. Her control was a way she made sense of the world filled with chaos. Her wildness in private was her guilty pleasure, only without the guilt.

THEY WATCHED *ALIEN* and *Aliens,* and he learned a new side of her. She was good at her job. He'd seen her with the patrons at the library, and she was always warm and welcoming. Had seen her with his family and with Tuesday. He knew she was a funny, generous personality, but with these women, she was utterly unguarded. Comfortable.

It made him appreciate how easy she was around him now.

They teased one another. Mocked. Poked and bickered. These women were family in every way but biological. She'd been right to say as much to her grandmother, though he doubted that point would make sense to the woman.

They all took turns poking at him, trying to figure out if he was good enough for Natalie. Natalie let most of it happen, only stepping in if they got too nosy. And they ignored her, anyway.

Finally, Zoe threw her hands up. "Okay, fine. Did you want to be a musician from day one?"

"I wanted to be a rancher, actually." He snorted a laugh. "I wanted to do what my dad did. What his dad did. But when we'd stay out of trouble, my parents bribed us with musical instruments. Ezra, that's my oldest brother, he was first, and then we all wanted to be like him. Then my parents bribed us for time in the barn to learn how to play. In the early days, it was a way to get girls. A way to rock and roll and get drunk and be away from the house."

"I'm going to guess you always had *it,* though." Natalie looked so good eating that ice cream, he wanted to lick her, too.

"*It?*"

"People who take it past success in media to become celebrities. Stars. You have charisma, Paddy. It rolls off you in waves and makes the ladies and probably a lot of the dudes, too, weak in the knees. You look at the camera in your music videos, and you know when to wink or give that sexy smile. You know how to work what you have, and yet you never come off calculated. The *it* factor."

He liked that she said it, maybe even wanted to blush. He couldn't deny being aware of it. Couldn't deny that he'd used it even when he was young, to get attention and keep it on their band. There were lots of great, talented people in the world. People who were better than Sweet Hollow Ranch who'd never get that attention because they didn't have that *it* she talked about.

The band loved to support up-and-comers, and they did it as often as they could. It was a key factor in who they chose to open for them when they went on tour, too. They liked using their power for something positive.

"My parents let us start doing small gigs when Ezra and I were done with high school. But we had to keep within an hour of Hood River. My mom and dad went with us most of the time, trying to keep us out of trouble." He laughed. "My mom is not someone to be messed with. Even early on, she protected us from getting screwed over. Anyway, I was twenty when we were all done with school and we were at a gig. A sort of battle-of-the-bands thing. There were execs from labels there. Ezra pushed me up front and said, 'the chicks dig that wink you do. Drop some panties so we can win this.'"

Natalie burst out laughing.

"Anyway, I can't say I'm blind to the charisma thing. Or that I don't know how to use it. It's another way to sell my band and that's part of it. But it's fun. Being a musician feeds a part of me that needs creation to be happy. I could sit around all the time noodling on my guitar writing songs and be ridiculously satisfied. But the rock-star part is why I get to travel all over the world. It's why I got to meet and eventually became friends with my musical influences. I can make sure my parents have a comfortable life and support all the charities my mom is involved with and start a musical charity of my own with some of my friends. It gets me great tables in restaurants, excellent seats at the theater. Flying is a hell of a lot nicer in first class, I can't lie. It sucks to be stalked by people with cameras, who want to know all sorts of stuff that's not their business, like when my brother got divorced and when my other brother got married last year. My friend had to move away from his place in West Seattle out to Bainbridge Island into a house with a gate and high security to protect his family from crazy fans and the paps." He lifted a hand, palm up. "It's not all perfect, but that's how it works these days, so you gotta work as hard as you can to wall that off."

And in the matter of a long Friday after Thanksgiving, he won his way into a provisional membership into 1022.

CHAPTER SEVENTEEN

DECEMBER SETTLED IN as Paddy spent more time getting this album on track with his brothers. He spent long hours daily writing, rewriting, working on arrangements and production.

And when he wasn't doing that, he was with Natalie. She had a busy life, too. She had her job and her friends, and she did volunteer work, a lot of it with his mom and Mary.

As the time to get into the studio approached, label people liked to sniff around to see what was going on. Because it was their studio and not time the label leased out, the Hurleys had more control, but they had advances to deal with and other basic industry bullshit.

Currently, Jeremy, their manager, was in town and staying with Paddy. He'd been with them since pretty much the beginning, and Paddy considered him a friend as well as a business associate.

It was late after a long night working, and they all sat outside the barn around the fire pit drinking beer and blowing off steam. "So when do I get to meet this woman you're seeing? You talk about her so much, I feel like I know her."

"She's got some sort of board meeting or other tonight, and then she's hanging with her girlfriend who's visiting from out of town." He'd gotten used to her awfully fast. It was sort of freaky. But the way she just accepted his life with all its noise and chaos comforted him. Filled him up and made him feel whole. "She'll be here tomorrow night for dinner, though."

Vaughan cracked open another beer. "We still going out afterward? We haven't gone to Portland since the spring. You have a girlfriend and Damien is breeding. We have lots to celebrate. Plus, we need to show Jeremy a good time before he heads up to Bainbridge Island to hang out with Adrian." Adrian being Adrian Brown, major huge rock star and also a client of Jeremy's.

Damien had met Mary at Adrian's wedding, and Sweet Hollow Ranch had done some tour dates a few years back with Adrian. Adrian's wife was one of Mary's best friends. Around the holidays, it was the craziest mix of musicians, ranchers, security people and cooks. And this year, there'd be a librarian to add.

He smiled, thinking of her.

Vaughan snapped his fingers in Paddy's face. "Stop thinking of nailing her for three minutes, please."

Paddy gave his baby brother the finger. It would be good to get out with his brothers. They hadn't done it in months and months. "What about you, D?"

Damien nodded. "Mary insisted. And by that I mean, she said, 'get out and do something so I can work on this cookbook in peace.'"

"She's not going to care if you go out with your brothers, Paddy." Ezra nodded his way. "Natalie trusts you. You just have to trust yourself."

"She the jealous type?" Jeremy asked.

"Ha. No. She's just wary about the wild and crazy aspects of this world we live in. It's cool. Yeah, I'm in. We'll have an early dinner and then go out."

THE NEXT MORNING, his phone rang, and it was Lykke Li's "Little Bit," Nat's ringtone.

"Hello, gorgeous."

"So I have a request. If it's weird and you want to say no, please do, and I won't even be mad or upset or anything."

Paddy smiled. "You can always come over and use me for sex. I promise to let you objectify me until we're sticky."

She laughed. "Well, that's good to know. Not that I didn't already know that. But anyway. Sometime when you guys are working, and you think it would be okay with everyone, and I'll be quiet and stay out of the way and never say a single thing, do you think I could watch you guys lay down tracks? It's just I love to hear you sing and I've never seen you do it. Which seems sort of weird considering all the other things I've seen you do."

He knew she blushed. His cock stirred, knowing she would have ducked her head, exposing the back of her neck with that downy bit of pale hair and all that soft skin.

"All you ever had to do was ask. And I hum and sing all the time." While driving, riding horses, when they hiked with Tuesday, when he cooked, hell, even when they took baths in his giant bathtub.

"Well, that's different. I mean, whatever. Anyway, I'd like it."

"Come over when you get off today. You're only on until what? Three?"

"Yes."

"Come here to the house. I'm working on something, and I'll give you a preview. You can hear it that way and then in the studio. It's the track we're going to lay down today. Or start, anyway."

"Really? Yay!"

"You're making me miss the hell out of you right now."

"Good. I'd hate to be alone in the missing stuff. I need to go, but I wanted to check in since we didn't connect last night and you left me a message."

"Okay. I'm going to be rolling out of here soon enough. I'll see you later, then. And Natalie?"

"Hmm?"

He nearly told her he loved her. He'd been wanting to for weeks by that point. But he realized maybe the phone wasn't the right way. "I miss you."

"Miss you, too. See you later today."

She hung up, and he managed to get out of bed, heading for the kitchen where he needed a seriously huge pot of coffee.

HUMMING, SHE PULLED into his driveway and got out, breathing in deep. It was cold and clear, snow maybe on the way. The air had that slightly electric feeling it sometimes did before a flurry. Up here it was higher than where she lived in town and more likely to get it.

He opened his door and the happiness on his face at the sight of her made everything better.

He was beautiful and handsome and masculine. Rumpled in his jeans and long-sleeved shirt. He'd been working; she could tell by the ink stains on the fingers he held out to bring hers to his mouth to kiss. His beard tickled.

"Hey."

"Hey, yourself. Come in out of the cold. Jeremy is off

with Ezra doing something or other, so it's just the two of us." He led her inside and she found herself backed up to the door after he'd closed it.

He seemed to love backing her up against things and she seemed to love it when he did it. When he used the power and size of his body to hold her in place and kiss her silly. Like he did just then.

"Ready to see me work or did you want to wade in?"

She laughed. "I'm ready."

He brought her up to his workroom but instead of the guitar, he headed to the piano. She sat in the cushy chair in a corner after taking her coat off.

"I'm actually sort of nervous. That's new." He looked confused by that, and it was so sweet, she got up, walked over and took his cheeks in her hands. He gave her so much. Bent over backward to be patient and sweet, even when he gave her hickeys on her boobs and left a bruise on her hip from his thumb where he'd held her as he'd thrust into her body.

She wanted to give this to him.

"Patrick?"

"Yes, gorgeous?"

"I'm in love with you." She swallowed hard but kept going, because she needed to say it, and she'd even practiced in front of the mirror after talking to Tuesday about it for over an hour the night before. "You're a miracle in my life and I want to hear you sing and play music. Not only because you're good at it, and you are, but because it's important to you and I want to share it."

His eyes widened and she put a finger over his lips.

"It's okay. I don't need you to say it back. I don't expect you to say it back. I just wanted you to know."

He kissed her fingers and moved her hand. "I love

you, too, silly. I was going to say it this morning on the phone, but I figured on the phone wasn't romantic."

Oh.

She blinked back tears and struggled past the wave of emotion that threatened to drown her. He loved her, too. Well wasn't that a wonderful thing?

"Now go sit down. I feel a little better and I want you to hear this."

She did and he began to play.

His voice was caramel and a little bit of smoke. His eyes went half-lidded as he began to sing about skin and curves. Of eyes as blue as the summer sky and hands and shoulders that held the weight of everyone's sins.

Those tears she'd been holding back washed through her along with wonder that he'd actually written this about her. *For her.* These were the words of a man who was head over heels in love with a creature he adored. No one had ever felt like this about her.

It was about being burned alive by need, by desire and love. About holding something so beautiful and strong in his hands that he could barely breathe.

Natalie just sat there and listened, tears streaming down her face, filled with a thousand different emotions she couldn't begin to name. Though chief among them was love and an aching sort of tenderness. She pressed the heel of her hand against her chest, over her heart, and when he finished, he looked up, meeting her gaze.

Seeing her tears, he smiled. "Yeah?"

She nodded. "Yeah. The woman you wrote that for is pretty lucky."

He moved to her, putting his arms around her. "Nah. I'm the lucky one." He kissed her and tore himself away.

He had his hand up her shirt, the cup of her bra

pulled down when the door slammed open downstairs, Damien bellowing his name.

"I'm going to kill him." Paddy nipped her bottom lip and helped her up. "Come on. I guess they're ready for me over at the barn. I'm going to warn you in advance, some people might think I'm sort of a perfectionist dick while we record."

She tried not to smirk but it was impossible. "I think, Patrick, your dickish perfectionism is sort of legendary."

"Really?"

"Hey, dickhead, where the fuck are you?"

"Are you speaking to me, Damien?" she called down and Paddy laughed, hugging her.

"Oh, shit! Shoot. Um, no, I'm sorry, sweetheart," Damien called as he got closer.

"Hand out of my shirt, Patrick."

"Aww." He frowned and did it, kissing her quickly as he stepped back and pushed her in front of him. "Best to stand in front of me until I don't have a really noticeable hard-on."

Which he pressed into the flesh of her butt cheek.

"We're in here," Paddy called out. "I take it you're ready for me?"

Damien came around the corner and grinned at Natalie. "Look at you making me all nervous." He kissed her cheek. "Like one of us already." He looked around her at Paddy. "Yes, dumbass, we're waiting on you."

He held his arm out and she took it. "You coming to watch us work? Maybe your presence will keep him in line."

"I'm just a spectator. I'm not interfering with your process. I promise."

Damien drew her downstairs where he held her coat

out for her, and she put it on. Paddy came down, stepping into his shoes and grabbing a coat. "Hands off my
woman. You got your own."

Damien rolled his eyes. "See? He's already in Make
It Perfect Patrick mode. Ugh. Come on, Natalie, and
walk with me. Mary said she'd come by in a bit. She's
having a nap."

"Is she all right?"

Damien's expression went soft. "She's absolutely
perfect. Gestating is hard business. She likes a nap in
the afternoon. Makes me slow down, too. It's all good.
Thanks for asking."

They headed out toward the barn, their high-tech,
super-duper recording studio and practice space. She
hadn't been in it while they were working, though she'd
been given a tour some months back.

But it was entirely different now. Ezra was in the
booth looking seriously at the console as he and someone else consulted.

"Hands off." Paddy inserted himself between Natalie and Damien. Damien laughed as he danced around
his brother to plant a smooch on Natalie's cheek before
he headed to his drums.

"He's such a punk," Paddy grumbled.

She held a smile back.

"Let me introduce you to Jeremy. He's been asking
after you."

Paddy took her into the booth where Ezra turned, his
face all business until he recognized her. "Nats, hello
darlin'." He gave her a hug.

"What is it with all you guys and your need to call
my girlfriend pet names and hug up all over her? Hands.
Off. Ezra. Jeez."

"But he's so adorable and huggable, Patrick." She gave Paddy what he called her puppy-dog eyes, and he grinned.

"Ezra huggable and adorable? Okay, well, that's gonna make me snicker for days. Jeremy, this is Natalie."

Their manager gave her a quick once-over and took her hand in his. "I'm pleased to meet you. They've all had such nice things to say about you. Even Sharon loves you, and she's the toughest judge of character I've ever met."

Well, that made her feel better, even if she was a little embarrassed. "Thank you. It's nice to meet you, too."

Paddy tucked her up in a comfy chair in the booth, well out of the way, but with a great view of the action.

Everyone got headphones on and took their places. Ezra made some adjustments on the board and then went out to join them. Jeremy sat at the controls, putting his own set of headphones on, and she just watched.

Something different came over each of them as they coalesced with Ezra clearly in the lead. Ezra took over with ease and confidence. Each of them did some sound adjustments, and Paddy got up and took over a few times until it all worked like he wanted.

His brothers just let him. A minor argument broke out as Paddy, who'd sat back at the piano, played a few notes and asked Vaughan to come in with his bass. They went back and forth, Paddy frowning, Vaughan pushing back, saying how he'd been doing it was best.

Ezra looked on, adding when he seemed to feel it was necessary.

She'd been concerned at times, hearing the stories about how they worked while recording. It sounded pretty awful and mean. But really, as she watched them, it wasn't so mean. Paddy wasn't attacking Vaughan personally, just his opinion on a tone. And Vaughan wasn't attacking Paddy personally, just his opinion on the same.

While there was no shortage of insults and curse words being tossed around, it was surprisingly professional as each played the same opening again and again. Ezra came into the booth and listened to both several times, asking Damien to come in here and there.

Finally, Ezra spoke.

"Paddy's right. I think, though—" he shot a quelling glare at Vaughan, who'd opened his mouth to argue "—that Vaughan has a point on a few things, so I adjusted a small bit." He took Vaughan's bass and fiddled a bit, playing. Paddy played along, and when he got exactly what Ezra had said, his whole expression changed.

"Got it. Yeah, I see what you mean."

"Let's do this. Paddy, let's do one whole take so I can get a baseline." Ezra handed the bass back to Vaughan, who seemed mollified by the response and being partially right.

Vaughan looked up and winked at her, and she laughed.

Paddy flipped his brother off and settled, his fingers tracing the keys for a moment. Damien set a beat, and everyone hit it, sliding into something altogether different from those four brothers who started a band to get girls and stay out of trouble.

He played the opening notes, leaning closer to the microphone and started to sing, a breath filled with emotion.

The song swelled through the headphones as "Silent No More" started.

In his workroom, the song had been stripped down, but there in the studio, it unfurled as the other instruments embellished it just right, as Ezra's voice on the chorus deepened it, sharpened it and polished it.

Once they finished, they all started writing stuff down, and then she was blown away by the level of energy they put into making the song perfect.

They argued over so many things. Played parts differently ways; sometimes one of them would take over the other's part to underline a point.

"Fascinating, isn't it?" Mary came in and settled next to Natalie. "It's easy to only see them as these laid-back, gorgeous boys who play music because they were born to. And then you see how much work they actually do, and it's like... I don't know. The first time I saw this it reshaped my perspective, to say the least."

"I've never been privy to any part of this process, so it's all been eye-opening. I have a whole new level of respect for what they do and for how they work together." Because if someone told her something she'd created sounded weak or needed more of this or that, she wasn't sure how easy it would be to take without it being personal.

"Damien once said it was like watching sausage get made. But I don't think so. It's like trying to create a recipe. It's good a dozen different ways. Less of this, more of that. Cook it longer, bake it, sauté it, whatever. But there's a way it should be. And while you can enjoy it one of those dozen ways it's good, there's a way it will shine brightest. They all have to work together to make that perfect recipe."

"Damn, you're good at this."

Mary grinned. "I only knew a bit of it when Damien came into my life. I saw the edges, saw the backstage, the travel. It was surprising."

They both looked back to the studio where the brothers poked and prodded and bickered their way toward a track that would make them all happy. Natalie wondered about the whole of it even as she tried to pretend it didn't make her wary.

SOME TIME LATER, Paddy came around the piano and headed into the booth.

"This is going to take a few hours more. We're going to skip dinner and then we're headed out with Jeremy. His last night here before he heads up to Washington in the morning. Sorry, I know we were all supposed to hang out."

She shook her head, cupping his cheek. "It's totally all right. You can't schedule this kind of stuff. It's good. Call me when you can." She kissed him and he blushed.

"You so rarely do that." He said it quietly as he hugged her.

Mary had gone in to talk to Damien and they were alone in the booth for the moment.

"Do what?"

"Kiss me in public. But you do in front of my family and your friends. That makes me happy."

She took a deep breath and allowed herself to accept his compliment the way she knew he meant it. "You make me happy, too." She vowed to try harder to be affectionate with him, knew he liked it, needed it, even.

"I'll touch base with you tomorrow. I'm sorry to

say it's going to be crazy like this for a while as we lay down tracks."

She brushed a kiss over his knuckles. "It's fine. This is your job. I have stuff to do, as well."

"As long as you don't forget I'm part of that stuff to do. Spend the night tomorrow night?"

She'd taken to spending the nights before a day off with him either at her house or at his.

"Yeah, I can do that. I'm going out with Tuesday in the day, though. We're seeing a movie and she's getting a tattoo touched up. I won't be back in town until after nine or so."

He pouted. So cute when he did. "Okay. Well, that's for the best, anyway, since we'll be working. Come out when you're ready."

"Have fun tonight."

He smirked.

"Don't get arrested, Patrick. Your mother isn't going to bail you out and neither am I."

He laughed. "Ah, gorgeous, I have an attorney on speed dial."

"Good Lord." She tiptoed up to kiss him one last time. "See you tomorrow."

She waved at everyone, reiterated that it was nice to have met Jeremy and left.

MARY CAUGHT UP to her outside. "Hey, come over to my place. Dinner is still made. Call Tuesday and invite her, too."

"Oh, good idea." She quickly called her friend, who said she was on her way up.

At Damien and Mary's, she slid her shoes off and

hung up her coat, smiling to herself that she'd done it enough times that it felt like a habit.

"There are sodas and juice in the fridge. Damien brought some back from his giant box-store run. Also, about four hundred pounds of Cheerios. Those boys and cereal, I swear."

"Great. I'll get it. What do you want?"

"I'm having water with some oranges. I can't do orange juice because it gives me heartburn. My mom says she had it really bad with all her pregnancies, too. Thank goodness I also have enough pregnancy-safe antacids to keep it under control. Also, a plus of the box-store run. Of course in his zeal to be sure I'm okay, there's probably enough for the next fourteen pregnancies. Not that I plan on fourteen pregnancies. Man, I shouldn't even have said that." Mary rapped the wood of the table quickly, making Natalie laugh.

Tuesday arrived, and they filled plates and headed into the dining room.

Natalie buttered her bread. "I've never had anyone so much as write me a poem before. A song? I don't know what to do with how it makes me feel. Damien declared his love for you in a concert venue in front of thousands. How do you process that?"

Mary put some spinach on her plate. "I don't know. From the start, my biggest hesitation in entering into a relationship with Damien was that aspect of his life. But then I just fell in love with him. I tried to resist him and I couldn't. I have to weigh that stuff, the harsh public fascination with everything about his life—which is now my life, too—with how much I want to be with him."

Tuesday sipped her soda. "Song? Fill me in."

Mary spoke, "Paddy wrote her a song. It's a gorgeous, sexy love song."

"It's a song, Tuesday. Oh, my God. It's beautiful and I'm filled with all this stuff he makes me feel. I didn't mean for him to happen, but he's so pushy and he's cute and really good in bed, and he loves his mother, and he's sexy, and he makes up poems about pigs, and I'm so out of my league here."

Tuesday's bemused smile made her feel better.

"So, Mary, tell me about the song. I know how Natalie feels and she's not one prone for overreaction. But a disinterested opinion is always good."

"He's… This song is… Wow. Paddy is in major love with Natalie. His writing, as you can probably tell, is very autobiographical. That wasn't just a run-of-the-mill love song about some random girl designed to make a hit. That song is how Paddy feels about Natalie. Damien told me about the song a week or so ago. Saying Paddy has been bleeding over it to get it right, and how they all think it's going to be the lead single."

"Yeah. Well. He's not alone." Natalie took a deep breath. "I told him I loved him today. Look, I know I'm not an easy girlfriend. I'm touchy. And I'm weird and messed up and he's so mellow. But he…he's my safe place. He had just been so sweet and he was nervous and I was touched and realized I needed to tell him what he meant to me."

"I love how you say that like we'd be surprised." Tuesday looked up at Mary, laughing. Mary snorted and rolled her eyes.

"It's pretty obvious to anyone with eyes that you're in love with him. And that he feels the same."

"I think so, yes. But stuff is coming up and I'm wary.

Not that he'll give in to temptation backstage. I can't worry about that. I just can't. If he's going to cheat, he'll do it no matter if he's on tour. But it all seems so chaotic. I don't think it's a secret that I have some control issues, and all that sort of unbridled insanity makes me anxious. I know it's stupid."

Mary waved that away. "It's not stupid. I've been backstage. It's crazy sometimes. I went with them on this last tour as their chef. They've already insisted on a short schedule because Damien absolutely doesn't want to be away once the baby is born, and I want to be home for a few months afterward. I don't mind traveling with the baby. Our friends have young children who travel with them on tour, so it's possible. But I want to be here when the baby is very young. I want to be totally selfish and cocoon with my husband and my friends and family.

"Which is a tangent, sorry. Back to the subject. Tour is an anomaly. Do you know what I mean?"

"Maybe."

"They're not normally on tour. It's this thing they do to push a new album dropping and because they love their fans and playing live for them. But it's not normal. It's like reality is distorted when they're out on the road. They don't get enough sleep. They're not in any one place very long. It's all about their public persona, like, all the time. Everything is catered to them. They have every bit of their lives planned by other people, taken care of by other people. Literally, every single day a sheet of paper is given to each one of them with a detailed schedule. They put all their energy into performing, and it gets frenetic, yes. Especially as they head into the last third or so and they've been away from home long enough to feel it every time they stop. It's hard not to sort of fall into the lure of that. To be a different person on the road."

"So you know you're not actually helping, right?" Tuesday peppered her ziti.

Mary laughed, and the knot that had been tightening in Natalie's belly eased a little. "I'm getting to that part. But I went with them. I was there every day with Damien. I brought home with me. I fed them, which kept me busy, and having me there reminded them they had lives away from hotels and backstage and groupies."

"So it's insanity but temporary insanity?"

"Partly. They still remember Ezra's meltdown. That's part of who they are now as a family and as a band. I think they all came away changed. What do you think about going? Not for the whole tour. I know you have a job. A reminder of home is good and maybe you'd feel better, too. To reconnect with him."

"So I have to babysit him?" This was her fear. That he'd be debilitated in some way, and she'd step in to help, to ease his burden, and slowly she'd end up resenting him and hating herself for doing it again.

"Nope. They play their hearts out every night across the country and back. It *is* wild back there. That part of their world is part chaos, part machine. It's controlled chaos, I guess. You can go and experience it with him so you can understand it that way, find a way to process it and accept it. You can wait at home and understand that you *will* see horrible stuff that makes it look like he's banging every woman he comes across—and you can understand it's part of that machine. That celebrity media machine that exists to create caricatures to try to both satisfy demand for celebrity news and create more clamor for it all at once. But he's still who he is."

Natalie blew out a breath.

"Essentially, what you and Paddy are? That's not going to change because of whatever happens on tour. He knows how to manage his shit. He's a multi-millionaire leader of one of the most successful rock-and-roll bands of all time. Right? Oh, sure, he's pretty and sexy and charming. He comes off laid-back but you know what? None of those boys is laid-back about their business. Touring is part of it. There are things I don't like about their world, but I had to weigh it all against how much I wanted to be with him. This is a hugely tangential way of saying *go if you want to see it for yourself.* In my case, it helps because I hate being away from him for months at a time. Travel is fun. It'd be even more fun if you came, too, and I had a tour buddy. Man, I can't keep coherent and on topic to save my life of late."

Natalie laughed. "It's fine. I get it. Sort of."

"They're going to do some dates to try out the material in front of a live audience. It's sort of a brunch version of what it's like out there. Maybe try that to see? I really can't do justice to what it's like. Good and bad. It's pretty amazing to see how they put a show together. They're really good together onstage, too."

Natalie nodded. "Makes sense, I guess."

CHAPTER EIGHTEEN

"COME TO PORTLAND with me," he announced when she answered her phone. "I need to do some Christmas shopping. We can stay overnight and order room service and have really filthy hotel sex."

"I have some shopping to do, as well, and I'm always in the market for filthy hotel sex."

He laughed. "I'll pick you up in two hours. We'll have lunch there."

She'd agreed and got showered quickly before packing an overnight bag. By the time she'd put on some lipstick and watered the plants he'd shown up and they'd gotten on the road.

"Don't you have to work with your brothers today?" she asked him as they headed west.

"We've declared a three-day break. We've got four tracks finished and Ezra wants to polish up the next two without any pesky interference from lesser human beings."

She snorted. "Okay, then. I'll take it. I've missed you." He'd been working at night, and she worked during the day so it made getting together hard. Even on her days off when she could adjust her schedule to his, it was difficult. He had his energy fully on his work and she understood it.

But that didn't mean she hadn't missed him.

"I miss you, too. It's not always like this."

"Paddy, I get it. It's part of your life. Creation takes time and energy. Really, it's all right. It's not forever. Soon enough your time will be filled with other stuff like promotion and appearances and then touring."

"The label likes what they've heard so far. Jeremy took them what we had. They want your song as the first single. They're interested in a branding shift."

"For what?"

"We're past the young guns getting drunk and nailing groupies stage."

"I should hope so."

He grinned at her tone. "Damien is married with a baby on the way. I'm writing love songs. They want to get out in front to create the buzz they can control. A more mature Sweet Hollow Ranch. Still sexy but grounded."

"And how do you feel about that?"

"To be honest? It had been something I was thinking about. This album is introspective. Not just my stuff, but Ezra's. Damien has contributed two songs, and at least one will make it. Vaughan's daughters are growing up. We're all changed by these major events in our lives. It's good they want to handle it and make it into a positive. Damien the wild man now a daddy. Paddy in love. They proposed an interview with us."

"*Us* meaning who? You guys? Mary? She's not going to want the baby exposed to any of that. Though I suppose a baby can't really be recognized the way a toddler or older child will be."

"No. You and me."

"Oh. That's a lot of attention." Her personal business

exposed to everyone? Her father might see and want a taste of the attention. A million what-ifs filled her head.

"Yes. I told them I'd talk to you about it, but it was totally up to you. I said you valued your privacy. They promised to keep the questions to whatever you were comfortable talking about, and you could have control over the photographs they used."

"You sound like you think it's a good idea."

"I think it's totally up to you."

"I'm asking you what you think. I'll make my own choice, but I'm asking."

"I like that I'd be showing you off. I know that sounds weird, but I want people to see what sort of person I've fallen in love with. Part of me realizes, though, that once we invite them in, even a little, others are going to feel like it's now open season on my romantic life. Which hasn't bugged me that much before, but now I'm in love with someone who values her privacy and who doesn't live behind big gates like I do."

"Publicity-wise? Will it help?"

"We're fine, Nat. We will be just fine without this interview."

"But if I do it, will it help with this new branding thing?"

"Probably. You're beautiful, but in a relatable way. We're a reunion story. People love second chances at love. You're a freaking librarian. The public will eat that up. But on the flip side, you're a librarian in a relatively small town. Easy to find. It might raise some money for the library, or it might end badly because people snoop around to get pictures of you. This isn't an easy decision, I know. And if you say no, I will totally understand."

"I need time to think about it."

"Of course. I didn't tell you to rush you. I just wanted you to know it had been discussed. I'm trying to be up front with you."

Her father had left her alone since that whole show-down with her grandmother before Thanksgiving. But if she was in the media, he might get it into his head to sniff around again. He craved attention so much. The lure of media attention would be too great to pass up.

At the same time, it was her life. She wanted to help Paddy. And to be honest, she sort of got off on such a public declaration of love. But would it be like getting someone's name tattooed on you? Like a curse?

Ugh.

She was being dumb, and she refused to think about it anymore.

"So they're also trying to get Ezra on the road with us for at least a few shows."

"Wow."

"It's totally his decision. I love playing with Ezra. He's the backbone of the band whether he comes out with us or not. But the road nearly killed him. He's got his life on track. There is nothing more important than him keeping his life together."

Paddy pulled up to a beautiful hotel that looked more like a grand old mansion than a traditional hotel. Right on the river, so the views would likely be fantastic.

The valet came out, and a bellman came to collect the bags.

Turns out their room was a suite that overlooked the Willamette as well as downtown Portland. Once their stuff had been delivered, he turned to her. "You like?"

"This is fantastic." There was even a wood-burning fireplace in the living room of the suite.

"I discovered River Place right before I ran into you again, actually. This is the first time I've stayed in this suite. It was booked when I was here before. But I love the park next door, and the views are beautiful." He stepped closer. "Like you."

"Oh, you're good, Hurley."

He grinned and kissed her slow and easy.

"First shopping and then when we get back, we'll get massages, and then I'm going to fuck you so hard, no one is going to look us in the eye when we check out because you're gonna make so much noise."

"That's a very bold promise."

"One that'll bring me a great deal of pleasure to keep."

"Win-win for me, then."

THEY HEADED INTO town to shop, walking hand in hand as they did. He wore a knit cap and sunglasses but even disguised he was gorgeous, so of course people looked twice, and when they did, they realized he was famous.

In Powell's, arms full of books, they were beset by a group of college-age guys.

"You're Paddy Hurley! Dude! We saw you guys six times on your last tour. We even drove to Utah for a show, and then we went climbing. But it was stellar. Can I get your autograph?"

Paddy gave her an apologetic look, but she smiled and took the books he'd been holding. One of the guys saw it and handed her the small basket he'd been carrying around.

"Oh, here. You can have mine. I'll get another."

"Thanks." He even helped her put the books in.

"When are you guys doing a new record? Been nearly three years now!"

Paddy signed things but kept an eye on Natalie, not failing to notice the way one of the dudes in the group had helped her with the basket and kept sneaking looks at her. Not that Paddy blamed him or anything, but she was his woman, after all.

"Finishing it up right now. It's set to release in January. We're touring starting in early February."

He signed for the next guy.

"Where are you going to be playing?"

"Keep an eye on the website. Announcements about all this will be coming soon." The label was working on all that. They'd drop the album and start the tour right then. It worked best for them that way, and they'd be out and back by the time Mary got too far along to be away from home. It was either that or wait until later in the year and have the tour with an infant. Damien was nervous about security and how it would be on Mary, so they'd opted for early in the year.

"Awesome. Thanks so much, man. It's an honor to meet you." The third dude pumped his hand, his smile from ear to ear. "Plus, your lady is plenty pretty. Damn."

"Totally agree, man. You guys have a good day. We're going to keep shopping."

They stumbled off, waving over their shoulders as Paddy took the basket. "Sorry about that."

"Nah. Nothing to be sorry about. They were pretty sweet, actually. You're good with them."

Better it be a group of dudes than women. It would happen eventually; it was part of the gig, after all. One he appreciated. But one he didn't want her to be freaked out by. That time in the grocery store was one thing, but that was a whole different sort of experience.

"Let's pay for this. I have a few more places to hit, and then we'll get lunch."

They did, and he got stopped twice more. The last one being the least pleasant.

"Oh, hey, Paddy!"

He'd been walking down the sidewalk toward where they'd parked when he'd heard the voice.

His arms were full of bags, but he kept close to Natalie as the women approached.

One of them full-on pushed Natalie aside so she could stand next to him.

"Standing here." Natalie's voice was not polite, though he had to give it to her, she kept her temper.

The woman turned and shrugged before looking back to Paddy.

"Hey, there, you maybe didn't hear. Or see. But someone is already standing there. Can you move, please?"

"Oh." She turned back, gave Natalie the once-over and then stepped in front of him, keeping her back to Nat.

"What do you ladies need? We're on our way to lunch."

"Don't you remember us? The Gorge when you were there with Adrian Brown?" She licked her lips and Natalie snorted.

"Okay, then. Well, I'm going to skip this trip down memory lane. Mainly because it's pretty rude with my girlfriend standing here. You two have a good day." He stepped around them, juggling the bags to put a hand at Natalie's back as they left.

He heard one of the women call Natalie a bitch and he stiffened, turning.

"No." Natalie shook her head. "Who cares?"

"I do."

"But I don't. They don't mean shit to me. Or to you, which is sort of sad and all, but that's how it goes. Come on. We have lunch, and you don't need to defend my honor."

He snarled, but turned and kept walking. "I don't like that. You deserve respect."

"I respect myself. You respect me. What they think? Doesn't matter to me."

He drove them back to the hotel and ordered room service. Once he'd done that, he pulled her close. "I'm sorry about today."

"About what? Spending the day with me instead of in the studio? Responding to your fans when they see you and want to interact? I don't expect to have one hundred percent of your attention at all times."

"No, but this was a day for you and me. We got interrupted over and over."

"Three times in three hours. That's not too bad."

"And the women. I'm embarrassed."

"Paddy." She heaved a sigh and moved away from him, standing to look out over the river. "Do I like it that you've fucked your way from one side of the globe to the other? Not really. But I'm not a virgin and I can't control what you did when you weren't with me. So I guess the real question I have is why you're embarrassed."

Sometimes she was sharply intuitive.

"It's sort of seedy. I clearly must have been with those women."

"Both of them at once, and I bet it wasn't the first time you'd been with more than one woman at a time. But so what? You're a man in the prime of his life. You're handsome and powerful. Charismatic and famous, too. It's not like it's a secret to women that dudes want to bone two women at once. We aren't dumb. Not even those heifers who came on to you earlier. So it's not the three-way."

"Notice you didn't argue that it was seedy."

She gave him a look, and he sighed.

"I'm standing here in a hotel room with you. With a woman I once had a fling with all those years ago, and I remembered you. Pretty much the instant I saw you. I don't want you to think you're like them."

She laughed. "But *they're* like them. Do you get my meaning? Are you maybe embarrassed that you've stuck your dick in so many women, it's like fast food? You don't remember which burger shack you ate in, and maybe that leaves you empty at the end of the day? Not every sexual encounter has to be deep, meaningful love. But after a while, if you're only giving yourself the dollar menu, you're treating yourself like you're only worth a buck."

"Ouch."

She reached up to cup his cheek. "I think you're worth more than the dollar menu. I don't want you to feel bad for being irresistible. I understand that better than those women ever will. I don't want you to feel bad because you take the time to talk to your fans. I don't even want you to feel guilty because you slept with so many women, you can't remember a threesome. If you look back and think it's seedy, maybe it was." Her expression was rueful. "But you can't go back and change it and let's face it, you wouldn't. It's okay that you took advantage of one of the very reasons young men want to be rock stars."

"But I have you. And I know the difference between what's real and what's seedy. It makes me feel disrespectful to you and what we have."

"I can't tell you how to feel. It's sweet and all that you're worried. But when I express discomfort over your lifestyle, it's not that you banged a zillion girls before I came into the picture. Respect me now that we're together. Right? That's what I need. I don't need you to feel bad because some catty bitch shoved me out of the way to try to hump you in the middle of the street. You handled it. We're here. Right now."

"I'm a lucky man. You know that?"

She nodded. "You totally are."

Before he could show her just how lucky *she* could be, room service arrived to set up lunch.

"Foiled."

She laughed as he moved to let them in. "It's okay. I'll just be thinking about it more now."

"That works, too."

SHE DISAPPEARED FOR a bit, coming back to find a fire built and crackling merrily and lunch laid out and ready to be eaten. He was in the process of taking a bite of the chocolate cake.

"What? It's totally okay to eat dessert first at Christmas. It's the American way. And stuff."

She rolled her eyes and sat, forking up a bite of her own and humming. "This is really good."

The soup she'd ordered was perfect and warmed her up. "The first time I tried pumpkin soup, I did not believe it could be good. I turned my nose up at it, and Tuesday shamed me into trying it. She's usually right. It was delicious."

"Was it just me, or were there some sparks when she and Ezra met?"

"It wasn't just you. But she's…well, she's not easy to reach. She's had a rough time since Eric died. I don't know if she's ready for more than sparks. She dates a little, mainly to have sex, I think." But her friend was way too comfortable with her inner darkness.

"The first time I really understood Ezra was in trouble, we were on the road. It was the second tour, right after we'd made it pretty big."

He hadn't shared this with her, so she settled back and listened.

"We all… Look, I'm not going to pretend I was an innocent. I had enough problems of my own. I just liked coke better than heroin. I did it with him a few times, but where he loved the way it sucked him under and smoothed him out, I wanted the opposite. I liked being up. Loved the creative jolt coke gave me. At first, until it fucked my voice up and ate all my money and made my dick soft. All that was enough to keep me away from it after a while. Anyway, we were on tour, and he started getting rooms on a different floor. And at first I was like, well, I like to get the hell away from them sometimes, too. But then I realized his dealer was with us in every damned city."

He stared off into the middle distance for a bit and then sighed, eating some more. "He was dropping weight like crazy. We were at dinner and he disappeared right in the middle of it. Like he said he was going to the bathroom and he just didn't come back.

We were eating with some people from *Rolling Stone* magazine, for God's sake! So I thought, maybe he fell or hurt himself, and I went to find him. He was still in the john, his goddamned rig in his arm, passed out on the toilet."

She'd seen it herself more than once, and bile rose at the memory. Just imagining someone as hale and hearty as Ezra like that was sick-making. Hearing Paddy talk about it, though, that was worse. She heard the anger, the hurt and she *understood* it so well.

At the same time, she resented it a little because her father never really had that experience of getting himself together. She'd never known him when he wasn't screwed up.

"I only managed to not kick his ass because Jeremy had come to find us. We got Ezra a cab to the hotel and Jeremy went with him. I went back to the table and made excuses saying Ezra was sick and Jeremy had taken him back to rest. An article came out in the next issue about us. And it wasn't good.

"But by that point, things were so bad in the band, it didn't matter what *Rolling Stone* had said. It was like Ezra had taken on addiction like he had making the band a success. He'd embraced heroin like it was family. He blew off sound check. One of us had to constantly be with him before a show or he'd be hours late. It's when I started filling in that space for him onstage and taking over more of the vocals. We had to because he just wasn't showing up. Hell, even when he was physically there, he wasn't really showing up. Then he fucking nodded off onstage. Just right there in front of thousands of people. He was already playing so bad, they'd turned off his amps so no one could hear him. And he just fell asleep. Standing up. It was like at that moment I was looking at a stranger who'd killed my brother. The rage just drowned me." And a lot of shame, she supposed. Fear. Helplessness. "I hated him so much in that moment."

She remembered this part. Remembered seeing the footage on television. Remembered, too, that sudden, cold-as-ice rage and hatred at another person.

"You charged him. Right there onstage and knocked him to the ground."

"I did. In front of the whole world, apparently." He snorted. "I should have known you'd have seen it. That film haunts me to this day. But I had just… He wasn't even my brother anymore. It was like something had taken him over. It was an ugly, horrible thing. An abomination. He'd been stealing from us. From his family. Let people into our lives who didn't care about fucking us over. They just needed money for drugs. And they were everywhere! Jeremy and the label people had stepped in, and they did a pretty good job at keeping them out of the backstage area. But Ezra would ditch his keepers to get drugs. My big brother never would have done that. Never would have abandoned what we'd built together. He endangered *everything,* including his own life. I don't think I've ever been so angry."

She reached out to draw the pad of her thumb over his knuckles.

Paddy looked up, his faraway gaze snapping into place, seeing her. Knowing she had been there. "You understand me. Sometimes it scares me how much you do. You understand the fear and the rage. The guilt. The moments when you just hate them so much for not choosing you over using."

She managed a smile, but she had her own fear to choke past. "Yeah."

"So we got in a fight in front of all those people. He hit his head on a corner of a speaker, split it open. Facial wounds are the worst. They bleed so much. But he didn't even get it then."

He drew a shaky breath. "I'm sorry, I shouldn't have said all that."

"Why not? That's how you grow to know someone. You share things with them."

"It's not really my story to tell. Ezra isn't that anymore."

"Sometimes you share a bad memory to let that other person share that burden. Or maybe you give them a piece of yourself to see if they can be trusted. You said it yourself. I understand. And I'm envious because Ezra is stronger than my father, and he got his act together. No, you weren't the one addicted, Paddy, but it's your story as much as it is his. Addiction isn't just about the person with the habit."

She had known in the back of her mind, even back in July when he'd first reappeared in her life, that to open the door even a crack would mean something she couldn't have expected. It was probably why she'd tried to hold him back. Why she'd tried to keep control of all those things that could hurt so very much if they went bad.

He was beautiful and clever and talented and funny, but he brought so much into her life that scared her so much. Caring about him the way she did meant he had the power to hurt her more than even those years growing up couldn't compare to.

Because this... These moments were about giving him access to all her wounds. Because his sharing meant she had access to his and the responsibility to be what he needed. Hell, to figure out what it was he did need, which was more than head-nodding. Sometimes he'd need the harsh truth, and she'd have to hurt him a little to help him in the big picture, and what if she fucked it up?

He brought the hand on his to his mouth and kissed it. "I guess you'd know that more than most. They patched him up backstage, and then he disappeared. We looked for him. Found him in a place that made that hotel at the bowling alley look like the Four Seasons. He was so ugly. Dope sick. He said some stuff we had to actually deal with in therapy." He shivered.

"But he went to therapy with you."

He nodded. "My mom made us lock her and Ezra in the room. We guarded the door and the bathroom window from the outside, and they were in there a long time. When they came out, he'd agreed to rehab. I'll always be grateful to Jeremy because they sent Ez to a really amazing inpatient rehab in the middle of nowhere. And when he came back, he was changed. He wasn't the Ezra he'd been before. Not entirely. He had shadows in his gaze. A seriousness he'd never had. But we all went to therapy with him and worked through a lot of stuff. He still goes from time to time if he feels like he needs to unload."

She liked Ezra, liked that he owned his shit and cared about his family the way he did. Was thrilled he'd gotten clean and stayed that way. But she couldn't deny the twist of envy in her belly.

"I'm sorry if I upset you. I just... He's got his own darkness. I said more than I'd intended to. I just wanted to say maybe he needs someone who is as familiar with that pain as he is."

"Maybe. I've teased her about it. I know she finds him ridiculously attractive and at the same time, hello, he *is* ridiculously attractive. As for telling me all that? Sharing with me? You didn't upset me. Not like that. Ezra isn't my dad. Ezra got himself together. He has a life. He's on track."

"He's still an asshole with a lot of jagged shit in his gut. I know that much. But he's the strongest person I know. He kicked and when he did, it was awful. But he did it. And he rebuilt his life. I admire that so much."

"So maybe he doesn't need to be back out on the road."

Paddy thought that over. "Or maybe he needs it more than I thought he did. In any case, what I do know is that he can make the choice, and I'll back him up either way. Thanks for listening."

"One of the services I provide."

He gave her a smile as the intensity of the moment shifted to something else entirely. He got up and dropped his iPod into the dock, spinning the wheel until *Natalie* came up on his playlist. He pressed it and the opening strains of Death Cab For Cutie's "Transatlanticism" came over the speakers, filling the room.

He turned to find her watching him.

"I think you need to stand up."

She looked at him briefly and then did it.

Every time he took the reins during sex and she let him, every time she trusted him to be what she needed, he learned something about himself as well as her.

"You're so beautiful."

Her lashes swept down as a pleased smile marked her lips, and a pretty pink blush flamed her cheeks.

"Show me. Get naked and show me all that pretty skin and that ink that's my own private work of art."

He leaned against the back of the couch, hands in fists to let her get naked on her own.

She toed her shoes off first, then unbuttoned and unzipped the soft pants she'd worn. Because she knew he watched, she left her panties on, deep blue against her skin, with ties at each side. Those were his favorite.

Something stirred in his belly that she'd put them on just for him to look at before she took them off.

For him.

Her socks made him smile. Wonder Woman socks.

"They were a gift from Jenny."

He could see that. "I approve."

"I knew you would."

That made him suck in a breath. This dance—her giving up control, his taking it—was delicate. She knew what she was doing. Everything she did was purposeful. Which made it all the more powerful. Because she was choosing to let him take over.

This tightly wound control freak who shared his life the way she did made a conscious choice to give herself to him this way. Which made him both proud she thought him worth it and freaked out that he'd screw it up.

He was trying to find the balance with her. He wanted her trust, loved when she gave it to him. But he was working still to find an equilibrium. He didn't want to walk on eggshells. Didn't want to be so careful they lost all the heat between them, either.

He was just taking it bit by bit. Trying to learn. Trying to listen. Definitely enjoying being in love with this woman who made every moment, even those of struggle, worth it.

She slid her hands up her belly, pausing to cup her breasts through her clothes and then up her neck. He hummed his delight at the sight. Bold.

She unbuttoned each small pearly button on the cardigan she wore, sliding it off and tossing it on the couch behind him. The wisp of her scent rose as the soft-as-sin cashmere caressed his skin as it landed.

The song ended and "Lightness" came on.

"Someone loves Death Cab for Cutie."

"This is your playlist. There are other bands on it, but shuffle apparently decided this was a good start. I agree."

"Yeah?" She sang along with the lyric about a heart being a river, and he finished it.

"How come I never knew you could sing?"

She crossed her hands over at her waist, grabbing the shirt's hem, and pulled it up and over her head, tossing it to join the sweater.

"Oh. Well, now."

The bra clearly matched the panties. Deep blue, coming to a V in the center, between the breasts it so lovingly cradled together, creating the most luscious curves he'd ever seen.

"I figured you'd like it."

"I'll like it even more when it's in a heap with the rest of your clothes."

She smiled, reaching behind her to unhook and with a shimmy that was more theatrics than necessary, though certainly appreciated, she ridded herself of the bra and indeed, tossed it to join the rest of her clothes.

Band of Horses' "No One's Gonna Love You" came on and her gaze swept up to meet his.

"So how come I didn't know you could sing?" He made himself stay still as he watched her really hear the lyrics to the song.

"It's sort of like telling Kelly Slater you surf. Anyway, it's not a hobby or something I do other than around my house and in the car. Not onstage in front of a zillion people."

"Panties can go. I like the socks, though."

Ever so slowly, she pulled one tie and then the other and tugged until the panties fell from her body.

"Seeing you naked is like being really hungry when you go grocery shopping. I want to rush and devour every inch of your body even when I know I'd be better off going slowly."

"You're really good at this stuff."

"Advance warning, a lot of this stuff goes into lyrics."

She blushed again and he moved, forcing himself to go slow.

He kissed from her shoulder to her neck, up to her ear. He breathed deep there, the scent of her skin settling things deep inside even as his cock was so hard it ached.

She turned her head to receive the next kisses, their tongues sliding and teasing. He could kiss her for hours.

"Before you, I totally underestimated kissing." He kissed her again and again until she clutched his shirt at his shoulders. "Your taste, God."

One corner of her mouth tipped up and he licked over the dimple it formed.

He moved to the other side, down her neck, nibbling

until he got to the side of her left breast. He sucked all that luscious flesh and gave her the edge of his teeth. "Gonna leave a mark. I like you knowing who makes you feel good. Like knowing it's our little secret."

She drew a choked breath and he smiled, dropping to his knees in front of her.

Her hands slid into his hair, holding his head as he kissed around her belly button, nibbling it. Her skin heated against his lips; he knew she was ready even before he spread her open and took a lick.

She made a strangled sound and tugged his hair, keeping him close.

"Love that you want it so much."

"So give it to me." She urged him again and he smiled against her before he took several more long licks. He'd give her this first climax hard and fast so she'd be slippery and ready for him. And then he'd take his time and give her more.

She came with his name on her lips. He loved that as much as her taste.

HE STOOD IN a fluid motion, his pupils taking up most of the color of his eyes, his lips swollen. She sucked in a breath, but it wasn't enough.

He kept a hand at her hip as he tore his sweater off and got his pants unzipped. She moved closer, pulling his cock out and into her hands, thrusting herself around him, up and down until he was slick at the head.

"Stop."

She did, licking her lips, loving the way he groaned at the sight.

With him this way, she felt powerful, even when

she let him control everything. Sexy and desired. Understood.

He finished getting naked and moved to sit on the nearby couch, laying out a condom within arms' reach.

"Suck me for a bit. Not too long because you know I want to be in you. I'll let you know when I'm ready for you to get on my lap and ride me."

The National went away and Ellie Goulding's "Burn" came on. No one had made her a playlist in a long time. Since college when someone made her a mixed CD. But this was better. Because these songs told her things about how he felt about her.

He moved to put a pillow down for her knees, but she shook her head. Sometimes the rub of the carpet added to things rather than detracted. Sometimes a little pain or discomfort was just what she wanted.

She took him in her mouth, knowing exactly what he liked.

Giving it to him.

Sometimes.

Other times she teased him, going just shy of it. Giving him just enough, holding back a little until he got restless, churning his hips, seeking more.

There was so much power here. Even on her knees, there was power. She knew his body so well, and he let her. She got to him, drew him out more. He opened to her in ways she knew without a doubt he did for no one else.

"Enough. Come up here."

She stood, licking her lips, loving his groan in response as she moved her thighs just outside his.

She took the condom from his hands, ripping the package open and rolling it on for him.

When she took him into her body, she locked her

gaze on him. Watched him as he watched himself disappear into her. And when he shifted up to look at her face, his smile was open in ways it so rarely was.

He reached up, sliding his hand around to the back of her head and pulled it down to meet his kiss. Which she did.

Kissing Paddy was as intimate as his being inside her. Because he put all of himself into the way he kissed.

He held her lips to his own as she undulated, rolling her hips to take and keep him deep. His hands roamed all over her body, caressing, fingertips teasing all her favorite spots and a few she hadn't even known existed until him. Like the hollow of her throat, where he played the pad of his thumb, slowly, back and forth, over and over. Shivers ran over the surface of her skin.

He followed his thumb with his lips, the edge of his teeth, his tongue, drawing her toward climax yet again. And all just with a touch at her throat. But when he cupped her breasts, pinching her nipples just how she liked it best, suspended right before pleasure became pain, she gasped, her body rippling around him.

He gave an answering gasp, that pinch tightening a little.

"You're going to kill me. But it'll be worth it."

She smiled, tipping her head back, arching to get him into her deeper. He cupped her throat and she gasped, shocked at how good it was.

"Someone likes that."

"How'd you know?" she managed to stutter out.

"Your pussy just clamped down around me. Oh, and the gasp of shocked delight. Christ, I wish I could sample that and use it on one of the tracks we're laying down next week."

He kept his hand there and moved the other to where her body met his, finding her clit and giving her just exactly the right amount of pressure. She had no idea how he could be so precise, knowing just exactly what she wanted and needed right at that given moment. But he did and she loved it.

"Give me another, gorgeous. Let me hear it. See how beautiful you are when you come."

She sucked in a breath as she went under, letting orgasm steal through her cells, take hold of her muscles, heating her, bringing little earthquakes around him as she continued to roll her hips, grinding herself against his fingers.

"That's it. So gorgeous and all mine."

She nodded. Because it was true.

He came shortly after she did, on a snarl, his arms sliding around her waist, his face against her breasts as he held her for long moments.

"I'm more relaxed than any massage could ever make me. But I will have some cake now, since I don't smoke cigarettes anymore."

She laughed, allowing him to help her stand on still-rubbery legs.

He put his sweater over her head and she let it swallow her body, surrounding her in warmth and his smell.

And she allowed herself to be deliriously happy.

CHAPTER NINETEEN

SHE WOKE UP when her bed got jostled.

Just a few days after that superdirty hotel sex, Natalie opened her eyes to a bunch of hugs from her friends, who'd come down to have a pre-Christmas celebration before most of them headed out to wherever their families resided.

Tuesday kissed her smack on the lips. "This is the first Christmas you won't be at my parents' house in seven years. That is freaky."

"You guys are going to break my bed." She laughed as Jenny settled on one side, spooning her against Zoe, who'd gotten on the other. Tuesday hugged them all the best she could. Dee and Rosie piled on.

"Just think of Paddy's face when you say all your girlfriends were in your bed snuggling you when they broke it."

More laughing came.

"He might nod his head and never hear a word right now. They're wrapping up this album, and he's so deep in it he barely remembers to sleep much less get tititlated by faux lesbian orgy stories."

"Aww, is he ignoring your basic biological needs?" Rosie asked as she rolled off.

She blushed. "Well, I wouldn't go that far."

"Good Lord, you need to elaborate. But Dee has gathered the ingredients for a massive breakfast pig-out so come on. Guzzle coffee and tell us about Paddy's technique."

Natalie rolled her eyes and got out of bed, stepping into her fluffy slippers and pulling on a robe because it was cold.

They rolled downstairs and settled at the kitchen table while Dee and Rosie cooked, Tuesday handling coffee.

"Now, sex?"

"It's not like I'd be with him if he didn't know what went where and what to do with it."

They all just stared. Tuesday laughed and turned music on. Dee started dancing around as she turned bacon and flipped pancakes. In different pans, of course, so Jenny didn't have bacon goo on her pancakes.

"Well, duh."

"God. You're all not going to let go until I tell you."

"Have we not all told each other about our sex lives? That's part of the contract." Rosie brought plates down from the cabinets. "Plus, Tuesday knows way more details, which is not even fair. You're hurting our feelings, Nats. How can you be so mean?"

"He's…"

Jenny put a dish towel over Natalie's head. "Now, you don't have to look at us when you tell. Though I hasten to remind you, you've told us plenty about other dudes while eating popcorn and cackling madly."

"They were different." She pulled the towel off. "He's… I'm…I'm so in love with him, I should be scared as hell, but I'm in so deep, I can't find it in me to not jump off that cliff with him. When we're together, especially sexwise, he gets me. You know sometimes there are things you want but you don't even know it until it's happening?"

"Like in the butt?" Jenny's bright smile after that statement only made it better.

Natalie guffawed. "Um, I guess someone could make that corollary if they wanted that. Sure. But in this case, I mean he takes over. I like being in charge. A lot. I'm always in charge but with him…"

"Well, it makes sense. You're in charge all the time. You're the biggest control freak I know, and that says a lot. So that you'd trust him to take over? That says so much about how you feel about him. And how he feels about you because you sure wouldn't do it if he didn't hit all the right buttons." Rosie kissed the top of Natalie's head as she passed a platter of pancakes down to the end of the table.

Zoe forked up a few and put them on her plate. "So are we talking whips and chains?"

"No. He sets the tone. Orders me around. Sometimes he, oh, God, I can't believe I'm saying all this! He'll spin me around to face a wall and fuck me. He talks really dirty in my ear. Tells me to do stuff and how to do it." She shrugged. "It pushes my buttons. Every time we're together and it goes like that, there's something deeper at the end. He gets me and he doesn't try to fix me. He doesn't give me advice on how to do anything. Other than the sex stuff." Natalie laughed.

"He accepts you." Tuesday laid a hand on top of hers.

Natalie nodded.

"He listens to me. I find myself telling him things I never intended to. And it's surprisingly all right."

"Plus, he's so hot. Man, that beard. I bet he's got

piercings. I've seen the ink in pictures of him onstage."
Dee winked.

"Both nipples and yes, lots of ink. He's…he's a bad
boy, no lie. But one with a big heart who loves his family and works hard. He's kind of perfect like that."

"No one is perfect." Rosie brought out some jam
and syrup.

And that was what worried her. "It's not like I have
rose-colored glasses."

"No, sometimes I think it's too much the opposite.
You expect everyone to mess up and disappoint you."
Jenny smothered her pancakes with butter.

"Keeping low expectations means you're not as disappointed when people mess up."

"No one is perfect, but most of them are not Bob
Clayton, either." Tuesday topped up her coffee.

"Thanks. No, that's true. But I had to have Bob in
my life growing up. As an adult, I have choices about
who I let in. I've never felt this way about anyone before. So I'm wary of it. When it's just the two of us, or
his family, it's fine. But his life." She lifted her hands
momentarily. "If I had made a list of all the things I'd
want to avoid in a man, he'd be in many of those cat-
egories. But I can't help it."

"So jump. Jump and know that you might get a wed-
gie when you hit the water, but you won't die if it goes
wrong. It might hurt like balls, but you're surrounded
by people who love you and who will make his life a
living hell for breaking your heart if he does." Rosie
raised her mug. "To love!"

PADDY WOKE FROM the nap he'd managed to steal on the
couch in the barn. They'd been working pretty much

nonstop for the past four days to get *Day Dream* in the can, and it looked as if it would happen a week or so before Christmas. Which was good because he was sick of seeing his brothers more than he saw Natalie.

He smiled as he shuffled into the bathroom attached to the lounge where he'd been sleeping. He splashed water on his face and brushed his teeth. He'd need coffee—and a lot of it—shortly. Damien had gone home to check in on Mary, and Vaughan was still sleeping on the other couch. Ezra? Hell, who knew.

He started a pot of coffee and caught sight of Ezra out in the distance, tossing a ball to the dog, a cigar between his teeth. Paddy pulled on a coat and boots and headed out.

Wild, joyous barking echoed with the pig's happy squeals. "I can't believe you have a pig that follows you around like a dog and a dog who forgets what he's doing even as he's doing it." Paddy nodded toward the cigar his brother held. "Got another?"

Ezra pulled one out of his pocket and a lighter followed.

He puffed and sighed happily. "Where'd these come from?"

"Jeremy sent them for my birthday. I figured finishing another album without any of us getting killed was worth a celebratory smoke."

They laughed until Ezra turned to him. "You should tell me what you've been holding back for the last few weeks."

"Damn. You're good."

"That's what she said." Ezra thought that was hilarious, and when he stopped laughing, he cleared his throat. "Sorry, you walked right into that one. I know you talked to Jeremy and the label people. You danced around some of it. You told me the rest. So it's not hard to figure out you're sandbagging on something."

"They proposed you come out with us this time. Either an open and close or maybe even the whole thing."

Ezra was quiet for a time as they smoked their cigars in the cold, crisp air.

"What do you think about that?" Ezra asked Paddy.

"I think I'm one hundred percent in support of whatever you want to do. The most important thing is what we do here in the studio. You're part of Sweet Hollow Ranch like that, and you always will be. The words I sing are the ones we create. The production, all of it. You're the backbone. You don't need to go on tour to prove that."

"I miss it sometimes. When you guys are all gone, and I'm here, and I hear about it via phone calls or see it on television, I remember what it was like. The heady fucking joy of standing on a stage in front of all those people singing words *I* wrote. Hitting that perfect moment in a song with you guys."

Paddy nodded. Not much he could argue with in that. He loved those things, too.

"True. And if you do open and close you can have that in a controlled way. A quick shot of it, blow the doors off the Rose Garden. Have a blast and then come back here. Or not." He paused. "Look, we don't often talk about it, but the road is hard. Your health is worth more than any of that shit."

"You think I'm weak, then?"

"No." He flipped his brother off. "Just the opposite. But you got tossed out of an airplane and hit the ground at full speed. It took you years to put yourself back together and you're *better* than you were before. I'm saying if you want to do it, I'm your biggest cheerleader."

"I'd rather see Natalie in a short skirt, thanks."

He flipped Ezra off with the other hand, too. "Not fucking likely. Anyway. Come out with us. I know you're strong enough to do it. Or don't come out. Do a show. Don't do a show. It's your choice. It's always totally Hurley against the world, right? Those dicks at the label want to make a buck and whatever, fine. But we make them more than a few bucks, and none of us owes our soul or our health."

"What about a few club gigs? I can do one and see how it goes."

They had three club gigs set up to preview their material in front of a small audience before they dropped the CD. They were fan club tickets mainly, which meant the crowd would be on their side but also would give good feedback. It was the kick off of the tour, gave them a chance to do the material live to work out any kinks, too.

"Been nearly three years since the last time we toured on new material. It'd be a big surprise for the fan club, too." Paddy snorted.

"I'll do the two secret shows and we'll see about the rest."

He clapped a hand on Ezra's back. "Gonna kick some ass with you. But no pressure, yeah? Do it, and if you feel like it isn't going to work, don't do another."

Ezra nodded. "Come on. I have a coffee date with your girlfriend later."

"The hell you do."

Ezra thought that was hilarious. "I do. I'm assisting

her with your present. Plus, I'm pretty to look at. Everyone says so."

"Oh, well, if it's for a present, I withdraw my objections. Also, it's good for her to be around the brother who is far less smooth so she remembers just why I'm so irresistible."

"Whatever. Let's get working so I can play."

EZRA PUT THE guitar in the case and grinned up at her. "He's going to love this. It's in perfect shape and yep, tuned."

She smiled back, happy. "Thank you so much for helping me find it. I wouldn't have known where to start looking, much less what to get him."

The *what* in question was a dark cherry-red 1981 Gibson 355. She'd had to cajole, charm and ruthlessly pursue it once Ezra had said it was a guitar Paddy had wanted for years, but the person who had the one he really wanted didn't like him.

Of course, she took that as a personal challenge and had been working on the guy for the past three months.

She loved the shape of it. Curvy, like her, she supposed. When he held it onstage, hopefully, he'd think of her.

"Honestly, I think you're a freaking wizard for getting Ed to sell this to you. Also, when Paddy gets over his freak out of joy he's going to frown at you for what this must have cost."

"It's my money. I wanted him to have it."

Ezra kissed her forehead and watched her wrap it. "I've never seen a package look so professionally wrapped outside a department store. You could slice tomatoes with those corners."

"I worked in a department store when I was in high school. I was the queen of the holiday wrapping counter." She huffed a breath on her nails, shining them against her shoulder.

"I bet. So you're staying up our way, right? I mean..." Ezra looked around the house. He'd insisted on accompanying her to Eugene where she'd taken custody of the guitar from Ed, a crusty old dude who'd been the one and only owner. "Tuesday's not around?"

She hid her smile. Both of them thought it was easy to hide their mutual fascination with one another from her.

"She flew out to Tennessee first thing with her parents. They're having a huge family reunion at her great-aunt's house. Apparently, all her extended family are coming in from all over the country to celebrate her great-aunt and -uncle's sixty-fifth wedding anniversary."

"Wow, that's pretty awesome. She's from Tennessee?"

"She was raised in Olympia. Her mom was born and raised there and met Tuesday's dad while she was going to college in Virginia. They came back to Olympia after they graduated and married. He's a former hippie who owns a roofing company, and she's an engineer. His folks are from Tennessee. Cookeville."

"Small world. My mom and dad are from Columbia and thereabouts. Both grew up on farms."

"You two have a lot in common. You should ask her to dinner sometime."

He gave her a look, and she tried to stay serious.

"What?"

"Her best friend is my brother's girlfriend. I'll wait

a bit to see how that works out before I make connections."

She picked up the case and put a bow on it. "Yes, I'm spending the night. Also, so are you saying you think Paddy and I are going to crash and burn?"

He choked. "What? No! How the hell did you get that? Christ, women. You're all the devil. As it happens, I think you and Paddy are good together, and thank goodness he does, too. You keep him calm. He didn't even bloody Vaughan's or Damien's nose. Not once."

"Pfft, he gave Vaughan a black eye, and he split your lip and Vaughan's. Twice. If that's calm, God help us the next time you guys record."

"Says the woman who charmed this guitar out of Ed Chasen to give to Paddy Hurley. Seriously, this guy hates my brother."

"How about we load this into the car along with those presents over there? I'll grab my bag and meet you at your car and then on the way over to the ranch, you can tell me the Ed and Paddy story?"

"Okay. But only if you tell me how you charmed him."

"Deal."

She ran upstairs to grab her bag with her clothes and toiletries. She already had stuff at Paddy's house, which made her happy. But she had some Christmas presents she'd give him in private, too.

She locked the house up and met him at his truck where he opened her door—Sharon Hurley didn't raise boys who didn't open doors for other people—and she climbed into the seat.

"Hang on a sec and the seats will heat." And they did. She sighed, relaxing and turning to him.

"Spill."

"Ed Chasen is sort of a legend. He's been in the music scene for sixty years. Few people can play blues guitar like him. He used to run a school and there was this competition. Paddy, with no formal training and no shortage of ego, talked some trash to this dude who was one of Ed's students. And Paddy kicked his ass. I mean, it was sort of crazy. The thing about Paddy is that he has this devil-may-care thing, but he's really, really good. A natural musician. He can play all the instruments his brothers play. He can sing. He's got that damned star-quality thing."

"Yes, the ladies really like that," she said dryly, and he laughed.

"Sorry, sweetheart. He's aware of that stuff and *before you,* he used it. He was a rogue but women like it as long as the guy is up front about who and what he is. But Paddy won that competition three more times. Ed, well, he got mad. Here's this kid from a small town with no training, and he's beating Ed's best?"

"For Paddy, his music just flows from him. He doesn't have to think about it. It just is. Oh, and he still uses it, only on me."

"I really can't have chosen anyone better for my brother. You're really smart, you know? People-smart. You get him in ways most people never will."

She blushed.

"So that started this thing, and Paddy never really thought about it much until the guitar. He wanted that guitar so bad, and he went to Ed and made a case to Ed but Ed told him to fuh—go away. How'd you do it?"

"At first, I tried logic. I came at him head-on, and he blew me off. Because I was a woman he was mannerly enough, but it was clear he had no interest in selling the guitar. So I started calling him a few times a week. Then I sent him Sweet Hollow Ranch CDs. He got mad at me at first. And then I drove down there and showed up at his house."

"You did what? Christ! I told you not to go down there alone. He could have been insane or a serial killer or something. Paddy is going to kill me."

"Hush. You didn't tell me that until after I'd already gone down there. So technically, once you told me not to, I didn't. But anyway. I showed up, and I followed him around pretty much all day until he finally agreed to listen to one track if I'd leave him alone. So I played him 'Be There.' And I said, 'Don't you think your guitar would make magic with this man playing it?'"

"You're ballsy, Nats. Jeez."

"Pfft. Why do men say that? Balls? If you kick them or bump them or they get cold or too warm, you guys go down for the count. I say I have vagina. Way tougher than balls. Though it does hurt to get kicked there."

He sputtered and then laughed and laughed. "We need to think of another term, though. Vagina up? No. I'll think about it and get back to you. So did he agree, then? To sell you the guitar, I mean?"

"No, but he started to consider it then. I called him still. Emailed him. And when he kept picking up the phone, I knew he was thinking of it. What finally did it? I said, 'Have you ever been in love, Mr. Chasen?' He said he had and had been married three times."

"Course, he probably drove 'em all off with his crankiness."

"One died in childbirth in the forties. Another he married about six weeks after he lost his wife, mainly to care for his newborn son. That fell apart a decade later. And then he met Suzanne. He called her Zany. They were married until she died two years ago. So I told him I loved Paddy and that he wanted that guitar because he loved music, just like Ed did, and that guitar couldn't go to a better person. Paddy would use it and love it and make music with it. He hung up on me. Three days later he called and agreed to sell it to me."

Ezra shook his head. "You're one tough cookie. And for what it's worth? Paddy will play that guitar all the time. And that you did all that for him is only going to make him love it more."

CHAPTER TWENTY

So of course, the Hurleys did Christmas in the same way they did everything else. In a crowd of noise, hugs, kisses and no small amount of brotherly trash talk.

Vaughan had the girls, who loved all over the puppy they'd picked out a few days before from the animal shelter. Vaughan watched them with a bittersweet smile.

"They're growing up so fast."

She wondered about their mother. Paddy had said his ex-wife was a really good mother who stayed nearby so Vaughan could see them and be a regular part of their lives. Mothering like that was sort of miraculous to Natalie.

Mary leaned against Damien, laughing at something her mother had said to Sharon.

"You could totally tell me what my present is now."

Paddy Hurley was absolutely useless when it came to patience over a surprise or a present.

"We're going to be opening stuff in like five minutes. I bet you hunted all over the place to find presents when you were a kid."

"Guilty as charged." He grinned, without any remorse at all. "You didn't?"

"I sometimes came up here to my grandparents' for Christmas. I got lots of presents. Never let it be said that the Claytons didn't shower me with things." Things too big or too small, things inappropriate for the weather or just clear evidence of how little they knew her.

"I'm sorry. I shouldn't have stirred that up."

"Hush." She kissed him quickly. "It's fine. It wasn't like this. Never. But once I got to college, things changed. I always spent Christmases with Tuesday's family. And 1022 tries to be together before or after the holiday. Delia is Jewish so she and I often hung out on Christmas if I wasn't visiting anyone's family. But this? This is pretty fantastic, and I'm happy to be spending it here with you all."

Sharon whistled and got everyone's attention, even the puppy. "Santa's superbusy, and he's appointed Poppa to do his job. So let's go on into the living room."

Natalie loved presents. Loved the process of finding the exactly perfect thing for each person. Over the course of the year, she was on the lookout for everyone. For holidays big and small. The closet in her bedroom was full of presents she'd found here and there.

And she loved wrapping them, too. Each present under the tree from her was something she'd genuinely thought about, from the awesome veterinary kit for Vaughan's oldest daughter, to the new gloves, three pairs, for Sharon, who lost them all the time. Mary's present was in the form of a promise. She was having a blanket made because she was awful at such things herself. But the blanket had little sayings all over it from songs and poems and things his or her parents and family said.

And while she was long past a crappy childhood full of disappointing Christmases, she wasn't prepared for what it felt like to be treated like one of the Hurlcys.

Michael brought her a present from him and Sharon,

a brooch to pin her scarves, a scarf to pin it to and a jewelry box Michael had made. There was a season pass to the theater in Portland from Damien and Mary, a coffee mug with art the girls had done; Vaughan had donated a sizable sum to the library in her name, and Ezra gave her gift certificates for a massage every month for the next year.

There'd been perfume and books—lots and lots of books—movies, cosmetics, pretty pins for her hair and then once the girls had been gifted enough to be sucked into playing with stuff, the couples gave each other gifts.

Paddy brought out a tier of boxes. She cocked her head. "What did you do, Patrick?"

"Open up and see."

It was…hats. Lots and lots of hats. Summer hats and winter hats. Knit caps, a beret, a beautiful hat he whispered she could wear to the Kentucky Derby because that was part of the present, too. Lastly, he gave her a cowboy hat. A simple, classic, elegant cowboy hat. Gray. She'd been admiring that hat two months before in town on a person at a table across from where she and Damien had been sitting.

"How?"

"When you went to the bathroom, I went over and asked where she got the hat. No big deal."

She hugged him. "Total big deal."

"You missed this." He handed her the box again, and she saw the envelope. She opened it to find an itinerary. Paris for a week. "I'd sweep you away for more, but I didn't know how much vacation time you had."

"Wow. You sure know how to give presents."

He grinned. "I did okay, then?"

"More than okay."

"Good. Gimme my present!"

Ezra groaned. "He's been like this since we were kids."

"Hang on. Close your eyes."

She got up and headed into the laundry room where she'd stashed it, knowing a guitar case was pretty recognizable, even wrapped in colorful paper.

By the time she returned, everyone had turned to watch as they'd finished their gift giving. She blushed, cursing that she hadn't done this earlier. She put it down on Paddy's knees. "You can open up."

He did and made a happy little sound when he saw the shape. He tore the paper like a wild man and it made her laugh.

"Love the case," he murmured and then flipped the latches, opening it up. He gasped, as did Damien and Vaughan. Paddy pulled it out and set the case aside, examining the guitar. "Sweet baby Jesus. Is this Ed Chasen's Gibson?"

She nodded.

"How did you even get him… Wow. Wow. Gorgeous, this is…wow." He kept looking down at it, brushing his fingers over the curves, against the strings, over the neck. He placed it back in the case and then grabbed her in a hug. "You're the best girlfriend in the whole world. Thank you. I'm going to take this on tour with me. I can't wait to play it."

He kept on and let her go, kissing her soundly right before he stepped away.

"She's not going to tell you the story of how she convinced Ed to sell her the guitar, so I'm going to because it's the best story ever." Ezra winked at her and proceeded to tell the room how she'd done it.

A FEW HOURS LATER, Sharon approached, putting her arm around Natalie. "You made his entire life. Thank you for being so good to my boy."

"Well, he's… It's not hard."

Sharon laughed. "Sure it is. He's a pain in the butt. But he's worth it, and you see through all that outer stuff straight into the heart of who he is."

She blushed. "Thank you."

"I should also tell you we met our goals two weeks early with the collection drive. Paddy and the rest have been so busy finishing up their record, Michael went with me to drop it all off. We made a lot of happy families at a time of major need. You were so integral to those efforts."

Sharon hugged her.

"That's great news! I have ideas for some things we can do next year, too. There are some food pantries in dire need, and I've spoken with a few of the restaurants in town about maybe doing a themed night where people can choose certain restaurants where a percentage of the receipts can go to the food banks."

Sharon beamed. "Let's meet after the New Year. Come over for dinner and we'll work on some plans. I'll invite some of the folks I've worked with in the past on different charity drives, too. Never hurts to have lots of ideas."

And that made the day absolutely perfect.

CHAPTER TWENTY-ONE

A FEW DAYS after the New Year, Natalie tried on and cast aside several different outfits. "I have no idea what to wear!"

"I told you." Tuesday pointed. "Wear those pants and that shirt with the boots. Supercute. They make your figure look fantastic. The boots are comfortable enough to stand in, and if anyone gets in your way, you can kick them in the face. It's on trend but not *trying too hard to be twenty.* And then I'm doing your hair and makeup."

She blew out a breath. "I agreed to having Paddy mention me in some interviews as the inspiration for the song. I am hedging on the picture and being interviewed myself, though. I am nervous about being pushed to the front. I'm not in the band. I'm not anything more than Paddy's girlfriend. Why that means I'm someone people want to know about makes me superuncomfortable."

"So why do it at all?"

"It's good publicity. He never pushed me one way or the other, but it does help, and I want to help. I just want to be careful where it leads."

"Fair enough."

Tuesday looked awesome in leather pants and a halter top covered in sequins. Natalie could not have carried it off in a million years, but it looked casual and fabulous and the bronze of the sequins brought out the bronze in Tuesday's skin, especially from the shimmer she'd rubbed onto her shoulders. Her hair had grown, too, so it was big and sexy and full-stop fabulous.

"God, you look like a magazine ad. Good call on the lipstick."

Tuesday and Natalie both were of the opinion that there was a shade of red for every woman, and because Tuesday's skin tone was so gorgeous, she could wear reds from coral to deep blue-red. She wore the latter and kept the rest of her makeup light.

Natalie took a look in the mirror at her outfit. She didn't have leather pants and would have been totally uncomfortable in them. But she did have on shiny silver trousers, formfitting, the bottom slightly tucked into the booties she had on with them. Her shirt was pale blue and dipped down in the front deep enough that she wore a camisole that was a darker blue.

Tuesday returned with a great belt to wrap around Natalie's waist a few times and a chunky cuff bracelet in blues with a little bit of earth tones in it. Warm to the pants' cool tones. And it worked.

She added earrings to match the cuff. "We'll let your boobs be the decoration instead of a necklace."

"As one does, of course." Natalie rolled her eyes, but smiled. They weren't hanging out, but they were there showing more than she usually did. "The perfect accessory."

"Truer words, Nats, truer words. Now into the bathroom so I can do your face."

First there was hair. Tuesday did something to give the top some height and slicked the sides back.

She then held still while Tuesday did her makeup with dramatic smoky eyes and liner and a red that was more neutral and sheer so it didn't work against the eyes or the hair.

Tuesday stepped back to survey her work, nodding approvingly. "You clean up nice. He's never seen you so gussied up. You totally look like Paddy Hurley's girlfriend. Like a woman a hot dude writes songs about."

They stood side by side, looking in the mirror. "We totally look fabulous. Thanks for handling my face and stuff. I'm so nervous. Thanks for coming with me."

Tuesday linked arms with her. "Duh. Where else would I be? Also, we look hot. I'm not gonna pass up a chance to go out looking hot."

"Sure, and if Ezra sees you looking sexy as hell, even better."

"Meddlesome." But Tuesday didn't deny it.

They headed down and Natalie grabbed her bag, checking for the credentials that would get them backstage and into restricted areas. Paddy and the guys went in separately. They had sound check and whatever else, including some publicity and interviews.

Tuesday drove, thank goodness, and they parked where Paddy told them to, and at the back entrance, she gave her name and showed her credentials. The guy marked them off the list and motioned them inside, telling her to keep the credentials where they could be seen.

It was sort of like what she thought it'd be on some levels. People milled around, some set stuff up, tested equipment, moved things.

"Where do you think they are? Or should I wait for them to go onstage?"

"What did he say?" Tuesday was calm, which helped keep Natalie calm.

"Come find me when you get there."

"So, your answer is, we need to ask around until we find them. Look, your badge thing is different than the others I see, which means, probably, that you get in places most don't."

She touched someone's arm as they passed. "Excuse me, have you seen Paddy Hurley?"

The person had an earpiece and a clipboard, and he looked at her. She held her badge up and he softened. "You're Natalie, right? Paddy mentioned you might be looking for him. Come on." He jerked his head, and they followed. "I'm Ross, Vaughan's guitar tech."

"Natalie, and this is Tuesday. Thanks for helping. I've never been backstage before."

"No problem." He pushed through a group of people all clamoring for the attention of a guy blocking another hallway.

Ross gave them all a look. "Blue badges. Taking them to the dressing room," he told the tree trunk of a guy blocking access, who then moved to the side.

She heard someone call her name but didn't recognize anyone.

"Shine it on." Ross waved down the hall. "Those are the dressing rooms. Paddy is in one of them. I don't know which, so knock first or you might get to know one of Paddy's brothers more than you want."

Natalie laughed. "Good advice."

Ross headed back the way they'd come.

"What do you think he meant, shine it on?" She listened and decided to knock on the nearest one.

"I think people know you're Natalie, Paddy's girlfriend, and they're going to try to be your friend to use you to get back here."

She looked back over her shoulder as Mary opened,

her eyes narrowed until she recognized Natalie. "Hey, there." She hugged Natalie and Tuesday.

Damien came over. "Coast must be clear." He saw them and also gave them a hug. He wore no shirt and low-slung jeans with heavy boots. He had as much ink as Paddy did. And seriously great arms.

"Hey, you two. Paddy is next door." He pounded on the wall.

Paddy stuck his head out. "What?" His gaze slid past Natalie and then snagged back. "Wow." He grinned, circling his finger to get her to turn, so she did.

"I'm pretty sure I'm glad I didn't know how gorgeous the two of you looked before you got here. Must have gotten quite a bit of attention."

Speaking of attention, Paddy's hair was artfully tousled, he wore a threadbare Sonic Youth T-shirt, leather pants, also low-slung enough to show all of his hip bones, and purple Puma sneakers.

"You look pretty gorgeous yourself." She was going to have to get him to do the outfit when they were alone. Maybe a private game of rock star and groupie.

He hugged her, kissing the side of her neck. "I don't know what you're thinking, but it looks like I'll enjoy it later."

"We don't want to be in the way, so let us know what you need."

"You want to see the stage from back here?"

"Yeah!"

Ezra came down the hall, brightening when he saw them, darkening in a distinctly sexual way when he focused on Tuesday.

"Nats, beautiful, nice to see you." He hugged her,

nervous tension in his muscles. She knew it was his first live show in years.

"I'm so excited to see you up there tonight. You look hot." She winked at him and loved the way he blushed.

"Tuesday, it's been a while." He took her hand, and Natalie's mouth nearly hit the dirt when he turned it to kiss the inside of Tuesday's wrist.

Tuesday's lids dropped just a little, her mouth curving up. "Hey, Ezra. Give me a tour?"

Natalie was torn between wanting to hug her friend for taking his mind off being nervous, and wanting to corner her and demand some facts because there was simply no way these two had only seen each other the two times Natalie had been there when they were in a small group, and the handful of other times when there was a large group. There was intimacy of some type between them.

"My pleasure." He turned to Paddy. "Check with Stuckey. He was looking for you." He drew Tuesday down the hall without another word.

"So you want to tell me what that's all about?" Paddy demanded.

"Me? I was going to ask you. Clearly, there's something going on, and she hasn't mentioned it, even when I poke at her over it. Who's Stuckey?"

"My guitar tech."

He placed a hand at the small of her back, waving at people who called his name, but he kept moving. "By the way, I meant it when I said you looked gorgeous." He leaned in close, ducking them into an alcove. "I want that shade of lipstick on my cock later."

Her heart pounded at his words, at the intensity of his

body against hers. They were in public and yet, wow, it was hot even as it made her a little nervous.

He smiled, that sexy smile that promised all sorts of dirty fun later, and moved back. "Let's find Stuckey. I'm playing my new guitar tonight, and I want to be sure there aren't any problems."

It was all sort of a blur from then on. It got more crowded as more and more people directed Paddy to do stuff, demanded his attention, especially the fans who saw him at the stage from their place up front. It was a fan club crowd so they were pumped up, but the intensity of it was a little nerve-racking.

He brought her to the side of the stage. "I'm going back with the rest of the dudes. We'll be out shortly. Just wait here."

She took his hands, kissing his fingertips. "All right. I don't know if I should wish you luck or if that's a no-no or if I have to wish for broken legs or whatever."

Again, that sexy grin. "Gorgeous, your being here is good luck." He kissed her. Not a quick peck but a full-on, openmouthed swoonworthy kiss that left her breathless and clutching his shirt to keep standing.

"Now, that's even better than wishing me good luck."

He was different. Not like a totally new person, but Paddy on fifty instead of fifteen. And he was already sort of overwhelming at fifteen.

He hustled back to the dressing rooms, and she watched him retreat, loving the way he moved.

"Dude." Tuesday sidled up, both of them watching Paddy's ass. "Spectacular."

"Um, yeah." She turned her attention back to Tuesday. "You totally have some explaining to do."

Tuesday bit her bottom lip for a moment.

"Don't worry, I won't hound you about it right now. But later I expect a full accounting."

"Maybe by then *I'll* understand whatever it is that's happening," Tuesday muttered.

There was a flurry of action—lights adjusted, sound done and the crowd hushed.

They turned to watch the Hurley brothers—no, more than that, Sweet Hollow Ranch—make their way up to the stairs where Natalie and Tuesday stood.

They were all the same, but more. Ezra was with them like he'd never left. Paddy took his guitar from his tech and winked at Natalie before he walked out, Vaughan behind him, and Damien jogged to his drum kit.

Ezra hung back. She took his hand, and he smiled at her. She stretched up to kiss his cheek. "Kick ass, Ezra."

"Thanks, sweetheart, that's my plan."

The crowd lost their shit when Paddy tried to talk. He waited and finally got them quieted. He pointed to his guitar. "Sweet, huh? This is what happens when you have the best girlfriend on the planet."

More hoots and shouts, and she blushed even in the dark.

"Hey, Portland, what's goin' on?" Paddy asked.

Something south of Natalie's belt buckle might have pulsed at how hot he was as he owned his role as Paddy the rock star.

The crowd cheered.

"Awesome. Here's the deal. Tonight we've got some new stuff just for you. We've been working our asses off for a few months, and before Christmas, we finished production on *Day Dream*. It'll be dropping in a few weeks, and then we'll be touring. You guys need to keep an eye on the fan club site for presales. As in, check tomorrow."

More insanity, and Mary came to stand on Natalie's other side.

"We're going to give you all a special sneak peek at the new album. You're the first people outside the studio and the label to hear it, and we figured, why not add something old to something new?"

Ezra stepped forward, taking the guitar his tech handed his way and walked onstage. And *then* the crowd went absolutely bat-shit crazy as they stomped and called EZZZZZZZZZ over and over.

He stepped to the mic and didn't pause at all, just counted into the first song, and they were off.

It was hard to remember everything that happened that night. Once they started singing, it was as though she was swept up into a weird thrill ride.

Mary hugged her at one point. "You look like a deer caught in the headlights."

"I'm overwhelmed by it."

And it *was* overwhelming. Mainly in a good way. Paddy was undeniably sexy. He owned the stage. He crooned and snarled.

He handed his guitar off and headed to the piano. Mary pressed a tissue into Natalie's hand and she nodded her thanks.

"Hush now or you won't hear the first single." He winked and she wasn't the only one swooning. "This one is called 'Silent No More.'"

He closed his eyes as he started to play, leaning in, his lips close to the microphone and began to sing.

She sang along at a whisper and when he opened

his eyes, it was to track her, lock on and sing the chorus to her.

Shivers ran over her skin.

When the song ended, the crowd went wild, and he blew a kiss to Natalie before he moved out to grab his guitar and head up front once more.

BACKSTAGE AFTER THEIR ENCORE, when the lights came up, it was insanity. She would have gotten swept up, but Mary grabbed her on one side and Tuesday on the other and tugged them through the crowds.

One of the security people stopped them but recognized Mary. "This is Natalie. She'll be around with Paddy, so don't give her a hard time."

He smiled at her and made some sex eyes at Tuesday, who gave him the once-over.

"Good Lord, come on."

In one large room, the green room, it said on the door, the guys were laughing, toasting one another and giving each other sweaty hugs and shoves.

Paddy glistened with sweat, his shirt off and tucked into his waistband. His eyes gleamed like he was high, and she supposed he probably was from adrenaline.

"Ezra, my man, you killed the hell out of it." Paddy clapped his brother on the back.

Ezra grinned. "I totally did. Wow, it's been a while. I'm tore up." He laughed. "Good thing I'm in shape, even so, I forgot what it was like to be up there for longer than an hour. An arena show would kick my ass."

He pulled his shirt up and off, mopping his face with it, and Tuesday made a sound under her breath. Mary nudged her with an elbow. "Right? Good gracious."

Damien then looked toward the door, bounding over

to his wife and sweeping her into an embrace. "Curly! How'd we sound?"

"Excellent." She laughed as he kissed her face and neck.

He put his hands on her belly, bending down. "How'd Daddy do, sprocket?"

Paddy wove his way over, looking pretty fierce and sexual, and her heart stuttered as he stopped a breath away. "I'm sweaty."

"Yeah. You totally are."

"You're doing that breathless thing. It makes me feel like a wolf, and you're the rabbit."

She swallowed, blushing.

All around them there was noise and celebration, so no one heard him lean even closer and say, "And I want to eat you all up."

She put a hand on his chest—partly to keep standing because he overwhelmed her. He was warm and real and sweaty or not, it was clean sweat from hard work. And it must have been laced with some major phero- mones because she wanted to lick him.

The Natalie that she was back at the beginning wanted to kick the door down, jump on him right there and ride him to the floor.

"You should see something," he whispered.

"I've seen it."

He laughed, sliding his hand up to cradle the back of her neck.

"It's in my dressing room. It shouldn't take too long to see."

"Better take long enough for *both* of us to see it."

He laughed again, kissing her. "Of course."

Tuesday was talking to Ezra and Mary. Natalie motioned that she was ducking out, and Tuesday waved a lazy hand at her to go on and get some.

He took her hand and dragged her out of the room and two doors down. He ignored the hails of his name, slamming the door once they were inside, locking it.

"Now, then."

Holy cow.

"I believe earlier, I mentioned wanting to see that particular shade of lipstick on my cock. But I'm all sweaty so it can wait. What can't is you dropping those pants and panties, facing the table over here, bracing your hands and waiting for me."

He pulled his shirt from his waistband, wiping his skin down and goodness help her, it probably should have been gross but it was sooo hot. She moved to the table, facing him as she got out of her boots but kept her socks on, and slid her pants and panties off.

He dug in his bag, pulled out a foil packet, and she turned, bracing her hands, sticking her butt out because why lie about how much she wanted it at that point?

"Damn, look at you."

The sound of his pants unzipping made her suck in a desperate breath. His heat at her back and then a kiss to her neck.

Ever the gentleman, even as he was ordering her around, he slid his fingers through her, testing her readiness. He hissed. "You want this as bad as I do," he murmured as he pressed inside with his cock.

She arched to meet him as a driven sort of heat settled in her gut.

"Yes. Give it all to me, Nat. I'm all worked up and I need you."

The table began to thunk against the wall as he thrust harder and harder.

He crooned to her all manner of dirty, sexy things. Some sweet. Some vulgar. All hot. He fucked her as though he couldn't possibly do anything else. His hands roved over her body until one found its way to the spot between her legs she needed him most.

Needed him to soothe that ache that was just out of reach of climax.

He'd gone quiet and she knew he was close. Knew he was waiting for her to go first. She opened her eyes and realized the glass frame on the poster hanging in front of them reflected what they were doing.

He had a smile on his face and she bit her bottom lip, tightening around him with her inner muscles, gripping the edge of that table so hard, her knuckles went white.

A roll of pleasure took her and she let it. Grabbed it, jumped in. Behind her—inside her—she knew he'd met his own end as he made that growling snarl he did when he came.

He kept deep and she gasped, sucking in air, letting go of the table to slap a palm against the wall, going up to her toes to receive him.

"Jesus." A harsh whisper as he pulled out.

She swallowed around a dry throat as she turned to watch him duck into the attached bathroom. She opened a bottle of water, drank half and handed the rest his way.

"Thanks, baby."

She watched his throat work, his Adam's apple going up and down as he swallowed. His gaze never left her as she got dressed.

He grinned, tossing the bottle into a recycle bin.

"You look like your boyfriend just fucked you hard and fast in his dressing room."

She laughed. "It's the new trend. I guess I know why now."

He stepped close, his arm snaking around her waist to pull her to him. "Let me kiss you before you put your lipstick on again."

She did, breathing him in. Loving his taste and the way he felt against her.

"I feel better." He grinned, stepping back.

"I'm glad I was here to help you out."

He could have told her he normally came back and jerked off in the shower to rid himself of the postshow adrenaline jitters. Or availed himself of the women who offered themselves. But Natalie was there now, and what they'd just done was better than fucking his fist or some stranger.

Even better, despite the chaos all around them, she seemed to be dealing with it well. Maybe the key was a good hard fuck to keep her mellow. He could be down with that.

"Let's go back and celebrate awhile. Then we'll go home, and I'll pretend not to scour the media to see what they thought of the material."

"I'm sure we can find a way to keep you occupied some."

He took her hand. "What did you think?"

"You were awesome. The band was awesome. The material sounds great live. I'm so proud of you. How are you going to do the piano thing when you're on tour? If Ezra isn't there to do your guitar parts, how does that work?"

"We have a guitarist and a few other musicians who

tour with us. I'll probably end up playing the guitar and someone else will do the piano."

The room was lively still, filled with friends and family and a few faces Paddy hadn't seen in some time—including Adrian Brown.

"Adrian! Dude, I had no idea you were going to show up."

He shook his friend's hand, grinning.

"Jeremy is around here somewhere. Gillian told me to come down and see the show. My house is overrun by women and babies and toddlers right now." Gillian was Adrian's wife and the mother to his teenaged son and toddler daughter.

"So you're excited to be going back home soon, then?" Damien approached, Mary along with him.

"Thing is? I am. I know my toddler is running around and getting into everything, dancing and singing. This is what happens when you settle down. I miss my gorgeous wife and my kids. My son who is now three inches taller than I am. He's more like his uncle Brody every freaking day. Miles just chose a college. A college. This kid thing happens really fast, Mary. Take lots of pictures because you blink, and they're driving and leaving home."

Paddy turned to Natalie. "Adrian Brown, this is Natalie Clayton."

She held her hand out, and Adrian shook it. "Hey, I've heard all about you. Mary is pretty tight with my wife and they talk about you, so I hear about it that way."

Mary sighed and patted Natalie's arm. "That sounds worse than it is. He means I tell Gillian, who's one of my very best friends, how wonderful I think you are."

"Sorry! Didn't mean for that to sound weird."

Natalie blinked, blushing and smiling, and Paddy put an arm around her shoulder, pulling her close.

They chatted, and Jeremy showed up with some champagne and some sparkling cider for Ezra.

Paddy needed to talk to his brother about all that had happened that night. Honestly. Because having Ezra up there with them had been so good, but not at the expense of his brother's hard-fought mental and physical health.

An hour or so later, Adrian had left to go back home. Jeremy was off to visit with another client, and it was time to wrap up and head back to Hood River.

"I wish you could drive home with me." He kissed her temple.

"Tuesday and I rode in together. Anyway, you probably need to decompress and what do they call it—debrief—after tonight with your brothers, as well."

She was right.

"You'll come to me, though? After you drop Tuesday off at home?" She had the following day off, and he was quickly getting used to waking up with her in his bed.

"Yes."

"Let's all walk out together, then."

They rounded everyone up and headed toward the door.

They walked down that noisy hallway. A woman stepped in front of him with a smirk. "Hey, Paddy. You and your friend here want some company?"

"Uh. No thanks. I've got plenty." He looked to Natalie with a smile, but she did not look happy at all and he got that, too.

He kept himself between Natalie and the other woman, and they went outside. He helped her into her coat.

"We're right over there." She pointed to her car. Tuesday gave Mary a hug and made her way over to where he stood with Natalie at her car.

He got close enough to whisper. "Sorry about that out there."

"We'll talk about it later."

Uh-oh.

"Okay. I'll see you in a little while."

"Yes."

He took her chin, tipping it so he could meet her eyes. "I love *you.*"

"I love you, too."

He brushed a kiss against her mouth and she kissed him back, so whatever she wanted to talk about, it didn't preclude a kiss.

CHAPTER TWENTY-TWO

SHE DROVE EAST, and Tuesday broke into her thoughts. "So, what's going on with you? That face isn't your happy one."

"You first! Oh, my God. I can't believe you held back about Ezra. Tell me every last detail right this moment."

"You're a bossy bitch."

"Damn right I am. Holder backer! You're a *holder backer*. Jeez."

"That's such a dumb insult, I can't even be mad at it. You have a master's degree, and that's the best you've got?"

"You're ducking the subject."

Tuesday sighed. "I don't even know what's going on with me. I haven't told you because I don't know what to think. He's... Oh, my God, he's so intense. I get near him and he looks at me and I can't hear anything else. I can't feel anything else. I see him. I hear him. He listens to me like there's no one else in the world."

"Did you do the sex with him?"

Tuesday burst out laughing at their longtime joke.

"No! We bumped into each other last week. He was in town, and I was walking from the shop to my car, and we saw each other on the street. And then we had dinner and then he walked me back to my car, and he kissed me."

"You kissed Ezra? Oh, my God! I can't believe you got your mouth up in all that, and you didn't say a word. I am so mad at you, but I'm willing to put it aside if you tell me how he kisses."

"How do you think he kisses? First. He smells really good. Not like leather and man or whatever, but he has this cologne and it smells like sex. And so does he. Also, he's superwarm. I was shivering. He opened his coat. He didn't even say anything. He just opened it and looked at me, and I walked into him, and he closed it and he had a hard-on. And then I was like, hello, sailor, and I looked up and he was looking at me, and he kissed me."

She took a breath as Natalie drove, impatiently waiting for the next part of the story.

"I've never in my life been kissed like that before. He just…got up in there and took over. He's the best kisser. The. Best."

"Why do you sound so miserable?"

"What about Eric, Nats? Huh? What about him?"

And suddenly, her annoyance about groupies and that whole backstage business was swept aside by something real. Something deeper.

What could Natalie say? For so long, the subject of Tuesday's dead husband and the wall of grief that had kept her from fully living her life had been one they'd danced around.

But Tuesday was her best friend. The person she loved most in the whole world. Natalie just had to hope she didn't screw it up too badly.

"He's gone, though, Tuesday. That you liked being kissed by someone else doesn't mean you didn't love Eric. Or that you don't still and won't always on some level."

Things stayed quiet as they headed home.

"You've dated here and there." It had been four years. But what sort of timeline can you put on that sort of grief?

"Yes. None of them were…"

"This is different."

"I don't know. I don't know, and I don't like that."

"Okay. But what kind of life is this? Eric wouldn't want you to date dudes you know you'd never care about just so you can have sex."

"Eric is dead, Natalie. He doesn't have wants anymore." Tuesday's voice went flat, her tone signaling the end of the discussion.

"Okay, then. He's gone. And you can't just turn your life off because you come across someone who makes you *feel* something."

"I don't know. I'm too tired to think about it anymore right now. Tell me what your grumpy face meant."

"Meh. Doesn't matter. So let's watch scary movies and make popcorn. We won't go to bed until after sunrise and sleep all day."

"You're going to Paddy's tonight."

"He's going to be buzzed on that show for days. You and I haven't really hung out since you got back from Tennessee. He'll understand, and it's not like I won't see him tomorrow, anyway."

Tuesday waved a hand. "I don't need to be babysat. Also, we have so hung out. Today. Yesterday. Stop. I'm a little blue, it's not the end of the world. Oh, my problems. A superhot dude laid a kiss on me! Woe."

"I don't want you by yourself wallowing in this stuff. Alone with your memories."

"I *am* alone in my memories, Nats. The person I

made them with is dead. Oh, I know I'm not supposed
to say this stuff. It makes everyone uncomfortable. But
it's still true."

"Who says you're not supposed to say it? I'm sorry
if I made you feel that way. I want you to talk about it.
I want to listen to you. I know I can't fix it, but I'm always here to listen."

"No, not you. You're the only one who will talk to
me about it. Everyone else wants me to move on because it's been four years now."

"It's not that I don't want you to move on. I do. Not
on, that's not right. Forward. Because you can't go back.
But I get that it hurts. And I know you're struggling, and
I wish I could make it better. I want you to say whatever the hell you want to. If you can't be open with me,
who can you be open with?"

Tuesday blew out a breath. "I don't want to talk about
it anymore. Thank you, and I mean that, for listening
and always being here, but I just don't want to deal with
it right now. I want you to drop me home so I can take a
long, hot shower and go to bed. I want you to leave me
there and go to your boyfriend's house. I need to be by
myself and you need to be with him. He's going to be
heading out on tour soon enough. Get as much of him
as you can before that happens."

PADDY LOOKED OVER at Ezra, who'd chosen to drive. He
was a great designated driver, but he was high on performing, too. And he was a control freak—a lot like the
one Paddy'd fallen in love with.

"You were on fire tonight."

Ezra grinned. "It felt really good to be up there. I
can't lie."

"We missed you." Damien spoke from the backseat. "It's not the same without all four of us up onstage."

"How are you feeling?"

Ezra blew out a long breath. "A lot of ways. I...I was wondering if I still had it."

Paddy had to face that each time they started a new recording session. Each time he started to write a new song, he wondered if his best work was behind him. So he understood it on one level. But for Ezra, he knew things were way more complicated.

"You do. You never lost it. You just lost your way for a while." Vaughan sometimes was the smartest of all the brothers. He was full of shit a lot of the time, but he was so much more insightful than Paddy gave him credit for.

Vaughan continued, "The question is, Ezra, not whether you have it or not. You prove that every time we make a new album. But how you want to go forward."

Paddy agreed. "You don't have to answer now, either. We have some time before we need to deal with tour musicians and all that."

"I need to think about it. But that aside? This material kicks ass."

"Loved the crowd response to 'Silent No More' and 'Bright Light.' I did not expect that reaction to 'Chemicals.'"

The discussion shifted to what songs seemed to be the crowd favorites and which might need some tweaking live. They poked fun at Damien for breaking a stick and at Paddy for forgetting a line in one of their new songs. It was normal and good, and he realized how much he'd missed having Ezra be part of this.

But his brother had asked for some time, and they'd

give it to him. And they'd be all right no matter what he decided.

"So. Tuesday." Damien prodded from the back. "You gonna share what's going on there or what?"

"Nothing's going on there. She's a beautiful woman. She's our Nat's best friend. Just being friendly."

Paddy laughed at that. "If I was that friendly to Tuesday, Natalie would smother me with a pillow in my sleep."

"That's because I'm the superior brother."

"Fine. Button up and don't tell us anything. You're stingy, Ezra. Selfish and stingy, and you're going to hell." Vaughan whapped the back of Ezra's head, making him laugh.

"Asshole. I'll see you there, I guess."

"Paddy has his own table. I guess he can make us all set it perfectly over and over until the end of time." Damien snorted.

"That's purgatory, though, right? Like when we finally get it right, we can advance to heaven?"

It went on that way the rest of the way back to the ranch.

HE'D ONLY BEEN home about twenty minutes, long enough to build a fire and change into a robe—he planned to sweet-talk her into a shower with him—when she knocked on his door.

He opened up. His heart always beat faster when he caught sight of her, and that night she'd looked so fucking gorgeous, so rock and roll in her unique, Natalie way that she stole his breath.

"Come in out of the cold, gorgeous."

She kissed him quickly as she passed, and he shut the door, closing the night away.

"I think we should shower, and then I propose food. I'm so hungry but I'm sticky and sweaty, too. So you can rub me clean, and I'll watch you look gorgeous and wet, and then I promise whatever Mary has left in my fridge."

She gave him a look over her shoulder and went upstairs. He followed, entranced by the switch of her hips as she led the way.

"I really like those pants."

"I forgot I had them. I suppose now might be the time to confess Tuesday is much better at this sort of dressing-to-be-the-girlfriend-of-the-lead-singer-of-the-band thing than I am."

He laughed, swatting her butt. He'd taken her bag downstairs so he tossed it in his bedroom, and then they headed into the bathroom to grab that shower.

"Let me." He pushed her hands out of the way and pulled her shirt off, and then the undershirt. "I like this bra." It was blue, like the undershirt had been. Blue against all that pale, creamy skin. He hummed and pressed a kiss to the luscious curve of her right breast.

"It's new. The bra, I mean."

"I love it when you do that."

He unhooked the bra and bared her breasts.

"Buy bras?"

He popped the top button of her pants and unzipped. And dropped to his knees to help her from the boots before he pulled the pants down.

"Well, now."

The panties had a corset sort of lace-up thing at the

front. Dipping enticingly low to expose the top of her pussy.

"Those are new, too." She turned, and he saw the back had the same lace-up V at the butt.

"Daddy like."

He slapped her butt.

She got the giggles, and he joined her, surging to his feet and pulling her close. "Damn, I'm lucky."

She sobered. "You are. Also, the hot *I just got off stage* sweat is now edging into *I stink* territory."

He shoved her underpants down and dropped his robe before stepping into the shower stall and turning it on full blast.

"Used to be I'd smell like sweat, booze and cigarettes. Now that you can't smoke in as many places, it's one less thing to stink me up."

"You can add women to that list."

He grinned. "Woman? Because my hands smelled like you after I fucked you in my dressing room. I like that way better than cigarettes."

"You sure you want to go down this conversational road while we're naked?"

He soaped up, watching her do the same. He might have had a death wish to talk about groupies—and he knew that was where the discussion was heading—while they were naked and in close quarters. But at least it'd be while he watched soap slide over her nipples.

"I hate it. Just telling you up front. I know it's part of your world and all, but I hate it. It's bad enough that you're gorgeous and charming and rich and famous. But that backstage stuff? Women just offering you sex every few steps? I don't know what to do with it."

"You know I'm with you, right? That nothing would happen ever? I get all I need at home, you got me?"

"And what about when you're out on the road and you're not home? What about when you come off the stage and you're all…well, the way you are and you want to get off, and I'm not there?"

"Are you so quick to assume I'd cheat on you instead of jerk off? God. I like to think you know me better than that. What have I ever done that would indicate to you that I'd fuck you over?"

She stood under the water and he realized he was dumb for pushing this discussion. He wanted her pliant and warm, not pissed off.

But now he was pissed off, too, because he hadn't done a thing to make her distrust him.

"As it happens, I don't think you'd cheat on me. I said the same to Mary last month. But what? Am I supposed to lie about how it makes me feel? Am I supposed to pretend? I'm trying and I know you are, too, but you asked me and kept asking until I answered. I'm sorry, though, that I hurt your feelings."

"It comes with the territory. Like booze and drugs and getting ripped off by industry people. I can manage to avoid all that other stuff. You can trust me to avoid the former, too."

She got out of the shower and he followed, catching the towel she threw to him. "You poke at me to be honest, and when I am, you punish me. That's an unwinnable situation, and next time I'm going to think twice before I answer."

He dried off, watching as she headed into the bedroom, naked while she rooted through her bag for her clothes.

He was crazy, but fighting with her turned him on. So stupid. She was angry, and he'd pushed her to that place. Worse, she was right. He couldn't ask for her trust and then punish her for giving it to him.

"You have no idea what it's like, Patrick." She turned, pulling a long-sleeved sleep shirt on and then stepping into panties. He groaned slightly when she put pants on over that. "You've never had to. Put yourself into that place, I mean. But try. For one moment, imagine if really hot men propositioned me multiple times every day. If I did a job where I got all worked up, and they were in my path, and I was away from you. How would you feel?"

"I'd trust you to remember what we have. And that's what I'm asking you to do."

"I *do* trust you. Asshole. I just said I did. I didn't flip out at the club. Or even just now. I came over here. I'm still with you. You kept at it, and I told you I hated it and didn't know what to do with it. Me being mad now is about your reaction."

Oh.

He sucked in a breath. And then he remembered, and heard the apology she'd given while they were still in the shower. "You're right. But I love you. I'm with you. I don't want anyone else. When I'm away from you, I'll still love you and I'll still be with you and I'll still only want you. It's a three-month tour. Come out whenever you want. I'll leave it open for you to show up. Always have credentials waiting. Hell, take a leave and come with us like Mary will." Mary would probably kick his ass if he did anything stupid, anyway. Ha. Probably. More like definitely.

"Ugh. I don't want to be with you if I feel like I have

to check up on you. I don't think you'll cheat on me. It's just gross and uncomfortable and it makes me unhappy. But it's part of the world you inhabit, so I just need to figure out how to process it. I do want to come out when I can, but not because I don't trust you. Because if I can't trust you, this isn't worth the energy. But I can't just take a leave. It doesn't work that way. I have vacation time, and I can shift around a little here and there with my coworkers, but that's what I've got to work with."

He sighed. He wanted to say—and wisely did not— that she could quit her job and hang with him. Wanted to ask her to move in with him. She could volunteer and do her own thing and not have to hold down a regular job. Hell, she had the means to do just that.

But she loved her job, and working to make her way meant something to her, so he kept his mouth shut.

Natalie took him in, clearly torn between annoyance and amusement. "If you're looking for an easy woman, you're with the wrong one. This isn't a problem that's ever really going away, so we just have to figure a way to deal with it."

He took a risk to get closer, and when she didn't maim him, he pulled her into a hug. "Okay. We'll just have to do this step by step."

"The only way we can is if we're honest. And I can't be honest if I can't trust you not to be mad when I tell you how I'm feeling. It's hard enough to admit being jealous."

He got that, too. It had taken him until that very moment as he held her, the warmth of her seeping into him, to *truly* understand a few things.

She had given him her trust. Every time she let him

take control, control he knew she held on to like a security object.

It was a continued reminder to be careful with it. To deserve it.

"I'm sorry I reacted that way. I just… I've never done this before. Never been with anyone like I am with you. I can't help what stuff comes along with my life sometimes. You seemed okay about it when it happened in Portland. I just…I'm sorry. I do want you to trust me. So we step carefully."

She nodded. "And I'm sorry if I made you feel like I didn't trust you. As for Portland?" She pulled away, and he would have complained but she looked back over her shoulder. "You promised food."

He laughed, taking her hand, relieved when that connection zinged between them again.

"Sit, and I'll toss something together." He pointed to a chair at the kitchen island.

"Want me to do any media checking while you do?"

"My iPad is there. Check the fan club site first. They'll be the best source for now."

She watched him work because he wore no more than low-slung sleep pants. So low slung the blades of his hips showed. Natalie shivered before she turned to the task she'd just volunteered to do.

She scrolled through, smiling at the comments in the live show forums. "They have a forum started for tonight's show and already have one for the new album, as well. Everyone thinks Ezra looked and sounded fantastic. Lots of *you're so lucky* comments from people who weren't there. They're very dedicated to be on this so fast."

The show had only been over for hours, and there were already a hundred posts. Including pictures.

"What songs are they talking about? Oh, and salsa on your burrito?"

"There are burritos?"

"Damn, I think you sound more excited about a burrito than me."

"I already fucked you a few hours ago. I haven't eaten since six. Priorities. Plus, it's only a matter of time before you jump me again. I need to keep my strength up."

"Okay, then. I'm glad you seem to have a fine grasp on the way things are." He winked, and she rolled her eyes.

"They loved 'Bright Light' and 'Silent No More' best it seems like. Not that I'm biased or anything, but the girl you wrote that one for is pretty lucky. Anyway, they also loved 'Chemicals' and 'Here Comes Trouble.' There are pictures here, too. Of you guys."

"We have a photographer and media guy. He was backstage tonight, and he also sends stuff to the fan club site for them to post."

"Yeah, hang on, there's a link to the band's official website." She clicked it to a gallery of shots taken from that show. "Your people are really efficient."

She paused, smiling at one, a candid, taken of the two of them in a hallway. Before the show. Her head was tilted to look up at him, a smile on her face, eyes wide. He looked like he was about to lick her. There was so much sex between them in that moment, it leaped off the page.

"Hot damn. I sure do want to get all up in whatever

you've got." He stood behind her, sliding a plate within her reach. "You're beautiful. Holy shit."

The note beneath it said, *"Silent No More."*

"Yeah, so I guess this is part of that rebranding thing."

He turned the stool so she faced him. "You said you were okay with it. I know you're sort of overwhelmed by my world right now, but I want to stay on the same page. I can call him and have them remove it right now if you want me to."

It was three in the morning and she had no doubt at all he'd do it and not be angry.

She shook her head. "No, you're right. I said I was okay with it and I am. I'd rather this than be interviewed. We talked about that."

He kissed her forehead. "It's a great picture."

She smiled and wrapped her legs around him to hold him close. "Yeah. Thanks for the burrito."

He grinned, kissing her quickly. "Eat up. We have time to have at least an orgasm or two before we sleep and rest up for the rest."

CHAPTER TWENTY-THREE

WINTER HAD SETTLED in and didn't seem to want to make way for spring, though March 21 had come and gone. The extended cold made Paddy's being gone even harder. Ezra had elected to do the second secret show in Seattle and the opening and closing shows of the tour itself, but passed on the rest.

They'd left nearly two months before and had been busily blazing a trail across the country.

He called her every single day so she knew he missed her, but she heard the excitement in his voice and knew, too, that this was an important part of his life. Their album dropped and was doing amazing.

She was incredibly proud of him, and she tried to keep really busy so she didn't have time to mope or miss him, much less think about what it might be like out there for them.

Speaking of Ezra, she needed to get a move on. She was having lunch with him in less than ten minutes at her favorite Mexican food place in town. The Hurleys had sort of taken her in while the band was out on tour. It had been…startling and yet really nice. She and Sharon had coffee or dinner at least once a week, and Ezra was her regular lunch date.

She closed the project she'd been working on, grabbed her coat, hat and gloves and headed out.

She hated driving in the snow, and Hood River was currently blanketed in it, so she walked over to the restaurant and was freezing cold by the time she hurried through the doors.

"Hey, Nats." Ezra waved from a table, standing and moving to take her coat and give her a hug and a kiss on the cheek. "Darlin', you're so cold." He enveloped her into another hug, rubbing his big hands up and down her back and arms a moment.

It didn't feel creepy or sexual at all. It felt…as though he was her family.

She grinned his way as he set her back with a kiss on her forehead. "Sit down. They just came by and took my order for some hot chocolate. I got two."

"You're the best Hurley ever."

He laughed as she settled across from him. "How are you? You look fantastic. Even the red cheeks make you pretty."

"Wow, I'm paying for lunch now."

They looked over the menu, but she knew exactly what she was going to have. The same thing she always had, the giant veggie burrito.

"Been two months now. How are you? Missing Paddy?"

"I haven't shaved my legs since he left. It's cold, and I'm always in pants, so no one's gonna see anything, anyway. That's a plus. Otherwise? Yeah, I miss him." She waited a beat. "And how are you?"

He looked up as the server brought more chips and salsa, and they gave their orders.

His smile was wry. "I could pretend I don't know what you mean. But…there's something about you that makes my tongue loosen up."

"Maybe you've just held on to the words too long. It's not good for you. Some things need to be said so you can be free of them."

One of his brows rose for a moment. "Someone's been to therapy."

She laughed, reaching out to pat his hand. "Yeah. It helped put some stuff into perspective. If you're interested, I can give you someone's name."

"Ha. I've got my own therapist. Though I haven't been in a while. Anyway, with performing? It's addicting in a lot of ways. Doing something you love. Being up onstage. Hearing the cheers. You can't so much see faces as you simply know they're all there. For you. They clap and stomp. They sing lyrics you wrote. They…they're into something you made. And that's… I'm not sure I can really explain just what it is. But it's amazing. An ego boost to get you through the days when everything else in your life is shit. It feeds your soul. But it's dangerous, too. Because it's easy to let that become normal. And it's not."

Their food came out, and they ate awhile in silence.

"Anyway, I love the road. I loved it before I fucked everything up. And it's not so much that I think I'm going to end up in the gutter again if I'm out there. Musicians do it every day. I'm around people who drink and to be totally honest with you, it doesn't bug me. It's not the alcohol that was my big problem, anyway." He snorted.

Natalie thought about how the depth of her father's addiction had shot down deep when he started using opiates. Wondered if Ezra ever was tempted.

Instead of asking that in a crowded restaurant, she

kept it fairly safe. "Mary said it's like a totally different reality on tour."

He nodded. "Time is different. You don't sleep enough. You don't eat right." He grinned. "Though now that Mary tours with them, that's not an issue. But you're off. And home is so far away. Every night you're filled with this adulation. The rush of it is like nothing else. Normal isn't so normal. Your life is filled with people who never question you, never say no to you. In the early days, it was worse. Backstage was like a three-ring circus of chicks, drugs, booze. It was wild every moment. So much that you start to believe your own hype machine. I'm not scared of doing heroin again. I'm scared of getting out there and losing the self I had to go to hell and back to find."

She took his hand again, squeezing it.

"I don't understand *your* journey because it's yours. But I know what it means to find yourself and be terrified of losing it. Of fighting every single day not to lose ground you fought so hard for. If you need to not go out there, or to manage your exposure to it so you can have what you love in the way it takes to be healthy, you know your brothers support that. They love you. More than that, they respect you, and they want the best for you."

"I can see, in so many ways, why Paddy loves you. Why you're different from all the others."

She needed to hear that more than she'd realized. She swallowed back the emotion the statement brought— or tried to.

She thought of all he'd just revealed to her and decided to share, too. "I needed that, Ezra. I miss him, and while I trust him, I do my best not to think on anything but what he tells me. Which seems like I'm hiding from the truth."

"Bullshit. You're managing your shit. That's not hiding. You've been to shows now, you know what it's like. It's totally normal to be overwhelmed by it. Wise to be suspicious of it. You letting Paddy fill you in is a lot more an act of trust than fantasizing about what he might be doing. That's what's important, anyway. Not the shit outside the dressing rooms or off the stage."

"I guess." She blew out a breath.

"You give Paddy something real. Something heavy to hold him, and that's not negative. He needs to be anchored. Everyone does so they won't blow away in a storm."

"You need to use that line in a song."

"I will." He winked, and she sipped the hot chocolate.

"So, if there was something in the media, and it was about you, but it would upset you, would you want to see it, anyway?"

Her happiness went sour. "What is it?"

Ezra pushed a sheet of paper across the table. "Jeremy sent it to me yesterday. He got it off a celebrity gossip website."

The title of the article was Father's Desperate Cry for Help for His Daughter. A picture of her father was below it as he held up one of the photos snapped of Natalie and Paddy at the secret shows Sweet Hollow Ranch had played before going off on tour.

Her father had gone off to some fucking tabloid and sold a story about her. She placed a hand over her stomach, pressing hard as she read the details of her life spilled through her father's self-centered perspective, which painted him as a self-sacrificing single dad who only wanted a relationship with a daughter who so cruelly rejected him.

"Jesus." Her skin had gone clammy. "I wish I could say I couldn't believe he'd do such a thing, but I can't. And I…" She looked up to Ezra to catch the empathy on his face. Not pity—that would have driven her away—but empathy. "Is Jeremy mad?"

Ezra shook his head. "Hell, no. Look, this is part and parcel of this whole thing. I know you have reservations about the life Paddy leads. I care about you and I like you with my brother. I could have kept it from you, but I didn't want you blindsided with it. Chances are? No one is going to run with this story. But if it's slow and someone wants to, the last thing you need is to have this shit shoved in your face without knowing about it first."

"I keep thinking I'm finally free of him. I draw my boundaries around myself clearly. I communicate to him that I don't want him in my life, and he never stays gone. He's told the world about stuff I've never said outside therapy. I've tried to not be bitter, to understand he's not a fully formed person, you know, like bread that's not cooked all the way through? But this is… He's accusing *me* of being an addict? Me?" She scrubbed her hands over her face. "You're not going to ask me why I won't forgive and forget?"

Ezra's laugh was entirely without humor. "Having been through the process and the programs and all the stuff that comes with it, I'm in a unique position. Forgiveness, like respect, needs to be earned. You can't just say you're seeking to make amends and not mean it. The amends can't be all about the person seeking them, either. My sponsor was really clear about that. I did ugly stuff. I'm lucky my family and friends forgave me. But I wasn't owed forgiveness, and I understood they needed to see that I was not only truly sorry, but that I was going to do my best not to do it again. Your father sounds like a piece of shit. And he's going to be a piece of shit even if he was straight because some people are just pieces of shit. You don't have to let that into your life now. You don't owe him anything. I do think, for your own mental health, you need to let go. But as far as I can tell, you're trying."

He lifted a brow. "Sometimes the only way you can survive and move on is to wall the people who are poison out of your life. And sometimes those people will never allow themselves to truly see what they are. He's a coward for that."

It was as though he had given her permission to feel the way she did. Not that she hadn't owned her feelings in the past. She had. But it meant something to her that he'd said all he had. And that he saw her father for what he was. Made her feel less of a jerk for not letting him back in one more time.

It hit her again, the depth of her father's utter lack of concern for anyone but himself. And she was caught in it, even when she desperately didn't want to be.

Ezra got up, moved to kneel next to her and encircled her in his arms.

"I can't. I can't fall apart. I need to go back to work. So go over there and sit and tell me about your pig or whatever."

He snorted but kissed the top of her head and did what he was told.

AFTER WORK, SHE showed up at Tuesday's shop at closing time. She slapped the paper down on the counter.

Tuesday read it, her eyes going wide. "That mother-fucker! I'm going to hunt him down and kick him in the taint for hours. What are we going to do?"

"First I'm going to thank you for being so wonder-ful and jumping straight to the taint-kicking threats."

"Number one rule of best friends, hello."

"And then I'm going to pack because I'm getting on a plane tomorrow to Chicago. I'll be back in a few days. I need…"

"You need Paddy." Tuesday smiled. "And thank goodness you're going to admit it. Does he know about this?" She indicated the interview.

"If he does, he didn't find out through Ezra. I asked him to let me tell Paddy in person. I don't think he's heard it anywhere else, either. He texted me a while ago. Today is a travel day for them, so he's sending me pictures from airports. He needs to know I'm coming to him with this, you know? That I trust him to share my stresses."

"In the past you tried on your own and it made him pissy. I'm glad you're doing this. Like a big girl and everything."

"He has been someone I can rely on. Someone I can count on, and you know what that means to me. He's really trying, so I'd be a jerk if I didn't, too. Plus? I want to hold him." Now that she'd started to be more open, it had become something that actually made her feel better. Even if all he did was listen.

"Nothing wrong with needing that, Natalie. Let him. He wants you to need him, too."

"Yeah, well, I do. Guess I have to shave my legs now. Either that or wear thigh-high socks the whole time."

They'd driven in together that day, Tuesday ever the

efficient snow driver and Natalie a snow wuss, even after years in Washington and Oregon. It worked out nicely.

Once home, Tuesday offered to make dinner while Natalie dealt with everything.

She made plane reservations and arranged for a car to pick her up at the airport to take her to the arena. She and Mary texted a bit, Mary assuring her she was welcome, that Paddy would love to see her and that she thought a surprise would be fantastic. She told Natalie she'd handle the hotel situation and gave her all the info she'd need to get from the airport to the hotel, to get her checked into Paddy's room and then to get to the venue from the hotel.

All that done, she headed downstairs to find a glass of wine and some hot soup and grilled cheese sandwiches.

She looked to Tuesday and sighed. "You're the best. Totally perfect. Thanks."

They ate as she filled Tuesday in on all the details. She'd head to Portland in the morning for her flight and would return two days after when Sweet Hollow Ranch moved to the next city.

They talked around Ezra and their lunch. Natalie pushed but kept it gentle because she didn't want to rip open any wounds and then leave town. There was something between Tuesday and Ezra, but her friend wasn't able to put it into words yet.

Because Natalie understood that, and loved Tuesday, she let it go.

AT THE AIRPORT the next morning, Natalie grabbed a latte and a stack of beauty and fashion magazines and settled in to wait for her plane's departure. That's when her phone rang with a private number.

It was automatic for her thumb to swipe and take the call. After all, sometimes Paddy called from a phone in his dressing room or the hotel.

But it wasn't Paddy.

"Natalie, it's your father."

She hung up and then with shaky hands, blocked that number.

Years ago, she might have listened to him, hoping he'd be calling to apologize for whatever he'd done to precipitate the call. But she knew better by then.

Her grandmother called next, and she let the call go straight to voice mail, and by the time her plane boarded, she was glad she let Tuesday convince her to take a Xanax when she'd arrived at the airport. She hated flying. Hated that loss of control.

But she was on her way to see Paddy, and that was worth it.

So she got on, slid the sleep mask over her eyes and settled in. Even better, she didn't wake until she landed in Chicago and found the car waiting for her.

ONCE SHE'D ARRIVED at the hotel to freshen up and drop off her bags, she smiled when she found the tray with chilled juice and snacks waiting for her on Mary's direction.

It was lovely to be taken care of.

Natalie did her best to mimic the stuff Tuesday had done with her makeup. She came pretty close, and once she'd swiped on some deep red lipstick, it worked. She'd just gotten a great haircut a few days before, so she managed to re-create most of what her hairdresser had done.

Her Tuesday-approved outfit was a pair of slim-legged dark pants with clunky boots. The bonus was they were warm, and she'd have some traction in the snow and ice. Her leather jacket was one she'd had since high school. A splurge of her meager summer job savings from a shop on Melrose. It had been worth every penny in the years since, though she'd had to have the lining done over twice; it was a great warm jacket and went well with the red T-shirt that mimicked the color of her lipstick.

She gave herself a look in the mirror as she slid on a wide cuff at her wrist and opted for studs in her ears instead of dangles.

No time like the present.

She tucked money into her pocket along with her identification and grabbed the credentials Mary had left, along with the snacks and headed to the car waiting out front.

"Wow, so did you win an all-access pass thing to this show?" The driver was chatty, which was fine because suddenly she was nervous, which was so stupid.

"No. I'm a friend of Paddy's. The lead singer?"

"Ah. So are you a musician, too?"

She laughed. "Nope. I'm a librarian."

"Really? My daughter is a librarian in Bloomington. Times are tough. Her hours keep getting cut. She's doing the job of three people."

"It's really frustrating out there right now. We've got the same issues. Most libraries do. I love my job, but I do get afraid I'll lose it."

He seemed to take that little bit of sharing to heart, because when he pulled up at the back entrance, and she showed the guard there her credentials, the driver handed her a business card. "If you need a ride again while you're here, give me a call. It's cold, and I'm better than a cab. You be safe, all right?"

He opened her door after shooing the guard away.

She shook his hand and thanked him.

Luckily, she had some good directions from Mary so she managed to get inside and down and around to where the backstage area was.

And stopped as she took it all in.

Women lined the hall, some drinking, some lounging, some clearly on the prowl. Someone, or lots of someones, given the level of scent, was smoking pot. On one level that was good because it was a smell that always made her think of college, especially if there was a hint of patchouli involved. It also slightly masked the gross, flat-alcohol smell and the acid whisper of puke.

She made her way through the first hall and reached another checkpoint. There was a clog, again, mainly of women claiming to be on this or that list. Mary had warned her not to bother waiting and to push her way forward.

So she did.

One woman grabbed her. "Wait your turn, bitch."

"I don't have to wait my turn. I belong here." She shoved past and waved her credentials, nearly slapping the hand of the woman who tried to snatch them.

"Seriously? Back up."

The massive bodyguard sort of waded in, grabbed Natalie and helped her through.

"I remember you from the Seattle show." He grinned, not looking nearly as scary. "Natalie, right? Paddy's gonna be happy to see you."

She smiled. "I hope so. Um…Ron! You're Ron."

"Good memory." He tapped another guy standing there on the shoulder. "Take Natalie to where the band is. She's with Paddy. This is Paul. He's going to get you to where you need to be. It's a bit of a hike."

Paul nodded and pointed her to a golf-cart-type thing that was clearly built to move in these back hallways.

"This is a great venue because we can keep most people back there. Some manage to get in who aren't supposed to, but it's easier to control. Here we go." He pulled to a stop in front of another checkpoint.

Their overhead for all this security must have been huge.

"Hey, Matt, I've got Natalie with me." Paul indicated Natalie as he spoke to the guy at the checkpoint. "She's Green access."

She held up her neck badge thing with a smile.

"Mary said to be on the lookout." Matt opened the rope thing and she went through.

"Thanks for the ride, Paul."

"No problem. Have a great show."

Matt jerked his head. "Head down that set of stairs right there to your left. The dressing rooms and green room are below. You'll probably hear them before you see them."

She thanked him and made her way down. Again stopping when she got to the main hallway.

More chaos but at least these were people she recognized. Paddy and Vaughan stood in one large room, the green room she remembered, taking shots. Paddy was shaggier than he'd been the last time she'd seen him. A little rough around the edges.

Mary sat tucked up on a couch, reading a book as Damien drummed on stuff relentlessly.

"Can I help you find something? Or someone?"

Natalie turned to see someone walking her way.

"Uh." She pointed into the room where Paddy was. "Found him. Thanks."

Paddy looked up from where he'd been sucking on a lime and his face lit at the sight of her.

"You're here!" He bounded over and swept her into a hug, swinging her off her feet before he put her down, kissing her soundly.

Man, she'd missed him enough to ignore the salt of tequila and the tang of lime.

She kissed him back, heard nothing else but the beating of her heart and the rush of blood in her ears as he took her from nervous to hot for him in seconds.

He broke, setting her back, looking her up and down. "You look fantastic."

She handed him a tissue. "You have lipstick."

He dabbed it off as Damien and Vaughan rushed forward to give her a hug. Mary was slower to get up as she was at the seven-month mark. "Glad you made it in all right."

"Thanks for handling everything. The food and juice were exactly what I needed after the flight."

"You knew she was coming and you didn't mention it?" Paddy slid an arm around Natalie's waist, hauling her close. "Best surprise ever."

He was tipsy. But it was okay. She realized this was different for him, part of how he was on the road. It wasn't like it had been before, either. He wasn't slurring and out of control.

"Show's gonna start in a few. Let's be sure we have you a headset and stuff."

Mary patted his arm. "Handled already."

"You're awesome. Thank you, honey. Now if you'll excuse us for a minute or two."

He took her out into the hallway and into a room two doors down and closed the door.

"Now. I need to kiss the hell out of you. *Months* without touching you. FaceTime is fine, especially when you let me talk you into dirty stuff. But this is a million times better."

He pulled her close, grabbing two handfuls of her butt as he did, grinding himself against her. "You've made me hard already."

Then he kissed her.

The kiss in the green room had been a nice one. But this one? This was a hot, dirty mouthfuck of a kiss and it sent shivers racing all over her skin as he slid his tongue between her gums and lip, against the inside of her mouth. He nipped her lips, sucked on her tongue, breathed her in like he had to simply to exist.

Her nipples hardened as the notch between her legs got slick and swollen. Her breath came shorter and it was filled with him. He kissed and kissed and kissed her until he broke away, chest heaving as he tried to breathe.

Her fists held on to the front of his shirt as she tried to keep her shaky legs. "Wow."

"I've missed you. So much. That kiss is a down payment on what's going to happen when we get back to the hotel after the show. I'm going to lick you until you beg me to stop. And then I'll lick you some more. And that's before I fuck you. How long do I have you for?"

She swallowed hard and cleared her throat to find her voice again. "Day after tomorrow. I'm here for tonight's show and tomorrow night's. I leave after."

"I'll take what I can get. Damn. Baby, I'm so happy

to see you." He tipped his forehead to hers. "You look so hot right now, it's taking all my self-control not to bend you over something."

A series of bells sounded, and he groaned. "We're up. Come on. You can leave your stuff here. By the way, love that jacket."

She grinned and told him the story as they walked, hand in hand, down the corridor and then up some steps to the stage. He paused, waiting for his brothers. The opening band, Subzero Supernova, had gathered to watch them play, and Paddy introduced her quickly.

She barely managed to keep herself from fan-girling all over them. She'd loved them for years, and it had continued to frustrate her that they didn't get the attention they so clearly deserved.

Paddy grinned at Shelly Avenida, their lead singer. "Did I ever tell you that Natalie was the one who suggested you guys as openers? She loves your stuff. Not more than my stuff. I mean, come on." He winked.

Shelly turned to Natalie. "Really?"

"I saw you guys at Evergreen. Like ten years ago. I bought a CD out of the trunk of someone's car that night."

"Wow. That's awesome. Thank you."

"Nah, thank you. *Soul Food Suicide* and *Atone* got me through grad school. Well, that and violent video games."

Paddy held her close, and she let herself be comforted by the way it felt. She'd tell him about her father later. Let herself simply enjoy this while she had it.

"Here we go." He turned Natalie in his arms to face him. "Kiss me for good luck?"

She stretched to kiss him. "Kick ass, Patrick Hurley."

He grinned, kissed her hard and fast and jogged out as their name was announced.

The smaller club show was one thing. She loved live music, had gone to shows pretty often. She could wrap her head around that, even with her boyfriend up on-stage.

But this? This was…so much more than she could even begin to get around. The crowd didn't just cheer, they *roared*. The sound echoed up from the floor she stood on, rattling her bones.

She couldn't have stopped the smile on her face if she'd tried.

The Paddy at the microphone was hers. Yes, long and tall, the width of his shoulders sliding down to nip at his waist. That ass his jeans only made hotter, his Puma sneakers she'd found out he had a collection specifically to wear on tour. Tonight they were poison-green with a purple stripe.

He caressed the guitar she'd given him in much the same way he touched her.

"Hey, it's you." He teased the words out like a sexy come-on line and given the reaction of the crowd, it to-tally worked. "Love that haircut." He winked, and she burst out laughing.

The crowd yelled out song titles, and he held a hand to his ear. "Did y'all have a request or two? Because I was thinking." He paused and turned to the band. They went into a huddle, with Paddy looking over his shoul-der in her direction a few times before he winked and headed back to the mic.

"Sorry, I had to be sure everyone remembered this one. This is 'Dive Bar,' and it goes out to my gorgeous blonde love."

She'd always sort of suspected that song was about her, but had never asked. He counted into it, and they launched into the song.

It was impossible not to shake her ass just then, so she gave over and danced, hands up, gaze locked on Paddy as he started singing about seedy bars, too many cigarettes, cheap beer and fucking against an alley wall.

She should have been embarrassed. Worried that someone might think she'd actually do such a thing.

But she had. She did. They'd stumbled out the back door. He'd pushed her against the wall, kissing her hard and fast. One hand up her shirt, pinching her nipple, the other managed to shove her skirt and underpants out of the way and he'd fucked her right then and there.

She'd loved it. The thrill of being wanted with such immediacy. The edge of the idea of being caught. Back then, she'd never have begun to imagine this future. She rarely thought more than a few months in advance, if that.

But she wasn't ashamed of those weeks with Paddy. Everything they'd done, she'd done willingly. Had loved every moment. It had been a turning point, a pivot point.

"Dive Bar" ended, and they launched into "Chemicals," and she kept dancing. Damien was a monster. He hit those drums so hard, a goofy grin on his face the whole time. Every once in a while, he'd lean in and sing.

"He's adorable," she said to Mary with a tip of her chin in Damien's direction.

Mary laughed and nodded. "He's a machine. But I like what it does to his forearms, and he's always hot for me when he gets off stage." She put an arm around Natalie's shoulders. "I'm so glad you're here."

For a long time, her family had been 1022. And she

realized as she stood there next to Mary, that these wily Hurleys with their noise and chaos had joined 1022 in her heart. They were part of her, too.

"Me, too. I needed to be here."

CHAPTER TWENTY-FOUR

PADDY CAME OFF stage after the third encore, handed his guitar to his tech and pulled Natalie close. Happiness had consumed him, made him a pool of contented male.

His woman had come to him and damn if he hadn't needed it more than he'd even known until he'd looked up at the sound of her voice.

"Let's go back to the hotel." He'd already arranged for a car to be waiting when the show was over. He usually rode back with everyone else, but he didn't want to share Natalie. Not for a while.

He led her through the crowd of people who seemed to materialize after the show. Just knowing he needed to be alone with her for hours and hours.

"Aren't there things you need to do?" she murmured as he kissed her neck.

"Just you, gorgeous. I have a tour manager for all the other stuff."

Their tour manager, Renn, would take care of everything that needed doing, so Paddy grabbed his bag and her stuff from his dressing room before catching sight of one of their security detail.

"Hey, Paul." Natalie smiled the guard's way.

Paul, who tended to frown more than any other expression, lit up. "Hey, there. I see you found him okay."

Paddy's brow rose, and he pulled her a little closer.

"Paul helped get me to you earlier when I arrived," Natalie explained to Paddy.

"Thanks, man. Can you get us to the parking lot?"

"Definitely."

There were fans there at the entrance, and he cursed under his breath.

"I'm not going anywhere for two days. Sign and be Paddy Hurley," she said quietly.

He kept her hand. "I'm sorry. I'll make it quick."

She kissed him, which only made him want her more. "Hush. Do your job."

"I'm going to make you come so hard," he whispered against the outer shell of her ear before he licked it.

She tried to move away, to let him do his thing, but he didn't want her away. He wanted her close. So he merely tightened his hold on her hand and pulled when she tried to sneak away.

He chatted, signed autographs and answered questions as they headed toward the car waiting for them. Paul was there just behind them to keep things under control in case trouble broke out.

It rarely did. They had great fans. Supportive and enthusiastic.

They called her name now, he noted with a smile. She blushed and waved at them when they did, which only made them more excited.

"Thanks for coming out tonight, all. Nat's only here for a few days, though, and I'm starving. I'm gonna head out." He stepped back as many of them called out that they'd be there the next night, too.

He turned. "What do you guys wanna hear tomorrow?"

They yelled out a lot of stuff from the new album,

which was already on the setlist. They liked to toss in a rarity here and there. Something they only played once or twice a tour, if at all.

And then he heard "Broken Open," and he nodded. "Okay. I'm going to add one of those to the setlist. You'll know which one tomorrow night." He waved one last time, and they got into the waiting car and headed out.

He pulled her close, not caring that he was a sweaty mess. He needed to touch her. Burying his face in her hair, he kissed the top of her head. "Damn, you're the best surprise present I've ever gotten. I can't believe you're here."

She snuggled in closer. "Me, either. You guys were incredible tonight, by the way. It's pretty amazing to see an arena show from the crowd, but backstage? I'm really proud of you, Paddy. What you guys have achieved is astounding. They love you."

That meant everything coming from her.

"Thank you, baby." He kissed her temple. "When did you get in? Why did you decide to come out now? I can't believe you didn't mention this yesterday when we talked."

"I didn't actually decide for sure until yesterday. Because of the library's schedule and some mandatory vacation hours I had to take for budgetary stuff, I figured it would be a good time to dart out to see you. I arrived just a few hours ago. Mary arranged everything from this end. My stuff is in your room, so I hope that's okay."

"More than okay. It's perfect. I've slept like utter shit since I've been away from you."

She'd come to him. He knew how she felt about the whole wildness of his life on tour, and he'd been careful to let her know he wanted her there but not to push. That she'd made the trip to him despite all that, that she was relaxed against him and not clearly freaked out, meant a lot.

Back at the hotel, they'd gone in a back entrance and headed straight up to his room.

He kicked the door closed, locking it and giving her a long look. "I need you naked. I also need a shower to wash the show off. I think we can combine those things."

Except she tossed her jacket and bag and stalked to him. One hand on his chest, she pushed him against the door and dropped to her knees.

"Holy fuck."

She smiled up at him as he uttered that strangled curse. Kept smiling as she unzipped his pants and pulled his cock from them.

"I'm dirty and sweaty."

"I know." She licked from the base of his cock up to the head, and he watched, snarling as she swirled her tongue around the tip, all while her gaze was locked on his.

Caught in the magic of her appeal, of missing her and the aggressive need to fuck he always had when he finished a show, he leaned against the door and wondered at how lucky he was.

"You're the sexiest thing I've ever seen. Jesus, I've missed this." He slid his fingers through her hair.

She knew him so well. Knew where to dig the tip of her tongue, where to lap at him, how hard to suck and to keep him nice and wet. It wasn't very long at all before his balls had pulled close to his body and orgasm began to gather in his toes.

He'd started off close. He'd been wanting her even before she'd shown up. Had jerked off in the shower before he'd left for the venue. Thinking of the last time they'd been together. He'd taken her from behind, which he loved because he could see her ink, touch all of her at his leisure. He'd come as he recalled the sounds she made, the way she'd felt around him.

Even after that, he'd wanted her as he sang and knew she waited just to the left. Wanted her as she'd patiently held his hand as they'd woven down the halls through the crowds back at the arena. Wanted her as he'd breathed her in like oxygen in the back of the car on the way over.

And the reality of her, the hot wet of her mouth, the contrast between the mellow, public Natalie and this dirty siren who sucked his cock and loved it, was more than he could take.

He strangled out a curse and blew, and she never shied away. Instead, she kept on as wave after wave of climax took him. Finally, he pulled her to stand, kissing her as he pulled up his pants with one hand and dragged them into the gigantic marble-accented bathroom.

"Jesus." He swallowed hard as he picked her up and set her on the counter.

"I told you, Paddy. I like it when you're dirty." She leaned in and kissed him, tugging on his bottom lip a little before sitting back.

"You're going to kill me." He kissed her once more and left her to turn on the double-headed shower.

When he turned back, she'd grabbed her shirt, pulling it up and off.

The red of her bra was perfect against her skin. Straps came up over the curves of her breasts, accenting them. The cups dipped so he caught the dusky pink of her nipple.

"I bought a few new things."

"I approve. Let's see if your panties match."

He helped her down and knelt to get her boots off and then ridded her of the rest of her clothes.

Paddy grinned at the stylized SHR. Sweet Hollow Ranch was the name of the place that lent the name to the band on the belt she'd worn. Like a not-so-subtle brand. That same SHR was on the big iron gates at the entrance to their land and also on Damien's drum kit and the custom work on their gear.

Seeing it on her revived his cock. *Mine.*

She looked down, a smile on her face. "Such recovery time. Another reason I keep you around."

"I'm loving those panties." Bright red, the same straps wrapping around her hips. Peeks of her ink here and there only added to that juxtaposition of her naughty/nice exterior.

"I'm sorry to have to take these off. But I need you in that shower with me so…" He hooked his fingers and pulled them down and off, tossing them over his shoulder. He slid his palms up her calves, over the muscles of her thighs. Standing as he kissed the curve of her hip.

When he popped her bra open, and she shimmied a little to get loose, he sighed. Happier than he'd been since before they'd left for the tour. He pressed a kiss against each nipple, licking them as they beaded to his touch.

Her fingers sifted through his hair as she held him to her.

He broke away, getting naked fast and pulling her

into the shower with him. He'd eyed that bench earlier. But he had a use for it now.

"Let me take care of you." She pressed a kiss on his chest, right over his heart before she took the shampoo. "Here, help me up."

She stood on the bench and he backed up to her so she could wash his hair. He leaned his head back, his body against hers, supporting her and being cared for all at once.

Her fingers on his scalp felt so good, he groaned, letting her massage him for a good long time before he turned and helped her down, letting her slide against his body.

He rinsed his hair while she washed and conditioned hers, and then he drizzled liquid soap all over her breasts and began to rub soap-slick circles around her breasts and to her shoulders and back.

She brushed herself against him, side to side, and then after washing his neck and arms and chest, gave plenty of slippery attention to his cock and sac. So much he had to make her stop.

"Quit that. Insatiable." He kissed the tip of her nose and then her mouth as his fingertips found her nipples. Tugging. Pinching. Rolling them between his fingers until she panted.

"What is it?" He laid teasing kisses over her face.

"You're killing me, Paddy. I want you in me. Please."

Before he'd left, they'd both been tested, and the results had been clean. He'd never been naked in any other woman but her. Though the temptation in the years before she'd come back into his life had been high, he'd known enough people with STDs to resist.

Desire hit, hot and hard, so dizzying, he had to bury his face in her neck and hold on until it passed.

"There's a big mirror in the living room. Across from the couch. I want to be in you. I want to watch you as I fuck you."

She shivered and it wasn't from the cold. They both rinsed off quickly and got out. He dried her off, kissing her as he did, and by the time he picked her up and she wrapped herself around him as he carried her out, he was beyond ready.

He set her down in front of the couch. "You need to be ready first."

"I'm totally ready. I promise." She took his hand, guiding it to her. "See?"

He teased her clit with a fingertip for a little while. Until she got that glazed look in her eyes.

"Now I need you to kneel facing the back of the couch. Hands on the couch. Ass out. Legs spread wide. I'm really hungry for you."

She sucked in a breath, and he smiled, letting her see in his gaze how much he liked that.

She did as he told her to do, and he settled on his knees on the floor behind her. The couch was low, and he was tall, so the part of her he wanted his mouth on was at eye level. He leaned in and spread her open before he took long licks, humming at her taste. Humming at how good it was to be like this with her.

Her taste rushed through him. Taking over, blotting out everything else but how he felt about her. This angle meant she was all he felt, all he saw and tasted. Her scent lived in him, and when she came on a sob of his name, he was up, getting seated in a flash.

"On my lap, Nat. I want to see your face in the mirror, watch as I push in and pull out of you."

He helped her get astride his body, facing away from him. His arm wrapped around her waist to brace her.

"Watch," she murmured, and he did. The sight of her sinking down on his cock was nearly as good as the heat of her hugging around him.

Her eyelids slid halfway down as a pretty pink flush worked up her skin.

He kept watching as he took her breasts in his hands as she rode him slow and deep.

Home.

He felt, as he slid into the embrace of her body, much the same as he felt when he drove up the hill to the ranch. She'd become home to him in a way he'd never expected another human being to feel.

She was so beautiful, reflected, his hands all over her, her eyes half-lidded, the muscles in her thighs flexing as she moved. Even with the orgasm earlier, he was already close.

Then she leaned forward, bracing her hands on his thighs, her gaze meeting his in the mirror. Frank. Full of need. No shame as she took what she wanted.

"Yes, gorgeous. Take whatever you need."

He held her hips, guiding her.

"Love being naked in you. Feel so good," he mumbled, and she gasped her agreement with that.

"Missed this. Dreamed of it every fucking night. Jerked off so many times while I imagined you, and it wasn't enough. Nothing is. Only you are."

She shuddered around him.

He reached between her thighs, finding her swollen and ready for him again. He kept his touch light, circling slow and steady, knowing how sensitive she'd be after her recent orgasm.

The hum she made in response seemed to vibrate through her straight to his balls.

Without a condom, the clasp of her inner muscles was something he felt along his spine. Was more attuned to the tiny earthquakes inside her.

She groaned, her head tipping back, and exploded around him. He held a hand at her hip, keeping himself deep as she rolled her hips, inferno-hot and wet around him until he couldn't do anything but come with her. So hard, so long, he wasn't sure if he'd actually come twice.

Finally, he picked her up, cuddling her, as they got their breath back.

CHAPTER TWENTY-FIVE

SHE STRETCHED AFTER she'd gotten out of the shower once more, smiling as she heard him singing in the other room.

He'd be naked, she knew. He rarely wore clothes in hotel rooms. He tended to run hot, anyway. She, on the other hand, pulled on another pair of new underpants she'd picked up with him in mind a few weeks before. Emerald-green this time, with the lacing at the ass that he seemed to love.

She grabbed her sleep pants and wandered into the bedroom where she found a stack of his clean T-shirts. Smiling, she took one and pulled it over her head.

He spoke when she came out. "I ordered some food. I know you must be tired, but I'm starving, and I'd love it if you hung out with me awhile."

"I can sleep when I get home."

He turned with a smile that grew even bigger when he noted she was wearing one of his shirts.

"Don't worry. I brought you a few to replace the ones I'll undoubtedly steal while I'm here with you."

He came to her, pulling her close. "I love that you steal my shirts. But you need to leave a few that you've worn so I can smell you on them. Once they get laundered, I won't have that scent of your skin on them anymore."

She smiled, incredibly happy. "God, I missed you."

He kissed her quickly. "Good. I'd hate to be the only one."

They settled on the couch as they waited for room service. She rested her head on his shoulder.

"We've sold out every single show. They want us to do more, but Damien won't leave Mary, and he won't be gone when she's close to going into labor."

"Good for him."

He grinned, turning to kiss the top of her head. "Yeah, they came at me, trying to go around him. Appealing to me to talk him into more shows. As if I'd talk my brother out of being where he should be? His wife's side when his baby is ready to come into the world? Who are these people? Sometimes, honestly, I just want to burn it all down and live on the ranch and make records and do small shows without all the label stuff."

She wisely remained silent. She knew it was a struggle for them sometimes. They put their family first, and sometimes they got blowback from the label executives about it.

"They like money. I get it. I do, too. But they think in terms of bottom lines, and they don't give a damn that Mary is pregnant or that Damien won't risk her health by having her so far from home and on a crazy travel schedule when she's eight months pregnant."

"But you do."

"Of course! We gave them a three-month tour. That's enough for now. Later, after the baby comes, we might think about Europe and South America. But for now, this is good, and they need to back off."

She patted his thigh. "Just underlining that. I know

you do. Should I deal with the room service when it gets here?"

"You?" He made a sound. "You rest. I'll handle all that."

"Well, then, you'll need pants."

He laughed. "Oh, yeah. That." He got up. "Be right back. Don't move."

As if she was going anywhere. It was warm where she was curled up, and the faint scent of sex hung in the air, making her smile.

Food arrived shortly, and she dived in along with him.

His phone dinged, and he glanced at it. "Jeremy sent me an email. It's about you."

Crap. She reached out, taking the phone. "I'd wanted to wait until tomorrow to tell you. Ezra said Jeremy would wait but not forever."

"What's up?" Paddy frowned but shoved half of the roll he'd just buttered into his face and in that moment, she loved him so much, enough to just share without hesitation. It felt so wonderful and real to unburden herself with him, like as a normal part of her relationship. Maybe she wasn't so damned broken, after all.

"My father spoke to some crappy tabloid. Made out like he was the injured party, and I was a drug-addicted slutty slut bagging a rock star and ignoring his attempts to reach out. The poor single father who had worked his whole life to raise me right."

Paddy's frown went away, and he very calmly put his fork down. "He said what?"

She got up to retrieve the printed version of the "interview," handing it to Paddy.

He read it over, his affable nature burning away into anger.

She felt horrible for ruining their night with her drama.

"I'm sorry."

"What the fuck are you sorry about?" He nearly snarled it, and she started. "He's the one who should be sorry, Natalie. He *will* be sorry by the time I'm finished with him. Don't you dare apologize for him and his crap."

Paddy pushed to his feet and began to pace. "He can't continue to be allowed to manipulate and hurt you this way." He shook the paper. "This mentions your mother. Again, he uses it to hurt you. And why didn't you tell me about this yesterday? And you said *Ezra* told you Jeremy wouldn't wait? How is Ezra involved?"

"I had lunch with him yesterday. He showed me this before I saw it elsewhere and someone brought it up for my comments. He didn't want me blindsided."

He went still, staring at her. "So you let Ezra fix it when I should have?"

"What?"

"How long did it take you to give me your trust? How hard did I work to gain it, and you just let Ezra have it?"

She blew out a breath, not expecting this at all. "I didn't just let anyone have it. Ezra told me. And then I came here. To you."

"That should have been my job. I *earned* that place in your life." She sucked in a breath. This was one of his buttons obviously, and she'd pushed it, so she needed to make it right.

She tried very hard to figure out what to say next. "I don't know why you're upset. I mean, I'm hearing your words, but they don't make sense to me. I need you to help me understand."

"Ezra did *my* job. I should have showed you that interview. Fuck that, I *wouldn't* have shown it to you. Ezra had no right to make that choice for me. He should have contacted me before he showed it to you. I'm your boyfriend, not him. Not only was it not Ezra's place, you don't need that emotional shit from your father. You don't need to struggle through any of this shit. You were better off not knowing. As for Bob? He needs a punch in the face."

"What?" Not only was she still confused, he was starting to piss her off. "I don't like that *for your own good* stuff. I make my own decisions because I'm a grown-up. I've been dealing with Bob my whole life. I decide if or when I deal with Bob. No one else gets to make that choice for me."

"For once in your life, you might let yourself be taken care of, Natalie. Ezra took that from me. And you let him. When it came down to it, you trusted him with it and not me." He looked at his phone and then made a call.

"What are you doing?"

"Calling Ezra."

"What? No!" She moved, but he turned his back, shutting her out.

He'd never done that before in an argument and her world shifted a little.

Ezra must have answered because Paddy started speaking into his phone, "Yeah, I'd say sorry I woke you up, but I'm not. What the hell, Ez? You kept this stuff with Natalie and her dad from me? Why would you do that?"

Natalie walked around him so she could look him in the eyes. "Paddy, you need to stop this now. I'm not kidding. This is spinning out of control and we need to work it out. Not by yelling at your brother."

"She's still taking your side. Do you hear that?" He wouldn't look at her, further shutting her out.

She touched his arm. "What side? There are no sides here. This happened to me. To. Me. If anyone gets to decide how to handle something or how to feel about it, it's me."

Paddy focused on her. "He took that from me, Natalie. I should have been the one to help you through this."

He wanted her to trust him by fighting with him? Okay then. "You're not even making sense. A bad thing happened to me and what did I do? I came here! *To you.* God, you're being such a self-centered asshole right now. You're making this about you when it isn't. And you're waking up your brother to yell at him for what? Being kind? Reaching out to me to tell me something awful? Something I could have found out by being blindsided by a reporter? You like to talk about how it's normal for couples to fight, and I'm trying to, but you're pulling Ezra into this, and he doesn't need to be."

"It *is* about me, though. If this gains speed, it's my girlfriend who looks like a dope-fiend skank. Sort of the opposite of what the rebranding push was about, no? Your father using me to get himself some attention. He's got himself a little bit of spotlight. You didn't trust me to handle this, and now it's fucked. Your need to always have control has wrecked everything."

Everything inside her went really still at his words. Even through the rest of this, she knew they'd get past it and work things out. But those sentences made a wound in a heart she'd trusted him with. How many times in her life had she been blamed for things other people did? All those voices threatened to swallow her up.

She heard Ezra yell at Paddy to shut up but the words were out, hanging between them. Slicing her open.

She managed to swallow her anguish and speak calmly to him. "I'm sorry you see it that way."

He and his brother continued to argue as she went into the bedroom and got dressed, leaving the T-shirt on the bed. She had to wall it out. Build a big moat around it and not feel. Not look at it because it hurt so much that if she spent even a second more on it, she'd break down.

As she reached the door she stopped, dropping her bag. Damn it, she was running, and she'd promised him she wouldn't. This was too big a deal to just walk away from. He'd hurt her, but they could get through it.

"Patrick!" Natalie yelled as loudly as she could, grabbing his shoulder and turning him to face her.

He was so surprised, he didn't prevent her from taking the phone and hanging it up.

She handed it back. "Now that I have your attention."

"What the fuck?"

"I nearly walked out just now." She jerked her chin toward the door where her leather jacket lay across her bag.

"Oh, you're going to run like you always do."

She shook her head. "Nope. I started to but when I got to the door, I realized if I left, I'd be using that to put distance between us." She'd be taking back control. "So I let go of that, I didn't run. I'm right here, trusting you to work this out with me."

"I don't want to deal with you right now. I'm pissed off."

"So you'd rather yell at your brother over the phone than work this out?"

"You can't just act like I'm a man to rely on, one you trust to protect and take care of you and then give that all to someone else, instead."

"I didn't do that." God, her chest hurt. She wanted to cry. Wanted to shake him to make him see reason. "Please listen to me. I came here to you. I *am* relying on you. Right this moment and ever since Ezra told me about this."

"I think you need to go. Cool off awhile. I'll be back home in a month." His voice had gone flat. "Have them get you another room here. Charge it to us. I'll have your travel taken care of."

Real fear was ice in her veins. Everything was falling down around her ears, and she didn't know what to do. Didn't know how to fix it. Wasn't sure he even wanted to.

"You're seriously asking me to leave right now? You're breaking up with me?"

"No. I'm not breaking up with you. I'll call you in a few days once I've processed all this. Right now I just don't want to deal. I'm on tour. I have to keep my head straight for that."

She drew a breath and licked her lips. She would not cry. Not in front of him. "This is going to do more damage than me staying here will. You have to know that."

"If you stay here, I'm going to say something I can't take back." He turned away from her, closing her out that last little bit so she stood there on the outside. Alone.

"You already have, Paddy." She took a step back. "I'll handle my own details, so don't bother. Have a good rest of your tour." She turned, hoping so much he'd call her back, but he didn't. So she picked up her jacket and opened the door, grabbed her bag and left.

PADDY HEARD HER behind him and didn't turn. Hurt anger burned through him. He didn't want to look at her right then. Couldn't.

He heard the door open and close, and she was gone.

He called Ezra back, who answered and started yelling before he could say a word. "Patrick! Get your head out of your selfish ass right now. Snap out of it. I can't slap the shit out of you to get your attention, but let me *call* attention to the fact that you're saying all this stuff in front of Natalie. To quote Pearl Jam, 'some words when spoken can't be taken back.' Dick. That last bit was me, by the way." Ezra's voice had that whip in it he used when he dealt with them in the studio.

And Paddy didn't want any part of it.

How long had he worked, really dug in and worked to earn her trust? With her, he'd been the man he had always wanted to be. The kind of man a woman would come to when she needed help and support.

And in the end, she'd trusted Ezra to do that and had treated him like a pretty second choice.

"Get your own girlfriend. Better yet, solve your own problems for a change instead of trying to solve everyone else's. Fuck off and stay away from Natalie."

He hung up and headed to the minifridge and grabbed a beer. Then he grabbed two more and a bottle of tequila he had already.

He drank them and wallowed. How could she have gone through all that and not called him immediately? Damn Ezra for not coming to him first and letting

Paddy decide how to tell Natalie. She didn't need to hear any of it. It made her unhappy, and Paddy would have known that. Ezra hadn't.

He'd spent the better part of a *year* with her, proving himself and in the end, it hadn't been enough.

Between Ezra and Bob Clayton, Paddy ached to pop someone in the nose, and since Ezra probably wouldn't answer his calls, and he'd already unloaded on his brother, anyway, Paddy decided to handle Bob Clayton.

Before he got any more drunk, he did just that, using the phone number Jeremy had given him a few months back when he'd asked their manager to keep an eye on the man just in case.

"Bob," Paddy said when he answered, "this is Patrick Hurley. Who the hell do you think you are?"

"Well, listen to that. A slurred phone call after midnight."

"Says the man with opiate slur totally awake after midnight. I'm confused. Do you even try to be a dick or does it come naturally?"

"I'm trying to save my daughter from the likes of you."

Paddy laughed at that. "From me? Yeah, because selling a lie to the tabloids for drug money is more your style than mine, old man."

"My daughter is the most important person in the whole world to me. She's gone to therapy, which has convinced her I'm the bad guy. I was an addict. I was a different person when I used, but that was the substance. Not me. You should know that. Your own brother was addicted to heroin of all things."

"You keep talking in the past tense but you're high right now. Try it on someone else. I've been around enough junkies to know. You're nothing like Ezra. He took responsibility for the things he did. He got clean. He doesn't blame everyone else for his bullshit. And he would never, in a million years, hurt his family the way you've made a hobby of. I know you're rich. Why are you selling stuff to the tabloids? Have you blown your monthly trust check or something? Looking for cash to shut up?"

"It's hard to get clean when no one believes in you. My daughter has abandoned me for you. You and your easy life and promises to her. If I had incentive to keep clean, I wouldn't have to tell my story. Of course, also yes, I'd love to have her back in my life."

Paddy snorted. "I'm not giving you a dime. I work for my money."

"My daughter doesn't. She's got a fourteen million dollar trust and then she sits and condemns my life?"

Holy shit. Her trust was fourteen million dollars?

"Your daughter *totally* works for a living. She volunteers. She helps people. Which is more than I can say for you. Leave her alone. If you really love her like you claim to, stop exposing her to people who'd do her harm for page views. She has a quiet, private life. She wants to be left alone. You're not helping."

"But she seems just fine with her picture all over the place with you."

Paddy got it right at that moment. Her father, that piece of crap, was actually *jealous* that Nat was getting coverage, even though she hadn't set out to get it and was uncomfortable with it.

"That's the real problem, isn't it? Oh, Bob." Paddy settled back, feeling vicious. He was so pissed off, and as he'd already hung up on his brother and chased Nat away, he had a better target for his rage.

"You can't stand it that she's got a life and she's happy."

"I'm going to pray for you. You're leading my daughter down the wrong path."

Paddy laughed and took another shot. "Save your prayers and use them on yourself. As for Natalie being led? If that's not the clearest evidence you don't know her at all, I don't know what is. I'm going to say this one last time. Leave her alone. Don't mention her. Don't paint her with your own sins to make yourself look like a victim. For once in your miserable life, don't use your kid and hurt her for your own benefit."

"Or what? Is this a threat of some type?"

"It's not a threat, Bob. It's a promise. Leave Natalie alone."

He hung up.

CHAPTER TWENTY-SIX

BONE-DEEP TIRED and emotionally wrung out, Natalie keyed open the front door and headed into the house. Tuesday looked up from her place at her worktable, surprised to see her back.

She put down the pliers and the piece she'd been creating. "What's going on?" Tuesday got up, concern on her face. "I thought you weren't due back until tomorrow night?"

"I... He..." Natalie burst into tears. Now that the door was closed, now that she was home and with Tuesday, the walls she'd built around everything that had happened in the hotel room in Chicago came rushing back.

Tuesday put her arms around her and guided Natalie to the couch, sitting with her. "Oh, honey, what happened? Did you find him with someone? Did he cheat on you? I'm going to run his ass over with my car!"

Natalie shook her head, getting herself together. "No. He didn't cheat." She laid out the fight. "You know, it was so good when I got there. It was... I felt like this could be it, that forever person. Even as we were fighting, I thought he was being a dick, but it was whatever, you know how dudes can be sometimes. And who am I to talk? He has a button I pushed, and I did it without knowing that. I figured he'd burn off his mad and we'd get to what it was really about. Then we'd have great makeup sex."

Tuesday blew out a breath. "And then what happened?"

"A few things. The main one is he walled me out. He took this thing between me and him, and he called Ezra. He was so cold. His voice was flat. He even turned his back on me. At the end. He told me to go. This was after he'd said to Ezra that my need to control everything had ruined things." He'd taken what vulnerability she'd shown him, and he'd turned it around to hurt her.

She'd hurt him so deeply, he'd done that. She hadn't meant to, but that's what happened all the same. And he had reacted with so much hurt anger.

Tuesday sat back. "Like that?"

"Yes. He said I always ran. So I stayed. He said I didn't give up control when I held things back so I went to him. And in the end, he flipped out when I shared because it wasn't exactly how he'd wanted, and he shoved me away."

"And you left."

"I tried to stay. He told me to go. He told me to get my own hotel room and charge it to the band and that he'd see me when he got off tour. Claims he wasn't breaking up with me. I did think about getting another room and trying to work it out with him again today. But by the time I got to the lobby, I was so humiliated. I just needed to come home. The really nice man who drove me to the venue to start with was around when I called, and he took me to the airport. He even stopped and made me get coffee."

"You look like hell. Did you sleep at all on the flight?"

"I tried."

"Go. Take a hot shower and get in bed. I'll crank up the heat and when you get out of the shower, there'll be some tea waiting. You'll sleep, and then we'll figure out what you need to do next. He's going to be sorry soon enough and call for you."

"I don't want to talk to him. I don't know if I ever will."

Tuesday started to say something but closed her mouth, pointing at the stairs. "Go."

THE POUNDING ON his door woke Paddy up from where he'd passed out on the couch sometime after sunup. He glanced at his phone and noted it was already nearly three.

Which meant he was about to miss sound check.

"Coming!"

He braced himself to see Renn's face, about to make an apology and run to the shower, but it was a very-angry, very-pregnant sister-in-law with an equally angry Damien right behind her.

"What did you do, Paddy?" She pushed him back.

"I'm sorry! I overslept. I'm going to jump in the shower now. It'll take me five minutes." It wasn't as if he'd never shown up hungover and still drunk from the night before.

He started into the bedroom and that's when Nat's scent hit him, and he remembered. "Did Nat spend the night with you? Sorry about that. I told her to get her own room."

"Are you actually kidding me? Because Patrick, I am in no mood for your jokes right now. This is serious business."

"Why isn't she here to be mad at me in person, anyway? She sends her pregnant friend to do her dirty work? Weak."

"You don't even know, do you?" Damien shoved a hand through his hair. "Jesus. How drunk were you last night?"

Suddenly, he remembered. He'd told her to get out.

"Sorry you got dragged into our fight. She and I will work it out. I should call her this morning at least since I told her to go."

Mary shook her head. "I'm leaving. Don't tell him anything, Damien. He doesn't deserve to know."

Damien groaned and moved to his wife, catching her at the door. "Curly, I nearly lost you. He pushed me to make it right. He made a mistake. But everyone makes mistakes. Go back to our room and put your feet up. I'll be back in a few. You stay here tonight. No use you going to the venue."

"I'm going. I have a menu planned. I made a commitment to do that for you guys at every show. There are three more weeks left, and I'll continue to do that until the tour is over." She shot Paddy a glare over her shoulder and left the room.

"I repeat. What the hell is going on? Is Natalie all right?"

"If you mean is she back in Hood River? Yes."

"She's not supposed... Oh. I told her to go home. She really fucking did it? And she came to your room to tell you all this?"

"Jesus, Paddy. How drunk were you?"

"I wasn't drunk when I had the fight with Natalie. I didn't start drinking until she left, and I'd hung up on Ezra. Then…I called her dad. I drank some more. I watched *The Matrix* and I passed out."

"Ezra called us about forty-five minutes ago."

"God, I went off on him. I was so pissed. But out of line." Paddy knew he had some apologies to make after losing his temper the night before. But still, the brother code. "I can't believe he called you to tattle, though."

"First, she didn't come to our room last night. She went to the airport. She left a thank-you card for Mary for handling all her arrival details. The front desk notes that was at nearly three in the morning. Ezra called Mary to let her know Tuesday called him at the ranch. To let him know Natalie just got back to Hood River. He figured you might want to know she was safe, but Tuesday says she's a wreck. What did you say to her, Paddy? Did you hit her?"

That question made him physically recoil. "I would *never* hit her. Fuck you for even asking me that question, Damien. *I love her.* Why aren't you asking what she did to me?"

"Really? Paddy, are you serious with that?"

"I've never in my life worked as hard to gain someone's trust as I did with her. I was patient. I put her first. Always. And she comes to me and shows me this bullshit interview her dad sold to the tabs. She knew for a whole day before she told me. She talked to Ezra about it first. And then when I was yelling at Ez, she took his side."

"So it's over, then? I'm confused because I saw your reaction to her last night. I saw you fucking light up when she came in. I saw the way you touched her, the way you spoke to her. Your entire being changes when you talk about her, when you're with her. I've watched

you fuck through dozens of women you didn't even remember the next day. Natalie is different."

"I'm not denying she's different, and who's saying
it's over? We had a fight. I told her we'd deal with it
when I got off tour. It's only three weeks at this point.
I was harsher than I should have been, but I said we
weren't breaking up. I figured she'd sleep it off, and
we'd probably make up today. I didn't actually expect
her to go. When I get back home, we'll work it through.
I need some time. I'm going to take a shower. We'll head
over to the venue in a bit."

"I just hope it's not too late."

Why was everyone making such a big deal out of
a dumb fight? Yes, he'd been a dick, but wasn't he allowed a button or two? "What the hell, D? Too late?
Why are you talking like this is something more than
it is? It was an argument. She and I have argued before.
You and Mary fight. That doesn't mean it's over. People
fight. Hell, Mom and Dad fight like whoa sometimes."

"Ezra's hurt. You said some shit to him. But he's your
brother. You two have that relationship. But whatever
you said to him, you said it in front of her. He refused
to say what it was, but he said you did some damage.
He's smart that way. Don't let your ego overrule your
common sense." Damien went to the door. "Text me
when you're ready. I'm going to have to cajole my wife
into not maiming you. She's pretty fond of Natalie."

"*I'm* fucking fond of Natalie. God. You guys are acting like I did something horrible. It was a fight. She'll
get over it. Let her lick her wounds. I'll lick mine. Everything will be fine."

Even as he said it, he ached. Having her with him

the night before had been so good. It had been right to be together.

Until he'd been slapped in the face with that old feeling of not being the guy people relied on. Which was stupid, he knew. She hadn't meant it that way. But it hurt nonetheless. He indeed needed to lick his wounds and then once he did, he'd do what he intended to do all along and fix things with her.

WHEN HE DIDN'T call her that day, or the next, or the day after, she realized she'd made the right choice to go. As much as she hated it.

She'd gotten used to him in her life. He'd filled the spaces she hadn't noticed were empty.

But now she did. She felt every place Paddy had been in. She'd become so used to texting him and sending him little stories about her day that she had to leave her phone home because she kept picking it up and realizing they were over once more.

Tuesday left little treats on her pillow. A pair of earrings, a pretty new mug for her tea, chocolates, a huge bag of bubble gum.

It got her through. That and a lot of writing in her journal and listening to The National and PJ Harvey while she cried.

Tuesday came home on a Saturday, and she took one look at Natalie and sighed. "You, pack a bag, we're going to Zoe and Jenny's for the weekend."

"Ugh. God, no. You'll all want to go out and do sporty shit, and it's cold. Plus, I'll have to get the pity face all weekend long."

"Pack a bag, Nats. You've wallowed and I've allowed it because that's what you needed. Your week is up.

Now you need to get the hell out of this house, brush your hair and do something with people who love you."

Tuesday gave her a look that told Natalie there would be no peace until she assented.

"And shower first."

On the drive up, Tuesday refused to let her listen to anything sad. "No. You're done with that. Look, I don't necessarily think you have to adopt an *it's totally over* mind-set. But you have to figure out how to move forward. Wallowing doesn't do that. You're bogged down and depressed."

"I love him. I wish I could just turn it off. But I can't."

"So call him. You said yourself he told you he wasn't breaking up with you."

"I know. But he hasn't even checked in. He shut me out, Tuesday. He punished me for sharing with him. His silence is making clear he's done."

"I talked to Ezra."

"Well, see? That's a conversation we can have instead of this one."

Tuesday rolled her eyes. "About *you and Paddy,* actually. Damien says Paddy is breaking down. He's drinking hard. He goes back to the hotel every night and holes up in his room."

"Alone?" Even as she said it, Natalie knew it was a dumb accusation.

"Whatever Paddy's sins are—and I agree what he said to you was shitty and hurtful, and he needs to grovel and grovel some more to make up for it—I am absolutely convinced cheating isn't on the list. As are you, so stop. The man is an idiot, yes, but he loves you.

Anyway, Damien told Ezra that Paddy has convinced himself you two are just fighting, not broken up."

"I hate that I'm worried about him. I'm the worst. The. Worst."

Tuesday made one of her *get the fuck outta here* snorts of dismissal. "Really? I can think of ten people I actually know right off the top of my head who are way worse than you. Your father. Your grandmother. Your mother. The guy at the post office who called me the N word last year. Just to name four. Why are *you* the worst?"

"Ugh, post-office bigot! Now I'm mad at him all over again. Jerky McJerkFace asshole."

Tuesday laughed. "You're like a kitten. So easily distracted. Back to the subject and why you think you're so terrible."

"I shouldn't worry about Paddy. And then I think, well, maybe I should have stayed overnight and tried again that next morning to get things resolved. He told me to go, and I just walked away."

Tuesday heaved a sigh. "You tried to stay. You made a conscious choice not to leave, but to stay. For him. And he used some words... Sometimes you say stuff, and it hurts, but you can move past it. Other stuff? He pulled all those triggers you have. And he should know that."

"Why is Ezra getting all this from Damien, anyway? He and Paddy are tight."

"They're not talking. He said some nasty stuff to Ezra, too. He sees Ezra as taking your side."

So Paddy didn't even have Ezra to lean on? "Ezra

is a guiding hand. Even from across the country. He's all alone."

Paddy had no one and damn it, she was worried about him. If he and Ezra were fighting, Damien would be put in the middle, and she knew from Mary that she was really angry with Paddy.

Paddy wouldn't admit it, but Natalie knew him, knew he was lonely, knew, too, that his family filled that need inside him. If he didn't have that when he was out there on the road, he would have been adrift.

She pulled out her phone.

"What are you doing?"

"Texting Paddy."

Stop being mad at Ezra and make up with him.

He replied. Really, Nats? Silence for a fucking week and when you finally say something you lecture me? Since you're obviously so close to him these days, why don't you tell him to make up with me instead?

Really, Patrick? What exactly are you saying here?

Nothing. Everything. You left.

I tried to stay. You told me to go, and I left with your back turned. You said I ruined everything in your marketing plan. Anyway, it's done. Ezra loves you and you love him and you need him. Call him. Text him. Don't let another day end with you two not talking.

What about us? You done licking your wounds?

It makes me sad that you see this in those terms.

So gut up, Natalie, and tell me what you feel! How can I know if you don't tell me? You say nothing for a whole week and I'm supposed to be psychic?

I tried. I came to you. I took time off work and got on a plane and I came to you. I opened myself up, my past, and I showed you that interview. I trusted you, and you accused me of fucking up your marketing plan. You accused me of betraying you by finding out from someone else, as if I could control that even if it did make a difference. How do you think that makes me feel?

I was angry. You should have trusted me to fix that situation with your dad.

I did! I told you, I got on a plane and I came to you. I put my heart in your hands. And you threw a tantrum because what? I couldn't bend space time and have you tell me instead of Ezra? And I've replayed exactly what you said in my head over and over and over again. You need to practice some introspection.

I have to go. It's showtime.

She didn't reply for a bit. Have a good show. Talk to your brother. You need each other.

She started to tuck the phone back in her bag when she got one last text. Don't give up on us.

CHAPTER TWENTY-SEVEN

AFTER THE SHOW, he took Mary aside. "I know you're mad at me. But I love you just the same."

She rolled her eyes but allowed him to kiss her cheek. "You have a lot of making up to do. My being mad at you is the least of your problems."

"There's less than two weeks left. I need to finish and go home, and then I can fix it."

They walked together through a gauntlet of people. Damien in front of Mary, Vaughan on one side and Paddy behind her. She was tired, and the last thing any of them wanted was her getting jostled.

Vaughan flirted as they went, but it was more automatic than genuine. Paddy had noticed his brother had been a little melancholy, but he'd been so wrapped up in his own stuff, he hadn't reached out. Being without Natalie, the silence that had yawned open where there'd been so much intensity of connection had done his head in.

And the text exchange they'd had right before he'd walked onstage...

Like he had every night since she'd gone, he headed straight back to the hotel. But instead of grabbing a bottle, he took a shower, and after he'd gotten out, he picked up his phone and listened to the series of voice mails from Ezra that he'd been ignoring.

And then he called.

"What?"

"Jesus, Ez, that's what you've got to say?"

"After a week and five voice mails to you that have gone unanswered, you're lucky that's all I said. I tried to help. She came to you. I'm sorry you think I should have circumvented her to give you a link when you were on tour on the other side of the damned country."

"I'm sorry. I'm… Fuck. I'm sorry, Ezra. Having her trust me and rely on me was this badge of honor, I guess. Something I'd worked hard for and earned. It made me proud. I messed up." All his life, it had been Ezra everyone thought was the responsible one. When his brother kicked, it was that Ezra was so strong. Finally, Paddy had felt responsible. "She made me feel important in a way I never have before."

"Because she loves you. You fucked up big-time."

"I'm sorry I said all that stuff to you about trying to do my job."

"You know I'd never step in between you and her. Asshole. Have you made things right with her? I talked to Tuesday. She told me every night Natalie holes up in her room listening to weepy music, crying and writing in her journal."

His stomach hurt just thinking about it. "She texted me today. Told me to make up with you. That I needed you." And she'd been right. Ezra was his compass in many ways. "She accused me of saying she fucked up my marketing plan."

"You did. Well, you accused her of fucking up the marketing plan because the tabloids were making her out to be a dope-addled skank, and if that story got legs, it would mess everything up. You said her need to control everything screwed things up."

"I didn't."

"You did. I yelled at you to shut up over and over, but you refused to listen. That's when she hung up and tried to get you to listen to her. Then you accused her of taking my side. I don't even know what came over you, Paddy, but you did some damage. You're lucky she loves you. You can make this right. Don't leave it undone."

She'd been away from him, alone as she had to process all the stuff he'd said. Yes, she'd hurt him, but he'd hurt her, too. He'd hurt her worse because he had thought it was a dumb fight they'd make up from, and she'd been thinking he'd broken things off.

Now that he had time to think on it, she had stayed. Even in the middle of a fight—and he knew how much she hated to fight—she'd given up the control of leaving. She'd stayed to work it out, and he'd pushed her away.

There was a knock on the door. "Hang on a sec," he told Ezra and opened to find Vaughan there holding his iPad.

"Paddy, what did you do?"

He took it from Vaughan, who followed him inside.

Ezra swore softly. "Jesus, Paddy, I just got an email from Jeremy."

"I'm reading it now. I was only trying to help."

Bob Clayton had done another interview, and this one was worse than the first because it included the phone call Paddy had made and the fact that he'd been slurring his words. The piece also contained references to her job as a silly-rich-girl hobby and had less than flattering things to say about her friends.

All in all, this would devastate her.

"You need to call her and tell her. If you want, I can go over there."

"I need to call Jeremy first. He's worked up. Then I'll deal with Natalie." Paddy paused. "We okay?"

Ezra sighed. "It'd take a lot more than you being a dumbass to chase me off. We all make mistakes, Paddy. Lord knows I have. Call her. Make this right."

"I'm heading into the last of a tour. I'll be back in Portland in ten days for our last dates. Hopefully, I can convince her to come to the Rose Garden show. But I'll call her. I promise." And he had to hope she'd forgive him.

Vaughan sat, tossing his feet up on the coffee table. "You are so in trouble. I thought *I* was the one who blew the best thing to ever happen to him. Guess you can sit at my table in the cafeteria in hell. Or maybe you can do what I didn't and own your shit. Make this right. She's worth it."

Paddy shoved a hand through his hair. "Yeah, yeah. You're next in line after Natalie. We're going to talk about your moping around. Let me put out these other fires. Don't go anywhere."

He dialed Jeremy.

"I take it you saw that interview. Did you call this guy?"

"I did. He made Natalie unhappy. I wanted to fly down to California and punch him. So really, a call was a far better outcome."

"Jesus. Okay, well, it's not the end of the world. The tour is nearly done. The album is doing fantastic. He's trying to shake you down for money to shut up. Don't give it to him. This guy will never go away. He's eaten through his own money, and he's living with his mother now in Washington. Let her carry his dead weight." Jeremy paused. "I hear through the grapevine that you and Natalie broke up. Over this? She's good for you, this dumb crap notwithstanding."

"*She* thinks we're broken up. I'm on it next. I'll see if I can't adjust her reality more toward my way of thinking."

"Good luck with that. If you need to say anything else to Bob Clayton, route it through me, and I'll decide if it's worth saying through an attorney. You got me?"

"Yeah, yeah." He hung up and took a deep breath.

He headed toward the minibar, and Vaughan stood up, blocking his way. "This is what got you in trouble to start with. It feels easier to deal with it this way, but you need all your wits to make this right, and you don't have that many to start with. Do you love this girl? Really love her?"

Paddy nodded. He didn't even need to pause.

"Then you need to put your pride and your ego aside. You said some harsh-ass stuff to her. And from what you've told me and what I know of her, the stuff you said was bound to have really done some damage. You pushed buttons, man. You gotta be careful. Because once something is really broken, you can't fix it. Not with another baby like Kelly and I failed at, not with diamonds or promises to slow down or go on a trip. You have to be truly willing to own it and get on your knees and beg her to forgive you and mean it. Because you might think you're over it. And you might find plenty of pretty thighs to get between and think you've forgotten. But you're going to look up in a few years, and there'll be an empty spot only she can fill. And it'll be too late."

"Aw, man." Paddy hugged his brother quickly. "You

have time to fix this. I know Kelly still has feelings for you."

Six years before, Vaughan and his wife had hit a rough patch and ended up divorcing. They'd been so young. Too young to get married. Definitely too young to have kids, and Vaughan had made big mistakes, and Kelly had stayed long enough after she should have left, that their end was bitter.

"She's engaged. She told me when I dropped the girls off before we left for the tour."

"Then do something about it!"

"Says you. You first. We'll talk about this when you're done with your call. Go in the other room so I don't have to listen to you debase yourself and beg forgiveness."

ZOE OPENED THE DOOR, and they all threw themselves to the couches right as Natalie's phone started ringing.

Natalie looked at it a moment as Paddy's face flashed on the screen and heaved herself up from the couch. "I need to take this." She answered as she headed out to the covered porch, closing the door behind her. "Hello."

He sucked in a breath on the other end. "I've missed your voice so much."

She tried not to cry because she'd missed him, too, and there he was. And then because she wasn't sure if it meant enough.

"I'm calling for a few reasons. I'm not even sure which is worse or better or which to go over first. But I'm sorry. We'll start with that. I'm so sorry I said all that and reacted that way. I... Never mind, I don't want to sound like I'm making excuses. I'm sorry. I'm sorry you tried to stay, and I pushed you away like a dick. I know it hurt you. I'm so sorry. Are you still there?"

"Yeah." She heard the tears in her voice and was too upset to even be embarrassed. "I'm sorry the way I handled this thing with Bob hurt you. I trusted you to stand in front of you after you said all that other stuff so we could work it out." She blew out a breath. "Even before that, I trusted you so much that I was raw with you. Trusted you so I could be open and free. To let you hold me down and order me to do all manner of things. And it was *good* because I didn't always have to be in charge and you…you cherished that. Took that and didn't make it a job, though you certainly saw it as a responsibility. You made me feel beautiful. You made me feel safe because I could be as dirty as I wanted to be with you, and you didn't think I was a skank, or a whore, or that I was fucking anything up."

Her tears came freely by that point, rolling down her cheeks as she looked out over the backyard.

"I spent years holding myself together, and then after we parted the first time, I made myself into an adult. With an education, which meant control over my life and my future. And a job that I loved. My house. My friends. I have all this money, and I can use it to help other people. What I had with you was a safe place. Like the library had been when I was a kid. Like school had been. You took that, and where you had been kind and respectful, you were dismissive and hurtful. I just… I tried to stay, and when you told me to leave and turned your back, I just couldn't stay. I should have. I'm sorry, too."

"I yelled at you about trust, and I'm the one who didn't trust you enough to be careful with you." His voice broke, and he cleared his throat. "Can we work this through? I love you, Nat. I want to be with you. I want us to be together. Please give me a chance to prove myself."

Before she could speak, he interrupted. "Wait. Before you answer, let me tell you the other reason I called. It's your dad. I was so pissed at him for hurting you that after you left...I thought you'd stay over. I'm a shit for sending you out into the night the way I did. Anyway, I called him."

She put a hand over her eyes. Part of her was undeniably touched that he'd do that. The other part was horrified because she knew whatever he had to say next wasn't good.

"I called him and he was such a smarmy bastard. He doesn't care about you at all. Or hell, anyone. And he hinted at me paying him off."

"Oh, my God, please tell me you didn't give him money!"

"Hell, no. But he gave another interview."

She sat because her legs wouldn't hold her up. Her face burned with shame. Damn Bob for making her feel this way. She'd sworn to never let him do this to her again and here she was. "Tell me."

And he did. He read it aloud to her and she listened to her father tear down her life. After repeated references to his own piousness and his being clean, her father referred to Zoe and Jenny in hateful terms. He'd inferred that Tuesday was her lover out for her money. Said she'd been a wild drug addict in college and how she was a lazy, spoiled, trust-fund brat who played at being a librarian to make herself feel better.

"My God." Her father had used the very things that

made her life special, and he used that to cut at her. And he did it in front of people.

"I'm so sorry. I fucked things up by calling him. I just hated that he hurt you. That he seemed to do it like breathing. I was stupid and I thought I could make him stop. Appeal to his sense of shame at least, if not his fear that someone was onto him. This is his revenge for that. What a self-righteous ass he is. That you're as amazing as you are despite him is a testament to your strength."

She wanted to ask if he believed any of the things her father had said. Swallowed it back because she would not give in to that particular shame. "How does this hurt you? Do I need to issue a response of some sort?"

"I was an asshole for saying that. It *doesn't* hurt me. I'm a freaking guitarist in a rock-and-roll band. I'm supposed to be wild. No one is going to care if your best friends are lesbians or if you were wild at college. It's not an issue. Not to me. That marketing thing was something you did for me, and that you pushed past your comfort zone to help my career when I asked made me feel worthy. I appreciated that you did it, and I still do. But the Bob thing only matters because it hurt you."

"I'm sorry, Paddy. Sorry he did this. Sorry about the fight."

"I just wanted to feel worthy," he said quietly and she had to swallow back emotion.

She truly understood why he'd been so upset in the hotel room. He was hers to protect, too, and she'd hurt him even if she hadn't meant to. "Paddy, you *are* worthy. Not knowing about a button doesn't mean I didn't push it and hurt you. I'm sorry for that. Sorry to have caused you sadness."

She let out a breath.

"I have to go tell them. I'm here at Zoe and Jenny's place."

"Okay. Are we…are we going to be all right?"

"I can't lie, this whole thing has messed with my head, but I don't want to let go. When you come back to Hood River, call me. You know my number. We'll go from there."

"I will. I'll leave you credentials for the Rose Garden shows if you want to come out. If not, I'll call you in ten days when I get back. I love you, Nat."

"I love you, too." But love wasn't always enough.

VAUGHAN LOOKED UP from his tablet when Paddy came back into the room. "So?"

"She cried." He slumped into a chair, tossing his phone to the table. "You don't know this, but she doesn't cry like that."

"About her dad?"

"Well, it stems from him originally. He fucked her up, gave her all these hot buttons. But this is on me. I was so fucking careless with her. My reaction, stuff I said, hurt her."

"You didn't use them on purpose to hurt her."

"Sure I did. I meant to hurt her like you do in a normal fight. I didn't think." He slapped his head. "I didn't fucking think about how what I said would make her feel beyond wanting her to know I was upset she'd let Ezra fix this thing instead of me. So she left, and I just let myself think we'd both lick our wounds and come back to each other. And I may have lost her because of it."

"So don't lose her. Look, Paddy, I've known you my whole life, right? I've never seen you fail at anything. In fact, this is the first, nonmusic thing I've ever seen you struggle over. Don't give up because it's hard. I'm telling you this from the other side of that mistake."

Vaughan was right. He was used to things working out easily for him. He knew he was charming and used it all the time to ease his way through life. His mom often joked that charm was his superpower.

But it had left him lazy sometimes. He'd let charm become a shortcut. And it had blinded him while the woman he loved had been suffering. He'd gotten so wrapped up in his sense of hurt that it was Ezra who'd helped her first and not him. All that time Paddy'd felt buoyed by her respect and the ways she shared herself with more, more and more. At last it wasn't just Ezra who'd been the reliable one. That had made Paddy feel ten feet tall, and he'd let that blind him.

But her apology, the way she'd taken responsibility for hurting him, for being willing to work it out, meant he simply had to up his game and earn back her trust.

Paddy put that aside to think on a bit and turned his attention away from his own troubles to his brother's. "So tell me about this thing with Kelly. Are you going to let her go? Forever and for real?"

"I need to figure out if I really still love her, or if it's one of those *I don't want you, but I don't want anyone else to have you* things. That's what Mary said."

"Who is this dude?"

"His daughter goes to school with the girls. Kelly's on the PTSA with him."

Damn.

"Man. So a nice guy. How long have they been together?"

"Yes. I've even met him. They started dating last year. I'm trying to get my head around it."

"What a bunch of dicks we are."

Vaughan laughed. "Well, you are, anyway. Damien has a gorgeous, pregnant wife who feeds us every day. He managed to get it together. I think we might, too."

"Countdown is on. In nine days we'll be in Portland. In twelve, we'll be done. Use the time to figure it out. Are you going to let your future be guided by your past mistakes and just give up and really move on? Find another woman and let yourself love someone other than Kelly?"

Vaughan made a face just as Paddy thought he would.

"Or you can accept the mistakes you both made in your early twenties and make up for it with a better future because you still love this woman who is the mother of your children."

"There's a lot of baggage there. A lot of hurt."

"And your babies. Don't mess up her future if you don't really mean to be the man she needs. Your girls don't need it, and neither does she."

"I know. But, dude, I hate the idea of their being parented by anyone else. He's a good guy, I can't deny it. But I'm their dad."

It put his own situation into perspective, at least. He didn't want another man to take care of what should be his, either.

"Well, do you want another man to be a husband to your woman? You can't do this just for the kids."

"I don't know. I do have to think it through, yes."

"I guess after the shows, we can think about how to claim our women instead of getting drunk." Paddy grinned.

"Maybe thinking and drinking. Let's not go wild." Vaughan winked.

CHAPTER TWENTY-EIGHT

"THERE YOU ARE."

Natalie turned to face Sharon Hurley as she came through the library. "Hi there, Sharon. I've got a few things I think you'll like."

Sharon linked her arm with Natalie's. "I've missed you. You haven't been up to the ranch in a few weeks now."

"I've been busy."

"I know you and Paddy are having difficulties right now."

Natalie blinked the tears back. "Sharon, I can't. Not here."

"Come to the house tonight. Let me make you dinner. Tuesday should come, too."

"Oh, I don't know if that's a good idea."

Sharon paused, turning to face Natalie. She put her hands on Nat's shoulders, squeezing gently. "Here's the thing. I consider you one of mine now. Paddy probably should have warned you about this, but to be honest, he's never actually brought anyone home before so he didn't know, either. So, I have a ham, and I'll be making fried potatoes and corn bread. I'll see you and Tuesday at six. You're off at five today, right? You can bring me the books you have set aside, too." Sharon grabbed a quick hug and dashed out before Natalie could argue.

Sharon had met a lot of people in her life. She came
from a big family and in turn ended up having one herself. Her sons' lives had introduced her to a lot more
people outside her normal circle. Most of them had been
a pleasant surprise.

Some of them, like the ones who'd circled around
Ezra when he was sick, ignited a bone-deep hatred and
rage. There'd been a battle for her son's very life, and
she'd had no intention of losing.

So she'd run them all off with Michael's help. They
were united in all things regarding their children. But
through all the good and the bad, she'd never met anyone who needed mothering more than Natalie Clayton.

Once she got back home, she dialed Paddy's number. "Patrick Michael Hurley, I'm going to save your
ass so pay attention."

"Hey, Momma. I'm going to take a guess you're talking about Natalie. I screwed up, but I'm working on it."

"I know you did. I've only heard the outer edges of
this whole thing because your brothers think they can
hide things from me to protect you. But I can't help you
if I don't know the whole story."

He told her everything, and her heart ached for both
of them. "Oh, sweetie. You messed up. But you know
what? People mess up. It happens. You're special, of
course, but you're not perfect."

"I'm afraid the mistake is too big for her to get over."

"We all have our hurts. You have yours and even
though she didn't mean it, she pushed your buttons and
when you reacted, you pushed hers. But there's love between you. You're a handsome boy with more charm
than a body has a right to. You love her and you're

clever. Use all that to fix this. On top of all that, you have me."

"I don't even know what to say."

"I raised four of the naughtiest, most unruly, lack-of-common-sense, no-fear-of-danger children into successful men. If I can get through all the hell you boys put us through, I can help you with this."

Sharon paused. "Honey, she needs a momma something fierce. Her grandmother is useless. Her father is worse than useless. Let me tell you, he won't even see me coming when I get my chance. But Natalie needs to be loved like a mother can love her."

"You'd do that for me?"

Sharon laughed. "Paddy, I'd brave the fires of hell for you. But this isn't a sacrifice. I truly do love that girl. She's got a big heart. And she loves my son. Enough to be flayed open by him and still not tell me to jump in the river instead of showing up here for dinner tonight."

"Thank you. I feel better."

"Good. You're on the home stretch now. Finish this tour and come home to her."

They said their I-love-yous and hung up.

TUESDAY ONLY LAUGHED and shoved her out the door and drove them both up to Sharon and Mike's house.

Course Tuesday didn't think it was so funny when Ezra showed up. Though he clearly had no idea they'd be at the table, either. When he came into the house, his hair was still wet from the shower, his smile for his mother was open and warm.

Then he'd turned to see them, and he gave his mother a narrowed gaze, but Sharon had pretended not to see it.

Sharon Hurley was the sneakiest person Natalie had

ever known. And she managed it with a cheeky smile that dared you not to like her even as she manipulated you exactly where she wanted you to be. It was masterful, and she wanted to be Sharon when she grew up.

Sharon was bold and unapologetic, but she loved her family fiercely. Exactly the kind of woman Natalie yearned to be, though she doubted she'd ever be quite as scary.

Michael just watched his wife, wearing a smile. He knew what she was up to but found it adorable. What would it have been like to have grown up with these two as parents?

"Thank you for bringing all those books."

Natalie knew Sharon loved historical novels and had recently dipped a toe into historical romance and found herself in love with all the options. So Natalie had brought her a bunch of Lisa Kleypas and Tessa Dare to try.

"Thank you for making chocolate cake."

Sharon laughed. "That chocolate sour cream cake is Michael's favorite."

"It's everyone's favorite, Mom." Ezra helped himself to another slice.

"Can't go wrong with cake," Natalie agreed.

"That needs to be on a shirt. I'd wear it every day." Tuesday winked at Sharon, who blushed, laughing.

"My sisters and some of my cousins want to start a reading group. We all live in different places, but we'll connect via Skype. It'll be a good way to keep in touch, and we all love reading. I'd appreciate it if you could recommend some books for us."

"The library has a few different guides for book clubs of all types."

"That Natalie wrote," Tuesday added. "What?" she asked at Natalie's look. "You wouldn't have said. I'm proud of you." She looked to Sharon. "They're great guides."

Sharon grinned at Tuesday. "I sure do like you, honey. Everyone needs a girlfriend who refuses to let them hide their light under a bushel."

It was Tuesday's turn to duck her head.

They talked about what the women in Sharon's group liked, and Natalie tossed out a few titles off the top of her head that she figured would work—a few her own book club had read over the past year.

She kept waiting for Sharon to bring Paddy up, but she didn't. Instead, she packed up leftovers and walked them out to the car. Ezra had hugged her and awkwardly patted Tuesday's shoulder and then mumbled that he had to be somewhere or something and loped off.

"I'm working on a quilt for the baby. I have to go into town to pick up supplies day after tomorrow. Want to meet me for coffee?"

Natalie nodded. Even as she knew this was about Paddy on some level, she also knew Sharon wouldn't be doing any of this if she hadn't wanted to.

They made arrangements and headed off.

"I like her."

"She's a hoot. I love how she pushes everyone around, and they all look at her with adoration, but there's fear, too." If Natalie ever had kids, she could only hope to have them look at her that way when they were adults.

"Oh, there's not a doubt in my mind that Sharon would cut someone if they hurt her family. I have to respect that. And she makes really good cake."

And gorgeous sons.

"You know she had us there to help Paddy get me back."

"Yeah. And I know you're perfectly capable of saying no when you want to. So maybe you should be thinking about what it is Paddy can do that will make it all right for you to give him another chance. Because you love him. You've been miserable without him. Your father pulled some ugly shit and that wasn't what made you upset. You were worried about *our* feelings. His included. You belong with him."

"I do love him. I've never felt this way about anyone."

"But?"

"But love isn't enough. I know I love him. I know he loves me. I just need to figure out the rest. I do *want* it to work."

Until she'd met Tuesday and the rest of her friends, she'd never been able to count on anyone. Not absolutely. Even something as simple as when or if she needed a ride somewhere—even if her father was in a pretty good place—she'd learned through experience never to rely on promises. Being disappointed by people had been a hard fact of her life.

It had sort of snuck up on her, the way her friends would say they'd do something and actually did it. The way they remembered things and promises was suddenly something she noticed in its stunning regularity.

She'd had to work to give that to Paddy, and he'd earned it. She'd never felt judged by him. He'd appeared to have accepted her weird triggers. Until that night when he'd dumped all that resentment on her the way he had. But she'd done a similar thing, not meaning to hurt, but doing it, anyway.

"Paddy said he was sorry, and I *believe* he is. It's unreasonable, given all the things he could have done to me, for me not to just say, hey yes, things are all right. I'm scared. Because this thing has reminded me what it feels like to be truly miserable, and I'd thought I was past it. I'm trying not to overreact because he's not that guy and I know it."

"You know what, Nat? Fuck apologizing for having feelings and for having whatever life experience put you here now. I don't ever want to hear you say stuff like that because it's bull. You are who you are. Everything you experienced in your life up to this point makes you who you are."

Well, then.

"Thank you for saying all that. I do love him. Being with him makes me happy. I want to put in the work to make it right. But there's a small part of me that is terrified that he'll fuck me over and I'll have walked right into it."

"Eric cheated on me once."

Natalie turned in her seat to stare, openmouthed at her friend. "I had no idea. When?"

"We were still in school. Our third year. He went to Central America for a quarter. It was one of the women in his program."

"Oh, my God. Why didn't you tell me?"

"I was embarrassed. I didn't actually know until about a week after graduation."

When she'd been planning a wedding.

"I'm so sorry. Do you want to talk about it?"

"There's a point here, I promise." Tuesday snorted. "I

always told myself that I'd never stay with a man who hit me or who cheated on me. He'd never have hit me, never. He just wasn't that person. But we were staying with his parents before our house was ready. I found a letter she'd written him when I was consolidating boxes. I left him and went to my parents' house. He followed me and laid himself bare. He betrayed me over something so stupid. But he was wrecked. We worked it out eventually. It took me a really long time to get over it. Not so much that he'd slept with someone else, but that I'd trusted him with something, and he'd misused that. He'd given to her what was mine. Anyway, I never regretted giving him another chance. But it took me a few years to truly trust him again."

Tuesday pulled into their driveway, and once she'd turned the car off, she turned to Natalie. "I have this wound now, because of that. But I loved him, and he loved me, and he made a mistake. I had to figure out if I could live with the humiliation and keep my self-respect. Being in love means you'll get scars. It's the way of it. But here's what I think you need to focus on. He was careless with you. Fights will happen. You'll both make mistakes. But you have to figure out if you can trust him enough to let him in again."

OVER THE NEXT WEEK, she had coffee with Sharon and hung out a lot with Tuesday.

And Paddy texted her every day. The first text had been simple.

Thinking about you today. The sunset was gorgeous. San Diego is one of my favorite cities. I wish you were here.

At first, she didn't know how to respond. It was agonizing trying to figure out what to say or even if she should say anything at all.

So she'd gone with I love San Diego. Hope you have a great show.

The tension of it, especially after they'd had such ease with one another, was awful.

The next day, he'd sent her a picture of the ocean.

Vaughan dragged me here so he could surf. I did, too. Got my ass kicked like a newbie.

But she made herself respond because she didn't want to let go. And it got a little easier each time.

You can take my place windsurfing with Tuesday, then.

Will you be watching on the shore?

Maybe.

More had followed. Just a few a day, but each time she responded back, things got a little better between them.

"So are we going to the Rose Garden shows?" Tuesday asked her at dinner a few days later.

The first show was the following night and while she knew Paddy had wanted her to go, he'd done his best not to pressure her.

Ezra would be playing both shows. She knew he was buzzing with excitement, and she knew he and Tuesday were back to circling each other, though neither of them said much about it. Natalie had the feeling both of them were waiting to see how this thing between her and Paddy worked out before they finally just jumped on one another.

She'd been tied up in knots over this decision. At first it was a total no. She'd just deal with him when he got home. And then she'd thought to go the last night and sit in the audience, but the shows were sold out. So then she thought she'd go backstage but just the last night.

"Ezra would love it if we went."

Natalie raised a brow. "Are we allowed to discuss this Ezra/Tuesday thing? Is there a *this* to discuss?"

Tuesday sighed. "I don't know what there is. But I can't seem to stop thinking about him. And before you ask, no we have not made the sex. *Yet.* It feels like there's a yet. But anyway, I think we should go. To both shows. So I can look at Ezra when he's being a rock star because as you're aware, it's really hot. And because I think Paddy is trying, and you want him to succeed."

"Okay. We'll go."

"Good, because I'm going to give you a manicure after dinner. Obviously not a pedicure because we know you're weird about that. But your nails should look nice."

"Yeah, I'm sure Paddy would be scandalized if I had a chip in my polish."

"You hush."

"*You* hush."

"Very mature." Tuesday sniffed, but a smile lurked at her mouth.

"You're the one all 'hey, ask Ezra if he likes me but don't tell him I asked.'"

"I know Ezra likes me, Natalie." Tuesday's arch look made her giggle.

"He wants to touch your boobies. Just be careful. Those Hurley boys, you get a taste, and they're trouble. Sharon was right when she said they dig in like ticks, and it's too late."

"The best kind of trouble, though. I mean, if Ezra fucks anywhere near as well as he kisses, I'm in."

"I can't speak to Ezra's sex prowess, but I can, of course, testify as to Paddy's. He gets an A. Also he's..." Natalie shivered, remembering. "So. Dirty."

Tuesday laughed. "Awesome."

"Not in a gross way. I don't know how he manages to be so filthy and yet not icky or predatory."

"I don't know. Ezra is outside my normal experience with men. As is Paddy. They're just oozing with something compelling."

And when it was all focused on her...Paddy had made her feel special in a way no one else ever had.

She blew out a breath. "Okay, so you choose what I'm going to wear so the nail polish can match."

"I love it when you give in to the inevitable so early. It's really easier that way."

"I'm perfectly capable of dressing myself and looking nice."

"You totally are. You're cute. You work that and keep it classic and pretty all at once. But I can make you look fabulous and sexy without looking like you're trying too hard. It's a gift, Nats."

"I feel bad you have such a problem with your self-esteem. You should do those affirmations in the mirror."

Tuesday tugged her arm and got her up. "Let's go look in your closet."

CHAPTER TWENTY-NINE

"HEY, BOBBI, WHAT do you have for me today?" Natalie would work awhile that morning before she headed to Portland with Tuesday later on. It'd keep her mind busy instead of thinking about seeing Paddy and how it would go.

Bobbi waggled her brows. "Spice doughnuts."

"Get out! Really? You're so awesome I could kiss you for that. I want them all and a mocha, too."

"I'd prefer that if you're going to hand out kisses, they're all for me."

Heart in her throat, she turned to find Paddy standing there.

"What are you doing here?"

He took three steps and stopped, just shy of touching her. "Missing you so much, my heart hurts."

Slowly, he cupped her cheek. "Natalie Clayton, right? We met before. You worked at that dive bar."

"I have to go to work."

One corner of his mouth tipped up. "Are you saying you don't remember me?"

"I don't know. I mean, I thought I knew you."

He frowned a moment and got a little closer, his chest against hers now. "I'm Paddy Hurley, and I'm the man who loves you."

It didn't matter then that she was in a public place. He was there with her.

"If you'll let me, Nat, I'll be the man you need every day for the rest of our lives. I'm sorry. I'm sorry I hurt you. I promised to take care of the trust you gave me, and I didn't. I was stupid and careless, and I hurt you. Please give me another chance."

Three weeks and she hadn't seen him. Three weeks and she'd thought things might have been over but there, with his hand on her cheek, his body touching hers, those eyes seeing right through her, she'd been lying to pretend she didn't want to be with him.

"Okay."

His smile grew. "Okay? I'm going to kiss you now. Right here in front of Bobbi and God and everyone walking by."

"Get to it, Patrick."

His mouth met hers, and she breathed him in. She slid her hands around his waist, under his coat and held on.

It wasn't a slow, sweet kiss. The heat of him slammed against her system, taking over. His tongue brushed over her bottom lip before he gave it a hard tug with his teeth.

It was only because it was so public that she didn't give in to the moan threatening to burst from her diaphragm. He kissed himself right back into her life and when he broke away, he rested his forehead to hers.

"I've missed you so much. It feels so good to have you here in my arms where you belong."

It did feel good. And right.

"I missed you, too. What are you doing here?"

"Groveling. We got in late last night. I wanted to

come to you then, but all the lights were off when I drove by. I knew you'd be here to get coffee before work, so I figured I'd wait here and pounce when you got all moony-eyed over doughnuts."

"You're diabolical."

He cupped her cheeks, holding her face as he looked at her so intently, it was like he was committing every bit of her to his memory. "I'll do anything I have to to get you back."

Someone cleared their throat, and Natalie looked around, realizing customers were waiting, and they'd been blocking the counter. Bobbi grinned at them.

"Sorry." She stepped away, paying and grabbing her things, and Paddy kept right with her.

The woman who'd been next in line shrugged. "No need to apologize. I'm going to call my husband when I leave here just to tell him I love him. You going to give this handsome devil a second chance for whatever he did?"

"Do you think I should?"

Paddy snorted.

"He looks at you in a way I hope someone looks at me someday. Plus, he's gorgeous and rich," one of the others in line piped up. "Unless he cheated, in which case, punch his Adam's apple really hard and dump him."

Paddy rubbed this throat. "I've got her, why would I need anyone else?"

"Good answer." Bobbi winked.

"Can I walk you to work?"

"Yeah. Come on." She sipped her coffee, and as he opened the door, she grabbed a doughnut and took a bite. When he turned to her, she offered him the other.

"You must love me to share your doughnuts."

"You're okay for a rich, gorgeous rock star."

"I was reckless with your heart and your trust."

They kept walking, his arm around her shoulders as she leaned in against him.

"Yes. I don't need every minute of your time or attention. I don't expect us to never fight because you're difficult, and you think charming gets you a pass for it."

She paused and jerked her head to a nearby bench. They sat, and she drank some more coffee before speaking again. "I'm difficult, too. I'm a control freak, which you've known since the beginning, so I can't apologize for that part. I don't expect you not to be flirty or charming with other women, that's all part of the Paddy Hurley thing. I know your life is wild, especially on tour. And I accept that, even when it makes me uncomfortable. I'm doing my best to work through it. But I have these, I don't know, buttons, wounds, whatever, triggers? Whatever you call them, I have them, and sometimes I may not know about them until they get pushed. And you have *always* accepted that. So now, what I'm saying is, I own my shit when I'm responsible for it. Clearly, I pushed your buttons with how I brought up the interview situation. I made you feel like I didn't trust you to help me through."

Paddy sighed. "We're both a pair. Jeez. Look, it was stupid. I just… I'd worked hard to gain your trust, and I was so happy that you'd come to me, and we'd just had some seriously stellar sex. It hit me wrong, and I just stopped thinking. I hit out and I hurt you. I wanted you to count on me to come to me when you needed something."

"And I did. And your reaction made me feel like I shouldn't have. Like I couldn't." She chewed on her lip.

"I know. I'm sorry. I wish I could take it all back but I can't. All I can do is promise to do my best going forward."

"I need to be able to count on you. Scratch that, I was totally able to count on you. I love you. So much, it was torture not to be with you. But I'd rather feel that than feel like I can't trust you. And I know it's unfair to expect so much. I'm a dick, too. And high-maintenance that way. But it's who I am and how all my broken pieces fit together. In turn, I have to own my shit, too. And stay."

"You're not a dick for that. I want it, too. You and your broken pieces need to be with me. They're the most beautiful broken pieces I've ever seen."

She looked into his face and saw love there. "Okay."

He kissed her again, this time long and slow, leaving her boneless when he broke away. "You're coming to the show tonight?"

"Did you just kiss me until you were sure I'd say yes?"

"Did it work?"

"I decided for sure last night. I'm only working a few hours this morning, mainly to keep my mind off you. Tuesday and I are heading to Portland in the afternoon."

He grinned, and she took his hand, winding their fingers together. "You're impossible when you get your way."

"I'll make it worth your while. Will you stay with me tonight? Go to tomorrow's show, too?"

"Are you staying in Portland?"

"Nah. It's only an hour away. I wanted to come home.

To you. I slept like shit in my bed, though. Because your stuff is in my bathroom. Your things are at my house, and you weren't, and I didn't know if you ever would be other than taking it all back."

"Enough of that, okay? I feel like we can't keep going over it if we're to move on. I don't need you to wear a hair shirt. You're sorry. I'm sorry. We're together."

"So you'll stay?"

"Incorrigible."

"Unmanageable, too. But goddamn, I love you."

CHAPTER THIRTY

PADDY BOUNDED UP the stairs toward the stage. One-handed, he took his guitar as Nat held his other. He paused before walking out and gave her a kiss. Letting her taste reassure him.

She was there with him. They were back on track. Everything was really, really good.

"Have a great show. I love you."

He grinned. "I love you, too." He walked out and let the sound of a hometown crowd wash over him. They'd made a few adjustments to tonight's lineup. Some because Ezra was with them, and some for other reasons.

"It's good to be home, Portland."

More cheers as he grinned out over the crowd. The lights meant he couldn't really see it all, but he felt their attention, and it fed into his mood.

"I think this is gonna be a good show. What do you guys think?"

The crowd cheered, hooted and yelled out song titles.

Paddy looked to the side. "Ez, what do you think? Gonna be a good show?"

Ezra walked out, slinging his guitar on, and the crowd lost their minds. Paddy grinned at his big brother.

"It will be now, yeah."

He counted into "Ground Down," a song off their new album, and they were off.

Paddy hadn't felt this good since before she'd walked out of his hotel room three weeks before. He was there onstage at the end of a supersuccessful tour. Their album was kicking ass and *all* his brothers were up there with him.

And she was there. When he looked to the right, he caught sight of the pale moonlight of her hair. He knew she'd be dancing, knew she'd be smiling.

They sailed through "Chemicals" and "Boots" before he handed his guitar off and headed to the piano. The crowd, knowing it was "Silent No More" roared their approval.

"This one is for Natalie, who makes me a lucky, lucky man simply because she exists."

He began to play, and as he sang, they all sang with him. His words echoed not just back to Nat, but to their special people, too. That filled him. The awe that something he wrote for her would also be something they'd sing to each other, play at weddings and proms. It was so damned special.

He fell into the lyrics. Speaking to her about his love and what she'd done for him. This time was different. This time he understood what it meant to not have her. So now he knew better what it meant to have her at his side. What it meant to fight to keep someone he'd been careless with.

He knew what he had. Wasn't sure he deserved her, but he'd sure as hell try to be worthy.

They played through to the first encore and left the stage. The lights didn't come up, so they all knew the band would be back. He headed straight to her and kissed her because he wanted to.

"Hey."

"Hey, Paddy Hurley. You sure know how to win a girl back."

"Glad it's working."

He excused himself and ran back to hit the john. On the way back, he chugged down some water and ate a protein bar, tossing one to Ezra as they met up just off the stage entrance.

Ezra tipped his chin in thanks.

"How's it going, old man?"

"Not bad. Not bad at all."

Paddy leaned in close. "So I'd really like to drive Nat home. Can you take Tuesday back with you?"

Ezra's brow rose, but he shrugged. "Already handled. You're doing the right thing. She looks happy."

"Working on it. You ready?" He looked around to catch Vaughan's and Damien's attention. Everyone gave a thumbs-up, and they went back out.

After a rousing version of "Dive Bar" and "Revolutionary," which was a song Damien had written for Mary, Paddy paused. "Forgive us if we butcher this cover. But a week ago, I was on a flight to yet another city after yet another show, and this one came on, and it made me think of the most important person in my life."

He and the guys only had a few runs at practicing "Titanium" but he thought they managed a pretty rock-and-roll version. She was fearless in ways he'd never fully understand, but he appreciated nonetheless.

She was strong and fierce and the best thing in his world. She made him better.

And when he got off stage, the tears in her eyes were good ones.

HE PULLED UP into his garage, and the door slid closed behind them.

"At long last I have you alone and in the vicinity of a shower and my bed. It's like Christmas morning."

She rolled her eyes as they headed inside, and he only paused long enough to reset the alarm before tugging her upstairs as he pulled his clothes off one-handed, leaving a trail down the hall.

"I'm a sweaty mess."

"You are. But you make it look really good."

He smiled. "Damn, Nat, you're here with me. I'm so happy right now."

She reached out and grabbed his cock. "Wanna be happier?"

"You first."

Instead of their usual quick shower sex to take the edge off, they both cleaned up fast, drying as they rushed to the bedroom.

"You, on that bed." He flicked the switch to get the fire going and turned on some music before moving to stand at the foot of the bed, watching her as she lay there, a flush from the shower pinkening her skin.

"There are so many things I want to do with you—to you—I don't know where to start. It's like trying to read a menu when you're really hungry. I'm afraid if I choose one thing I'm going to really want something else."

She spread her legs, putting her feet flat against the mattress as she drew her knees up.

All the spit in his mouth dried up.

"Plenty of time to eat more than one thing."

He cursed, moving to her, over her, sliding his body against hers until his cock notched up against her.

"Trouble."

She laughed and stretched up to steal a kiss. "The best kind, though."

She moved, counterbalancing him, and sat astride his body. He tried to sit up but she pushed him back against the mattress. "Oh, no. I'm in charge right now."

Trixie Whitley's "Undress Your Name" came on, and she gave him a smile. "I love this one."

He had planned to respond but she slid herself down his cock hard and fast and everything wisped away, replaced by pleasure, sharp and raw.

Then she began a slow rise and fall, undulating her hips as she came down on him fully.

"I was really sad without you. I never expected to actually get used to having someone in my life."

The only light in the room was from the fireplace and the warm orange glow against her skin made it appear as if she glowed. He slid his hands up her thighs and the nip of her waist.

"I'm—"

She put a fingertip against his lips. "I'm not telling you to make you sad or sorry. I'm telling you so you understand what you mean to me."

He lifted his hip and rolled, flipping her to her back. "Now I'm in control." He thrust in harder and deeper. "Now I'm going to tell you how every night I'd go back to my hotel room and try to convince myself everything would be fine. In between bouts of drinking too much and jerking off while I thought about you. I came into the coffee shop this morning. Bobbi was excited when I told her I was going to surprise you. So I gave her the doughnuts."

She laughed, wrapping her legs around his body,

her heels on his ass, pushing him, urging him deeper. "Those were your doughnuts? So sneaky."

"It's merely an indicator of what I will do to get you back. Anyway." Damn, she felt so good around him, he lost his words for long moments, just falling into that sensation as the heat of her rippled all around him.

"That's so good." He kissed her before he moved, keeping inside her while he got to his knees.

She was flat on her back, legs spread with him between them, looking up at him with those big blue eyes burning with a light made just for him.

"I love you this way. Laid out all for me." He caressed over her stomach and up to her breasts. He got back to his story. "And then you walked in. Your cheeks rosy from the cold. Everything had been chaos in my head since Chicago, and when I saw you, everything stilled. Got quiet until I didn't see or hear anything but you. You're the one."

"Even after you talked to my father?"

"Don't spoil this moment with that asshole. We'll talk about that later. For now, let me declare my love."

She snorted a laugh, and then he nearly swallowed his tongue as she slid a hand down her belly and began to stroke herself slowly.

"This. You're like my diamond. So many facets. On the surface, you're cool and elegant and then here, when it's just us, you're raw and sensual. It's like the best secret I have. Here, what we have is all ours."

She caught her bottom lip in her teeth, and her inner muscles tightened. "Don't hold back. I know you've got a lot more in you after this one. I'm just going to watch."

She arched, her head going back, exposing more of her neck, enough that his mouth watered, but he held

LAUREN DANE 379

back kissing her there because he'd miss the way she looked as she made herself come.

She didn't close her eyes, her gaze on him as his roved over her body. Over the way her nipples had darkened, pulling tight, the flush on her belly, the peekaboo nature as her hand moved, her mouth as she dragged in air and then to her eyes.

"Love you, Nat."

Her body heated around him, making him gasp as she did, as all that hot wet squeezed him in waves, dragging him closer to his climax with nails dug deep.

Once she'd come down a little, he bent to lick up her neck, tasting her skin. "You're the most gorgeous thing I've ever seen."

"Gotta give you something to use the next time you're in a hotel room without me."

He laughed, changing his angle, so impossibly deep inside her, they both gasped. "That's the way. I want all of you."

She reached up to cup his cheek. "You have all of me. I love you."

And he planned to spend every day for the rest of his life deserving that gift.

She loved it when he took her like this. When he poured all his desire into his gaze, into the way he touched her, possessive and wild but gentle at the same time.

This man would hurt her again, she knew. She'd hurt him, too. They'd step on one another's feelings, sometimes on purpose but mostly by accident. But they'd get through it.

Because he saw her in ways no one else did. And that was a gift.

He was close, but she was rising again, halfway there because he'd stripped her bare and loved what he found, wounds and triggers and all.

He pulled one of her legs up over his hip, turning her a little sideways, getting deep in rolling thrusts. She gasped at all the places he brought to life each time he plunged into her body. And that was before he wet his fingertips in his mouth and found her clit.

"Not alone. You come with me."

She couldn't deny him; instead, she tightened around him, concentrating, and when it hit, it was a bone-deep wave of sensation that started at her toes.

He cursed under his breath then. "So damned good. Never want this to end."

He thrust harder and faster until he gripped her tight, holding her, staying deep as he fell into his own climax.

Long moments later, he fell to the bed next to her, pulling her close after he brought the comforter up over them. "Makeup sex is not overrated."

She smiled and let herself know she was loved and that this was good.

* * * * *

Look for the next installment of
the HURLEY BOYS, *Ezra and Tuesday's story*
in BROKEN OPEN,
coming from Lauren Dane
and HQN December 2014.

ACKNOWLEDGMENTS

SPECIAL THANKS GO to Angela James who has been my editor since 2006. I don't know really if I can do justice to how amazing a great editor/author fit is, but I'm so fortunate to have it. Thank you for all the work you put into helping me write the best book I possibly can.

My agent, Laura Bradford, who spent part of the offer and negotiation of this book deal while I was on another continent and never even broke a sweat.

My assistant, Fatin Soufan, who capably and ably handles all the kooky stuff I send her way.

My friends who are always around when I need them.

My family—my wonderful husband who deals with a crazy writer for a wife with grace (and never complains when entire conversations from our life end up on the page) and my children who are wild and never stop talking and who remind me why it's important to love with all your heart.

Kings of Leon—thank you for being the spirit animal of this series and for these brothers.

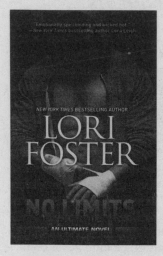

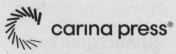